D1617577

HENRY IRVING'S
WATERLOO

FRONTISPIECE. *A Story of Waterloo*, from a drawing by Arthur Rackham (*Westminster Budget*, 10 May 1895). (Courtesy of the Garrick Club)

Napoleon is reported to have said: "In life there is much that is unworthy which in art should be omitted; much of doubt and vacillation; and all should disappear in the representation of the hero. We should see him as a statue in which the weakness and the tremors of the flesh are no longer perceptible."

Gordon Craig, "The Actor and
the Über-Marionette" (1906)

HENRY IRVING'S

WATERLOO

THEATRICAL ENGAGEMENTS

WITH

ARTHUR CONAN DOYLE
GEORGE BERNARD SHAW
ELLEN TERRY
EDWARD GORDON CRAIG

LATE-VICTORIAN CULTURE

ASSORTED GHOSTS, OLD MEN, WAR

AND

HISTORY

πόλεμος πάντων μὲν πατήρ 'εστι
WAR IS THE FATHER OF ALL THINGS
HERACLITUS

BY

W. D. KING

UNIVERSITY OF CALIFORNIA PRESS
BERKELEY   LOS ANGELES   LONDON

UNIVERSITY OF CALIFORNIA PRESS

BERKELEY AND LOS ANGELES, CALIFORNIA

UNIVERSITY OF CALIFORNIA PRESS, LTD.

LONDON, ENGLAND

© 1993 BY

THE REGENTS OF THE UNIVERSITY OF CALIFORNIA

PRINTED IN THE UNITED STATES OF AMERICA

9 8 7 6 5 4 3 2 1

Library of Congress Cataloging-in-Publication Data

King, W. Davies.
  Henry Irving's Waterloo : theatrical engagements with Arthur Conan
Doyle, George Bernard Shaw, Ellen Terry, Edward Gordon Craig : late-
Victorian culture, assorted ghosts, old men, war, and history / W.
Davies King.
    p.   cm.
  Includes bibliographical references (p.   ) and index.
  ISBN 0-520-08072-6 (alk. paper)
    1. Doyle, Arthur Conan, Sir, 1859–1930. Waterloo.   2. Doyle,
Arthur Conan, Sir, 1859–1930—Stage history.   3. Theater—England—
London—History—19th century.   4. Waterloo, Battle of, 1815, in
literature.   5. Craig, Edward Gordon, 1872–1966.   6. Irving, Henry,
Sir, 1838–1905.   7. Terry, Ellen, Dame, 1848–1928.   8. Shaw,
Bernard, 1856–1950.   I. Title.
PR4622.W33K56   1993
822'.8—dc20   92-31013

This book is dedicated to my grandparents—
Miriam Paar McKown & Herbert William McKown,
Marion Davies King & Clair Boyd King—
who in their lives and in their deaths
brought me close to the subject of this book.

CONTENTS

ILLUSTRATIONS

PREFACE

This book began with an anecdote. Here is the anecdote of that anecdote.

Late in my theatrical education, at an ill-tempered moment, I indulged a taste for unashamed arrogance by reading the dramatic criticisms of George Bernard Shaw, his *Saturday Review* columns from 1895 to 1898. The only collection of these writings available at the time was a small assortment of them in a cheap paperback. The editor had made his selection on the basis of several rules: all the writings on Ibsen, Shakespeare, and other well-known authors, and also all the writings that concerned Henry Irving, about whom I knew little. I was surprised to discover so many pieces devoted to this actor, each of them so hilariously nasty, and yet almost all dealing with plays that according to the standards of my training were of marginal interest at best. I soon discovered, upon reading these many severe attacks, a rule of thumb in appreciating Shaw's criticism: he often rises highest on the lowest occasions. Further exploration in the collected volumes confirmed this impression. He can be wrongheaded, noisy, even mean (though never less than brilliant) when writing about the play of merit, the play of continuing interest. On the other hand, one never notices any of that, except the brilliance, when reading of the obscure work.

One particular piece seemed to me the pinnacle of ruinous reviews. Here, Shaw systematically carried out the process of devastation, meticulously removing everything that had been *there* in the production until nothing could possibly have remained. The review was called "Mr Irving Takes Paregoric" and concerned a triple bill that opened at the Lyceum Theatre in London on 4 May 1895.[1] The first work on the bill was an adaptation of *Don Quixote* by W. G. Wills; Shaw took this occasion to make fun of the solemn Irving for his abuse of a literary masterpiece and his odd appetite for making himself look ridiculous. The third work was Arthur Wing Pinero's *Bygones,* which received little notice. Shaw's analysis of the middle work, Arthur Conan Doyle's *A Story of Waterloo,* was the one that caught my attention.

Shaw describes this work in merciless detail, from beginning to end,

exposing each melodramatic gimmick, each mechanical trick of dramaturgy, each histrionic ploy to win the audience's heart. Furthermore, his
description makes antagonistic reference to the many cries of acclamation
already evoked by *Waterloo* from Shaw's professional peers as well as to
the whispers of enthusiasm from spectators in the theatre. Almost all had
been rhapsodic about the piece, especially about Irving's acting. Shaw, on
the other hand, shone the cold light of analytical prose on the production
and found it void, especially Irving's acting. So thorough is his description
that I felt my reading of it must be largely equivalent to the experience of
having witnessed the performance. The review seemed to provide a complete package; critic had upstaged actor-manager in "producing" a coherent
experience of the play that included everything one ought to feel and think
about it. As with much of Shaw's writings, however, I could not help wor-
rying that I was being led astray. On impulse, I decided to indulge a taste
in reading opposite to that which had led me to Shaw in the first place: a
taste for benevolent estimation, for sentimental abandon, even for the indulgence of an actor's arrogance. A worn Samuel French edition of the
play, last checked out of the library in the 1940s, gave me what I needed to
find out if a play could be as empty as I had been told this one was.

Well, no, not precisely. Several of the effects—comic and sentimental—still worked, though the machinery was rusty. It was certainly not
among the worst plays I had read. But here was no forgotten jewel. It was
what I knew to be claptrap, and a modest example even at that. With Shaw
as guide, I could visualize an actor named Irving pressing for every cheap
effect, using ready pieties, outworn humor, convenient minor characters,
and contrived situations, all building to the big curtain line. This led me to
investigate what those other critics had said, to see how they could possibly
defend such a play. Using the index of Austin Brereton's two-volume *Life
of Henry Irving,* I located A. B. Walkley's review, which was quoted there
in its entirety. I knew Walkley, who was dramatic critic for the *Star* from
1888 to 1900, to be one of the two or three most respected critics of the
day, one of the early champions of Ibsen in England. He gave credit for the
play's powerful emotional appeal precisely where Shaw had withheld it—
to Irving's acting. Without the actor's "distinction, tact, delicacy, measure," he admits, it might have been "a chromolithographic inanity from
the top of a grocer's almanac." Instead, it was "a finished picture, and, to
my mind, one of the most actual, 'observed' things Mr. Irving has ever
done."[2] This diametric contradiction was enough to intrigue me. My next
step compelled my attention.

I came upon Bram Stoker's two-volume *Personal Reminiscences of Henry Irving* (1906), a delightfully overstated, often pretentious, finally wonderful book about the theatre. Stoker told memorable anecdotes of the play's production and testified that it was "perfect," and Irving's acting "the high-water mark of histrionic art." "Nothing was wanting in the whole gamut of human feeling," he went on. "It was a cameo, with all the delicacy of touch of a master-hand working in the fine material of the layered shell. It seemed to touch all hearts always."[3] He added that Irving had acted the piece 343 times. Something in the tone of euphoria and confirmed belief in Stoker, in contrast to the professional enthusiasm of Walkley, seemed to bode revelation.

Turning to the front of the book, I stumbled upon his reminiscence of one night in 1876, when Stoker, then a petty bureaucrat and part-time drama critic in Dublin, had dinner with Irving, along with a dozen friends. Following the meal, Irving recited Thomas Hood's poem "The Dream of Eugene Aram," a thriller which Stoker (and I, too) recalled reading as a boy. Here, perhaps, was a clue to what had held the attention of the audience at *Waterloo* (excepting Shaw). I must quote this extraordinary description at length:

> But such was Irving's commanding force, so great was the magnetism of his genius, so profound was the sense of his dominance that I sat spellbound. Outwardly I was as of stone; nought quick in me but receptivity and imagination. That I knew the story and was even familiar with its unalterable words was nothing. The whole thing was new, re-created by a force of passion which was like a new power. Across the footlights amid picturesque scenery and suitable dress, with one's fellows beside and all around one, though the effect of passion can convince and sway it cannot move one personally beyond a certain point. But here was incarnate power, incarnate passion, so close to one that one could meet it eye to eye, within touch of one's outstretched hand. The surroundings became non-existent; the dress ceased to be noticeable; recurring thoughts of self-existence were not at all. Here was indeed Eugene Aram as he was face to face with his Lord; his very soul aflame in the light of his abiding horror. Looking back now I can realise the perfection of art with which the mind was led and swept and swayed, hither and thither as the actor wished. How a change of tone or time denoted the personality of the "Blood-avenging Sprite"—and how the nervous, eloquent hands slowly moving, outspread fanlike, round the fixed face—set as doom, with eyes as inflexible as Fate—emphasised it till one instinc-

tively quivered with pity. Then the awful horror on the murderer's face as the ghost in his brain seemed to take external shape before his eyes, and enforced on him that from his sin there was no refuge. After the climax of horror the Actor was able by art and habit to control himself to the narrative mood whilst he spoke the few concluding lines of the poem.

Then he collapsed half fainting.

There are great moments even to the great. That night Irving was inspired. Many times since then I saw and heard him—for such an effort eyes as well as ears are required—recite that poem and hold audiences, big or little, spellbound till the moment came for the thunderous outlet of their pent-up feelings; but that particular vein I never met again. Art can do much; but in all things even in art there is a summit somewhere. That night for a brief time in which the rest of the world seemed to sit still, Irving's genius floated in blazing triumph above the summit of art. There is something in the soul which lifts it above all that has its base in material things. If once only in a lifetime the soul of a man can take wings and sweep for an instant into mortal gaze, then that "once" for Irving was on that, to me, ever memorable night.

As to its effect I had no adequate words. I can only say that after a few seconds of stony silence following his collapse I burst out into something like a violent fit of hysterics.[4]

Several things caught my interest in this story, but above all I was captivated by his testimony to something *beyond* the willing suspension of disbelief. In contrast to this, as it seemed to me, rather perfunctory requirement for the enjoyment of fiction, like a legal disclaimer one must sign, Stoker attested to an effect between miracle and madness, a leap of faith or an entry to the unconscious, produced by the artistic effort of this actor and the imaginative compliance of his auditor. I decided in a flash it would be necessary to know more about this experience and the actor who had sponsored it. I wanted to understand the power manifested in this scene and its transmission to the audience. The range of vocabulary that Stoker used— from "soul" to "hysterics," from "magnetism" to "genius," from "passion" to "art"—suggested to me the broad field I would need to explore. These same words had been used repeatedly by Stoker and others in reference to *A Story of Waterloo* and other works enacted by Irving, perhaps especially those works of no permanent literary importance.

The initial purpose of this book, then, became clear: to attempt to understand how and why *A Story of Waterloo* worked for its audience, soaring beyond all reasonable expectation, and how and why Shaw refused to be carried along. In pursuit of this topic I encountered many fine complicating factors. The historical record is inconsistent and conflicting. It would make no sense to add that the record is incomplete as well, for what could it possibly mean to have a complete record of a performance, or of 343 performances, each attended by 1600 or so spectators? What "record" does a performance leave at all? And *Waterloo* seemed, if anything, to leave a fainter trace with each year following Irving's death.

The anecdote of *Waterloo*—its miraculous incarnation, extravagant reception by the public, and ruthless castigation by Shaw—is usually told in a paragraph or two, if at all, in biographies of Irving, Shaw, Doyle, or in surveys or memoirs of the London theatre in the 1890s. Older works tend to give it more space; more recent books, almost none. It seems the story has the status of cherished memory, important so long as it holds a place in recollection, and no longer. Does *anyone* now survive who saw Irving perform this piece between 1894 and his death in 1905? It stands at the limit of memory's reach. Even the legacy of Irving's tradition stands at the boundary of living connection. John Gielgud was born one year before Irving's death. Laurence Olivier, who has just died, was born two years after.

Walkley had described the play as "one of those *mortalia,* those signs of mortality in human affairs, which, as Virgil said, *mentem tangunt,* do come home to the mind and touch it."[5] As I reflected on the temporal distance separating *Waterloo* from my own time, and the "death" of this particular moment in historical awareness, it suddenly occurred to me that this play had again, unexpectedly, come home to the mind and touched it. The play is about the death of a last living survivor, a man who can tell the story of the battle of Waterloo from a hero's perspective. The man is Corporal Gregory Brewster. His story gets told, in surprisingly humble and unimpressive terms, to a few assembled characters, before death comes in a brief, astonishing burst that is also an instant of recognition of the past. And now this old script sat before me, another of those *mortalia,* containing in some fashion a remnant of "the high-water mark of histrionic art," now on the verge of dying from awareness. It is in surprisingly humble and unimpressive terms too that the playscript testifies to this supposedly heroic moment in the history of acting. "Could this, indeed, be the last of that band of heroes," thinks Colonel Midwinter, the last of Brewster's visitors, upon seeing the corporal's decrepit form. Could this, indeed, be all that remains of that heroic tradition of acting, I think, as I survey the bony frame of Conan Doyle's "perfect" play, which "touched all hearts always." "Better, surely, had he died under the blazing rafters of the Belgian farmhouse," adds the colonel.[6] Perhaps, too, it would have been better if the text of this play had died, leaving only the impressive facts of Irving's career: twenty-five years the acknowledged leader of the profession; unparalleled popular and critical success in London, the provinces, and America; first actor to be knighted; burial in Westminster Abbey. This play threatens to undermine all that, especially when one comes to it through Shaw's review.

In the moment before Brewster's expiration comes a surge of vitality. "Staggering to his feet, and suddenly flashing out into his old soldierly figure," he shouts out the brave line that had propelled him into heroic action sixty-six years earlier.[7] Then he dies, and the curtain comes down. The question that occurs to me is this: would it be possible to perceive a similar flash of recognition across the almost one hundred years since this play was first performed? Would it be possible to achieve an instant of contact with the histrionically heroic past of this play? Or, to put it another way, what connection might I establish with those distant moments of great acting, given the few documents, the bits of testimony, the pictures, whatever history happens to have offered to the material and textual trail of this production?

My research led me into what I think is a thrilling and resonant story of the theatre, though its occasion might seem trivial at first. What's more, *Waterloo* provides a point of entry into an especially complex moment of cultural history, a moment of paradigm shift, seeming to organize a great deal of information by its terms. A story about an old hero of bygone wars, on the verge of death, becomes the battlefield where a veteran actor defends the English stage against the invasion of New Drama. The Old Guard, Irving's Lyceum faithful, give their hearts and souls to his ideal of art. But a new opponent appears in the midst of that crowd, resisting the spell of its leader, challenging his hypnotic techniques, and calling for a new realism and overthrow of the old order. Irving is their imperial leader, and a few years later he plays (Sardou's) Emperor Napoleon on that same Lyceum stage, but not before the invading critic has proposed a different Napoleon to him, a fierce fighter with Shaw's face. Shaw's *The Man of Destiny* was initially accepted, later rejected by Irving in a two-year battle for the heart of the "Empress" Ellen Terry, leading lady of the Lyceum. Her son Gordon Craig belatedly joined the fight and pursued it long after Irving's death, as an Orestes returned to the hearth (from his point of view) or a Polynices exploiting his "father's" charm (from Shaw's point of view). The end of the tale is death for all, the final curtain, and Doyle's little curtain-raiser sets the pattern for that as well.

On one level, I suggest that in the conflict between Shaw and Irving over this play one might gain insight into the changes taking place in the theatre during this period: the rise of the New Drama, the end of the era of the great actor-managers, the ongoing struggle between romanticism and realism. On another level, I believe there is a *danger* in neglecting a case such as this. It marks a crisis, and it demands an action, as much as the crisis in which Corporal Brewster found himself at Waterloo demanded his action. The story of *A Story of Waterloo* reflects on an emergency; a flashing light calls us back to this moment as an example in which we may witness the emergence of a certain sort of control through sentimentality, as well as of a cultivated resistance to emotional appeal. "Waterloo" is a noun, "a decisive defeat," according to Webster. In the case of the *Waterloo* of Irving and Shaw, the decision seems to cut different ways. *Waterloo* rings a bell; it echoes alarums and calls me to battle on both sides of the conflict. Thus, beyond providing a point of entry, this anecdote continually surprised me by appearing to become a point of return as well, as if it were somehow prophetic. This uncharacteristically superstitious recognition on my part alerts me to a basic instability in the concept of history I import to this study, an instability that I believe is pervasive in historical writing. It comes down to an ambiguity: is the past staged by a ghost or by a machine? An inquiry into the inspired and mechanistic theatre as a metaphorical agent of historical inquiry is a general project of the book. Instability is an inescapable part of that metaphor.

I could hardly have asked for a more extraordinary cast of characters for this study, singularly powerful men (men, almost without exception), each of whom has left a vivid record of his career. The literature on Henry Irving, along with his pictorial record, is as vast as that of nearly any other English-speaking actor. Irving carefully saw to it that his name would appear in print as often as possible, to keep his image alive among the public, and he also attended to the memorialization of his achievements for posterity. Shaw, of course, has no rival among English-speaking playwrights, except Shakespeare, for command of library shelf space, and much of that space is devoted to his discussion of himself. His plays, criticism, and letters from the mid-1890s form an exciting and remarkably detailed story of a genius determined to take command of the theatre. The rather melodramatic plot he attempted to enact was to draw Ellen Terry from her keeper, Irving, whom he cast as the evil tyrant and exploiter of her beauty and talent. Terry has also left a marvelous record of her more oblique perspective on this drama, in her memoir, in her correspondence with Shaw, and in her influence on her son and Irving's godson, Edward Gordon Craig. Craig preferred to cast Irving as the decent protector of Terry, Shaw as the villainous tempter. Terry was torn between these conflicting plots, Shaw's and Craig's, but on the whole she chose to play dutifully her role as empress in Irving's stately pageant of the theatrical profession. Craig's many writings on himself recur frequently to the influence of Irving and Terry on his ideas. As he grew older and crankier and more frustrated with his work, he became somewhat obsessive about Shaw's devilish part in breaking up his artistic family. He wrote books about Irving and Terry to appease their ghosts, and to avenge the violator of their graves, Shaw. Arthur Conan Doyle was not directly involved in this circle, but his many writings effectively form the constellation of military and mystical images in popular and historical literature within which *Waterloo* must be located. He stood at a distance from the conflict, always mindful of the possibility that popularity, fame, and commercial advantage were the root issues after all, and that the whole fray had a comic, as well as a political, aspect. These are the principal players, and they speak a rich dialogue in this extended anecdote, but, with the exception of Shaw's review, none of them wrote more than a few incidental remarks about *Waterloo*. Nevertheless, I found that one can detect traces of the play in their writings by examining closely all that adjoins the space where it might be.

Just a bit further from the center of action one finds other remarkable characters—comic relief, minor heavies, and clever confidants. These include people such as Bram Stoker, Clement Scott, and William Archer, each of whom was a prolific writer with special interest in the controversy between Irving and Shaw. They were also at the theatre on the evening of 4 May 1895 for the Lyceum premiere. Then there are background figures, including the giants who give this theatrical event a surprising sense of proportion: Gladstone, Napoleon, Victor Hugo, Byron, and many others. Poetic license permits them to speak in this drama, though they took no direct part in the action.

My way of telling the story of *A Story of Waterloo* is like the method described by Émile Zola in his advice to the naturalistic novelist—to dwell among the voices or documents of the subject and allow *them* to "write" the story. In fact, I would like to think that in creating this book I have not so much *written* the story as *read* it. Unlike Zola, though, I will not insist that the categories of the natural and the mythic can be separated with rigor. Indeed, my personal bias is to doubt that it makes sense ultimately to apply the concept of truth to any document. Rather, I conceive of documents as inherently dramatic, implicitly dialogical, and founded on conflict. Like most dramas, they are finally resolved, but it is essential that one question the resolution. There is something indispensable, though dangerous, about Hugo's *pensée:* "Poets of the drama put historic men rather than historic facts upon the stage. You are often obliged to make events false, you can always make men true. Write the drama not following, but according to, history."[8] Still, I trust the stories to be told here will touch reliably on "a scrap of human life" or, possibly, death.[9]

The book scrutinizes the structures of power to be discerned within the cultural configuration of *Waterloo,* and each chapter takes a different tactical approach. The first chapter introduces the core anecdote and explores its situation with respect to "sensibility"—the actor's and the critic's. The second chapter surveys the topography of crowd emotion in such a work and the particular handling of the crowd which was to be found at the Lyceum. The third chapter looks at the ways in which authority is imposed upon an audience and Irving as a crowd leader. The fourth chapter considers the play's aesthetic, the juxtaposition of realism and idealism implied in the representation of an old man on the verge of death. The fifth chapter situates the historical perspective of Doyle's play in the spectrum of myths/histories of the battle of Waterloo, while the sixth analyzes Irving's inscription of himself into myth/history through the play of *Waterloo.* The seventh chapter tells the story of the aftermath of Irving's battle with Shaw. The eighth chapter maps out the psychic/spiritual configuration within which the uncanny power of Irving's "personality" might be analyzed. The ninth chapter considers Gordon Craig as a historical and artistic mediator of Irving's presence in the twentieth century—or, indeed, as a medium in contact with his ghost. The final chapter takes up the multiple figurations of death in this study, as well as providing some concluding thoughts.

Many of my arguments have taken shape in part on the basis of reflections triggered by theoretical writings, but I bring no single frame to this material. A reader familiar with the range of theoretical discourse will find elements of many of the modern pieties. No case is made here for any of these. I have, in fact, attempted to keep my prose free of any special terminology that would call into service the important and often fascinating writings that work so hard to create and sponsor such terminology. There is one important exception to this declaration. The writings of Walter Benjamin—or rather, a particular mystery contained within many of them—I consider to have parental authority over this work. Benjamin confronted boldly the untrustworthiness of the historical process, the danger of relying upon the received past as a guide to origins. He viewed sceptically the reconstitutive efforts of historians, and chose instead to attend to certain intimations of the past which he recognized in the metaphor of "flashes": "The true picture of the past flits by. The past can be seized only as an image which flashes up at the instant when it can be recognized and is never seen again." He also writes: "To articulate the past historically does not mean to recognize it 'the way it really was' (Ranke). It means to seize hold of a memory as it flashes up at a moment of danger."[10] These flashes cross the gap in time not to give a picture of "the way it was" but to answer a critical need in the present, to respond to an alarm. The concept is distinctly mystical, but it is a concept necessary to explain where this work finally tends. My writing of this book has been in answer to a "flash," a compulsion to understand the correspondence of moments between the present, including the moment of this text, and something that occurred on 4 May 1895.

Benjamin aims to discover the mechanism of historical materialism at work within culture, the struggle of oppressed voices to overcome the dominance of the ruling class, and when he writes of the memories that flash up at a moment of danger, the danger includes those threatening forces which at last ended his life. The struggle between Irving and Shaw and the conflicts that arise from that struggle are of a different order of criticality, perhaps, but are no less politically significant. As Benjamin writes, "every image of the past that is not recognized by the present as one of its own concerns threatens to disappear irretrievably."[11] It is by no means obvious what lesson can be adduced from this story of *Waterloo,* what right and wrong meet, what justice is served or abused, but it should be clear that the struggle here is indeed critical. Fortunately, the immediate danger of the present moment impinges less than that which Benjamin saw, but, for all its disguises, it is no less real.

In my readings, I have preferred to search those parts of a text which have heretofore seemed slippery or less important than other parts. Of secondary sources, I have often favored the less reliable works—popular biographies, actors' memoirs, magazine stories—because of the relatively wild and unconcealed quality of their insights and rhetoric. The usefulness of such dysfunctionality will become clear in context. At the same time, I have benefited greatly from the authoritative scholarly literature on the period, and especially from the recent influx of important works, such as Nina Auerbach's *Ellen Terry,* Dan H. Laurence's volumes of Shaw's letters, Michael Holroyd's *Bernard Shaw,* and various writings by Joseph R. Roach, Richard D. Altick, Michael R. Booth, Alan Hughes, Cary M. Mazer, and Thomas Postlewait. Above all, Martin Meisel's two masterpieces of scholarship—*Shaw and the Nineteenth-Century Theater* (1963) and *Realizations* (1983)—have provided superb guidance.

I have been very lucky to have had close at hand during the writing of this book the Geraldine Womack and Norman D. Philbrick Library of Dramatic Arts and Theatre History, recently donated to Pomona College. This collection is housed in the Honnold Library of the Claremont Colleges and includes among its extraordinary holdings many books, letters, prints, and other material obtained from Edward Gordon Craig by his bibliographer and book dealer, Ifan Kyrle Fletcher. Many of these items have to do with Craig's lifelong devotion to Henry Irving and antipathy to Shaw. Tania Rizzo, Jean Beckner, and Susan Allen have been very generous with their time and advice in helping me make use of this collection.

I am also grateful for the assistance of Kay Hutchings at the Garrick Club in London, where I learned much from the extraordinary Percy Fitzgerald collection, twenty-two volumes of scrapbooks filled with myriad clippings and pictures concerning most of Henry Irving's career, conveniently indexed by George Rowell. Sadly, most of the headings of the clippings—dates, title of periodical, etc.—were cut off when the scrapbooks were made, so it is difficult to cite them properly except by reference to this collection. Nevertheless, these scrapbooks are beyond doubt the best introduction to Irving available.

I have been given friendly assistance by the staffs of many other libraries and collections, and in particular by Susan Naulty and Sue Hodgson at the Huntington Library; Mary M. Huth and Peter Dzwonkoski at the Department of Rare Books and Special Collections, The University of Rochester Library; Jeanne T. Newlin at the Harvard Theatre Collection; Francis Collinson of the City of London Museum.

Also, I wish to thank the staff members of the Shakespeare Centre Library, Stratford-upon-Avon; the Theatre Museum, London; the Wellcome Institute, London; the Billy Rose Theatre Collection, New York Public Library at Lincoln Center; the Folger Shakespeare Library, Washington, D.C.; the Library of Congress; the British Library; and the libraries of Yale University, the Colorado College, and the University of California.

I have been assisted in my research by a Summer Stipend from the National Endowment for the Humanities, as well as research grants from the University of California at Santa Barbara. I would also like to thank Peter Sellars and the staff of the American National Theater for a partially supported leave that allowed me to spend time in England.

Among the individuals who have assisted me in the research, I thank Gayle Harris, Peter E. Blau, Val Daley, Kathleen Barker, and Roy Porter. I have benefited from discussions with Frank Ries, James Malcolm, Joel Schechter, Laura Kalman, and Wolf Garr. Simon Williams, Bert States, Robert Potter, Robert Egan, Robert Dawidoff, and Michael Roth read early drafts and offered good guidance and timely encouragement. I am very grateful to Karen Branson, Doris Kretschmer, Paul Michelson, and Mark Pentecost for their close attention to this book during its transit through the University of California Press.

Stanley Kauffmann was the one who first interested me in Shaw, and it was with him in mind that I began this project, which was at first to have been a brief essay. Soon, I saw that a whole book might be written on the intersections of this topic, a book that might have something of the scope of different interests to be found in Stanley Kauffmann's writings and teachings and sayings and doings. The essay was published in *Before His Eyes: Essays in Honor of Stanley Kauffmann,* and I thank University Press of America for permission to use some of that material in my first chapter. Above all, I thank the teacher, advisor, and friend to whom, from the beginning, the book has been addressed.

Rena Fraden has been a constant friend and inspiration during the years of this book's making, and many more beyond that. Her encouragement and counsel have been of great value to me. Ruth Fraden King, on the other hand, has been of no help whatsoever, but she and her mother have made it worthwhile.

W. D. K.

CHRONOLOGY

1792		Fictional birth of Corporal Gregory Brewster
1815	18 June	Battle of Waterloo
1838	6 February	Birth of John Henry Brodribb (Henry Irving)
1847	27 February	Birth of Ellen Terry
1856	26 July	Birth of George Bernard Shaw
1859	22 May	Birth of Arthur Conan Doyle
1871		Irving becomes leading actor of Lyceum Theatre
1872	16 January	Birth of Edward Gordon Craig
1878		Irving becomes manager of Lyceum Theatre
		Ellen Terry becomes leading lady of Lyceum Theatre
1881		Fictional setting of the play, *A Story of Waterloo*
1891	21 March	Publication of Doyle's "A Straggler of '15"
	September	Publication of Shaw's *Quintessence of Ibsenism*
1892	ca. April	Irving buys rights to Doyle's adaptation of his story, which is retitled *A Story of Waterloo*
1894		Publication of *Trilby* by George du Maurier
	21 April	Premiere of Shaw's *Arms and the Man*
	21 September	Bristol premiere of *A Story of Waterloo*
	17 December	Charity matinee performance of *A Story of Waterloo*, Garrick Theatre, London
1895	5 January	Shaw's first column as dramatic critic for *The Saturday Review*
	4 May	Lyceum Theatre premiere of *A Story of Waterloo*
	10 May	Shaw begins writing *A Man of Destiny*
	11 May	Publication of Shaw's review of *Waterloo* ("Mr Irving Takes Paregoric") in *The Saturday Review*
	24 May	Announcement of knighthood for Irving

	October	Opening of Beerbohm Tree's production of *Trilby*
	28 November	Shaw sends copy of *A Man of Destiny* to Ellen Terry
1896	July	Beginning of intensive correspondence between Shaw and Terry
	22 September	Lyceum Theatre opening of *Cymbeline*, reviewed by Shaw ("Blaming the Bard")
	26 September	Shaw meets with Irving concerning *A Man of Destiny*
	19 December	Lyceum Theatre opening of *Richard III*, reviewed by Shaw ("Richard Himself Again")
1897	10 April	Lyceum Theatre opening of *Madame Sans-Gêne*, reviewed by Shaw ("Madame Sans-Gêne")
	May	Irving finally rejects Shaw's *A Man of Destiny*
	1–3 July	Copyright performances of *A Man of Destiny*, Croydon
	18 May	Copyright performance of Bram Stoker's *Dracula*, Lyceum Theatre
1898	18 February	Fire burns the Lyceum stock of scenery
	April	Shaw's *Plays: Pleasant and Unpleasant* published
	4 May	Lyceum Theatre premiere of *The Medicine Man*, reviewed by Shaw ("Van Amburgh Revived")
	21 May	Shaw's final column in *The Saturday Review*
1900	16 December	Premiere of Shaw's *Captain Brassbound's Conversion*
		Shaw-Terry correspondence nearly ceases
1902		End of Terry's professional association with Irving
	19 July	Irving's final performance at the Lyceum Theatre
1905	10 June	Drury Lane Farewell performance of *Waterloo*
	15 June	Testimonial matinee performance of *Waterloo*—Irving's last appearance in London and in this play
	13 October	Performance of *Becket* at Theatre Royal, Bradford—Irving dies shortly afterward
	20 October	Burial in Westminster Abbey

1906		Publication of Bram Stoker's two-volume *Personal Reminiscences of Henry Irving*
		Production of *Captain Brassbound's Conversion* at Royal Court Theatre, with Ellen Terry as Lady Cicely
1911		Publication of Craig's *On the Art of the Theatre*
1930		Publication of Craig's *Henry Irving,* reviewed by Shaw ("On Gordon Craig's *Henry Irving*")
	7 July	Death of Sir Arthur Conan Doyle
1931		Publication of *Ellen Terry and Bernard Shaw: A Correspondence*
1932		Publication of Craig's *Ellen Terry and Her Secret Self*
1950	1 November	Death of Bernard Shaw at the age of 94
1966	29 July	Death of Gordon Craig at the age of 94

CHAPTER I

"HAPPY THE PLAY THAT HAS NO CRITICISM IN THIS COLUMN"

In 1891, Arthur Conan Doyle wrote and published a short story called "A Straggler of '15."* The following year he turned it into a one-act play, a "curtain raiser," which, "greatly daring," he sent to his theatrical idol, Henry Irving.[1] Doyle was then a dissatisfied physician and a writer whose career was just beginning to explode with his new character, Sherlock Holmes. Irving was "Governor" or "Chief" of the Lyceum Theatre and the foremost actor-manager of the English stage from the 1870s to the turn of the century. Several of his Shakespearian productions were thought unsurpassed in his day, complementing a variety of melodramatic plays which became polished masterpieces of theatricality in his hands. He was the first actor to be knighted, on the occasion of which the Queen was heard to say, "I am very, very pleased," and he was buried in the Poet's Corner of Westminster Abbey.[2] Bram Stoker, who as Irving's acting-manager during those years was chief factotum at the front of the house, said that Irving "was on the mimic stage what Napoleon was on the real one."[3] In brief, Irving was utterly dominant, and at the same time greatly loved by his followers; enormously successful, and at the same time honored as a true artist and an intelligent, sensitive, magnanimous man.

Stoker's memoir of Irving records that one day in 1892 Irving asked him to give his opinion of a manuscript that had arrived in the morning mail. The actor gave no clues as to his opinion but went on to a rehearsal. Stoker had read the play twice by the time Irving returned, "touched by its humour and pathos to [his] very heart's core." Irving inquired:

"By the way, did you read that play?"
"Yes!"
"What do you think of it?"

*Note: the texts of A Story of Waterloo and "Mr Irving Takes Paregoric" are printed as appendices.

I

"I think this," I said, "that that play is never going to leave the Lyceum. You must own it—at any price. It is made for you."

"So I think, too!" he said heartily. "You had better write to the author to-day and ask him what cheque we are to send. We had better buy the whole rights."

"Who is the author?"

"Conan Doyle!"

The author answered at once and the cheque was sent.[4]

This anecdote is a blend of miracle and machine, conjuration and high-efficiency engineering. The compression of events into a short space of time ("write to the author to-day"), the absolutism of the action ("You must own it—at any price"), and the precision of the fittings ("It is made for you"): these are the details of a cartoon laboratory with "Eureka!" as a caption. What a marvelous convenience that this should be Conan Doyle's *first* attempt at drama, as all the production publicity emphasized (no matter that it was by then his *second* play to appear). The very announcement of the play would guarantee publicity; a special train had to be arranged to bring all the critics to Bristol, where the play opened.

And what productivity: high-water mark attained, perfection achieved, "Nothing . . . wanting in the whole gamut of human feeling," and the whole rights bought and paid for.[5] Stoker's diary further itemized the yield: "New play enormous success. H. I. fine and great. All laughed and wept."[6] Crowd sentiment was the medium of manufacture in the theatre, and the "All" was the site of transubstantiation, from matter to marvel, from machine to miracle. *Waterloo* effected this passage thoroughly: "It seemed to touch all hearts always."

Doyle noted in his autobiography that his eyes "were moist as I wrote it and that is the surest way to moisten those of others."[7] Before submitting it to the Lyceum, Doyle sent the manuscript to the novelist George Moore, asking for advice. Moore replied, "I do not know if your play would act—that is to say if a few alterations would fit it for the stage, but I do know that it made me cry like a child. I think it is the most pathetic thing I ever read in my life."[8] Doyle took Irving's few suggestions for its improvement and volunteered several more himself. With that, the piece became an efficient and effective property—four characters, one set, and nothing to up-stage Irving's forty-five minutes of virtuosic acting, in the role of an old soldier of about ninety years of age.

Even so, two and a half years passed before Irving found a way to work the piece into his repertory, under its new title *A Story of Waterloo,* later simply *Waterloo.* What resembles a miracle to reminiscence often looks like random circumstance at the time. Irving told an associate it was the mischance of a sudden illness in the company, knocking out another one-act play, that led him to remember Doyle's play. The humble scenery was quickly gathered, as the company had just set out on its provincial tour, and thus the play appeared first at Bristol, on 21 September 1894.[9] Eleven years later, Irving made his last appearance on a London stage in this play. Almost to a man, the critics exclaimed over the production, many in terms as extreme as Stoker's. Because the piece was introduced near the beginning of the tour, a steady stream of reviews poured attention upon it, each stop on the tour gaining the notice of all the local newspapers. Even after the first wave of reviews in the London papers, stories continued to appear about its triumphant progress from Bristol to Birmingham, Leeds, Liverpool, Edinburgh, Glasgow, Dublin, and Manchester. The local reviewers took a good deal of pride in the fact that they were seeing Irving in a new role well before the London audience did.

The provincial reviews are nearly carbon copies of one another, each remarking the "spontaneous outbursts of enthusiasm" and the "thunderlike crash of applause."[10] The praise was universal for Irving for having "undoubtedly made . . . one of the most remarkable stage pictures of our time, perfect in its verisimilitude, infinitely touching in its human pathos, and . . . a signal achievement even in Mr. Irving's long roll of dramatic triumphs."[11] A number expressed reservations about Doyle's play, which was seen as little more than a sketch to which the master artist had brought vivid color. Several took it as an encouraging sign of the "revived association of literature with the drama" that Doyle should have ventured to write a play, and that Irving should give it his attention.[12] But others were willing to give Doyle a bigger share of the credit: "Mr. Irving's acting throughout kept the house silent except when it was sobbing, and . . . Dr. Conan Doyle's little play carried all before it with its perfectly symmetrical and balanced art."[13] Virtually all clung to the principle expressed by a Glasgow reviewer: "To tell the narrative is far more potent for art's sake than any exacting criticism can be."[14] *A Story of Waterloo* was told over and over, until it must have become common knowledge by the time it appeared in London. The "story" of *A Story* is the memory of a gallant act at the Battle of Waterloo, told by the old soldier who performed the deed, and now retold by the aging actor who performed the role. Since then almost forgotten again, the story must be retold.

The curtain rises on the humble lodgings of the octogenarian Corporal Gregory Brewster. Enter, a bit uncertainly, his grandniece, Norah Brewster; she has journeyed here to keep house for the old man and does not know quite what to expect. She surveys the meager details of his existence—medicine bottles, a few sticks of furniture, and poor food—and promptly sets out to make things right. He has not been well attended by the previous housekeeper, who has been dismissed. One thing in the room stands out; over the fireplace, "a rude painting of an impossible military man in a red coat with a bearskin." Underneath is a newspaper clipping, and a framed medal—a memorial to a heroic deed.

A man about Norah's age, Sergeant Archie McDonald, R.A., knocks and enters. He's come to pay his respects to the venerable survivor. He has heard rumors that the "old gentleman" was not looked after well, but is reassured by Norah that all will be well now. His attention directed to the corporal's medal, he reads aloud (somewhat haltingly) the newspaper clipping, which is headed "A heroic deed":

> SERG[EANT]. "To Corporal Gregory Brewster of Captain Haldane's flank company, in recog—recognition of his valour in the recent great battle. On the ever memorable 18th of June, four companies of the third Guards and of the Coldstreams held the important farmhouse of Hugymont at the right of the British position. At a critical period of the action these troops found themselves short of powder, and Corporal Brewster was dispatched to the rear to hasten up the reserve am—ammunition. The corporal returned with two tumbrils of the Nassau division, but he found that in his absence the how—howitzer fire of the French had ignited the hedge around the farm, and that the passage of the carts filled with powder had become almost an impossibility. The first tumbril exploded, blowing the driver to pieces, and his comrade, daunted by the sight, turned his horses; but Corporal Brewster, springing into his seat, hurled the man down, and urging the cart through the flames, succeeded in rejoining his comrades. Long may the heroic Brewster—
>
> NORAH.   Think of that, the heroic Brewster!
>
> SERG[EANT].   "Live to treasure the medal which he has so bravely won, and to look back with pride to the day when, in the presence of his comrades, he received this tribute to his valour from the hands of the first gentleman of the realm."

The story impresses them both; it is true legend from the age of giant heroes, but strangely reduced now to a bit of newspaper beside the liniment bottle in a sparsely furnished room.

It is important to know something of the battle of Waterloo to appreciate the significance of this commendation. On the night of 17 June 1815, rain fell on the sixty-seven thousand English, Dutch, Belgian, and German soldiers under the command of the Duke of Wellington gathered on a vast muddy field near the village of Waterloo. Their intent was to join forces with the Prussian army of Marshal Blücher before Napoleon and his army of some seventy thousand could divide them. The ultimate confrontation began late in the morning, when Napoleon, who had ranged his soldiers on the opposite side of the field, gave the order to begin a diversionary attack on a château on one flank of the field. The château, known as Hougoumont, was surrounded by walled gardens and orchards enclosed in hedges. It was occupied by British infantry—Guards—who proved able to resist the fiercest of attacks. Later analysis of the battle showed that it had been a tactical error on the part of the French to waste their efforts on this farmhouse, in part because the stalwart resistance of the Guards clearly took on a symbolic significance. Since it was an enclosed position, supply of ammunition to the defenders was a problem. Another château, on the opposite flank, fell to the French largely because of a lack of ammunition. The story of Hougoumont was well known from history books, but also from literature, most famously Victor Hugo's *Les Misérables,* which was completed not far from the battlefield. Hugo's retelling of that battle begins at Hougoumont, the house that stood fast against Napoleon and eventually proved his undoing—"the first knot under the axe-blade."[15] Corporal Brewster was a crucial (fictional) figure in that pivotal fight. As Norah puts it, "It was as much as to say that uncle won the battle."

Though the old soldier has still not appeared, the sergeant is "due at the butts," and so, promising to return later, he departs. It is not long, though, before the "Straggler of '15" (played by Irving) makes his heartrending entrance:

Enter Corporal GREGORY BREWSTER, *tottering in, gaunt, bent, and doddering, with white hair and wizened face. He taps his way across the room, while* NORAH, *with her hands clasped, stares aghast first at the man, and then at his picture on the wall.*

This pathetic fragment of the Waterloo hero does not recognize Norah, taking her for the daughter of his brother, "Jarge," and when she explains that George, her grandfather, "has been dead this twenty years," he seems not to hear.

Indeed, it soon becomes apparent that Brewster has but a dim awareness of the past across the sixty-six years since 1815. His health has declined—his "toobes" give him trouble, and he "cuts the phlegm" with paregoric, an odd choice since the principal use of paregoric, a tincture of camphor, alcohol, and opium, is as a treatment for diarrhea. Paregoric was often an ingredient in cough elixirs of the day, owing probably to the mild euphoria it induced from the opium and alcohol, if one could stomach the unpleasant taste. Probably the term is here to be understood in its earlier, more general sense of a soothing agent, a pain reliever, though it is also possible that his Doctor Joyce, whom he calls "a clever man," has chosen a poor treatment. Doctor Doyle would know better. In any case, although Brewster's health is failing, his spirit is still active in the service. He presents himself as ready at any moment to be called up to "the glory to come" when he joins his old "ridgement" as they march to the "battle of Arm—Arm—The battle of Arm—." He struggles with the word "Armageddon" as he struggles with the "owdacious" house flies, but he "'spec's the 3rd Guards will be there" at the battle, and they need only him to make up a full muster.

He has evidently been the good soldier these many years, dutiful even in following the terms of his commendation: living long to treasure his medal and looking back with pride to the occasion of his valorous behavior. As he puts it, "I've not got the smell of the burned powder out o' my nose yet." But when the sergeant returns, it becomes clear that he has not kept up with change; the ways of the modern army are different. Always, when faced with modern advances such as the new rifles or regimental titles, he defers judgment to Wellington. A Victorian commentator remarked on this habit of Wellington's soldiers, saying that he became "a sort of ultimate arbiter; and discussions usually were closed by—'the Duke agrees to it!', 'the Duke will see to it!', 'the Duke says it must be done!' "[16] In Brewster's case, however, the "ultimate arbiter" can only be invoked in the past tense: "It wouldn't ha' done for the Dook. The Dook would ha' had a word there." The years have eaten away at his fortitude. When he breaks his clay pipe, "he bursts into tears with the long helpless sobs of a child." Nothing but time could defeat the man, and time now—thirty minutes from curtain rise, fifteen from curtain fall—is having its way.

The corporal is surprised and honored by the arrival of the colonel of the regiment, Colonel Midwinter. He snaps to attention, then almost collapses from the effort. Midwinter has come to hear of the historic battle from the heroic survivor himself. The old man contrives to recreate the scene, using his medicine bottles and other items to represent the various units and landmarks. The battle is so clear to him that he "sees it afore me, every time I shuts my eyes." The phrases of commendation are almost present in his memory—this was the moment given to him alone to treasure, and it is more vivid to him than the life that surrounds him now:

> CORP[ORAL]. The Regent he was there, and a fine body of a man too. . . . He up to me and he says, "The ridgement is proud of ye," says he. "And I'm proud o' the ridgement," says I. "And a damned good answer, too," says he to Lord Hill, and they both bust out a laughin'.

The record is nearly complete; the spectator has had ample certification of the greatness of this man and his deed, amounting to victory over the Emperor Napoleon. But the heroic picture is imperfect. The passage of time has made it difficult to fit the action to the broken and childish figure of the man.

Before the colonel departs, he grants Corporal Brewster's request that he be given a proper military funeral when he's "called." Then the veteran sinks back in his chair, exhausted by the visit and soon asleep. Already, one might say, the slow descent of the curtain has begun, but one effect remains to close the work and bring the moment of the past together with the moment of the present. Otherwise, the work is weirdly skewed: too quaint for the heroic, too heroic for the pathetic, too pathetic for the comic, too comic for the inspirational, too inspirational for the quaint. So the sergeant enters yet again and finds the old man asleep in his chair at center stage. He offers Norah a comforting opinion: "Yes, he don't look as if he were long for this life, do he? But maybe a sleep like this brings strength to him." The young folk, who are about the same in age and social standing, and who are both unmarried, converse for some time, sketching, merely hinting at, a possible romantic interest if this piece were somehow to extend beyond its one act. But their scene is literally beside the point. Marriage and domestic comfort have had no place in the corporal's life, and the spectator's attention does not stray from the figure of the sleeping man. He is the play, and his life, his past, his present, in one, form its sole action. Suddenly (how marvelous! how horrible! how pathetic!) the figure stirs:

> CORP[ORAL]. [*In a loud voice.*] The Guards need powder!
> CORP[ORAL]. [*Louder.*] The Guards need powder! [*Struggles to rise.*]

NORAH.   Oh, I am so frightened.

CORP[ORAL].   [*Staggering to his feet, and suddenly flashing out into his old soldierly figure.*] The Guards need powder, and, by God, they shall have it! [*Falls back into the chair.* NORAH *and the* SERGEANT *rush towards him.*]

NORAH.   [*Sobbing.*] Oh, tell me, sir, tell me, what do you think of him.

SERG[EANT].   [*Gravely.*] I think that the 3rd Guards have a full muster now.

Curtain. Slow.

Waterloo is a play of contrasts: the old and the young, the present and the past, the quaint and the heroic, the real and the ideal. The final moment brings these contrasts together in a full figure, a transfiguration of the impossibly real into the really impossible, uplifted by a surge of feeling, before the curtain descends. The corporal becomes his past self, grappling with death in the same heroic spirit with which he defied the burning hedge around Hougoumont. His death transcends the mean circumstances of his life by replicating (or reincarnating) the legendary past and thus becoming the stuff of a new story (or new testament). The biblical echoes are numerous—Brewster's disciples gathering at the last supper to witness his pious preparations for death and hear of his faith that God (and the "Dook") will redeem his life for a greater battle to come. He testifies to the fearsome battle he has fought against the great adversary, and then in death he undergoes a miraculous transfiguration. These are the elements of the inspirational story that critics repeat in their stories of *A Story of Waterloo*.

The provincial critics, as well as the London critics who had journeyed to the premiere, pressed this story upon their readers as the new gospel of Irving's career. These critic-evangelists prepared the way for the play's triumphant entry into the capital. In December, when his tour ended, Irving with customary generosity gave *Waterloo* its London premiere at the Garrick Theatre in a charity benefit, prompting another wave of ecstatic reviews and repetitions of the story. It was only toward the end of the season, on 4 May 1895, after a long run of his popular new production of *King Arthur,* that he opened Doyle's one-act at the Lyceum, on a bill with two other short pieces. And then the story was told yet again. The production became a classic in anticipation, on the strength of the story and of the report that Irving had made something immortal of this story of mortality.

"THE GUARDS NEED POWDER, AND, BY GOD, THEY SHALL HAVE IT!"

FIGURE 1. *A Story of Waterloo,* from a drawing by Arthur Rackham (*St. James Budget,* 28 September 1894). (Courtesy of Harvard Theatre Collection)

Student or art life of this century can scarcely be complete without one glimpse of Irving's "Straggler."

Amy Leslie, *Some Players* (1900)

There were discordant notes along the way, but the momentum of *Waterloo* as a cultural phenomenon swept them aside. A Glasgow reviewer, for instance, noted that the enthusiasm inspired by the piece had not seemed as spontaneous as when the play was done in Edinburgh:

The audience, indeed, appeared to be only partly *en rapport* with the spirit of the thing, for many of the humorous points were allowed to pass in silence, while two of the most pathetic touches in the whole, the spasmodic attempt of the decrepid [*sic*] old soldier to rise and salute his colonel, and the words, reminiscent of the part he played in the great battle, with which the warrior leaves this earth and goes to complete the muster of his regiment, were actually greeted with laughter! All the same there was plenty of noisy demonstrations at the end, the curtain being rung up four or five times in response to the continuous applause.[17]

In this performance the emotional effects seem to have misfired entirely, and yet the importance of the work has sufficiently impressed the audience and critic that they treat it with great respect.

The London audiences for the most part received the production as they had been told they would, honoring it as a new jewel in Irving's crown, preferring to think that his contribution had been more weighty than Doyle's, and in general responding wholeheartedly to its emotional effects. One historian of acting during the period, Sir George Arthur, who witnessed the triumphal progression of the play, wrote that "Pinero, in one of his plays, insists that in the life of every individual there is one supreme hour which is never repeated; it is possible to think that on a dark December afternoon [at the charity matinee] Henry Irving as an actor had his hour." [18] Another London critic called the piece "charming because it is full of what (in defiance of physiology) I can only call 'heart,' " and added, "I am not ashamed to confess that I dropped a tear or two. . . . But pray don't tell this to our friends the 'Anti-sentimentalists.' "[19] The record shows that at various performances of this work, a remarkable number of spectators responded with similar enthusiasm. Each time the "hour" was repeated, the work was met with "a surge of emotion" and "thunders of applause," and the spectators told others the story of their experience of the story of Irving's miraculous achievement in A Story of Waterloo, based on Conan Doyle's story—a story of a story of a story from the heart.

Waterloo might be described as an apotheosis of the spirit of the nineteenth-century English theatre, in the form of a heroic actor, amidst a thunderous crowd, thrilling the emotions, illuminating the ideal. And, in a way, the slow curtain at the end of Waterloo, at the end of Irving's "supreme hour," might be seen as the closing of an era, the passing away of something called "spirit" at the opening of the twentieth century. Spiritual transcendence was an idea at the heart of this play—spirit rising above the crude machine of the body and the physical world. Spiritual transcendence was, on another level, at the heart of Irving's acting of the play—spirit rising above the crude machine of Doyle's play. And on yet another level, it was at the heart of the audience's appreciation of the play—spirits rising above the insubstantial images offered by the crude stage mechanism. Waterloo provided the occasion for an investment of belief, in defiance of the crudely mechanistic tricks that might account for all that they would attribute to spirit.

In writing an "acting play," as Stoker calls it, Doyle had neatly set up this opportunity for the actor, carefully constructing the ground (aged, quaint, real) from which the figure (youthful, heroic, ideal) would rise. Irving was praised for his detailed portrayal of old age, and in general the alternation of humorous and pathetic moments was accepted and admired as a means to realism. But the moment that shook critics and audience was the apparition of Brewster / Irving / spirit rising mightily to death. Sir George Arthur describes the tremendous effect of this moment:

> When the curtain sank there was a silence, intensely significant but almost unbearable in its tension; men who had never before been "moved by theatrical stuff" were furtively wiping their eyes, women were quite unashamedly "having a good cry," a wave of emotion swept the whole house. . . . The stage manager knew his job and kept the drop down until people had a little recovered themselves and were able to give Irving an ovation which admittedly, in volume and sincerity, exceeded anything he had hitherto enjoyed.[20]

Alfred Darbyshire proclaimed, in *The Art of the Victorian Stage,* that Irving's creation of Gregory Brewster (and Charles the First) would not only be thought of as "works of high art," but would also "remain as exquisite memories 'as long as memory shall hold her seat.' "[21] An "exquisite" memory is a memory literally without question, and yet without question Irving's performance stands now as merely a strange, rather obscure anecdote, a memory without seat, in a number of dusty theatrical annals and *Personal Reminiscences.* That is perhaps the fate of the actor's art: it commands attention without question, and then without question it passes. It was question—one voice of question amid all the exclamation—that arrested the passage of Irving's *Waterloo* into nothingness and turned it devilishly against itself. If *Waterloo* is without question a forgotten play, it has become outstandingly forgotten because of the extraordinary, deviant retelling of its story by Bernard Shaw. Shaw made the play unforgettably forgettable, immortally dead, in the course of his review. He did so by standing alone and outside the concealed position of the other critics, outside their participation in the mechanism, and by breaking the mechanical laws of their complicity with the theatre.

To be sure, other London critics were unenthusiastic about the play, but cautiously so since by this time Irving was preeminent on the English-speaking stage. What's more, he was respected, admired, and loved for his service to the art and the country, and for his generosity, dignity, and good nature. Still, critics must be critics, and *Waterloo* presented a fine test of tact and discrimination. Those who had qualms about the piece tended to blame the playwright, not the actor. They pointed to the slight plot, the awkward structure, the functional minor characters, while reserving for the star all credit for elevating the piece above its faults. Others maintained that Doyle's play was more nearly faultless than might be supposed and that it had been a key to Irving's success. If there were any problems, then they must be laid to the supporting actors. This sort of disagreement, known as a healthy dispute, makes for a good show of independent thinking, while serving the fundamental purpose of promoting the theatre, and especially its most powerful exponent. That was, at bottom, the contract of service to which the critic, as a theatre professional, subscribed.

It was Shaw who completely buried the work and marked the tomb with an unforgettable epitaph. "Mr Irving Takes Paregoric" was the heading of his column in *The Saturday Review* of 11 May 1895. Shaw's idea is that Irving used *Waterloo* (and the concurrent production of *Don Quixote*) as a drug to clear himself, temporarily, of the "sustained dignity" demanded by serious drama on the stage and professional eminence in life—the (constipative?) pains of the art. But how much more severe the anguish "at the point of the pen" when Shaw began to cut through Irving's Brewster to show that the "toobes" had been clear of vital essence all along: "There is absolutely no acting in it—none whatever." Doyle, Shaw said, deserved all the credit for his "ingenious exploitation of the ready-made pathos of old age," while Irving's contribution amounted to "a little hobbling and piping, and a few bits of mechanical business with a pipe, a carbine, and two chairs."

And yet the machine handles the sentiments of the audience so neatly that the simplest business appears to them inspired. Shaw indicates as much in his inventory of the play's effects, alternating between objective description and subjective exclamation:

He makes his way to a chair, and can only sit down, so stiff are his aged limbs, very slowly and creakily. This sitting down business is not acting: the callboy could do it; but we are so thoroughly primed . . . that we go off in enthusiastic whispers, "What superb acting! How wonderfully he does it!" The corporal cannot recognize his grandniece at first. When he does, he asks her questions about children—children who have long gone to their graves at ripe ages. She prepares his tea; he sups it noisily and ineptly, like an infant. More whispers: "How masterly a touch of second childhood!" He gets a bronchial attack and gasps for paregoric, which Miss Hughes administers with a spoon, whilst our faces glisten with tearful smiles. "Is there another living actor who could take paregoric like that?"

Shaw does not deny the effectiveness of the machine in stimulating strong feelings. His references to the "enthusiastic whispers" register the pure subjection—subjection without objection—of the audience to the sentiments of the scene and performance.

Shaw does not, at least at first, detach himself from the subjected mass, but neither does he relinquish his objectivity. He represents this condition of semi-detachment rhetorically in his review, not explicitly but implicitly in his playing out of the entire sequence of events in *Waterloo*. In effect, he dramatizes the role of the critic, showing the critic as an actor who stands apart from the crowd and yet participates in its sentimental involvement. In many of his reviews, as in this one, Shaw addresses the issue of the critical sensibility—that admixture of engagement and disengagement, of subjectivity and objectivity, which the critic must control.

The problem of critical sensibility mirrors that of the actor's sensibility, and Shaw's inquiry into the issue reflects interestingly on Irving's close involvement in the ongoing debate over Diderot's *Paradox of the Actor*. Diderot argues that the actor must remain emotionally disengaged from the performance in order to preserve the degree of self-control necessary for the most artful execution of the role. Irving disputed Diderot's conclusion, allowing that detachment is possible and even essential to the extent that it is necessary for the technical demands of the part—i.e., for the efficient operation of the machine—but arguing that a great actor must go beyond the limited power that detachment permits, beyond the machine in a burst of spirit. The lore of acting uses a range of rather mystical concepts to account for that power of origination, especially the romantic notion of an actor's lyric inspiration, vested in the voice. Shaw would remind his readers of the machinery—the hard copy—that lies within those mystical concepts. Even Irving's supporters, however, had to admit that Irving could not claim many of the outward characteristics associated with the ideal. As one textbook on elocution put it: "Mr. Irving has a bad voice, a plain face, and an ungainly figure, is ungraceful in action, and is singularly lacking in force; while Mr. [Frederick] Warde has a good voice, a handsome face, a symmetric figure, is graceful in action, and has abundant force; yet Mr. Irving has an undisputed place among the first, while Mr. Warde is, as yet, hardly accorded a place among the second."[22] The author's explanation for this anomaly is that Irving has a quality of "intelligence," but it was not easy to explain just how this intelligence became manifest, particularly in his more simplistic and melodramatic works.

In 1877, William Archer and Robert S. Lowe anonymously issued a pamphlet assailing the London public for making Irving "the apostle of popular dramatic culture" given his obvious faults: "Night after night he has filled the dingy old Lyceum from the front row of the stalls to the back row of the gallery, with audiences which applauded every jerk, every spasm, every hysteric scream—we had almost said every convulsion—in which he chose to indulge."[23] A few years later, Archer issued a more temperate analysis of "Irvingmania" and "Irvingphobia," both of which he decried, though he leaned toward the latter. He reiterated the familiar criticisms of Irving's diction and mannerisms, but he also sought some means of defining the paradoxical, if not mystical, effect Irving exerted: "By intellect he produces the effect of masterful decision of purpose, which saves even his worst parts from the fatal reproach of feebleness. By intellect he makes us forget his negative failings and forgive his positive faults. By intellect, he forces us to respect where we cannot admire him. By intellect he dominates the stage." Archer sharply limits how he applies this term "intellect" to Irving by suggesting that it is not a spiritual wholeness, not an originative artistic essence, but a mask concealing a *hollowness* inside. At the end of his pamphlet, he asks, "Will Mr. Irving never turn his attention from revival to creation?"[24] In other words, will he never enlist a writer to fill that hollowness? Shaw, of course, saw Irving's usurpation of the literary or generative aspect of theatre as his prime offense and took a still narrower view of his intellect. He saw Irving as an outgrowth of obsolete romantic ideals, packaged in such a way as to flatter the public's social pretensions. It was essential for this purpose that he appear the genius, the eminence, the hero, the artist, the paternal lord, but all of these guises, in Shaw's view, were masks, indistinguishable from the illusionistic mechanisms at work in the culture at large. These the critic must expose in order to free the crowd from its subjection, and yet that last frontier of the mystical within the mechanism—the sensibility—would resist strict definition, by Diderot or by Shaw.

In his hostile preface to an 1883 translation of Diderot's dialogue, Irving quotes the great French actor Francois-Joseph Talma as his authority:

> "I call sensibility," says Talma, "that faculty of exaltation which agitates an actor, takes possession of his senses, shakes even his very soul, and enables him to enter into the most tragic situations, and the most terrible of the passions, as if they were his own. The intelligence which accompanies sensibility judges the impressions which the latter has made us feel; it selects, arranges them, and subjects them to calculation. It aids us to direct the employment of our physical and intellectual forces—to judge between the relations which are between the poet and the situation or the character of the personages, and sometimes to add the shades that are wanting, or that language cannot express: to complete, in fine, their expression by action and physiognomy." That, in a small compass, is the whole matter. It would be impossible to give a more perfect description of the art of acting in a few words.[25]

Thus, Irving takes the "emotionalist" position in the controversy. Although he does not deny the need for self-possession or "intelligence" in order to avoid errors and excesses, he implies that it is secondary to the "faculty of exaltation," which propels a performance beyond mere mimicry. Both Talma and Irving describe the effect of this exaltation without being very explicit about how it works. Irving prefers to consider it a professional mystery: "Every actor has his secret." He adds that "volumes of explanation" would not fully clarify the matter, which stands beyond the horizon of discourse: "The exaltation of sensibility in art may be difficult to define, but it is none the less real to all who have felt its power."[26] Writers can barely approach the power of "exaltation," which is a spiritual elevation beyond the capacity of judgment, beyond description, beyond criticism. But if the actor is the one who exercises this "faculty of exaltation which . . . enables him to enter into the most tragic situations . . . as if they were his own," what about the member of the audience or the critic who is also expected to "enter," in some fashion, these situations? To what degree should the *critical* sensibility follow that of the performer?

An agitation, possession, soul-shaking, similar to that described by Talma, swept the audience of *Waterloo,* and the critics mostly attempted to represent this sensation in descriptions, identifying the actor as the source of the exaltation. It could be said that they credited the actor with the emotions of the audience, such that the actor represented the feelings of the crowd "as if they were his own." This appropriation of sentiment seems to be a basic condition of "acting" plays and the "actor's" theatre—a giving over of sensibility to the actor. The actor must, as Talma writes, be disciplined by the "intelligence which accompanies sensibility," retaining clear judgment as a guide and regulator. Meanwhile, the audience is allowed the free play of sensibility, since the responsibility is deferred or transferred, even to the extent that the member of the audience is permitted to enter into the tragic situations as if they were *not* his own. The audience can receive the stimulation—the agitation—without being obliged, as the actor is obliged, to select, arrange, and subject the impressions to calculation according to "intelligence."

But the essence of criticism is judgment, which amounts to intelligence in league with sensibility, or even in command of sensibility. When the critic is deprived of responsibility by a work that overcomes discrimination through the appropriation of sensibility, then he can do little more than register the surge or stimulation of the work, without the discipline of intelligence, without differentiating among the causes of the various sentiments, without judging "the process" as a process. Shaw's revolution in criticism (indeed in the theatre generally) was the reappropriation of intelligence and the establishment of a critical "sensibility" dramatically opposed to the actor's.

Consider the second quotation that Irving cites from Talma: "The inspired actor will so associate you with the emotions he feels that he will not leave you the liberty of judgment; the other, by his prudent and irreproachable acting, will leave your faculties at liberty to reason on the matter at your ease." [27] Thus, inspiration disarms a critic—or, more to the point, the acting that produces a reasoned critical discourse and a range of different opinions cannot by this definition be inspired acting. Inspired acting asks only for acknowledgment of its power. In effect, Talma (and Irving) turn the paradox of the actor into the paradox of the critic. The inspired actor seizes the crowd, with the critic in its midst, and deprives them of their "liberty of judgment." Shaw, like Talma but from an opposite point of view, dramatizes the paradox of the critic in terms of the paradox of the actor. The one reflects the other. For Shaw to give way to the emotional exaltation he feels (and hears) in the crowd around him would be to grant the actor a power he cannot define. It would be to lose control. And yet that is what is expected of him. On the other hand, a supreme critic might subordinate sensibility to intelligence, thus placing himself in opposition to the inspired actor. Such a critic might rescue the audience's lost liberty of judgment by *dissociating* them from the emotions they feel. The Lyceum opening of *Waterloo* was the occasion of a great battle of inspired actor and supreme critic, Irving and Shaw in conflict over the power of sensibility.

In the late 1890s, the Hungarian philosopher Max Nordau contributed to this discussion with his assertion that the distinguished actor should not be a genius but should rather have the psychological disposition of a child or a savage. That is, the actor should be a simple medium, able to convey the impressions of a role with a minimum of mental interference:

> The distinguished actor must be like a gun with an exceptionally ready action of the trigger. Just as in the latter case the slightest touch produces a discharge, so in the case of the former the most trifling external impression will produce the mental condition which is to be represented, and which then automatically of itself completes its manifestation to the senses. It must be quite clear that such a relationship is only to be looked for in a brain the highest centres of which are as a rule unoccupied, that is, perform no mental labour of their own, and for that reason are ready to respond to all sense-impressions with the corresponding temperaments and conceptions.[28]

Perhaps this is the actor Shaw would prefer, an actor at the opposite extreme from Irving, who always conveyed the impression of immense mental effort in executing his part and who undisguisedly asserted his authority. Shaw, of course, doubted the intellectual substance of this show of mental labor. Irving was, in his estimation, no perfectly susceptible medium but an obtrusive presence, a domineering figure as well as a skillful confidence man who could, nevertheless, undeniably throw *the audience* into a condition like that Nordau describes. The Lyceum audience, at least in Shaw's opinion, unthinkingly, automatically responded to the external impression received from Irving. Nordau's model of the distinguished actor does not differ significantly from Talma's definition of sensibility except in the value judgments that are derived from it. Both suggest an actor who is, in some sense, passive to the role, a medium through which an emotional discharge passes. But Nordau presents an unflattering picture of the impressionable actor, asking, "Where is there room left for a man of genius here?" while

Talma regards that susceptibility as the essence of the actor's genius. Finally, though, both Shaw and Irving recognize that the game dictates that both actor and critic must play it both ways to succeed, conjoining within their sensibilities as much of intellect and impulse as possible.

The one critic and the one actor on the two-way stage of the theatre play out the drama of crowd control. When there is "none whatever" of acting, then the critic can come forward to object against the subjection of the crowd, as Shaw does in his review. When there is none whatever of criticism, then the critic remains in the crowd, indistinguishable, wholly subject, as in most of the other reviews of *Waterloo*. More often, both critic and actor come forward, in conflict, the former objecting, the latter subjecting, until one or the other accedes. The critic accedes when the acting, as Talma says, "takes possession of his senses, shakes even his very soul," denying him, the critic, the "liberty of judgment." It is open to debate in this century (since Shaw, one might argue) whether this subjection is the proper goal of theatre.

On the other hand, the actor must accede in the conflict when the criticism is as powerful as Shaw's. His exposure of the machine and his stout objection to its intelligence-depriving effect should show the actor that he has lost one individual from the crowd. Shaw insists upon his liberty of judgment, insists upon seeking to define. He finds positively offensive the notion that the proper response is simply, mutely to feel the power of the acting. His review of *Waterloo* provides a model of how an alert spectator might respond to this production, and in that sense he competes with Irving for the attention of the crowd. However, the critic must fight for the crowd outside the theatre, in publications (though the judgments are presumably born in alienated privacy within the theatre), and so there is an unavoidable time lag in the conflict of actor and critic. The critic works on a larger time scale, changing the future of the theatre on behalf of the future crowd. Shaw accepted that fact. As he wrote to Ellen Terry in 1896, "I like a state of continual *becoming,* with a goal in front and not behind."[29]

Shaw pushed for that future by satirizing the theatre of the present, hurting in order to improve, and he involved the crowd of the present in his satire. He worked for *their* improvement by allowing them to read their actual and potential sensibilities in the figure of the critic. In his review of *Waterloo,* Shaw shifts his mode of addressing the audience (and his position toward them), first addressing them as individuals, then joining them in the crowd, then leaving them alone among themselves. The account begins in the second person, with the private moment before the individual is drawn into the crowd ("You read the playbill; and the process commences at once with the suggestive effect of . . ."). Soon the singular meshes with the plural, since "the process" ensures that the effects are universal ("You are touched: here is the young soldier come to see the old—two figures from the Seven Ages of Man"). Then the review switches to the third person and it becomes clear that the "you" is not personalized, not flattered into a sense of individuality. In other words, the play addresses the audience as an undifferentiated crowd, a herd of low aptitude ("the pair work at the picture of the old warrior until the very dullest dog in the audience knows what he is to see, or to imagine he sees, when the great moment comes").

The "great moment" is the entrance of Irving, and it is at this point in his account that Shaw introduces the first person plural. It is as if Irving's entrance brings Shaw into the crowd to join "you" and "the very dullest dog." Irving is the force that draws together the production, the crowd, the critics, and especially Shaw. Irving binds the group into a "we," but Shaw does not soon forget the undistinguished role that had been accorded him, a role no more demanding than that given the dull dog and certainly no great opportunity for the exceptional critic. So the "we" becomes more and more ironic; one doubts that a tearful smile broke on Shaw's face as he watched the corporal take his paregoric. Shaw pushes the limit when he parodies the absurd claims of those who praise the minutiae of naturalistic acting: "We feel that we could watch him sitting down for ever." He grouses at the predictable clichés, Doyle's capitalizing on the public's sentimental reflexes ("The band being duly exploited for all it is worth, the bible comes into play") and the crudely manipulative dramaturgy ("Mr Fuller Mellish, becoming again superfluous, is again got rid of"). These comments come from the experienced professional who has seen these tricks many times, in contrast to those simples who, upon hearing about the clergyman who reads to Brewster about "them Israelites [who] was good soldiers, good growed soldiers, all of 'em," are wont to exclaim, in Shaw's words, "How sweet of the clergyman to humor him! Blessings on his kindly face and on his silver hair!" The "we" has dropped out altogether, and the quoted exclamations appear unattributed, still more enthusiastic, and *wholly* ironic ("A masterstroke! who but a great actor could have executed this heart-searching movement?"). Shaw's resistance grows as the figure of the corporal grows more decrepit and the effect on the surrounding crowd becomes overwhelming. "The curtain falls amid thunders of applause," of course, but one feels sure that Shaw did not join in.

He was already in the next paragraph, where the subject of address changes once again: "Every old actor into whose hands this article falls will understand perfectly from my description how the whole thing is done." As Irving is concealed by the curtain of seriousness, drawing waves of emotion and thunders of applause from the crowd, Shaw is concealed by the curtain of the ludicrous, laughing scornfully but envious of the actor's opportunity. In another review of *Waterloo,* Austin Brereton, who was among those who disparaged the play (mysteriously finding it "deficient in virility"), waxed enthusiastic about Irving's performance. Along the way he pointed to the boundary that Shaw undertook to enforce: "In dealing with such a part, an actor might be forgiven if he overstepped the bounds of common sense and lapsed into the ludicrous. For the dividing line is extremely shallow. It is easy to conceive that an actor, even of average talent, could not wholly retain the serious interest of any audience in such a part. Mr. Irving, however, succeeds, unquestionably, in so doing."[30] In Shaw's view, though, Irving succeeded *questionably,* and Shaw is more than ready to press the question and challenge Irving's hold on the "serious interest" of the audience. Brereton implies that the actor ought to stay within "the bounds of common sense," but suggests that the same bounds apply to the audience. When the audience oversteps these bounds, failing to question their assumption that the part deserves their "serious interest," then they lapse into the ludicrous, as Shaw demonstrates in his review. Shaw does not question the common sense of Irving, who, like "every old actor," understands perfectly how the whole thing is done. It is done by drawing the audience beyond the bounds of common sense under the guise of "serious interest," leading them to "go off in enthusiastic whispers" over "the commonest routine of automatic stage illusion." Shaw catches the audience out, in ludicrous posture, then serves them their due of scornful laughter.

Shaw's satire enforces a realistic perspective on the construction, the machine, that had held the audience captive to an ideal. In the preface to his "Pleasant Plays," Shaw declares that his intention is not "to please the less clear-sighted people who are convinced that the world is only held together by the force of unanimous, strenuous, eloquent, trumpet-tongued lying." The theatre, especially Irving's theatre, appeared to Shaw an insidious mechanism for fostering in the crowd those imaginary constructs that prevent an accurate perception of the world. The preface quoted above concludes: "To me the tragedy and comedy of life lie in the consequences, sometimes terrible, sometimes ludicrous, of our persistent attempts to found our institutions on the ideals suggested to our imaginations by our half-satisfied passions, instead of on a genuinely scientific natural history."[31] The crowd itself presents a problem, both within and without the theatre, when its binding force, its unanimity, is not well-founded. Unanimity is, literally, singleness of spirit in a crowd, a contract binding the numerous "half-satisfied passions" to an ideal. It is a construct, even a rhetorical figure or mode of expression, having more to do with the enforcement of belief than the recognition of truth.

During his apprentice years as a music, art, and literary critic, Shaw had become an emphatic and provocative political orator who repeatedly showed that "politics" resides as much in habits of thought or speech as it does in governmental functions. Quietly held opinions, even unconscious assumptions, about worldly values might ultimately prove as dangerous as open abuses of the system. The theatre was a place where people were regularly faced with imaginary situations, contrived according to vaguely understood ideals. The theatrical mechanism offered a ready device for influencing those habits of thought and speech in large crowds of people, and for refounding the audience's perception upon the real. Shaw wrote his earliest plays as a self-conscious "dramatic realist," then encountered a predictable reluctance among managers to carry out his reform. In 1894, his essay "A Dramatic Realist to His Critics" answered those who disliked the attack on conventional notions of military heroism in his *Arms and the Man,* a play that stands about as far from *Waterloo* in its attitudes as it is possible to stand. His lengthy rebuttal includes quoted documents from actual participants in military conflicts in an effort to show that his play was grounded not in theatrical tradition but in the real world. He concludes: "I declare that I am tired to utter disgust of imaginary life, imaginary law, imaginary ethics, science, peace, war, love, virtue, villainy, and imaginary everything else, both on the stage and off it. I demand respect, interest, affection for human nature as it is, and life as we must still live it even when we have bettered it and ourselves to the utmost."[32] The mission of the critical persona he had developed and had recently dubbed G. B. S. was to challenge all sacred cows, and in this work his target was dramatic criticism itself: "No class is more idiotically confident of the reality of its own unreal knowledge than the literary class in general and dramatic critics in particular."[33] Nevertheless, by the end of the same year, he had accepted Frank Harris's invitation to become dramatic critic on the *Saturday Review.*

Harris, whom Shaw called a "buccaneer" and "blackguardly enough to stand my stuff," had just bought the notoriously caustic and Conservative magazine, with ambitious plans to change it, and thought immediately of Shaw as the one to write a column of theatre criticism for him.[34] He sought to bring together the best writers of the day, and he largely succeeded. Under his editorship, the magazine was transformed from a failing organ of Tory prejudice—the "Saturday Reviler," it was often called—into a widely discussed source for urbane and stylish commentary, often distinctly progressive. The idealists and traditionalists were displaced by writers who shared Harris's respect for the term "Modern," including H. G. Wells, Arthur Symons, Max Beerbohm, and Shaw.[35] It is reported that Harris instructed Shaw on his reviewing policy, "I've asked all the reviewers only to review those books they can admire and praise; starfinders they should be, not faultfinders."[36] Shaw's promotion of Ibsen, in open defiance of the fact that the English stage had generally ignored the Norwegian, satisfied Harris's dictum nicely. His disparagement of Shakespeare, on the other hand, greatly annoyed Harris, who was to publish early versions of his own study of *The Man Shakespeare* in the magazine. However, he could not argue with Shaw's success in drawing attention and subscribers to the magazine and so he let it pass with no more than stern words of counsel that Shaw did not know Shakespeare well enough to gibe as he had. Ibsen and Shakespeare, however, were relatively remote and timeless subjects. The current plays and productions were accorded a full measure of the faultfinding Harris had discouraged. Shaw said it best: "Happy is the nation that has no history, and happy the play that has no criticism in this column."[37]

Harris was hardly consistent in his policy against hard-hitting reviews, and indeed later conceded, "These too are necessary when dealing with be-puffed mediocrities."[38] Just two weeks before Shaw's first *Saturday Review* column appeared, a truly nasty, unsigned review of Irving's benefit performance of *Waterloo* appeared in the magazine, and Harris is as likely a candidate as any for its authorship.[39] Harris did not particularly like Doyle, who was too commercial in his literary ambitions, too Conservative in his politics, and too sentimental in his taste. (In the 1920s, Harris wrote a rather Shavian story in which a character calls God uncreative, unless creation means "mediocre, fishlike productivity"—in which case "He is prodigious, a gigantic Conan Doyle.")[40]

In one of the last issues of the *Fortnightly Review* before Harris was fired as *its* editor, William Archer published a retrospective of the 1893–94 sea-

son's plays, which became the occasion for his meditation on the rise of
what he called "an inconsiderate and dangerous policy" of antagonistic
criticism: "Our work has had a purely destructive, what I may perhaps call
a *sterilising*, tendency; whereas criticism of real dignity and value must
always be, in the main, constructive, helpful, fertilising." Archer remarks
that during the season of 1893–94, not a single serious play had been produced with success. Though a retrospective analysis revealed a number of
works which, if not masterpieces, "might have harmlessly and not quite
trivially entertained the public, while preparing the ground for stronger and
sterner work," these had been massacred by bloodthirsty critics along with
the genuinely weak plays.[41] He blames a sharp division in the ranks of
critics between the old and the new, brought about by the controversy over
Ibsen and the advent of Pinero. The younger critics, disappointed that Ibsen was not being given a fair chance on the English stage and greatly
excited by the promising new work of Pinero, were inclined to apply new
standards of artistic excellence to the run of new plays, standards that were
not germane to the taste of the average theatre-goer and producer. The older
critics, meanwhile, had grown "tetchy and suspicious" of vile Ibsenism.
Clement Scott, of the *Daily Telegraph,* had led the charge, writing of
Ghosts: "Realism is one thing; but the nostrils of the audience must not be
visibly held before a play can be stamped as true to nature. It is difficult to
expose in decorous words—the gross, and almost putrid indecorum of this
play."[42] A few brief exposures to these plays on the stage and a great many
lengthy defenses of Ibsenism in print had, Archer wrote, "rendered [the
older critics] morbidly acute to scent the accursed thing in the most improbable and even fantastic quarters; while it [had] enriched their vocabulary with a fine stock of terms of opprobrium which it would be sinful to
leave unemployed."[43] Archer concluded that the "acidity of temper" of
these conservative critics had spilled upon any work of conspicuous novelty, while plays that were merely conventional began to seem predictably
dull. Hence, the divided community of dramatic critics was not inclined to
give full support to anything that came along.

Archer's critical protégé, Shaw, though he was not yet writing dramatic
criticism, was already making his views known, showing that he was beyond the opinions of even the younger critics. Shaw regarded Pinero's
plays as tepid imitations—Ibsen alone would suit him—and saw little
logic in the idea that as a critic he should compromise his values for the
good of the institution. He and the anonymous reviewer were quite willing
to stand conspicuously outside the crowd of admirers of Irving and *Water-*

loo. The alternative was anathema to Shaw and the younger critics, Archer included. Archer is eager to insist that he is not advocating "a return to the bad old days when criticism meant perfunctory puffery, and no one paid the slightest attention to it."[44] Indeed, he argues at length that criticism can exert great power, not just upon managers and authors but upon the public. The key word in this discussion is "power" or "strength," as in his hope for "stronger and sterner" plays. Given this critical measuring stick, it is easy to see why Shaw and the anonymous reviewer were not inclined to like *Waterloo.* They both insist upon the word "little" and its pejorative cognates in their reviews, Shaw calling Irving's performance a "pitiful little handful of hackneyed stage tricks," and the anonymous reviewer alleging that "nothing weaker was surely ever written for the stage." The twin vices of powerlessness and obsolescence, which both critics charge to the play and production, echo within the description of Brewster, an enfeebled old man.

Meanwhile, however, the older critics (and many of the younger) withheld their "fine stock of terms of opprobrium" and praised *Waterloo.* Irving, of course, exerted enormous influence over the whole publicity mechanism, of which criticism was, for him, merely a component. Beyond that, Archer's analysis suggests why this production had stirred the critics so: "In their heart of hearts they demand that impossible, or at any rate improbable, combination, a conventionalist of genius."[45] Doyle and Irving, perhaps, came close to supplying just that combination: a play that is new and somewhat different, modern but not superficial or morbid, written by a popular writer whose potential was unknown, containing a part that is out of the ordinary for the old master, Irving, calling for the usual stage business of the old man but also an extra layer of detail and a final effect that make the character real *and* sublime.

Archer wrote his assessment of the crisis in modern criticism as "the cry of an awakened conscience to other consciences as yet, I fear, unawakened." At its end, he proclaims himself willing to adopt a new attitude: "If a play seems fitted harmlessly to entertain the particular public to which it is addressed, we may surely, without betraying the cause of Art, or dissembling our preference and desire for work of larger inspiration, permit and even help it to live its little day."[46] Archer shows little difficulty in following this guideline when, within a year, he writes his two reviews of *A Story of Waterloo,* after the Garrick matinee and the Lyceum opening. Some perspective on Shaw's distinctive attack on this play might be gained by comparing these analyses.

Archer's first review consists mainly of a plea for Conan Doyle to write more plays, given the skill he has exhibited in this one. In fact, he anticipates Shaw in asserting that even an ordinary actor might make this play reasonably effective. He (strangely) declares it "the finest thing Mr Irving has done in comedy," and (more strangely) asks, "I wonder if it would not have been more artistic to have left the old man alive?"[47] The too "theatrical" ending of the piece receives no comment in the second review, but Archer does raise the question of the balance of art and nature in the performance. He gives the impression that the representation of Brewster might have been "unnecessarily ugly." His qualms nearly echo the older critics' qualms about Ibsen: "In studying an essentially painful phenomenon, such as senility, the artist should be not only permitted but enjoined to choose, out of many possible cases, one of the less repulsive rather than one of the more—except when repulsiveness happens to be of the essence of the dramatic problem, as in this instance it is not." Other than this, he is prepared to give high marks to Irving's performance ("a piece of acting no one can afford to miss"), to Doyle ("a true humorist") and to the whole effort: "A trifle it is, no doubt; but a trifle well worth doing, both on the author's part and on the actor's." In only one passage in this appreciative or "fertilizing" review does he betray any possible anxiety, any sense of strain about commending a work that Shaw, among others, might call a mediocrity. (And, of course, Shaw's review would appear just three days after Archer's.) Archer writes, "It must not be subjected, of course, to realistic or anti-idealistic criticism. It is a piece of unblushing idealism—a frank appeal to our most rudimentary emotions. Yet, if there were not a large infusion of truth in this *Arms and the Man's Old Style,* as it might be called—perhaps quite as much of the essential truth as in *Arms and the Man: New Style*—we may be sure it would appeal to our emotions in vain."[48] Archer had taken a beating from Shaw for writing of *Arms and the Man:* "To look at nothing but the seamy side may be to see life steadily, but is not to see it whole."[49] Shaw responded that the review might have been written by a "Bulgarian idealist," more out of touch with reality than anyone.[50] Archer's comparison of Shaw's play to *Waterloo* must certainly have satisfied some deep need to lash out against one who would resist all challenge.

Shaw was, indeed, intolerant of the sort of compromise Archer proposed in 1894—that the highest standards be relaxed in the short run in order to serve the cause of progress in the long run. Archer had said that criticism is advertisement and had argued, "If we massacre everything but masterpieces, we kill the masterpieces as well; for there are not enough masterpieces in the market to keep one theatre, much less five or six, in profitable activity."[51] This was as much as to concede that the critic is but a functional adjunct of a business enterprise. Of course, in Archer's case, there was no question of his being corrupted by the managers, as Shaw well knew and later wrote in a pen portrait of his friend of over forty years.[52] Still, the notion that a critic should write "for the good of the theatre," or representing the interests of the audience, might involve slight deceptions, exaggerations, omissions that would be in conflict with the goal Shaw was soon to declare, of a "genuinely scientific natural history."[53]

It would be inaccurate to suppose that Shaw took himself for a purist or a model of rectitude as a critic (Archer would be his candidate for that). On the contrary, in 1929, speaking at a gathering of London critics, he said, "Criticism is, has been, and eternally will be as bad as it possibly can be. I am speaking as a critic myself. I did it myself. I am criticizing myself. It never can be worse. It is always down to the limit."[54] When his *Saturday Review* columns were later collected for republication, he wrote:

> In justice to many well-known public persons who are handled rather recklessly in the following pages, I beg my readers not to mistake my journalistic utterances for final estimates of their worth and achievements as dramatic artists and authors. It is not so much that the utterances are unjust; for I have never claimed for myself the divine attribute of justice. But as some of them are hardly even reasonably fair I must honestly warn the reader that what he is about to study is not a series of judgments aiming at impartiality, but a siege laid to the theatre of the XIXth Century by an author who had to cut his own way into it at the point of the pen, and throw some of its defenders into the moat.[55]

He does not aim at "impartiality"; instead, he adheres to "the bounds of common sense" as the proper field for *partiality,* allowing and even expecting the part to stand out from the unanimous whole.

To free the crowd of its dependence on unanimity is to demand growth or maturation beyond constructed ideals, beyond the institutions that protect or preserve the immature. In a musical review some years earlier, Shaw had written, "When the critics were full of the 'construction' of plays, I steadfastly maintained that a work of art is a growth, and not a construction. When the Scribes and Sardous turned out neat and showy cradles, the critics said, 'How exquisitely constructed!' I said, 'Where's the baby?' "[56] The strategy of opposing question to exclamation and always asking who or what will *grow* in the work of art continues in his review of *Waterloo.* In refusing to acquiesce to the half-satisfaction of his passions, Shaw demands the growth of the theatre *and* of the audience. The delight of cradles is beyond question, is exquisite, but the concern of serious theatre should be the "baby" of full potential. Near the end of his review, Shaw offers a surprise, confessing that he enjoys sketches such as *Waterloo,* "with their ready-made feeling and prearranged effects," *when* they are performed in the music hall: "I enjoy them, and am entirely in favor of their multiplication so long as it is understood that they are not the business of fine actors and first-class theatres." Vulgar and second-class enjoyments have a place in the world, he implies, in the realm of fantasy, but the leading theatres should pursue goals in the realm of actuality. Shaw attempts to jar the crowd to this somewhat elitist conclusion by showing them the ludicrous consequences of their belief in a false ideal—and this is painful for them. The pain involves the loss of a fulfilled past: the loss of exclamatory feeling in the opening of questions, the loss of the subjection in the opening of an objection, the loss of the crowd in the opening of the individual. In a sense, Shaw asks the crowd to accept (or even precipitate) the downfall or death of their paternal leader, as a necessary stage of growing up, *or* of growing into the groove cut by Shaw, which they are to believe is the groove of individuality, self-sufficiency, freedom to judge, critical independence, adulthood. In other words, growing into Shaw. And *Waterloo* functions as a ritual staging of this revolution and even as a rite of passage from the nineteenth into the twentieth century.

Shaw sacrificed *Waterloo,* sacrificed even his own acknowledged enjoyment of the performance, for a higher cause, killing in the name of progress. *Waterloo* survived this Waterloo seemingly unharmed—for ten more years and hundreds of performances, for the remainder of Irving's life, and it was later revived by none other than his eldest son, H. B. Irving, with similar success. Laurence Irving (the grandson) wrote of his father's performances, "Many times I watched Corporal Brewster die as he relived the defence of Hougoumont, and as often I was borne along by the surge of emotion that broke over the footlights with the thunder of applause."[57] It is as if the work were immortal, living on from performance to performance, generation to generation, or so the myth seems to suggest. But the work became a landmark in theatre history chiefly because of its fall, soon after its opening, beneath the fatal hand of Shaw—beneath the curtain he lowered on an era that would become the theatre's Past so that a new theatre could become the Present.

Shaw was having trouble attaining this new stage for his dramatic works. Few had been performed by 1895, and their reception (not to mention their presentation) had been, in his view, all wrong. Irving, because of his eminence and the idealist aesthetic to which it seemed to bind him, appeared to Shaw as a main obstacle to his own theatrical ambitions. For histrionic fireworks, he preferred the idol of his early theatre-going, Barry Sullivan, and for sheer voltage Irving made poor competition. What Irving had offered Shaw, much earlier and perhaps again at the time of *Waterloo,* was a glimpse of a new sort of actor, the actor for a realist theatre, the actor to play Ibsen's Dr. Stockman or John Gabriel Borkman. And he could envision Irving in the roles he had written or would write, if only the actor's steadfast resistance could be surmounted. In the meantime, though, Shaw wrote his weekly column for the *Saturday Review,* and the Present theatre was *Waterloo,* so it was through his reviews that he began to "cut his own way."

Shaw took the art of theatre criticism to its limit, to the point where the critic's writing itself becomes the occasion of theatrical discovery. Instead of assisting the *closure* of the work in memory—elaborating its impressions with description and evaluation—Shaw *reopened* the work to further play, taking positions or parts according to the premises of the work and testing the conclusions that resulted against a hard and responsible logic. The rhetorical fireworks for which Shaw's reviews are famous—long sentences that become an avalanche of wit, a multiplicity of voices, and especially the playful posturing and elaborate turns of the G. B. S. character— do not merely amplify the principle point he addresses but they also manipulate the reader's experience. Shaw operates on the reader's memory and understanding, using a play's performance as a pretext for exposing the artifices—tricks and mechanisms—that lie behind the seemingly natural processes of apprehending a performance and, by extension, behind any human action.

Shaw continually makes a show of upsetting the hierarchy of opinion by breaking all the "laws"—speaking the unspeakable in the name of honesty, taking advantage openly where it had always before been taken covertly. No mode of address could be more vexing to a self-proclaimed guardian of the law and order of public opinion, as Irving was. But in some of his reviews, Shaw goes beyond this positional rhetoric to a fully dramatized sense of his text in which conflict stands as conflict. And *Waterloo* was a particularly ripe occasion for this sort of review—because its substance was compact and simple enough to represent completely, and because the disparity between its apparent effect and its actual cause was especially enormous. Shaw reduces the audience's profound impressions to mere reflexes triggered by "the commonest routine of automatic stage illusion." He does this, as outlined above, by re-creating the whole work and anatomizing its impressive effect, piece by piece, to show that it works by "machinery."

At the same time, Shaw admits his own susceptibility to the "routine," his *enjoyment,* which cannot be denied because it comes from feeling genuinely felt, even if mechanically produced. It was the machine at the core that brought out Shaw's will to challenge, because machines do not die a natural death:

> The whole performance does not involve one gesture, one line, one thought outside the commonest routine of automatic stage illusion. What, I wonder, must Mr Irving, who of course knows this better than anyone else, feel when he finds this pitiful little handful of hackneyed stage tricks received exactly as if it were a crowning instance of his most difficult and finest art? No doubt he expected that the public, on being touched and pleased by machinery, should imagine that they were being touched and pleased by acting. But the critics!

Yes, the critics, too, might be haunted, beyond disbelief, by an effective spirit—the ghost in the machine—which no amount of violent stabbing or funerary rite can lay to rest—*in the theatre,* that is. In a review, though, a different order of burial applies—scientific methods of counterattack, killing, entombment, and commemoration, at the cost of the spiritual effect, which is left behind, untouched.

Shaw thus plays the role of subversive or double agent in his representation of *Waterloo,* the converse of the role he accuses Doyle of playing: "Mr Conan Doyle has carried the art of constructing an 'acting' play to such an extreme that I almost suspect him of satirically revenging himself, as a literary man, on a profession which has such a dread of 'literary plays.'" Shaw, the literary man, describes *Waterloo* to death in order to give it new and delightful life. He makes a literary play on words, a satirical figure, out of Doyle's "good acting play," and in this action, this upstaging of Irving, he posits a different sort of play. This is the "literary play," as specifically defined by Shaw in his review: "a play that the actors have to act, in opposition to the 'acting play' which acts them." Shaw places his textual performance, his literary playing, in the abyss that Irving opened ("There is absolutely no acting in it—none whatever"); he metaphorically "acts" *Waterloo* by showing how *Waterloo* acted Irving.

This is the way of satire—ridiculing by a substitution of point of view. Replace performance with description and watch how the spirit drops out of the machine. Irving sinks, and Doyle rises, but finally it is Shaw who comes forward, vengeful and marvelous, as the one who really acts, the one who makes a performance of the text. The "ready-made feelings and prearranged effects" work for him as they do for the actor, although with opposite results, and the trick that Shaw performs is the same as the one performed by Irving—to make a moving presentation, a performance that goes beyond what can be described. This is precisely Shaw's new direction in criticism: going through description to something beyond what can be described—towards a new theatre. His criticism leads rather than follows the theatre. He presents the new actor by outlining the void that will be left by the demise of the old, and then he begins the work of filling that void.

The sceptic will challenge Shaw's interpretation—maybe it is itself a piece of cheap magic, a sham substitute for the real thing—but it is *Shaw* who must be addressed, and only through a reexamination or *review* of memory and understanding. *Waterloo* itself recedes into the past, and a new drama begins in the present of reading, on Shaw's stage. Thus, even in his criticism, as in so many of his plays, Shaw writes a drama of the forgotten or repressed or misunderstood in the act of becoming present.

AFTERWORD

Through time, the critic has the last laugh, and Shaw, who is rarely out of print, always seems to win this particular battle of *Waterloo*. But there are other voices to figure into the all-important afterword that is the historical construction of this event. Gordon Craig writes:

> I think that no one on the English stage will deny that there is nothing to-day, in England, comparable with the Lyceum Theatre under the rule of Irving. I think there are many who would like to see England with another incomparable theatre. After Irving's time, we opened the flood-gates, and there has been a general inundation. It has done no harm. After Irving should come a flood! . . .

You will ask me why there should be a flood after Irving. You may perhaps not be satisfied in your mind that there was sufficient reason for it. The reason is that Irving was the end of a great line of actors.[58]

After *Waterloo,* the deluge. Shaw and his kind constitute what Craig saw as the flood. The singular actor's theatre gave way to a flood of ink in an era associated with the writer. But Irving left a fierce advocate in his godson, the son of Ellen Terry and the architect and aesthete E. W. Godwin. Craig was the most important of the people who took the conflict between Irving and Shaw beyond its one Punch-and-Judy act.

Godwin was a figure absent from Craig's life, and Irving became for Craig a substitute authority figure, as well as a model of the great artist. From an early age, Craig took roles in Lyceum productions and soon became a regular member of the company. He was seen as a highly promising actor (by Shaw, among others) when, in the mid-1890s he left the Lyceum and soon after that quit acting entirely. Around the turn of the century, he directed and designed a number of experimental productions in pursuit of a new approach to the theatre. His visionary books and articles on the theory and practice of the theatre began appearing shortly thereafter. He left England in 1904, disdaining what he saw as the nation's decline into mediocrity, to work with some of the more progressive artists of the day, including Reinhardt, Duse, and Stanislavsky. Eventually he found it impossible to gain the requisite support for his iconoclastic ideas and extraordinary but impractical designs, and he turned more and more to writing, sketching in the abstract an ideal theatre, in which, it turns out, actor and author were to be completely subject to the control of a single artist. Craig took Irving as his model for this supreme creator.

As Shaw saw it, though, Craig was essentially a talented actor, with skill in drawing, who had overestimated the force and originality of his ideas and had attempted to conquer the world on the basis of those ideas. Predictably failing in this aim, Craig had become a "literary propagandist" and finally "an irresistible sort of goose-genius in artistic biography."[59] The subject he had chosen to mine in this latter phase was the beatified memory of his "master," Henry Irving, and also of his mother. In these adulatory writings, he singled out Shaw as the satanic enemy who had, he thought, sought to desecrate the sacred memory of these honored forebears. The flood that followed Irving was, according to Craig, a nightmarish vision of replicated Shaws: "Our Theatres have lately somehow been clogged with men of action, Napoleons of the Stage. Open the doors—let them and their glorious self-importance escape . . . or we shall have a thousand little Napoleons. What we have been working for years in our Movement Towards a New Theatre is *to grow Artists not Men of Action.*"[60] The war that had been waged over *Waterloo* and Irving's "incomparable" theatre continued to be fought on the slippery ground of history, and finally it is hard to discriminate between the fierce ideologist of the *Über-Marionette,* Craig, and the domineering spirit of his dead father-figure, Irving, as they square against the comparably Napoleonic Shaw. Craig and Shaw argued over the body and departed spirit of the fallen hero, Brewster/Irving, fighting for control of the historical record of who he was. Which epitaph would stand in place of a career that no longer existed except in its verbal and pictorial residues? In this conflict, they also assumed different attitudes toward that other departed being of the Lyceum history, of which even fewer traces remain: the crowd.

CHAPTER II

HEART OF THE CROWD I:
"THE JUDGMENT OF CONTEMPORARY
EXPERIENCE"

> The play met with a success extraordinary even for Irving.
> The audience followed with rapt attention and manifest
> emotion, swaying with the varying sentiments of the scene.
>
> Bram Stoker, *Personal Reminiscences*
> *of Henry Irving*, I, 249

There is a vision of the nineteenth-century crowd in this and many similar accounts of Henry Irving's theatrical triumphs. The writer here naturally measures success in terms of emotion, and not in an abstract sense but in the concrete imagery of the *motion of emotion* across or through a crowd. Thus, Stoker sees the audience "swaying." This is a relatively mild description, fitting for the gently contradictory movements of *A Story of Waterloo*. Often the physical metaphors of a crowd's emotions had a more extreme character or, so to speak, more weather than Stoker's image; floods, earthquakes, torrential storms stood for sublime feelings. The nineteenth-century crowd follows and is rapt and is commonly swaying and swept with emotion that surges from the heart toward the object of attention— flowing, pouring, washing in waves. Approval thunders, and disapproval blasts, and both can rend the air or explode like a volcano or crash like an avalanche.

Perhaps it was in theatrical literature that this elaborate poetic conceit for describing crowds emerged most profusely, in descriptions of dramatic performances furnished by sympathetic critics and publicists. There is, of course, a direct relation between this descriptive diction and the "nature" of the theatre that it addressed—both are typically caught up in an essentially romantic view of the world. Both the individual in the audience and the actor on the stage experience the porous quality of the self, the deep interfusion of the outside and the inside. The heightened emotions felt in the theatre would, therefore, seem to permit insight into the hidden forces and structures of nature. On the other hand, the spectacle of a world in upheaval, out of balance and full of danger, such as that presented in many theatrical productions, would seem to reflect the hidden forces and structures of the self. But the interfusion becomes still more complex in the theatre than in literature, since the crowd takes the place of the individual as the object of address, and the crowd becomes more and more a part of the spectacle, both as figured on the stage and as a public fact within the increasingly vast auditorium. The spectator feels with the crowd, and the actor feels for the crowd, and the crowd itself becomes a natural fact, a landscape, in which hidden forces and structures can be glimpsed.

Irving's Lyceum productions set the late-Victorian standard for the romantically inspired theatrical landscape, which extended throughout the enthusiastic crowd. The various writings about this landscape are virtually all that remain of what was once an emotionally vibrant scene. They might be regarded as poems for their attempts, deliberate or incidental, to represent something of that environment. By 1895, however, a new element was making itself felt in that landscape, antithetical to the old assumptions about its nature. Many have written about the profound change that was at hand in terms that echo those of St. John Ervine: "I did not know that my beginning was almost simultaneous with Henry Irving's end, that Irving and the actor's theatre were about to die, that Bernard Shaw and the author's theatre were rising to great renown."[1] Some writers, such as Clement Scott and William Winter, felt sure that the change was for the worse, with the latter proclaiming in 1913 that the "pinnacle of beauty" had been attained in the best days of Irving and Edwin Booth: "The period extending from about 1878 to about 1890 displayed so much and such variety of opulence [of acting] that it would seem invidious to set the Present in comparison with it."[2] Writers about the theatrical environment of the 1890s who were more conservative faced the poetic problem of overcoming a growing turbulence, evidenced by an increasingly divided audience. The revolutionaries, on the other hand, faced the problem of overcoming a tremendous inertia—of bringing more weather into the landscape. One would like to know more about the extension and effect of the theatre of this period upon its audience, but, for these conflicting rhetorical reasons, the portrayals of its landscape are difficult to interpret.

The case might be made that the much-discussed transition from actor's to author's theatre was itself something of an optical illusion, created by an unprecedentedly populous and influential critical community, sharply polarized over the subject of Ibsen. A few revolutionists promoted him vigorously, and a few reactionaries resisted him with equal vigor, but the conflict affected the whole critical community to some degree. Those who were opposed to the idea of substituting *Little Eyolf* or *Rosmersholm* for a lavish historical contrivance by W. G. Wills or Comyns Carr or a new one-act play by Conan Doyle found themselves having to defend what were, in fact, mere vehicles for a certain sort of acting. Ibsen would never prove popular to the extent that those other works had and would not become a fixture on the London stage until the nonprofit and nationalized theatre movement took hold. (*Both* Shaw and Irving actively campaigned for that.) The critics who preferred the status quo and were leery of Ibsen, however, found themselves defending some fairly trivial plays, largely on the basis of strong acting. The aging Irving, who had so long dominated the stage, formed a convenient symbol for the passing of a heroic era. Indeed, his life and death had been so sentimentalized by the end, so thoroughly constructed as a vehicle for nostalgic regret, that nearly all critics participated in the mythicizing, even someone like Archer. But relatively inconsequential plays designed for strong performers continued to be the staple of the commercial theatre, and actors of remarkable power continued to act in them. Perhaps all that had changed was that the artistic air that Irving had given to such productions, the intellectual pretension and the allure of high culture, had been removed to the protected environment of a small theatre like Shaw and Granville-Barker's Royal Court Theatre. That is, at any rate, one way of interpreting this notion of an epochal change at the turn of the century.

Reviews are slippery documents, often carrying out an agenda far removed from any sort of personal poetic representation of the emotional or intellectual experience of a performance. And yet the attempt to represent or influence the public's taste, using the audience's response to a specific performance as an occasion, gets directly at the function of a crowd in Irving's sort of theatre. Becoming part of a larger entity, such as a trend or fashion or swaying audience, was part of the aesthetic of that theatre. The critical frame that was placed upon the theatrical landscape did undergo a change around the turn of the century, emphasizing the playwright over the actor as the primary motivating agent of the crowd. The rhetorical shift that accompanied this change was great, turning critical attention away from the production that *was* (the actor's theatre) to the production that *might have been* or *might be* (the writer's theatre). In that conditional future, the

goal of the crowd becomes staying ahead of the critic, rather than having
been (literally) behind the critic on the original landscape.

The passing of the age of great acting was the passing of Henry Irving,
of the nineteenth century, of Victoria, of the empire, of the old guard. Irving spent the last ten years of his life within the mechanism that would
make of his career a milestone, a legend, a coiled history that might continue to exert pressure through time. Theatre historians have made many
efforts to register that effect, but it becomes apparent when one picks
through the artifacts and records that the spring is difficult to locate or define, though the force continues to be felt. Histories that trace the career
over decades *and* histories that elaborate on a moment frame an empty
square where something one fears to call presence must have been—an
actor's presence.

An actor produces adequate or sometimes overwhelming texts in the
moment but leaves behind a fragmentary and insufficient record. This, the
central problem of the history of performance, was well expressed by Stoker in the preface to his *Reminiscences:*

> The fame of an actor is won in minutes and seconds, not in years.
> The latter are only helpful in the recurrence of opportunities; in the
> possibilities of repetition. It is not feasible, therefore, adequately to
> record the progress of his work. Indeed that work in its perfection
> cannot be recorded; words are, and can be, but faint suggestions of
> awakened emotion. The student of history can, after all, but accept
> in matters evanescent the judgment of contemporary experience.[3]

A performance is constructed as a discourse that responds appropriately to
a variety of collateral discourses—those of the playwright, the other actors, the business manager, the audience, and so on—in order to achieve a
momentary effect which is only later, serendipitously, given consequential
form by another set of discursive events, such as reviews, memoirs, eulogies, or by the influence that might have been exerted on other performers
or on the audience. Stoker's complaint is familiar to readers of the history
of acting; indeed, it might be called a motif in writing about actors, especially dead actors. The actor's art depends on those "poets," strong or
weak, who register in well-chosen terms the evanescence of a moment in a
crowd. Dramatic critics often have no particular qualifications for the job,
and sometimes fail even in the basic task of reporting. (In place of the great
curtain line of *Waterloo*—"The Guards need powder, and, by God, they
shall have it!"—one critic heard "The Guards want more powder!" and

another, simply, "Napoleon!")[4] Then, too, since many of the documents that survive—reviews, advertisements, official biographies, and so on— participate in the business mechanism of the theatre, their representational or historical function is distinctly secondary. And yet, these bits of histori- cal writing are remarkably resonant. The interpretive discourse of acting, especially in the late nineteenth century, typically sets one performance in dialogue with a range of others, assessing differences in terms of an im- pressively wide range of circumstances, including the temperament, phy- sique, background, and reputation of the performer; the location and type of theatre; the taste, class, and historical moment of the audience on the occasion; and the self-consciously reported personal history of the inter- preter. Still, the literary exercise consists largely in finding terms in which to memorialize and even immortalize, and in which to universalize the val- ues of the work by means of a variety of tropes and devices, including the use of the classic literary universalizer, Shakespeare, as the true validator of an actor's merit. In one caricature from the period, Shakespeare places a laurel wreath on a bust of Irving; in another, a laureled bust of Shakespeare looks on as Irving and David Garrick drink a toast on the occasion of Ir- ving's receiving his knighthood. The acting of Shakespeare gives a ready access to immortality for those who succeed.

Still, in an art where dying is figured as often as it is in acting, where the passing of the actor's "hour upon the stage" is played out again and again for its poignant or terrifying or even ludicrous effect, there is general acknowledgment that an actor's art does not transcend the historical mo- ment. Instead one finds a steady stream of complaint against the inade- quacy of the verbal record, as in this impressive elegy of Irving. The title is the date of Irving's death:

October 13, 1905

If all the poets' pens in their bright verse
(Like glorious tapers flaming round thy tomb)
Could light these times to see, and they rehearse
Their loss in losing thee, for times to come;
Yet would that age not guess what magic lay
Within that face which marble pictures ill;
The poorest fool that saw it yesterday
Can o'er the lettered future triumph still.
O let me thank thee for the riches given
By thy great spirit to my barren youth,
When in the listening crowd the skies were riven

Before the lightning flashes of thy truth.—
Moved by no vain ambition to be read,
But for my love, I give this to my dead.[5]

Two lines only of this poem attempt to register the actual impact of Irving's presence, and they employ a metaphorical strategy of universalization by implying the extension of the poet through the crowd, which is seen as a stormy landscape, "in the listening crowd the skies were riven / Before the lightning flashes of thy truth." That is the landscape that must be explored in order to see what access is afforded to the "student of history" by what Stoker calls, in a theoretically fraught phrase, "the judgment of contemporary experience."

Weathery descriptions offer, one might say, an inversion of what John Ruskin called the "pathetic fallacy." Ruskin laments the tendency of the weak poet, through an excess of undisciplined feeling, to project human characteristics onto natural objects, e.g., the "weeping sky": "The temperament which admits the pathetic fallacy, is . . . that of a mind and body in some sort too weak to deal fully with what is before them or upon them; borne away, or over-clouded, or over-dazzled by emotion." The poet of the second order perceives wrongly because of this cloud or sea-swell or sunblaze of feeling. The poet of the first order "perceives rightly in spite of his feelings" and "whatever and how many soever the associations and passions may be that crowd around it."[6] Thus the poet faces a sort of crowding, a superabundance of natural tags for the multiple forces of inner turmoil.

Another sort of extreme emotional occasion tests the perceptive and descriptive powers of the writer in the theatre. Here, by contrast, the writer frequently projects images of nature onto the manifest emotions of the human crowd and the dynamic actor who sets off the turmoil—"thundering applause," "ground swell of feeling," "showering the stage with cheers." The feeling is projected over the whole crowd and is claimed to issue from the *heart of the crowd*. This ruling metaphor of sentimental theatre criticism might be taken as a limit case of the pathetic fallacy. The multitude is perceived as an organic whole, moved by the spectacle and expressing in a mass a unified emotion that is shared by or driven by the individual who offers the description.

In a crowd, there is a blurring of the within/without membrane of individual and environmental, self and other. The wash of uncontrolled feeling across this membrane produces delusions similar to those of the pathetic fallacy. The individual is perhaps "borne away, or over-clouded, or over-dazzled," as Ruskin puts it, but it is by the feelings of others in the crowd. A landscape of feeling overbears the individual, a landscape with characteristics of texture and topography, of changing weather, and composed of human beings held in sway by the emotional climate of a performance. The "poet" of crowd description aptly attends to these characteristics, appealing to natural imagery to convey a sense of subjection to the environment. While Ruskin's poet must reach beyond the concentration of feelings *within,* the crowd is concentrated *without,* in intensities toward which (rather than beyond which) the individual reaches. The crowd concenters on the actor at its core.

The nineteenth-century theatre gave a point to this pursuit of feeling beyond the self by providing an intensity toward which a crowd might move. The images of the crowd join almost without boundary—on the same landscape—those of the nineteenth-century starring actor, such as Edwin Forrest, who "could sigh like a zephyr or roar like a hurricane."[7] The theatrical work of this period cannot be appreciated properly without considering its extension through the crowd, on a continuum with the performance, because its spirit moved there as well as on the stage. And perhaps the stage was only a generator, the machine that *inspired* the crowd.

A historical account of *Waterloo* must in some way register its meteorological passing upon the crowd, the resonating phenomenon of its mass reception. Here, if anywhere, was the wonder of the work. But the historian faces a desperate lack of documents attesting to that significant, indeed artful, effect. One must begin with a look at the pressures Irving applied to the crowd and to those various "poets" who would represent the crowd for the moment and for posterity.

One of Henry Irving's main contributions to the profession of acting and to the social definition of the role of the star was his acknowledgment and finally sentimentalization of the role of the audience. Many writers commented on the Lyceum audience, the powerful force that Irving, as Stoker puts it, "had won—had made":

> Here was an audience that *believed* in the actor whom they had come
> to see; who took his success as much to heart as though it had been

their own; whose cheers and applause—whose very presence, was a stimulant and a help to artistic effort. . . .

The physicists tell us that it is a law of nature that there must be two forces to make impact; that the anvil has to do its work as well as the hammer. And it is a distinguishing difference between scientific and other laws that the former has no exceptions. So it is in the world of the theatre. Without an audience in sympathy no actor can do his best.[8]

Irving and his associates used a remarkable variety of methods to take command of the public image of the theatre and reform the very concept of the audience/crowd. Outside the theatre, he bound the audience to his cause (and hence to himself as leader) by his public discussion of the actor's calling, the moral stature of the theatre, the progress of the art. The audience that attended the Lyceum then, as it were, selected itself from the crowd, the public at large, on the basis of its association with that public discussion. This limited homogeneity was further refined by emotional associations with Irving as celebrity, which were heightened by publicity or gossip about such matters as his suspected relationship with Ellen Terry or his opinions on his sons' careers. Then, too, Irving quite often tied his productions to a specific charitable cause, thus binding the audience into a unit that had little or nothing to do with the play being performed. Thus, he shaped the crowd into an audience, even before they entered the doors of the theatre. The often-mentioned "revolution in the attitude of the English people towards the calling of the actor," which Irving sponsored, coincided with a revolution in the attitude of the English people towards itself as an audience.[9] Irving helped instill a sense of higher motive in the audience, through which they were able to recognize a new sort of unity among themselves, and that unity specifically disallowed the (vaguely defined) lower motive. The remarkable thing was that he was able to foster elite expectations without recourse to class prejudice and without disrupting the essentially middle-class base of his audience.

Inside the theatre, Irving took unusual pains to dignify the role of the audience, regularly addressing them in the warmest terms, praising them in interviews, and, in a variety of ways, insuring that the house was always full so that the impact of massed emotion could be felt. Sir John Martin-Harvey, who was a member of the company, remembers that the houses were always full. Even he did not know the well-kept secret by which the houses were papered, when necessary.[10] George Arliss, a novice actor at the time, recalled that it was customary for unemployed actors to write to the acting manager for available seats, but they never bothered to write to the Lyceum because it "was always crowded—at least, we believed it was."[11] The evidence suggests that Stoker, who was something of a name-dropper, made good use of a VIP list to secure the attendance of noteworthy figures, later seeing to it that their attendance was noted in the press. Irving cultivated association with prominent members of English society and of the artistic elite, and he took care that the bulk of the crowd should feel at one with them, contiguous with eminence and wealth and authority. On the other hand, Irving took particular care to express his appreciation of the pit and gallery patrons, who he claimed were the best audiences.

The Lyceum was structured like most English theatres of the day, with pit, stalls, boxes, circle, and gallery, providing an array of classes and tastes, which Irving, to a remarkable degree, was able to bind. His several alterations of this theatre over some twenty years suggest that his managerial strategy was to improve conditions (and capacity), especially among the cheap seats. Upon assuming the lease in 1878, he provided the plain benches of the pit and gallery with backs and rails and generally refitted the interior of the house. In 1881, he enlarged the pit by two hundred seats with good sight lines and installed new seats throughout the pit area. He also increased the capacity of the dress circle, enlarged the main staircase (used by all except those in the pit or gallery), and removed an arch that had impeded the lines of sight from the upper part of the gallery. The seating capacity increased with each improvement, from about 1250 (1871) to 1455 (1884) to 1600 (1899), which made the Lyceum larger than most London theatres.[12] Stoker follows theatrical custom in describing the increase in size following the 1881 renovation in terms of gross, not capacity—from £228 to about £420.[13] Irving and Stoker had no scruples against boasting about the size of the audience for a particular production in these monetary terms. Irving's early biographer, Austin Brereton, includes a great deal of information (much of it unreliable) about Irving's profits, all intended to illustrate his command of crowds and his skill in capitalizing on them. On the other hand, Brereton is usually scrupulous about adding a sentence such as the following: "And the artistic result was equal to the financial aspect of the case."[14]

In 1885, Irving attempted to cope with what was perceived as the serious problem of the crush of people at the pit entrance to the theatre. Pit seats

were customarily unreserved, and the wait outside the door, in all weath-
ers, without a formal arrangement for a queue, was known to bring out a
"rough-and-tumble, weakest-to-the-wall barbarism," as William Archer
described it. Archer began his report on Irving's change in the system as
follows:

> Everyone who has stood sweltering in the Black Hole of Calcutta
> which must be endured for an hour or two by whoever hopes for a
> tolerable place in the Lyceum pit, will welcome the radical reform
> whereby Mr. Irving proposes, so far as in him lies, to do away with
> this disgrace to our civilization. . . . Whoever has seen delicate
> women elbowing, struggling, gasping, shrieking, fainting in the
> wild-beast-like battle which has hitherto formed, for the poorer
> classes, such an incongruous prelude to the elevating enjoyments of
> the Temple of Art, will thank Mr. Irving for a reform demanded alike
> by common sense and common humanity.[15]

The proposed solution was to institute a scheme for booking the pit and
gallery seats, which in the meantime had been "reseated throughout in a
most luxurious fashion." When, on the opening night of the season, Irving
gave his curtain speech and broached the subject of the new arrangement
for pit seating, "At once out burst a storm."[16] There were some partisans
of the reform, but there were at least as many who clamored for a return to
the old system. Two weeks later, the system was abandoned, and soon
thereafter the controversial queue system, an innovation of the French Revolution, was adopted at the Lyceum and other theatres. In an interview on
the occasion, Irving stated:

> From more than one point of view, I was not sorry that [booking the
> pit] failed. Had it been successful it would have made a small revo-
> lution in the theatrical world, as even during the six weeks that the
> pit seats were bookable we found that the dress circle and stalls
> people had begun to avail themselves of the privilege of a booked
> seat at a cheap rate. I believe that ladies drove up in their broughams
> to the pit doors. Under the present system, they would go to the
> higher-priced seats. Then, from an artistic point of view, the booked
> pit did not applaud, and the applause of the pit is most inspiring, for,
> as I have said before, the pit is the backbone of the theatre. . . . You
> urge upon me what you are pleased to call the orgies at my pit door,
> . . . and you ask me whether I should be willing to adopt the 'tail'
> system. Certainly, but you cannot form a tail without space. I have

naturally thought much about these things, but even if the Lord Chamberlain were to inaugurate compulsory queues, how could we do it? Why, the line might sometimes wind down to the Embankment, and only police could enforce it. . . . On first nights the scene is, I think I may admit it, a remarkable one. Pittites have come as early as eight in the morning, bringing camp stools and luncheon baskets with them, and waiting until the doors open. Those *are* enthusiasts. I cannot help thinking that John Bull likes a scrimmage. There is the same crush if a popular man is announced to preach. But look at any English crowd, whether it is a first night or Lord Mayor's Day. Why, even the women would be disappointed if, when they got home, they couldn't say 'Oh dear! look at my bonnet strings'; or, 'Bless me if I wasn't half killed at that Lyceum pit!' [17]

On arriving in America for a tour in 1883, Irving discussed with reporters his misgivings about the very different configuration of a Boston theatre, lacking both pit and gallery: "The actor needs applause. It is his life and soul when he is on the stage. The enthusiasm of the audience reacts upon him. He gives them back heat for heat. You have no pit . . . your stalls cover the entire floor . . . in England our stalls are appreciative but not demonstrative. Our pit and gallery are both." [18] Irving fed directly on the willingness of people to form a crowd and become absorbed in the spectacle of inspiration. The "heat for heat" ratio must be considered in examining the cultural construction of Irving's career, but how does one read the text of applause? When the "life and soul" of the actor passes into silence, when the crowd disperses at the end of an evening, at the end of a career, what record remains of its incorporation into the event?

Irving's manipulation of the press insured that all the applause, all the associations with the rich and powerful, all the profits he had generated—his success itself—would register at least momentarily in the form of publicity. He had a staff of writers who supplied paragraphs for the popular and trade newspapers, wrote speeches for his many public appearances, and produced souvenir programs and several celebratory volumes. They strove to portray Irving as glorifying the theatrical art, elevating it to new intellectual heights without losing touch with what Archer called "common sense and common humanity," and one of the chief means toward that end was, in effect, to glorify, if not flatter, the crowd that honored him. He offered them extravagant spectacle, untold wonders, exalted performances, rare

beauties—in short, theatrical wealth. Virtually everything that emerged
from the Lyceum Theatre was calculated to impress the crowd with rich-
ness—lavish, finely tuned productions, elegant graphic design in souvenir
programs and books, supremely dignified and courteous curtain speeches,
nothing vulgar, abrasive, or untoward. The key was to associate his theatre
in the public mind with everything that betokened power—wealth, high
position, reputation, virility, intellectuality, beauty, Shakespeare—and
then to make plenty of moderately priced seats available to all who wished
to absorb some of that power. Apparently, Irving was not cynical about this
approach, concentrating instead on the morally uplifting effect of the stage.
But the promise of power is coded into much of the Lyceum's promotional
material and was picked up and amplified by most journalists, as in this
alluring passage by a New York journalist in 1895 (on the first American
tour during which Irving presented *Waterloo*):

> For intellectual men, the presence of Henry Irving upon our stage
> has from the first been not less a benefit than a delight. Mind answers
> to mind; and it is one of the signal peculiarities of this great actor
> that, everywhere and under all circumstances, he is the cause of in-
> cessant intellectual activity. Without tumult, and simply through his
> tremendous energy and unresting labour, he arouses and stimulates,
> in every quarter, the intellectual force of the time. Every thinker is
> aware of his presence and conscious of his influence. For nearly a
> quarter of a century his power in this respect has been advancing—
> the power to stimulate thought, to awaken interest, to vitalise ambi-
> tion, to refresh weary minds, to diffuse alacrity of spirit, and to hal-
> low common life with the charm of romance. . . . Such a conquest
> is achieved only by the wise use of imperial powers, the most stren-
> uous labour, and the most conscientious devotion to those ideas and
> agencies which are naturally tributary to human happiness.[19]

The linkage of "unresting labour" with "intellectual activity" and "imperial
powers" suggests the range of his appeal, from the common life in need of
hallowing or vitalization to the epitome of intellectual force, all in the context of world dominance. The diction echoes period advertisements for
self-improvement literature, miracle treatments, and other keys to success.
The pitch is aimed at those who know their own deficiencies, those most
likely to refresh their weary minds in the pit or gallery. An Irving production was an ideal site for what Thorsten Veblen would soon call conspicuous consumption.

The central concern of the publicist is, of course, to procure an audience, but also to frame or give shape to the audience's perception of the theatre or of a performance. The documents produced by the publicist thus reflect the experience of the crowd, but in a manner at least as unreliable as that of the critic. The exaggerations and deceptions follow hidden strategies, which are never fully disclosed. Still, their texts might also be read as lyrical embellishments of the crowd experience. Bram Stoker was Irving's acting manager, but in that capacity also one of his publicists. His custom was to stand in the foyer before the performance and oversee the arrival of the audience, resolving any problems that might arise, but, more generally, greeting and chatting with those who were friends of the theatre. He also lobbied the critics. He would invite them, even Shaw himself, to join Irving for the customary opening night banquet following the production. Shaw termed this sort of bribery "Chicken and Champagne": "I always accepted the invitation as a princely favour; but I never went."[20] After Shaw had proved as antipathetic to the Lyceum as possible, he was stricken from the critics list, and Stoker appears to have instructed the box office manager to refuse him a ticket. Shaw answered with threats, and the manager capitulated. Shaw was a maddening case for Stoker because he so completely resisted the blandishments with which the Lyceum handled critics. The point was to gain their sympathy so that they might blend in with the acquiescent crowd. Stoker's writings on Irving give a sense of the crowd that is diametrically opposite Shaw's. They are poems of enthusiasm, such as the following: "When the dying veteran sprang from his chair to salute the colonel of his old regiment the whole house simultaneously burst into a wild roar of applause."[21] A review of an Irving performance in Tennyson's *Becket,* late in his career, epitomizes this portrayal of the crowd: "A last impression is of a vast crowd cheering itself hoarse, of people standing on their seats waving hats and handkerchiefs, and of a dignified figure, still in austere monk's raiment, standing before the curtain—on the shore, as it were, of a great ocean of applause."[22] In this theatre, actors and audiences contrived among themselves to form a landscape amid civility, where wildness and abandon, as well as the heroic inspiration that dominates disorder, might be experienced.

Irving went to some lengths to obtain this poetic representation of his work. Early in his career as Lyceum manager, without public announcement, he paid one thousand pounds for a journal, *The Theatre,* which thereafter kept up an almost unmixed flow of flattering coverage of Irving, his associates, and his friends, especially after Irving signed over the journal, without remuneration, to Clement Scott in January of 1880. As dramatic critic for the *Daily Telegraph,* the *Sunday Times,* the *Observer, Figaro,* and other prominent publications (three or four at a time), Scott was the most influential critic of the day. He was among those high-minded *and* corruptible journalists for whom Irving generously demonstrated the warmest affection. Scott conveniently devoted a good portion of his career to idolizing Irving. He was, in fact, something of a sycophant, cultivating his associations with many prominent figures in the theatrical community. It cost Irving considerable effort over several years to procure for him at last, in 1892, an invitation to the Garrick Club. Their words of mutual esteem on all sorts of public occasions tested the limits of Victorian eulogy.

Irving wrote to Scott well over one hundred times during twenty-three years, apparently beginning soon after the transfer of the journal. From the start, one finds passages like the following:

> Put in a par[agraph] like a good fellow—about the money cleared at the Bazaar in aid of the Perry Bar Institute—Birmingham.
> I opened the Bazaar, you know. . . .

and

> You will be glad to hear, I know, that last night was the biggest 2nd night we ever had in the Lyceum—£278—& the play [*The Corsican Brothers*] went splendidly—enthusiastically.
> Thank you with all my heart for the pains you took to do it justice to the production [*sic*]—(which is without doubt the finest we have yet seen)—& for the spirit of your admirable article throughout. Yours is certainly from the pen of a gentleman & a critic—two things inseparable.

A year later, at an unrelated libel suit brought to trial by Scott, Irving's gift of *The Theatre* to the critic was made public, causing some embarrassing comment in the press. By then, however, Irving was so completely in command of his public image that he wrote to Scott: "I am not at all sorry that my name was brought in. . . . I would have no possible objection to my interest in the paper being known, as it was to very many." Through these years, the magazine had the look of the Lyceum—dignified and tasteful, with florid prose and beautifully reproduced photographs and prints. It was

FIGURE 2. William Archer. (Both photographs courtesy of Harvard Theatre Collection)

FIGURE 3. Clement Scott.

also expensive for the publisher. Scott was no more able to make it profitable than Irving had been, and in 1888 he related his troubles to Irving, who told him, "Certainly I would advise you to sell by all means if you think best & whatever it may fetch look on as your own completely."[23]

In a discussion of this incident, Irving's grandson and biographer, Laurence Irving, offers a fine analysis of the corruptibility of the press in those days *and* demonstrates by his argument how a clever player like Irving might be spared any imputation of guilt in this obvious case of bribery or tampering. Irving was a master at bringing out the finest casuistry from his defenders:

> In acquiring *The Theatre* Irving was pursuing a carefully calculated policy regarding the press which, for some time, he had prosecuted with vigour. When he came to London, dramatic criticism had been at its lowest ebb. It was regarded as the least reputable of journalistic activities. Nearly every dramatic critic was a successful or frustrated playwright. Notices, on the whole, were written in terms either of indiscriminating praise by those who hoped for or enjoyed the favour of theatrical managers, or of scurrilous vituperation by those whom the managers had failed to placate with promises of the purchase of options on their plays. Nearly all were corrupted, if not

by the bribe direct, from puff-seeking actors or managers, by too intimate association and traffic with the theatrical profession which coloured their criticism with the pale cast of self-interest. At its best, dramatic criticism was, for the most part, highly coloured reporting; in general it was apathetic to the conditions into which English drama and acting had fallen.

This sets out the reprehensible condition of an institution in need of reform. Next he turns to Irving's "carefully calculated policy":

While studying carefully the criticism of the few [critics] whose opinion he valued and respected, in the main [Irving] regarded critics and paragraphists with indifference or contempt. He looked upon himself as the public's humble servant. If he was able to win their support and approval without lowering the high standard which he had set himself, he accepted their verdict as that alone worthy of consideration. Directly his popularity with the public was beyond doubt, he exploited with cynical amusement the venality of the press in furthering his aims and in publicising his activities, while striking ruthlessly at those journalists who, by the vulgar or scandalous nature of their comments, undermined his conception of the dignity of the actor's profession. [24]

There is thus nothing venal about Irving's actions, just good business practice in humble service to the public. When Richard Mansfield came to London in 1889 and asked Irving about the best thing to be done to secure his success, Irving was rumored to have replied, "Bribe Scott!" [25]

From the late 1860s, Scott was the leading "picturesque" critic, going beyond the duty of evaluating plays and players to produce highly detailed, evocative sketches of the emotionally intense moments of a production, including the response throughout the audience. Scott's example was followed by most of the day's critics, who themselves formed a sort of crowd, echoing and amplifying the responses of the crowd at large, among whom they sat. And yet, during the 1890s, the crowd came to bear increasing dissent within its ranks, in the form of a small group of individualistic critics antagonistic to Irving, headed by William Archer, Bernard Shaw, and A. B. Walkley, sometimes called the "three musketeers" of criticism. Gordon Craig gives a mordant picture of the divisive presence of such critics in his hagiographical book on Irving. Following a description of the enthusiasm at a Lyceum opening, he writes:

And in the midst of this spectacle sat a number of men, grave, grieved, ridiculous. . . . Archer bewails—Bernard Shaw shakes his head—the *Athenaeum* sneers, and the *Figaro* is glum. Enjoying nothing, anon they leave the theatre, to say that the audience were all fools, suffering from Irvingmania. They say it in print, and what they do not say they reveal; they reveal an ignorance of all art, of all that is lovely, of all that is enchanting the judicious. They stubbornly "won't"—and they hate the very thought of enjoyment and enchantment—"so there!"

We will come to them by and by. For the moment the sound of a tumult of applause is in our ears—"Irving is loved and appreciated" is the only thing it says, and the only thing which matters.[26]

For a long while, of course, there had been critics who expressed their dissatisfaction in defiance of the majority, but in several ways, the new wave of antagonists differed from their predecessors. These critics, especially Shaw, made a point of detaching themselves from the crowd and challenging the theatrical devices and sentimental trickery that did so much to stimulate crowd feeling. In effect, they made a topic of the crowd, evaluating it as a component of the theatrical mechanism, a means as well as an end, a part of the spectacle and a part of the institution. And they made a point of inquiring into the ideological significance of the crowd's compliance, while at the same time resisting compliance themselves.

But this stance awkwardly suggested that they would resist any emotional excitement in the theatre, as Craig would argue. They vehemently denied this, and so were often at pains to discriminate between proper artistic effects and claptrap, insisting on objectivity and attempting to identify an appropriate emotional response to drama. Shaw, Archer, and Walkley, of course, had the additional impetus of promoting Ibsen and the New Drama, and Shaw forthrightly sought to promote himself. Even they acknowledge that there could be no possibility of true objectivity, whatever that may be, in their writing, but their "grave, grieved" and unmoved attitude might have indeed substantially altered the landscape of the crowd, thus altering the phenomenon to be observed, the theatrical event as such. In an open letter to Archer in 1896, J. M. Barrie reports observing the critic from a box. He saw a ripple of laughter running along the stalls until it reached Archer, but it could not leap over him: "You are like the ground that is cleared in a forest when a fire is approaching."[27] The self-consciousness of the antithetical critics opens another view of the crowd— the solitary individual amid the crowd—complementary to that of the critic who represents and partakes of the massed emotion. Shaw identified some of the characteristics of the other sort of critic in an 1896 review of a volume of Clement Scott's collected criticisms of Lyceum opening nights:

> The main secret of Mr Scott's popularity is that he is above all a sympathetic critic. His susceptibility to the direct expression of human feeling is so strong that he can write with positive passion about an exhibition of it which elicits from his colleagues only some stale, weary compliment in the last sentence of a conventional report, or, at best, some clever circumlocutory discussion of the philosophy of the piece. . . . The excellence of Mr Scott's criticisms lies in their integrity as expressions of the warmest personal feeling and nothing else. They are alive: their admiration is sincere and moving: their resentment is angry and genuine. He may be sometimes maudlin on the one hand, sometimes unjust, unreasonable, violent, and even ridiculous on the other; but he has never lost an inch of ground by that, any more than other critics have ever gained an inch by a cautious, cold, fastidious avoidance of the qualities of which such faults are the excesses. Our actors and actresses feel the thorough humanity of his relation to them. . . . The public believes in Mr Scott because he interprets the plays by feeling *with* the actor or author—generally more, perhaps, with the actor than the author—and giving his feeling unrestrained expression in his notices.

Shaw contrasts Scott, on the one hand, to "the average young University graduate," who shuns expression of emotion, and the results of whose "genteelly negative policy are about as valuable as those which might be expected by a person who should enter for a swimming race with a determination to do nothing that could possibly expose him to the risk of getting wet." On the other hand, he describes William Archer as "complementary and antidotal" to Scott. Shaw elsewhere makes apparent his admiration for Archer's criticism, but here it seems he would like to identify an alternative ground of "sympathetic criticism," neither maudlin nor unjust, where he might stand as well. Shaw disapproves of Scott's overly affected crowd, seeing in them the germs of bourgeois taste, reproducing uncontrollably in a medium of cultural capitalism. Scott held a position that was ideal for exploiting their voracious appetite, taking advantage of "the growth of mammoth newspapers like the Daily Telegraph, the multiplication of theatres, and the spread of interest in them."[28] He also made canny use of the unparalleled popularity of the crowd-master Irving.

Shaw obviously plays upon an elitist disapproval or fear of mass interests in his attacks on Scott and Irving. His first concern was to break what might be called the mesmeric thrall that held the crowd, and which critics such as Scott so effectively served. A refraction of opinion and attitude among the critics might be taken as the first step toward the disbanding of the crowd in the theatre, dividing and differentiating the audience to sever those close ties that make for group sentiment. Contiguous individuals in a highly charged emotional atmosphere can make for an organized mass sentiment, a unanimous surge of feeling greater than the sum of its parts. But by the same token, an element of difference introduced into such a mass can instantly fracture the group and redirect its interest toward the difference itself. Shaw was eager to fight for the progressive drama, "which is polemical rather than instinctive in its poignancy," and to turn the theatre into a battlefield if need be, and the crowd into soldiers, under different banners—banners of difference.[29]

Gordon Craig, too, disdained the crowd's intelligence and its influence on the performance. He often cited approvingly the example of Stanislavsky's Moscow Art Theatre for its discouragement of applause. Applause is the conventional sign by which a crowd registers and measures its enthusiasm, but for Craig, in an essay he wrote in 1909, it was "a vulgarity" and "the flattery of the strong by the weak": "Applause is the gross expression of our fear and envy awakened by the sight of a man in a position unattainable. The sooner applause is banished from the theatre the better for actors and audience. The way partly to prevent it is to leave the curtain down at the end of each act, and not raise it again until the beginning of the next act, and to give up the bad practise of the actor appearing before the curtain."[30] In other words, the curtain should not answer to the crowd, extending its power by going up again with applause or parting to disclose the star, but should seal the strength and dignity of the art from the control of the weak and vulgar. Irving, on the other hand, was fond of quoting the words of George Frederick Cooke: "Ladies and Gentlemen, if you don't applaud, I don't act."[31] Stoker clarifies these words by adding, "The want of echoing sympathy embarrasses the player."[32] In his book on Irving, Craig continues to quote Stanislavsky's opinion that applause is inartistic and offensive, but he declares that Irving must be considered an exception. On this occasion, he seeks to call the crowd back to the memory of Irving's performance to animate his description of what would otherwise seem a prosaic moment. The moment was no more and no less than the appearance of the hero at the heart of the crowd. Craig had been there, in the crowd, feeling that enthusiasm, and he knew that it would be necessary to bring back that ghostly crowd from the dead in order to write the poem of Irving's presence in that moment:

> In *The Bells,* the hurricane of applause at Irving's entrance was no interruption. It was no boisterous greeting by an excitable race, for a blustering actor—it was something which can only be described as part and parcel of the whole, as right as rain. It was a torrent while it lasted. Power responded to power. This applause was no false note, whereas silence would have been utterly false; for though Irving endured and did not accept the applause, he deliberately called it out of the spectators. It was necessary *to them*—not to him; it was something they had to experience, or to be rid of, or rather released from, before they could exactly take in what he was going to give them.[33]

Craig's ambivalence about the crowd is threaded all through this passage, but especially in the sequence of terms, "something they had to experience, or to be rid of, or rather released from." Power responds to power in this passage, where, in effect, authorship of the applause is in question. The crowd both *takes* and *is given.* The crowd makes the curtain go up by its applause, makes the absent actor appear again, even from the illusion of death, and satisfies a need for ideality and the heroic by generating a transcendent leader from its enthusiasm. In this, the audience rivals the authority of the actor who, in Craig's view, releases them from their herdlike submission to give them something more important than enthusiasm.

Still, even in his ambivalence, those inversions of the pathetic fallacy—the hurricane, the torrent of applause—reflect Craig's contiguous sympathy with the crowd that is, as Ruskin puts it, "borne away, or over-clouded, or over-dazzled by emotion." Shaw worries about an audience of weak poets, so "borne away" by their feelings that they lose contact with rationality and fail to perceive rightly. The danger of being reduced by the crowd to the lowest common denominator of thinking alarms the critic who would prefer to maintain his individuality at all costs in order to preserve that intellectual edge. Walkley, in an essay called "Applause," complains about the custom of "a loud clap," saying it "suggests the monkey tricks of primeval man." He complains, "But in the realm of dramatic art where we are supposed to be under the spell of illusion, inhabitants for the time being of an imaginary world, applause is an interruption, a rude reminder of

reality, a really impolite distinction between the player and his part."[34]
Walkley seems to be asking for an audience cleared of the crowd, a perfectly undisturbed scene of writing for the individual critic who strives to
represent the performance "in itself." Shaw, also, addressed what he saw as
the problem of an audience too manifest in its appreciation. He inserted a
"personal appeal" into the programs of the 1913 revival of *John Bull's
Other Island,* asking for the audience not to applaud or laugh during the
performance.[35] On the other hand, with his acknowledgment that he en-
joyed *Waterloo* (as a music hall turn) and his confession in the same review
that "I, too, have something of that aboriginal need for an occasional car-
nival in me," Shaw registers an ambivalence similar to Craig's.[36] Finally,
though, Craig credits Irving with a full measure of belief in his mastery,
whereas Shaw, far more ascetic, will only credit Irving with a full measure
of devious skill in the manipulation of his crowd.

Craig's writings on Irving tend to construct his memory as a prophetic
embodiment of Craig's own theories about the artist of the theatre. Irving's
popularity figures as a backdrop to his solitary mastery, confirming Craig's
own choice of a life of isolation rather than compromise, but then, suddenly, the crowd springs to life in his descriptions. The crowd was something that Craig "had to experience, or to be rid of, or rather released
from," in order to become his own master. He adopted the famous Byronic
pose of Childe Harold:

> I have not loved the world, nor the world me;
> I have not flattered its rank breath, nor bow'd
> To its idolatries a patient knee,—
> Nor coin'd my cheek to smiles,—nor cried aloud
> In worship of an echo: in the crowd
> They could not deem me one of such; I stood
> Among them, but not of them; in a shroud
> Of thoughts which were not their thoughts, and still could,
> Had I not filed my mind, which thus itself subdued.[37]

He also liked to assert that Irving, too, had taken this attitude, but the
adoration of his audiences shows that this could not have been the case.
Irving's thoughts were entirely their thoughts, and his knee bowed repeatedly to their idolatries. That was how the theatre functioned. Craig, taking
the stricter line, found himself alone in Italy, constructing an imaginary
theatre for an audience that existed only in the abstract. Finally, when the
impossibility of such a theatre alienated even him, he returned to his mem-

ories of Irving and the enthusiasm of those crowds. Like Corporal Brewster, he returned in reflection to a heroic moment in his past, and a bolt of
vivid memory crossed the gap in time. His "poems" of Irving are illumi-
nated by such bolts.

Shaw, meanwhile, continued to dismiss Irving's memory coldly, calling
him an "infinitesimal actor-nothingness." He rationalized the passing of
Irving's theatre in terms of historical logic: "Life is a constant becoming:
all stages lead to the beginning of others. The Lyceum business, on its
present plane, cannot be carried any further than it has been carried: con-
sequently we have now reached *a beginning.*"[38] He made no secret of his
belief that he was the agent of that new beginning: "The change for the
better in the British drama, in this century, is more than a mere change: it
is a Transfiguration. And our young critics lament its decay and sigh for
the golden age of Irving, Tree, Alexander and Wyndham, God help
them!"[39] This satiric "poem" (*Don Juan* to Craig's *Childe Harold*) of Irving's memory has had the greater influence on historical appraisal of
Irving.

There is a tendency now to regard Craig as the weak poet of the two, the
one who was borne away by his affection for Irving and by the frenzy of a
hypnotized or sentimentally infected crowd. Shaw had the clear view, the
presence of mind, etc. Ruskin might have identified Craig as "the man who
perceives wrongly, because he feels, and to whom the primrose is anything
else than a primrose." Ruskin gives a marvelous vision of the sort of great
"poet" Shaw might typify: "But it is still a grander condition when the
intellect also rises, till it is strong enough to assert its rule against, or together with, the utmost efforts of the passions; and the whole man stands
in an iron glow, white hot, perhaps, but still strong, and in no wise evaporating; even if he melts, losing none of his weight."[40] The very self-
sufficiency of this whole man, "in no wise evaporating," tells us of his
situation in the crowd, strongly asserting the rule of intellect. Shaw over-
mastered the enthusiasm of the crowd and his own susceptibility to sentiment in order to express his impassioned understanding of the theatre as he
saw it. Or perhaps Shaw should be classed among those poets who perceive
rightly because they do not feel. Shaw could be said to have described
Waterloo to death in his review, to the point where the play came to seem
lifeless. He replaced subjection and subscription with objection and description, and thus it was inevitable that he saw something other than the
crowd did. He saw "machinery." But does that necessarily imply that the

crowd saw inaccurately the landscape that was before them and of which they were a part—at the heart to the extent that they felt moved?

Shaw's concern was with the written play that gives rise to a performance and the written interpretation that might be carried away from it in a criticism. Craig's concern was with the performance, but only with the performance as it was filtered through his ideas about the values that should be demonstrated by a theatrical work, and further filtered through dewy-eyed memory. It might be said that they both failed to perceive rightly, that both were influenced by misdirected feelings. An actor performs on the margins of a text, inscribing a different text, which is the performance. The performance operates on the landscape of feeling in a crowd, beyond the frame of the prescribable or describable, beyond the capacity of any individual to represent because it withholds or controverts the authority of the individual. One can resist this controversion of individuality, questioning the authority of the performance to produce such an effect, or mistrusting the apparition of spirit at the concentrated core, or otherwise imposing the power of the resolute individual upon the landscape—in short, criticizing. Or one can accede, faithfully, to the higher force, the "natural" sweep of emotion, which may, of course, prove to be nothing other than the mechanism of some social control. The poet's description will discover only the describable, his logic only that which is susceptible to logical analysis. That is to lay bare the machine, but such a writing does not and cannot show the spiritual effect, which might be defined as precisely *the acting of the text,* a superfluity capable of flooding the crowd with feeling.

This is to say something more than that the acting of the text moved the crowd. One must add that the emotion of the crowd *was* in a sense the action of the performed text. It is an illusion, a fiction, that the acting of the text comes from the actor and in some manner goes to and acts upon the audience, which passively receives this gift, or this assault. The crowd, *like the actor,* longs for and strives toward a full or fulfilled text, in the sense of a writing that would represent the self acting in the face of what acts upon it, a writing that might be both reading and writing at once, suggesting the reflexivity of active and passive in time. That is the "nature" of the theatrical landscape, and anyone might, like Corporal Brewster, seize the heroic opportunity opened upon this landscape in its time, its history, by that surge of feeling, that effect of spirit, which is action and passion, active and passive, acting and passing. The audience, like the actor, surpasses individuality by acting on the point of death, passing from death *and* passing from life in a burst of willful and dutiful feeling: "The Guards need powder, and, by God, they shall have it!" There is certainly something ghostly in this writing, which can never quite be grasped, which constantly seems to perish as the efforts fail.

The spirit around which the crowd concenters—symbolized by the inspired actor—represents the feeling of "contemporary experience" in the face of "matters evanescent." (Recalling Stoker: "The student of history can, after all, but accept in matters evanescent the judgment of contemporary experience.") The momentarily glimpsed writing of the theatrical landscape, showing the interplay of act- and pass-, permits of no record for the student of history. All that will remain is the attenuated writing, in the dual form of machine and pathetic fallacy, logical reduction and emotional afterglow. As Stoker writes, "It is not feasible, therefore, adequately to record the progress of his work." The historian A. E. Wilson put it more simply: "The more one reads of [Henry Irving] the more one fails to discover the real Irving."[41]

There could be no adequate record of the fact of his acting, no fit memorial or framed commemoration. Of course, that is the weak point of the art, its mortality—the passing of acting. But, just as the actor's fame "is won in minutes and seconds, not in years," so does this mortality occur in the moment. The drive for an adequate writing fails continually but perhaps in no other context does it so nearly succeed as in the theatre. That the student of history must grapple with the notion that "words are, and can be, but faint suggestions of awakened emotion," is true but not by any means a situation unique to the historian. From faint suggestions or weak signals out of the past, come occasionally the clearest messages, inspired and capable of awakening the future.

One must not forget the deceptive similarity between shocks of helpless weakness and impulses of the greatest strength. After carefully enumerating the ranks of poets according to their capacity to perceive rightly and to feel, Ruskin reminds us of this difficulty: "Only however great a man may be, there are always some subjects which *ought* to throw him off his balance; some, by which his poor human capacity of thought should be conquered, and brought into the inaccurate and vague state of perception, so that the language of the highest inspiration becomes broken, obscure, and wild in metaphor, resembling that of the weaker man, overborne by weaker things."[42] In such cases, the reader must exercise judgment, careful discernment, but ultimately he might have to go on faith. *Waterloo* might indeed be a weak point in Irving's career and in the nineteenth-century theatre and in the taste of the late Victorian public, in which sentiment overcame the capacity to perceive rightly on a grand scale. How does one remember such a time, such a moment of weakness for the pathetic fallacy? There is a profound, pathetic temptation to accept "the judgment of contemporary experience" in the words of Gordon Craig:

> Irving was astonishing us always—he was terrible in tragedy: not terrifying as a sudden thunderclap, but as when the whole of nature seems to suffer and to become more still and more and more quiet, so did Irving do. There is a flash—something is struck—something terrible has happened, without rumblings or crash. These come afterwards; then the clouds conspire, and like a crowd of actors, create a fearful noise—but the tragedy, the terrible thing, has happened. The force which struck and blinded us has withdrawn, and is once again veiled within its secret temple. Irving in tragedy was not like the storm which splutters out, but like one which gathers and then strikes—once. Once aware of this we were awake.[43]

MR. HENRY IRVING WATCHING A REHEARSAL

FIGURE 4. From a drawing by Bernard Partridge. The figure in the background resembles Bram Stoker. (Courtesy of Harvard Theatre Collection)

To match his concentration at rehearsal, you must go to Napoleon at a military council.

Christopher St. John,
Henry Irving (1905)

CHAPTER III

HEART OF THE CROWD II:
"THE MAINSPRING OF ALL AUTHORITY"

> I think it has not been your fortune to hear what is called
> "the house coming down." Even in the epoch of Irving it
> was seldom that anybody else "brought down the house"—
> but Irving brought it down. A terrific sweep of applause is
> not "bringing the house down." "Bringing the house down"
> is when everybody simultaneously calls outs and applauds
> simultaneously and electrically.
>
> Gordon Craig, *Henry Irving,* p. 22

Corporal Gregory Brewster is dead. The roller curtain of the Lyceum Theatre falls slowly, leaving the theatre in dim light; then it rises, and Henry
Irving rises and brings down the house. Then the curtain descends, rapidly
now, until a slight thud is heard, after which it rises again. Eight times the
process is repeated (on opening night and on many occasions afterward) on
eight signals from the stage manager in the prompt corner; eight times the
counterweights fall and the big wheel turns and the curtain goes up and
down, until the crowd does what is called "dying down." Then the stage is
refitted for the next play, the longer work that would finish the evening with
another slow curtain on another death. That is the way the machine
worked.

In the course of the play, the corporal appears first as a picture of pathetic old age, then of amusing senility, then more of the pathetic followed
by more of the amusing, with nuances of quaintness and dignity varying
the pattern of alternation between the tragic and comic. This is what Stoker
called "the whole gamut of human feeling." In his mutability, his moving
away from his past through the stages of progressive infirmity toward
death, he evokes a tragic response. In his immutability, his clinging to routine, his sense of duty, his habits and mannerisms, he evokes a comic response. Gradually, through these alternations, the core of his character is
revealed in the uncovering of his past, which concenters on Waterloo, the

distant scene of origin where his changing and his unchanging began. His whole life appears to reverberate from that moment.

Sixty-six years seem not to have registered at all on the man—he barely grasps the mechanical innovations that have intervened and the passing of the generations of his extended family. On the other hand, the corporal's repetitions—the same anecdotes, the same phrases again and again in different combinations—are like a clock marking a different sort of temporality. The compression of the original in the terminal soldier, and the past hero in the present ruin, begins to unsettle the spectator's accumulated responses, with the tragic inflecting the comic, and vice versa, by the end of the play. The alternations of response, rhythmic but growing more and more intense, become violent, tearing one loose from the grounding of detached sympathy and interest, like a machine that develops an eccentricity, strips its ground bolts, and careens dangerously. One feels the surges of sentiment pushing beyond control. The play reaches for well-known reservoirs of sentiment, the passing of a father figure and of the sublimated form of father worship, patriotism. The man has in effect become his own child, planted as a seed at Waterloo, when the "Dook" turned back the Antichrist and redeemed all the children of England. That is the mythic dimension. On the other hand, the naturalist scene of an otherwise ordinary, infirm, old man living in meager circumstances and creeping toward an inevitable end turns into a heartening celebration of the stability and singularity of his goodness, loyalty, and honor.

In one moment only, the last, does he break from this continuum of his life, this rhythmic alternation of dramatic effects, tragic and comic, and in a flash the past rushes forward. Across a gap of sixty-six years shoots an arc of invigoration, and the same surge of life that carried him through the burning hedge with his tumbril of powder now carries him over the verge into death. The flash is at once all those clustered metaphors of powerful response—illuminating, electrifying, shocking, and magnetic. The very impulse that turned an ordinary soldier of the crowd into a hero becomes visible once again on a plain of ordinariness, and again it serves to concenter a crowd for the recognition of a kind of heroism (in Brewster's brave defiance of death), compounded with another sort of heroic accomplishment (the completion of Irving's impressive performance and the near-completion of his distinguished career). The curtain brings the crowd to a noisy acknowledgment of this point of intensity on the landscape, and an acknowledgment also of its willingness to submit to their ideal.

Waterloo is effective beyond the curtain in space and time, in the subjection of the audience to its time and tempo and in the vigorous show of spirit when the audience is left as just a crowd on the landscape of feeling. The curtain seals off the mystery, veiling the machinery that produces this effect. It is, as Shaw says, the "machinery of a 'good acting play,' " but it is also the machinery of organizing expectations and generating a crowd response. As Archer wrote in the mid-1880s: "The Messrs. Willing [pioneering advertisers], more than Faraday or Edison, deserve to be called the magicians of the nineteenth century; but their 'bold advertisement' is ineffectual compared with the subtle, penetrating, all-pervading influences which keep Mr. Irving in perpetual notoriety."[1] Beyond accomplishing the miracle of reaching across space to touch an audience, plays such as *Waterloo* actually harness the power of the crowd and convert it like a hydroelectric dynamo. *Waterloo,* simpler than most of these plays, shows the mechanism of this public works project. The crowd rises spiritedly as one in the sentimental landscape of the theater, where its impulses are safely sublimated into romance and the heroic, before falling back into the "natural" landscape outside the theatre, with those impulses now safely channeled into fervently held beliefs. The play ebbs and flows and then produces a *coup,* and the crowd reflects this movement. They follow with "rapt attention and manifest emotion," pushing and pulling, laughing and weeping, "swaying," until the *coup* at the end—the point of transcendence—mirrored in the rising of the audience to *strike* the air with applause. The corporal falls as his life expires and the curtain seals the scene. The applause, too, expires at last, and a metaphorical curtain seals the feeling in memory throughout the crowd. The crowd is always naturally bound to the landscape above which rises the hero, the spirit, the actor. The actor is the one who acts so that the crowd can remain passive—or who acts in such a way as to *keep* them passive. They stand within the frame of the picture, not just as background, but in order to make it work through their concentration. They make it beautiful, whole, inspiring, and absolutely authoritative.

As with any other industry, the manufacturers of theatre saw the need for close attention to the engineering of such a vital part of their mechanism. Of course, whatever actual study of this phenomenon might have been undertaken, the knowledge remains a trade secret. The scientific study of crowd or collective psychology arose mainly in France during the nineteenth century, particularly among those who engaged in antidemocratic polemic and who believed that the congregation and agitation of greater and greater masses of people in cities represented a threat to individualism and state authority. The spectacle of powerful crowds in the Paris Commune, the Boulangist demonstrations, and other instances of mass uprising led to much fearful discussion among social scientists and others about the dynamics of crowd behavior. Various psychological models were proposed to account for the formation of a collective will, for the spread by mental contagion of ideas and impulses for which no individual would take responsibility.

Foremost in influence and popularity among those who wrote about the crowd phenomenon, and first to attempt a thorough synthesis of existing ideas, was Gustave Le Bon. He was trained as a physician but made a career as a popularizer and synthesizer of scientific theories, especially psychological and sociological, and has been called the founder of crowd psychology, as well as the "supreme scientific vulgarizer of his generation."[2] Utilizing an organicist view of society consistent with that of Comte, Taine, Durkheim, and others within the mainstream from which he was excluded, he developed the notion of the racial mind or soul as the key to crowd behavior. A crowd, like a nation, might be moved by forces that trigger deep-rooted sentiments, atavistic recurrences of the racial identity. In his view, this sort of collective unconscious was created over generations, carried over by inheritance in the form of various affective states, which he called "sentiments," following the psychologist Théodule Ribot, who posits a "moral sentiment," generally altruistic and sympathetic, as the binding substance of human groups. Ribot, like Le Bon, argues that the driving force of a group is "a powerful emotion leading to action, and, by contagion, communicating its own impulse to others."[3]

In 1895, Le Bon published his seminal study *La Psychologie des Foules,* which sold widely, was quickly translated into many languages, and remains in print to this day. Here he makes no secret of the fact that a fear of the political power of the masses had provoked his "purely scientific" study: "To-day the claims of the masses are becoming more and more sharply defined, and amount to nothing less than a determination to utterly destroy society as it now exists, with a view to making it hark back to that primitive communism which was the normal condition of all human groups before the dawn of civilisation."[4] By his definition, a "psychological crowd" can form without coming into physical proximity, simply through collective abandonment of individuality and a uniting of the thoughts and feelings of the group in one direction at the instigation of a leader. His imagery in describing crowds and his examples, however, show that his argument derives mainly from observations of mob behavior, the crowd of the streets and barricade. The specter of revolution gives his book its rhetorical force. When a crowd forms, he asserts, the individuals might share a common heritage, but the thinking of the group takes place at the level of the lowest common denominator, and different and dangerous psychological characteristics become apparent. As one philosopher put it, "I may seem to know a man through and through, and I still would not dare to say the first thing about what he will do in a group."[5] Le Bon several times compares the growth and virulence of crowds to microbes spreading by contagion, as each individual "acquires, solely from numerical considerations, a sentiment of invincible power which allows him to yield to instincts which, had he been alone, he would perforce have kept under restraint." In other words, crowds pose a risk to society because they allow a return to primordial sentiments without the restraint of reason, and that seems to Le Bon a fearful prospect as the world entered what he deemed "the era of crowds": "Crowds are only powerful for destruction. Their rule is always tantamount to a barbarian phase. A civilisation involves fixed rules, discipline, a passing from the instinctive to the rational state, forethought for the future, an elevated degree of culture—all of them conditions that crowds, left to themselves, have invariably shown themselves incapable of realising."[6] Le Bon was careful, however, to leave open an alternative view to this dire outlook, indeed the possibility of a heroism that does much to undermine the conventional idea of the hero. In this view, heroic actions are regarded as expressions of the generally irrational crowd will, which is as likely to be aimed at a good end (a rescue, a defense of authority) as at a bad end (a lynching, an overthrow). The abatement of self-protective instincts and the combining of powers within the crowd create the occasion for a superhuman (or heroic) effort, so the individual deed, whether brutal or heroic, must be interpreted as an effect of crowd behavior. In the interest of controlling this effect Le Bon and his followers sought, as the First World War approached, to apply crowd theory in the manipulation of armies.

The crowd that Le Bon has in mind is at first glance quite different from that which gathered in the Lyceum Theatre in the mid-1890s, and yet Le Bon does include the theatrical audience in his discussion of "the exaggeration and ingenuousness of the sentiments of crowds":

It has been justly remarked that on the stage a crowd demands from the hero of the piece a degree of courage, morality, and virtue that is never to be found in real life.

. . . The art of appealing to crowds is no doubt of an inferior order, but it demands quite special aptitudes. It is often impossible on reading plays to explain their success. Managers of theatres when accepting pieces are themselves, as a rule, very uncertain of their success, because to judge the matter it would be necessary that they should be able to transform themselves into a crowd.[7]

Finally, there is nothing in Le Bon's book or, it appears, in other studies of crowd psychology of the period, French or English, to distinguish the crowd of the theatre as a separate or different phenomenon. The narrator of Guy de Maupassant's *Sur l'Eau* makes the connection explicit; following a précis of Le Bon's theory, he writes: "In short, it is not more surprising to see an agglomeration of individuals make one whole than to see molecules, that are placed near each other, form one body. To this mysterious attraction must without doubt be attributed the peculiar temperament of theater audiences." The same narrator declares:

I cannot go into a theater, nor be present at any public entertainment. I at once experience a curious and unbearable feeling of discomfort, a horrible unnerving sensation, as though I were struggling with all my might against a mysterious and irresistible influence. And in truth, I struggle with the spirit of the mob, which strives to take possession of me. . . .

The inherent qualities of intellectual initiative, of free will, of wise reflection, and even of sagacity, belonging to any individual being, generally disappear the moment that being is brought in contact with a large number of other beings.[8]

But it should be noted that Le Bon indicates that not every grouping of individuals in a small space results in a crowd; a transition—involving loss of self-consciousness and uniting of the sentiments in a common direction—must occur.

The experience of this transition, it appears, was one of the effects that was eagerly sought by the crowd at Irving's Lyceum Theatre and at many other theatres of the period. It is this effect that was resisted and scorned by Irving's staunch critics, who challenged its morality as well as its aesthetic value. The crowd did not become a topic of English thought to the same degree or with the same emphasis as in France, and in general, English political reaction to mass behavior lagged behind the French. Carlyle's euphoric portrayal of the crowd in *The French Revolution,* as well as the writings of Hugo, Flaubert, and Zola helped to fix the idea that crowd behavior was more or less something that French people did. English discussion of socialism did not, even in its more nervous manifestations, avail itself of the vivid metaphor of Le Bon, for in fact his term, the "psychological crowd," allows for the substitution of the vivid image of a seething mob in place of a mass political phenomenon that was not localized and that was of a scale much vaster than even the wildest vision of a shouting, jostling throng. Le Bon's choice of words was a way of miniaturizing a vast social movement and provoking a visceral response among its opposition. An English reviewer of Le Bon's book makes a telling point when he observes that in a crowd, the "mutual annulling of individual interests may evolve a higher form of impersonal mind, just as the mutual annulling of individual intelligences produces a lower."[9] This picture of the benefits of conformity stands at the opposite pole from Le Bon's rather paranoid view. In England, therefore, the degree of self-consciousness among those who took pleasure in the crowd phenomenon at the theatre might not have extended to the recognition of warning signs about political potential. The critical reaction to that phenomenon by Shaw and others, however, especially to the lower form of "impersonal mind," can be seen paradoxically to echo the critique of the crowd that was carried out by Le Bon and his followers.

According to Le Bon, crowds operate in a nonrational and automatic manner, subject to "collective hallucination." They are highly susceptible to suggestion and can be made to accept as true even the most improbable assertions. Most often they are induced into this state by a leader who exerts authoritarian power over them, similar to that exerted by the hypnotist over a subject, such that the individual becomes "an automaton who has ceased to be guided by his will." Le Bon places great importance on the influence of the leader, who must be a "strong-willed man, who knows how to impose himself," and yet the leader most often starts as one of the led: "He has himself been hypnotised by the idea, whose apostle he has since become." Leaders command by force of prestige:

> Prestige in reality is a sort of domination exercised on our mind by an individual, a work, or an idea. This domination entirely paralyses our critical faculty, and fills our soul with astonishment and

respect. The sentiment provoked is inexplicable, like all sentiments, but it would appear to be of the same kind as the fascination to which a magnetised person is subjected. Prestige is the mainspring of all authority. Neither gods, kings, nor women have ever reigned without it.

Nor actors, he might have added, including the one whom Stoker and others called the Napoleon of the mimic stage. The great example of prestige, to whom Le Bon returns over and over, is Napoleon, who was, in 1895, when the book was published (and when *Waterloo* opened at the Lyceum), much discussed and analyzed in a series of centennial reminiscences of his rise to power. The year 1895 was a crisis point in the French democratic republic, when the specter of Napoleon as leader haunted the crowd, benevolently or malevolently. As Le Bon observes, the "greatest measure of prestige is possessed by the dead." [10]

Bram Stoker says Irving had always been interested in Napoleon and had for years kept a beautiful print and bust of him in his room. He adds that Irving was always delighted to talk of Bonaparte and to speculate on how he might play him on stage. "An actor of character," writes Stoker, "finds his own pleasure in the study and representation of strong individuality." [11] It was inevitable that Irving should finally take on this character, as he did a few years later in a play by Sardou, but an earlier glimpse of Napoleon at the Lyceum came indirectly in Conan Doyle's *Waterloo,* through the eyes of a common soldier, one of the crowd, who through his heroic action in seizing a moment was instrumental in bringing down the "man of destiny." The prestige accorded Napoleon derived from command of the field based on inherent abilities combined with inexplicable magnetic power. Corporal Brewster's prestige came almost accidentally to a man otherwise indistinguishable from his crowd, and came in an extraordinary burst that left him permanently a hero even if circumstances would eventually return him as suddenly to the crowd. The magnetizing power of the corporal springs from his past and from the shared history of the Lyceum crowd that gathers in fascination before him. Irving masters this role of the accidental hero who bursts from the crowd on the strength of an inspiration. And in the play as well as in the production, this figure approaches death, which is a transcendence into immortality, into superhuman power. One modern scholar elaborates on Le Bon's observations:

> It is also true that the only leaders who keep their charisma intact and go on attracting the unlimited admiration of the crowd are dead

ones. When they are alive, they are venerated and execrated, loved and hated: venerated because they have the courage to lead the crowd, execrated because the crowd allows itself to be led by them. But there is no restriction on the cult of the dead, who are simply at one with collective ideas and illusions. They are gods, in short, and that is why a dead leader is more dangerous than a living one. [12]

In effect, Irving sought before he died to exploit the advantage of the dead leader, in figurations of death that would have the effect of deifying him, if only temporarily.

Freud theorized that the secret of the leader's power is a libidinal attraction, an illusion of love that binds the individual to the leader in an identification with the ego ideal, similar to that which binds the boy to the father. Many individuals, bound in a similar love for a common object, identify themselves with one another to form the group. They are also bound by common envy and aggressiveness toward the leader, as in the Oedipal relation with the father. Freud agrees with Le Bon that hypnosis, which resembles love without sexual elements, offers the key to understanding group behavior, because through suggestion one can activate repressed instincts and desires, paralyze the will, and command extreme behaviors. He admits there are certain basic mysteries concerning the *rapport* or transference involved in hypnosis that hinder his analysis, but he postulates a primal memory that is tapped in the hypnotic process, as well as in group behavior:

> By the measures that he takes, then, the hypnotist awakens in the subject a portion of his archaic heritage which had also made him compliant towards his parents and which had experienced an individual re-animation in his relation to his father; what is thus awakened is the idea of a paramount and dangerous personality, towards whom only a passive-masochistic attitude is possible, to whom one's will has to be surrendered,—while to be alone with him, 'to look him in the face', appears a hazardous enterprise. It is only in some such way as this that we can picture the relation of the individual member of the primal horde to the primal father. [13]

In his performance as Gregory Brewster in *Waterloo,* Henry Irving sets out for the crowd an image of the reduced and isolated old hero, the figure who stood up to the primal father in a moment of insanity or ecstasy and prevailed. That character reaches back in collective English memory to the primal scene, a fearful moment when English mettle was tested to the limit, and in death he summons that moment into the present, where it might serve to inspire the crowd at another critical moment. But compounded in the image is the figure of Irving, the actor who for thirty years had stood before the crowd and commanded its obedience. And now, like his character, the leader weakens and nears death.

Le Bon assigns gender characteristics to the crowd and its leader. The suggestible crowd is seen as feminine, the imposing leader as masculine. The crowd is fickle, credulous, submissive; the leader, self-assured and dominant. However, as Le Bon has pointed out, the leader comes from the crowd and is hypnotized in a similar manner. The difference has to do with accidental circumstances of time, location, special abilities. The opportune moment transforms the submissive member of the crowd into its willful leader, but the leader remains subject to the collective hallucination that encompasses the crowd. The dreamlike experience of the crowd, or more precisely the liminal condition between waking and sleeping, between perception and fantasy, both frightens and entices the outsider. A similar condition exists in the crowd at a theatre such as Irving's, where, in the intercourse of actor and audience, masculine and feminine, it is as if one might glimpse the primal scene. From within the crowd, the actor appears allpowerful, completely in command, and Irving above most other actors appears in that magnified form of virility, the Great Man, the historic figure. From the outside, however, when the actor's power is measured against that of the leader who directs the greater crowd of which he is a part, he diminishes in size and authority, becoming (in Le Bon's scheme) feminine. Thus, an actor's androgyny is iterated by the passage back and forth through the membrane, masculine and feminine, through the proscenium arch, or inside and outside the theatre. Typically, the price of his power within the theatre is that on the outside his leadership is undermined by a perception that he is a fool or, as in Le Bon's charming formulation, that he exhibits those characteristics typical of the crowd, "such as impulsiveness, irritability, incapacity to reason, the absence of judgment and of the critical spirit, the exaggeration of the sentiments, and others besides—which are almost always observed in beings belonging to inferior forms of evolution—in women, savages, and children, for instance."[14]

One of Irving's remarkable qualities was his ability, through force of personality and canny manipulation of his public image, to play the role of *actor as Great Man* on the world stage as well as on the mimic stage. He is the one responsible, in large measure, for the creation of the unofficial role of "leader of the profession." In *Waterloo* and several other plays, he displayed the conservative credentials—respect for the past, for tradition, for English honor—that would qualify him for the designation "leader." When the role of leader is performed within the theatre, in a role such as Brewster, the effect is to substitute for the usual theatrical sentiments those sentiments which specifically bind the society into a compliant mass. Shaw, of course, abominated Irving for his slavish complicity in this retrogressive effort, arguing that the credit was due to the playwright. He might more accurately have said that the credit was due to the vested authorities whose power such a representation would only reaffirm.

Gordon Craig wrote that "Irving was one of the first actors thoroughly to understand the public . . . but thoroughly." Irving, in Craig's opinion, had made a conscious decision at an early stage in his career to develop his powers of mesmerism, in order to entrance and take advantage of "a public which had been allowed to fall in love with itself." In short, Craig asserts, Irving "had not a very great opinion of the public."[15] It is also frequently asserted that Irving showed little enthusiasm for the performances of other actors, and that he employed a weak company so as to show himself to better advantage. But it is difficult, given the fervor of his approach to acting, the extravagance and care of his preparations, the wholeheartedness of his playing, and the drive with which he championed the actor's art, to conceive of him as anything less than completely committed to the image he set forth for the crowd—a supremely affectionate, if not selfless, benefactor.

From another point of view, however, one also maintained by Shaw, Irving might be seen as a mere vehicle or utility—a "psychic automaton"—for some transpersonal agency. He might be regarded, in a sense, as the puppet of the crowd, serving their self-interest. One writer on crowds put it this way: "Hero worship is unconsciously worship of the crowd itself, and the constituents thereof. The self-feeling of a crowd is always enhanced by the triumph of its leader or representative."[16] He might also be regarded as a puppet of those at the source of power—the holders of wealth, of state authority, of control over cultural discourse. Irving, with his skill at generating and directing emotion in his particularly influential and well-publicized crowd, undoubtedly served an important function on behalf of those powerful agents. Le Bon observed that the crowd might

appear to have a revolutionary aspect, but ultimately they prove conservative, reestablishing the order they overthrow. They have too much respect
for the past to do otherwise: "Their fetish-like respect for all traditions is
absolute; their unconscious horror of all novelty capable of changing the
essential conditions of their existence is very deeply rooted." [17] An actor
who could mobilize this attachment to tradition, generating the crowd's
present agitation within the safe confines of the theatre in order to produce
an ultimate attachment to the past, might indeed further the ends of vested
power.

A recurring theme of the anecdotes that emanated from the Lyceum was
Irving's inflexible will. One biographer, in 1899, reported, "A dozen newspapers and magazines have given descriptions of Irving's autocratic manner of conducting rehearsals, and a pamphlet might be made up of his
sometimes sarcastic, sometimes humorous, rebukes of those who failed
promptly to do his behests." [18] Edwin Booth was quoted describing him as
"despotic" on the stage: "He commands all points, with an understanding
that his will is absolute law, that it is not to be disputed, whether it concerns
the entry of a mere messenger who bears a letter, or whether it is the reading of an important line by Miss Terry. From first to last he rules the stage
with an iron will, but as an offset to this he displays a patience that is
marvellous." [19] Terry confirmed this general impression, even though in private she remarked how little Irving attended to her part in rehearsal, rarely
if ever instructing her in a line-reading. His image, though, was summed
up well by another writer, who said simply: "His success lies in his authority." [20] The Lyceum thus operated as a site for the spectacle of absolute rule,
a place to witness the operation of an iron will, like a prison or fort or the
Tower of London—common attractions for the anxiously curious public.
Elias Canetti, in his strange and exciting book on crowds, makes a case
that the national crowd symbol for England, the metaphorical key to crowd
identity within that country, is the ship at sea. As captain, the individual is
surrounded by a cohort of subordinates, who must be strictly obedient, and
a vast and threatening ocean. The danger (and excitement) of going to sea
is complemented by the security (and boredom) of remaining at home. [21] A
ship is a fascinating site for some because it is shut off from normal controls, subject to absolute rule, even to the extent of cruelty. One might see
the Lyceum Theatre as a site like a ship, where Englishmen could go to

sea, temporarily and vicariously experiencing the autocracy at the head of that pivotal, purposeful crowd, only to retreat comfortably to their home harbor.

The Court Theatre of the Duke of Saxe-Meiningen visited London on its first tour, in 1881, playing at Drury Lane. Irving paid close attention to the innovations displayed by this group, particularly their famous handling of crowds as a character in the scene. The Duke was renowned for his autocratic method at rehearsal, where he tirelessly drilled controlled disorder into his loyal performers. His influence on subsequent Lyceum productions was noted by many writers. Through the years, word about the Lyceum as a model of a strong theatrical organization worked its way back to the Duke. In 1897, he awarded Irving high orders of his duchy (Order of the Komthur Cross of the Second Class of the Ducal Saxon Ernestine House Order), said to be the first such orders given by a foreign government to an English actor. Stoker tells a revealing story of Irving's first meeting with the Duke in 1885. One day Stoker encountered a "tall, distinguished-looking old gentleman" on the stage and advised him that the rule was that no one was allowed on the stage without special permission. The man bowed and said:

"I thought that permission would have been accorded to me!"

"The rule," said I, "is inviolable. I fear I must ask you to come with me to the auditorium. This will put us right; and then I can take any message you wish to Mr. Irving."

"May I tell you who I am?" he asked.

"I am sorry," I said, "but I fear I cannot ask you till we are outside. You see, I am the person responsible for carrying out the rules of the theatre. And no matter who it may be I have to do the duty which I have undertaken."

"You are quite right! . . . I shall come with pleasure!" he said with very grave and sweet politeness. When we had passed through the iron door—which had chanced to be open, and so he had found his way in—I said, as nicely as I could, for his manner and his diction and his willingness to obey orders, charmed me:

"I trust you will pardon me, sir, in case my request to leave the stage may have seemed too imperative or in any way wanting in courtesy. But duty is duty. Now will you kindly give me your name and I will go at once and ask Mr. Irving's permission to bring you on the stage, and to see him if you will!"

"I thank you, sir!" he said; "I am the Grand Duke of Saxe-

Meiningen. I am very pleased with your courtesy and to see that you carry out orders so firmly and so urbanely. You are quite right! It is what I like to see. I wish my people would always do the same!"[22]

The order of the stage takes precedence over all others. The only title that counts within the vessel that sails over oceans of applause, through surges of feeling, is captain of the ship. Other titles might be attached to him, but they are secondary to the fact of his mastery of the crowd. The Lyceum made a noble entertainment of subordination.

Theatre of this sort creates a crowd by recontextualizing its audience, giving them a new point of focus in the form of a leading actor of prestige and hypnotic potential, an emotional charge to jolt them from self-conscious individuality, and a socially acceptable means for expressing enthusiasm. English theatrical literature of the nineteenth century contains little more than incidental and anecdotal discussion of the crowd of the theatre. One would like to know what emotional and intellectual associations an audience might have carried into the sort of crowd behavior produced within the Lyceum Theatre. Moreover, one would like to gain insight into the aesthetics of crowd composition—the framing of the collective experience—around the central action. Unfortunately, the historical record touches even more lightly on the experience of the crowd than on the evanescent performance of the actor. A certain amount of fanciful, if not precisely documented, speculation is therefore inevitable.

The nineteenth-century crowd has the form of landscape or seascape— a picture of nature in its diverse unity. Individual figures within the scene are different—a tree, a rock, a cloud, a man—but they are bound together by the dynamic, intermingled, and abrasive forces of nature that would tear them apart: the wind whitens the sea and tears at the clouds and turns the leaves; the water cuts the rock and mounds with the tides and coarsens the air; and so on. There is no standing apart from the landscape/crowd as a discrete entity (a certain envelopment is inevitable), but there is not yet that unfocused homogeneity of the twentieth century because the changing natural forces and forms contain points of extreme intensity that dominate the picture. The crowd is both extensive and concentrated; it goes beyond the frame of the picture and has no distinct edge, but the core, which is internal to the scene and intensely focused, epitomizes and defines the whole. The core is an emotion, a heart or spirit, and one is part of the crowd to the degree that one is proximate to the *moving,* the inspiration.

The related concepts of heroism and leadership during the period take their definitions from this crowd form. The nineteenth-century soldier operates within an articulated crowd, with a specialized role in the organization—both leading and following—and with a distinct set of opportunities limited by his location on the battlefield and his assigned role: infantry, cavalry, or artillery; officer, skirmisher, or reserve. The core of the battle shifts. *If* a soldier occupies and takes advantage of the right moment in space and time, then the opportunity to occupy the inspirational center of the crowd arises. This contrasts with the chivalric knight who steps boldly forward, moved by the cause, to prove valor in an individual fight. Le Bon described an individual in a crowd as "a grain of sand amid other grains of sand, which the wind stirs up at will," but, as he admits, each individual has the capacity to commit *the* significant act that stirs the crowd—the power to kill, to break through the line, to speak the crowd's will, even to assume leadership, if only momentarily.[23] One individual can drive the ammunition wagon through the burning hedge. Such actions derive, in some way, from the crowd sentiment and are propelled by its energy. They are expressions of collective will, even if executed by a single member. The agent of such heroism might be an individual who enacts the will of the whole, but this seized opportunity is not to be confused with the chivalrous heroism of individual achievement. The crowd functions as an integrated mechanism, utilizing individuals for its end, including the heroes whom it creates. It covers the field and fills the hour, and when and where a signal act is required it identifies the one who should commit, or, perhaps more accurately, be committed. (Compare Bluntschli's view of heroism in Shaw's 1894 play *Arms and the Man.*)

The hero concenters the crowd. But the hero is not necessarily the individual of superior qualities, and the individual of superior qualities does not necessarily become a hero, because there is no standing apart from the landscape, which is time and circumstance, as much as hill and valley. There is only the seizure of the point of intensity amid the crowd, and the opportunity for such a seizure shifts within the natural form of the landscape. It might be within the grasp of anyone and then fall away onto some other terrain. There is no guarantee of possession. The natural relationships of the landscape are the overwhelming fact. Perhaps the rock now resists the abrasion of the sea, but then perhaps the tree triumphs by rising from the rock; again, perhaps the wind tears down the tree, but the rock resists the wind until it is weakened by the water. Napoleon's artillery disorganizes the English squares of infantry, and then his infantry advances, but its front rank is decimated by the hastily reassembled English squares, which had been partially concealed by a ridge. English skirmishers take what cover they can find behind trees, rocks, or dead soldiers and attempt to interrupt the advance of the French, whose squares, however, are too deep. Their fire on the English squares is too sharp, and the English fall back for a time. Napoleon's cavalry takes this opportunity to sweep up the hill and assault the stragglers, but his cavalry is cut down by flanking squares of English infantry, followed by a countercharge of English cavalry. English artillery fire completes the momentary rout, then charge follows charge, pulse follows repulse, over hills, around promontories, along roads. An accurate map is essential for the leader—for command of the landscape, which is of a piece with command of the forces. At any one moment, this organized and purposeful crowd, which is focused but not limited by the frame, bears a core that is the heroic opportunity, the spirit of the picture, and just about any soldier can occupy that core. It might, for instance, be the cavalry countercharge that proves decisive, and it might be one soldier, desperately trying to rein in his horse, who finds himself at the crux, on impulse delivering the decisive blow that concenters the soldiers behind him. Or, it might be one foot soldier of the Third Guards, who, after watching his comrade blown to smithereens, delivers the vital ammunition through a burning hedge at the moment of near desperation. He calls on God for inspiration and miraculously comes through, which is to say, no flame happens to have ignited his powder, no bullet to have pierced his skull, no cannonball to have crushed his tumbril or maimed his horse, and his comrades have not, in the meantime, abandoned the house they have been defending inside that hedge. Finally, his deed is noted and remembered and as a result he is a hero. At the spectacle of his death, decades later, audiences will weep, applaud energetically, roar wildly.

Framed within the walls of the Lyceum, as well as within the bounds of the public discourse of the theatre, the audience and the general public concentered on a point of heroic intensity at their core: Henry Irving. The landscape of these devoted crowds was notable for the diversity of its terrains— men and women of different classes, different ages, different politics, different appreciations of the art. The leader on whom their emotions focused had come from among them: a traveling salesman's son, of limited education, physically ill-equipped for his profession, unhappily married, a man as much at ease talking with a cab driver or a journeyman provincial actor as with prime ministers and presidents, distinguished poets and members of the Royal Academy, bishops of the Church of England and stars of the foreign stage. Within the "natural" scene of English culture, he was just one element, but an opportunity opened for him to compose that scene into a heroic picture, in which all those crowded elements seemed to organize around him. In this pathetic fallacy, the environment of English society generally, and a self-selected segment of it each night in the Lyceum or another theatre, seemed to express the feelings generated by the actor at its core. They became, in his presence, not a quantity of individual and separate figures, but a surging, swaying, exploding crowd, a totality of feeling in answer to this one among them who seized the moment.

Doyle's Corporal Gregory Brewster was, of course, a hero of this sort, having found himself in a situation where he could be a hero, not because of any particular condition of birth or position or ability but because the landscape and the crowd took on a configuration that focused the point of intensity on him. In that fortunate charge he became a hero and was recognized as such "in the presence of his comrades" and the prince regent, "the first gentleman of the realm." For a moment, the crowd had concentered on him. He was given that one moment to live a hero, and years later he recalled that same moment to die a hero.

The case of Brewster (and of Irving as Brewster) illustrates that there can be no heroism at all if the crowd does not organize around the actor (in the word's widest sense) at its core. The example of Brewster organizes a crowd through the patriotic sentiments he evokes. The example of Irving works by artistic sentiments and convictions about his fulfillment of the purpose of the theatre. If the crowd does not know the emotional intensity at its heart, but remains a collection of disparate elements—rock, tree, cloud, wave, sunbeam—then the landscape never will answer the longing for higher order that the hero supplies, never will become a stirring picture. The army creates the opportunity for military heroism, the kingdom creates the opportunity for knighthood, the society for honor, the public for leadership, the audience for stardom. Unless each of these crowds is willing to project its desires onto a focal point, these distinctions and titles will not exist. It is important, of course, to ask whether these distinctions are granted in spite of or in defiance of serious disunities within the crowds from which the "hero" deflects attention. What are the costs of the sort of idealism that creates a hero? No doubt they are often great, but these heroic or honored figures represent in some fashion the spirit of the community. The culture perhaps requires such figures to nullify difference and celebrate wholeness. Certainly these ends were accomplished by Irving's Lyceum and his Corporal Brewster.

There is a long tradition of measuring the greatness of an actor by the cataclysmic power exerted on a crowd. Consider G. H. Lewes's famous description of Edmund Kean: "He stirred the general heart with such a rush of mighty power . . . no audience could be unmoved . . . because it was impossible to watch Kean . . . without being strangely shaken by the terror, and the pathos, and the passion of a stormy spirit uttering itself in tones of irresistible power."[24] The tendency is to conceive of this power as a real attribute of the performer, in other words, in terms of the human (and superhuman) powers exercised in accomplishing the work. But that is, literally, to go against the nature of the landscape. It is as if one would show the triumphant tree without showing the rock from which it rises, or the high wind without the cloud which it torments. There *is* a superhuman element in an actor's performance, but it is in the form of humans crowded beyond the proscenium arch, "strangely shaken by the terror, and the pathos, and the passion of a stormy spirit." The actor did not produce the "rush of mighty power" unless he "stirred the general heart." The actor, like the hero, occupies a point in the landscape, with all nature crowded around. The actor stands in the landscape of the heart. Irving's Brewster stood in "all hearts always."

CHAPTER IV

"A STUDY OF THE HOMELIEST REALISM": PICTURES OF *WATERLOO*

In March of 1897, Shaw began one of his weekly *Saturday Review* columns with a long digression on retrospective exhibitions of the works of Ford Madox Brown, G. F. Watts, and Sir Frederick Leighton, leaving his curt dismissal of two insignificant dramatic works for the final two paragraphs. He does not neglect, however, the general relevance of this discourse on painters to dramatic criticism. In the array of styles and attitudes among these artists, he finds a parallel to the tendencies (or possibilities) among theatrical artists. As usual, Shaw finds a way to orient himself to Henry Irving within the conceptual constellation, Irving among the misty idealists, himself alongside the steadfast realists. The use of visual artists as a frame of reference for the discussion of Irving's theatrical presentations is appropriate, as Martin Meisel has shown in the superb concluding chapter of *Realizations,* "Irving and the Artists." Irving's career can be seen as an effective culmination of the nineteenth-century dialogue between the visual and dramatic arts. Much of his achievement as an actor-manager, especially during the 1890s, can be attributed to his collaboration with various painters, including some of the leading lights of the aestheticist movement. Meisel argues, contrary to Shaw, that Irving's role in developing the theatrical art of the last quarter of the century was "essentially progressive." One secret to his popular success was that he managed to make use of aestheticist values "not in opposition to the philistines, but in response to their need for reassurance against the high-cultural snobbery that proclaimed their incapacity."[1] Such productions as *King Lear, King Arthur, Macbeth,* and *Faust* are susceptible to an analysis of this sort. However, *A Story of Waterloo* seems to be an exception to this rule and requires further investigation. An inquiry into the question of just what aesthetic, pictorial or otherwise, *Waterloo* embodies will also provide an opportunity for comment on the few pictorial representations of the production.

In Shaw's study of the spectrum of possibilities open to painters, Brown is the realist and "most dramatic of all painters," Watts is the visionary idealist, Leighton, "a mere gentleman draughtsman." This trio of terms echoes his tripartite division of humankind in *The Quintessence of Ibsenism*—realist, idealist, and (his term for Leighton's sort) philistine. The philistine accepts the world as it is, substituting "custom for conscience." Of the three sorts of artist, the last strikes him as the most dangerous (and increasingly prevalent) on the stage, because its exclusive preference for a decorous representation of life springs from a negative principle: "To suppress instead of to express, to avoid instead of to conquer, to ignore instead of to heal: all this, on the stage, ends in turning a man into a stick for fear of creasing his tailor's handiwork, and a woman into a hairdresser's window image lest she should be too actressy to be invited to a fashionable garden-party."[2] In a letter to Ellen Terry, a few days later, he made his assessment of Leighton more precise: "Leighton's plan was to give an elegant air to life, to soften and beautify what could be softened and beautified by fine art and fine manners, to help the deserving but not quite successful subjects by a little pretence, and to ignore all the horrors."[3] There was plenty of this sort of theatre in the glib chatter of drawing room plays, but Shaw in no way accuses Irving of harboring such an attitude. Irving was, if nothing else, says Shaw, determined to carry forth his vision in the theatre, a vision that embraced a far wider spectrum of imagery and ideas than that supplied by polite convention. Irving's preeminence was, Shaw later recalled, "abstract and positive," a mission of artistic ennoblement of the stage, even if at the expense of the playwright.[4]

Brown receives the longest discussion and Shaw prefers him for his Ruskinian pursuit of the beauty of the world as it really is. Shaw confesses somewhat disingenuously that when he was an art critic in the late 1880s he had not grasped the full boldness of Brown's project, and instead had adopted the customary prejudice that an artist should aim for "the sexual beautification and moral idealization of life into something as unlike itself as possible." He now feels that triumphant art comes when the artist's "sense of life" can overpower his "sense of beauty." Brown's achievement was

> to find intense enjoyment and inexhaustible interest in the world as it really is, unbeautified, unidealized, untitivated in any way for artistic consumption. This love of life and knowledge of its worth is a rare thing—whole Alps and Andes above the common market demand for prettiness, fashionableness, refinement, elegance of style, deli-

FIGURE 5. Drawing of Henry Irving as Corp. Brewster, probably by Bernard Partridge, printed by Hentschel. (Courtesy of the Garrick Club)

He is a reality during the 40 minutes of stage life, and when the curtain drops he is dead. It would be a sacrilege to your impressions to see him again. To those who once see him he is dead forever, but you may advise others who have not, most heartily and with unbounded enthusiasm, to go and see Irving's Corporal Brewster, the Waterloo veteran, and never hope to see anything in that class of work again.

Review of *A Story of Waterloo,*
Boston Standard, 14 October 1895

cacy of sentiment, charm of character, sympathetic philosophy (the philosophy of the happy ending), decorative moral systems contrasting roseate and rapturous vice with lilies and languorous virtue, and making "Love" face both ways as the universal softener and redeemer, the whole being worshipped as beauty or virtue, and set in the place of life to narrow and condition it instead of enlarging and fulfilling it.[5]

Shaw, of course, detects all too little of this attitude within the theatre, and he notes the similarities between the public derision provoked by Brown's work and the angry dismissal of Ibsen's prose plays. Ibsen had once been an idealist and had changed. Shaw had once stood among those who ignorantly attacked Brown, had since changed, and now sought to bring the impetus of that change to the world. Meisel contends that Shaw had seen in Irving, at some earlier time, an indication that Irving might achieve on the stage something of Brown's sense of realism. Possibly this glimpse had occurred in Irving's 1892 collaboration with Brown on *King Lear,* or more likely in Irving's early triumph in Albery's *Two Roses,* of which Shaw much later recalled, "I instinctively felt that a new drama inhered in this man, though I had then no conscious notion that I was destined to write it."[6] But Irving, in 1897, seemed to stand resolutely in the pathway of both Ibsen and Shaw. He had changed for the worse, particularly in *King Arthur,* which was staged in 1895, a few months before the London premiere of *Waterloo.* This "picture-opera," designed by Sir Edward Burne-Jones, came under Shaw's scrutiny during his third week as dramatic critic and set the pattern for his assault on the Lyceum as a bastion of pictorialism, which had left the art of literature "shabby and ashamed amid the triumph of the arts of the painter and the actor."[7]

This assessment of the artistic values of the Lyceum was firmly set by 1897. In Shaw's eyes, Irving was by then proving himself positively reactionary. But Shaw attempts to be precise and even tolerant in his delineation of Irving's place within the constellation. He compares Irving to Watts: "Sir Henry Irving stands on the Watts plane as an artist and idealist, cut off from Ibsen and reality by the deplorable limitations of that state, but at least not a snob, and only a knight on public grounds and by his own peremptory demand, which no mere gentleman would have dared to make lest he should have offended the court and made himself ridiculous." The problem with the idealist's art is that it turns away from life and embodies "imaginings of nobility and beauty": "The gallery [of Watts's paintings] is one great transfiguration: life, death, love and mankind are no longer them-selves: they are glorified, sublimified, lovelified. . . . To pretend that the world is like this is to live the heavenly life. It is to lose the whole world and gain one's soul."[8] Of course, Shaw deems the last a bad bargain. In the letter to Ellen Terry quoted above, he calls Watts "an idealist of the finest as well as a gentleman and artist." And then he cannot resist the question, "Well, why did he not hold you?" referring to the fact that Watts had been Ellen Terry's first husband in a marriage that did not last long. More re-cently, Terry had teamed with Irving in a long-standing figurative marriage. Shaw, here, in his coy, flirtatious way, insinuates that her rejection of Watts represents a rejection of Watts's idealism, and Irving's as well. Shaw can see that she is blinded by the "dear silly old fashioned things that *you think you think*"—a perfect expression of Shaw's attitude toward Irving's ideal-ism. Shaw, on the other hand, flatters her with the idea that the two of them share the realist approach: "My secret is that I learn from what you *do,* knowing that that is the reality of you." What they "*do*" is trade on (or cheat on) idealism.

And yet, assuming that Shaw is correct, and given Irving's famous pre-dilection for pictorial amplification, if not overstatement, how odd that Ir-ving should embrace such a play as *Waterloo.* How odd for a man who had spent his career concealing the theatrical tricks of his transcendent mo-ments, and resisting the upsurge of a new, more naturalistic drama, from cup and saucer plays to Ibsen and Shaw, at last to put on the shabby cos-tume, the powdery makeup, to lift the curtain on an ill-furnished chamber, and make an evening of the way an old man lives and then, in one excep-tional moment, dies. Indeed, Walter Pollock states that Irving had sworn off "coat and trouser" pieces following his performance as Digby Grant in *Two Roses* (last revived in 1881, the year of Brewster's death), a play that had been very successful. (Pollock adds that Irving adhered to this resolu-tion with the exception of *Waterloo,* which, he says, "would have made its enduring mark in any costume of any century"!)[9] Another writer recalled in 1906, "I do not think [Irving] appeared in any modern costume on the Lyceum stage more than once in twenty-five years. In a dramatic sense the clothes would have been too small." The same writer described Corporal Brewster as "a portrait in miniature . . . finished to the point where it is just divided by a nicely calculated shade from painful realism."[10] It was especially in his studies of old age and natural death that Irving explored "painful realism," as if in anticipation of the fact that his death from the stage would usher in a decided change in aesthetics. The interpretation of death, more than any other subject, separates the transcendentalists from the realists. And Doyle's play vividly poses the question by juxtaposing the grim mechanics of a life at its end with a brief moment that intimates miraculous transfiguration.

The dramatic portrayal of old age was seen as a difficult test for an actor. Irving's Brewster was compared favorably to Frederick Robson's Daddy Hardacre, Joseph Jefferson's Rip Van Winkle, and fine performances in roles of old men by the French actors Lafont, Lesueur, Regnier, and Got. Irving, however, had not always succeeded in such portrayals. In 1892, he developed his production of *King Lear* from a series of drawings and paintings on that subject by Ford Madox Brown himself, and with the artist's consultation. Martin Meisel provides an incisive analysis of this collaboration. Irving's Lear was described as a remarkable, perhaps exaggerated, "paradox of 'violent and weak.' " Indeed, Irving was criticized for offering a Lear "more physically infirm than he need be in his opening scenes," yet also exhibiting "paroxysms of rage, . . . almost inarticulate curses, . . . rare moments of unnatural self-control." [11] Irving perhaps stretched the capacities of his audience by exhibiting the full range from the king who had been to the king who would, inevitably, be, and then not be.

There is, throughout this period, an underlying notion that all sorts of expression, the experiences of a whole life, lie dormant within the enfeebled frame of an old man, capable of appearing at any moment. Hence, the actor must contrive by fine mimicry to suggest this reservoir of experiences and expressions despite the fact that he is relatively young. Then, too, the characterization of old age often demands an imaginative leap into the realization of death, and Irving's minutely considered death scenes were suitable for lingering word portraits, like Edward Russell's 1878 account of Irving's Louis XI, which claims that "never was there such a picture of moving prostration and animated decay" and that "no physical detail is neglected that can help to realize a sinking of mind and body into annihilating death." [12] Louis XI was another of the roles Irving performed until the year of his death (twenty-eight years later), and, like Brewster, it gained in pathos as the role came more closely to fit the actor. Arthur Symons wrote a description of a later performance of this role that perfectly captures its pictorial quality, and shows that Watts's idealism was far from being the only style Irving commanded:

It is a study in senility, and it is the grotesque art of the thing which saves it from becoming painful. This shrivelled carcase, from which age, disease, and fear have picked all the flesh, leaving the bare framework of bone and the drawn and cracked covering of yellow skin, would be unendurable in its irreverent copy of age if it were not so obviously a picture, with no more malice than there is in the delicate lines and fine colours of a picture. The figure is at once Punch and the oldest of the Chelsea pensioners; it distracts one between pity, terror, and disgust, but is altogether absorbing; one watches it as one would watch some feeble ancient piece of mechanism, still working, which may snap at any moment. In such a personation, make-up becomes a serious part of art. It is the picture that magnetises us, and every wrinkle seems to have been studied in movement; the hands act almost by themselves, as if every finger were a separate actor. The passion of fear, the instinct of craft, the malady of suspicion, in a frail old man who has power over every one but himself: that is what Sir Henry Irving represents, in a performance which is half precise physiology, half palpable artifice, but altogether a unique thing in art.[13]

The final sentence marvelously defines this production's qualities. The first three clauses precisely identify the moral ingredients of the character; the next clause points to the dramatic irony at work. Louis is captured within this truth about human nature, which he is not good enough to recognize himself until death forces him to see. The lesson of the first part of this sentence forms a little picture of correct feeling or sentiment, and it is this picture which Irving represents or realizes. The second half of the sentence identifies the artistic ingredients of the performance and the curious twist that Irving manages to put upon them. Although the artistry might appear distinctive, however, there is exactly nothing unique about this sentiment or about this moral encapsulation of a character. But Irving, in his enactment of it, makes it unique by reversing the irony: he is the man who has supreme power over himself. No frailty, moral or physical, limits his self-control ("precise physiology"). The emotional conditions that cripple and distort Louis belong to the mask ("palpable artifice"); Irving stands behind the mask as the singular artist and superior man who can utterly control the outward form.

Clement Scott singled out Louis XI as "the one character in which [Irving's] picturesque force, his variety, his humour, and his artistic method

MR. IRVING IN "LOUIS XI."

FIGURE 6. From a drawing by Hugh Thomson. (Courtesy of Harvard Theatre Collection)

are shown to the greatest advantage." [14] Even Shaw predicted Irving's Louis XI would never be surpassed, calling it a limit achievement in its genre, but he termed such outstanding portrayals by Irving "mosaics of bits of acting thought out touch by touch." [15] The idea expressed here, and in Symons, of an intensely studied, minutely detailed performance, reveals the close affiliation to Victorian pictorial realism in Irving's acting, even when a "grand manner" controls the style of the whole. In general, Irving's performance in Louis XI was regarded as a series of pictures, slowly developing out of one another, but amounting to an extraordinarily detailed and unidealized portrait. As a manager, Irving often sought what Shaw called the "glorified, sublimified, lovelified" qualities of visionary idealism, but as an actor his analytic discipline and scrupulous care conveyed the impression of realism.

Irving's Corporal Brewster relied upon a similar compounding of separate, small details and led to intensive descriptions, like Symons's, capped always by a moral encapsulation of the character's life. This summary, a kind of epitaph, is justified or given weight by the truthfulness of the picture. A typical review speaks of Brewster's "fountain of youthful memory springing ever fresh and bright within his heart, while all else in spirit and in frame is dry and parched and withered, while 'second childishness and mere oblivion' are chasing away the things of this world one by one, little by little, and he, frail mortal, lingers 'waiting for his call.' "[16] Here is the sentiment that the production enacts or realizes. So picturesque is it in its very syntax that it could stand in place of the production, and on a moral plane, it does. But much emphasis must be placed on the performer who operates this device, because it is his imagining of pathetic frailty that creates a vision in negative space, and in the final interruptive moment, realizes the "heavenly life" that Shaw recognized in Watts's paintings. Those pictures, however, were "glorified, sublimified, lovelified" to suggest the transfiguration, while Irving's picture, taking the opposite strategy, was "just divided by a nicely calculated shade from painful realism," as the critic quoted above wrote. Certainly this was not a production in which Irving's "sense of beauty" took precedence over his "sense of life," though it would be hard to claim that the world of this play was, as Shaw claimed for Brown's paintings, "untitivated in any way for artistic consumption."

Charles Kean, Irving's great predecessor at the forefront of the English stage and particularly in the role of Louis XI, was esteemed for a realism that at least one critic identified as pre-Raphaelite. Meisel, in his discussion of pre-Raphaelite drama, explains the distinction between this sort of realism, which depicts extraordinary stories in minute detail, and the sort that favors ordinary, unparticularized views of life. The latter generalizes about experience, about typical realities, while the former can give substance and texture to the stories of individual beings.[17] Kean's Louis, and still more Irving's, made convincing realities of this legendary figure by filling in as many details of the character's individuality as possible, in a manner comparable to Thackeray in the novel, Hunt, Millais, Rossetti, and Brown in painting. Meisel argues that all these artists attempted to take their forms beyond a concern for effect as an end in itself. He quotes Edward Mayhew's 1840 study of stage effect: "To theatrical minds the word 'situation' suggests some strong point in a play likely to command applause; where the action is wrought to a climax, where the actors strike attitudes, and form what they call 'a picture,' during the exhibition of which a pause takes place; after which the action is renewed, not continued; and advantage of which is frequently taken to turn the natural current of the interest." [18] The artists of the second half of the century, he maintains, continued to emphasize the importance of "situation" but invested the term with an opposite sense, closer to its current meaning—not as the climactic effect of action but as the occasion and circumstances from which action arises. The "natural current of the interest" should not be subject to the "picture," but rather the opposite. The pre-Raphaelite painters, of course, sought to create a picture, and with a climactic effect, but they also sought means to suggest the drama's integration into or subordination to nature. The theatrical artists, on the other hand, tried to work away from the static pictures that mark climaxes and instead emphasized the ongoing quality of action and character, without, in the process, losing the strong emotional effect.

Waterloo begins in a manner that points to generic realism, the typical ways of middle-class people. But Corporal Brewster becomes sufficiently individualized as an extraordinary character, bound to a heroic past, yet particularized and integrated into his situation, that the piece might be regarded as pre-Raphaelite or Thackerayan realism or their dramatic equivalent, the Robertsonian "cup and saucer" drama. The final moment of the play, however, puts strain upon the category. The picture created in the moment of Brewster's outburst and death seems to operate as a "situation" in the older sense, almost as if deliberately to evoke an archaic theatrical mode. It is an interruption to mark the climax and is treated as an end in itself. Here, of course, the moment *is* the end, and the "natural current of the interest" must necessarily be turned. Meisel observes that the nineteenth-century theatre exhibits a "severe tension . . . between picture and motion; between the achievement of a static image, halting (and compressing) time so that the full implications of events and relations can be savored, and the achievement of a total dynamism, in which everything moves and works for its own sake, as wonder and 'effect.' " [19] *Waterloo* offers a simple, sharp juxtaposition of these two interests, in which the latter (motion) is associated with ordinary life and the former (picture) with heroic death.

The idea of a graphic component to Doyle's play (usually described as a "sketch") and Irving's animation of its outlines pervades all critical discussion of it. The reviewer for Liverpool's *Daily Post* represents the typical opinion, using a key critical term: "Finish founded on intense realisation: finish which supplies every detail of physique, of habit, and of speech in minute and vivid perfection; realisation which goes to, or rather comes from, the very core of the being."[20] Realization, in its technical sense, refers to the actualization onstage of an image that has been established by a painting or drawing. One writer compared Irving's Corporal Brewster and his Don Quixote, which Irving played on the same bill. The latter he described as "an almost ideal embodiment of this famous conception, . . . as if, by some miracle, one of Doré's studies had been brought to life." On the other hand, the same critic writes:

> Mr. Irving, as the old soldier, made a study of the homeliest realism, which was in the broadest possible contrast with his idealistic portrait of the Don. Marvelously 'made up' he filled in Dr. Doyle's outlines with minute, almost painful veracity, with innumerable touches of grim humor and simple pathos, and with an infallible sense of theatrical effect. In all the details of senile speech and action his study was one of pre-Raphaelite precision.[21]

In the metaphor, Irving puts paint to Doyle's drawing, finish to his rough sketch, and together they realize an image that seems to come simultaneously from life and from a tradition of realist art.

Part of this tradition can be traced in the pair of pictorial references that Arthur Symons chose in order to describe the aesthetic tension in Irving's Louis XI: Punch and Chelsea pensioners. The two terms reflect the paradox of comic and pathetic, humorous and terrible in the Boucicault version, which Irving used, of Delavigne's more severe play. Punch, of course, refers to the traditional clown figure, or perhaps more specifically to the jocular old cartoon figure, a leering colonel who personified the magazine *Punch*'s prankish but hardly disrespectful attitude toward English ways. The second term refers to the retired career soldiers who lived in the vicinity of the army barracks at Chelsea, or who occupied the Royal Hospital nearby. David Wilkie established Chelsea pensioners as a stock subject of nineteenth-century genre painting in 1822 when, under commission from the Duke of Wellington, he painted *Chelsea Pensioners Reading the Ga-*

zette of the Battle of Waterloo. This work, which caused a great stir at the Royal Academy, shows a group of young and old soldiers and other citizens in front of a public house, rejoicing in the first report of the victory. The picture commemorates the impact of a historic occasion on those along the margin far from the center of action.

The Bavarian emigré artist, Hubert von Herkomer, also caused excitement at the Academy, in 1875, with the exhibition of his painting *The Last Muster,* which also takes note of the impact of history upon Chelsea pensioners. This work, based on an engraved drawing Herkomer had printed in the *Graphic* in 1871 (see Fig. 7), shows a congregation of old soldiers at a church service in the Royal Hospital. The faces are unlovely, ravaged by time, though of course filled with simple dignity. For one man in the foreground—a common soldier, white-whiskered, stooped, bearing a walking stick—this gathering has become his "last muster." He has quietly expired, and the man next to him, an aged corporal, is caught at the moment of discovering him. Here is another historic moment on the margin, at the outer edge of the noteworthy, which nevertheless bears on the center as a reminder of past glory. One imagines that many of these white-haired soldiers would have fought in the Napoleonic campaigns. (The dead man's uniform bears no medal in the painting but does so in the engraving. It is a fact that all English soldiers who fought at Waterloo received a medal. The corporal by his side does appear to wear at least one medal. Could this be Gregory Brewster himself ten years before his own death?) The picture initially came before the public at the time of the Franco-Prussian War and the Paris Commune, shortly after the military defeat of Napoleon III and his deposition as emperor. England had maintained neutrality during these conflicts, but the spectacle of the communards in open defiance of imperial rule had an impact on the reform movement. Herkomer's picture affirms the dignity of England's common citizens, who offer their service to country and to God with constant loyalty. Perhaps the picture also signals a growing anxiety that citizens like this are dying out. Who will take the places of these proud warriors on the front line?

During the 1870s, the *Graphic,* a new weekly journal, offered the English public a distinctly grim perspective on modern life, a social realism in hard-hitting prose and black and white pictures. (The young Vincent Van Gogh was greatly impressed by the work of this group.) Herkomer was among the artists who supplied material of this sort, later turning some of his images into oil paintings. The work of this group inspired a number of theatrical realizations, influenced to some extent by Émile Zola's pronouncements on the theatre. Herkomer's works proved difficult to trans-

FIGURE 7. Hubert von Herkomer, "The Last Muster," engraving in *The Graphic,* 1871. (Courtesy of Los Angeles County Museum of Natural History) Compare Fig. 15.

late, even from black and white into oil. Meisel observes that "[w]hat is reportorial and specific in one medium becomes—relatively speaking— poetic and universal in the other."[22]

Clement Scott, in his review of *Waterloo,* introduces the possibility that "Dr. Conan Doyle desired to paint in words and action what a Hubert Herkomer would have depicted on canvas. Here was a portrait straight out of Chelsea Hospital." [23] It is interesting that Scott here makes clear allusion to Herkomer's painting, not his engraving. Scott praised some of the experiments in stage realism that grew out of the *Graphic* drawings, but drew the line at some images, which seemed "all too real, too painful, too smeared with the dirt and degradation of London life." [24] His continuous call was for the "poetic and universal." When he comes in his review to "the artistic idea of the actor," he writes: "[Irving] wants to paint a strong, vigorous hero—who in the old days would fell an ox—reduced to mere impotence and babyhood." The "painting" that Doyle and Irving, in their realizations, have added to Herkomer's picture, if indeed either one had it specifically in mind, conveys a great deal of the "poetic and universal." Yet Scott returns constantly to the realist aspect of the piece, calling it an "absolute photograph of childhood in old age." [25] The comparison with photography has strange reverberations, however, since this mechanical process for capturing an image of reality was often associated with the scientistic approach of the European aesthetic movement known as naturalism, which for critics like Scott included the much-hated Ibsen.

The term "naturalism" did not take hold in England during the nineteenth century, and, as Shaw and others indicate, Irving would be loath to associate himself in any way with that movement. Nevertheless, when the critics quoted above say that Irving's performance was almost "painful," they register its contiguity with the naturalistic. There is reason for this association. When Doyle was a young writer and still a physician, he collected his "A Straggler of '15" in a volume of stories meant to exemplify medical phenomena, and thus adopted on some level the attitude demanded by Zola in his manifesto of naturalism, "The Experimental Novel" (1880). The physiologist is Zola's example of the expert fit to write about the human being because of his concentration on empirical phenomena. Doyle later traced his Sherlock Holmes to Dr. Joseph Bell, a master diagnostician he had observed early in his career, and a parallel fascination with character analysis of a scientific sort can be seen in much of his fiction. On the whole, his medical career was depressing to him, in part because of its associations: "I had my own visiting list, also, the poorest or the most convalescent, and I saw a great deal, for better or worse, of very low life." [26] This was, of course, the milieu made famous by the naturalists. Literature, on the other hand, represented for Doyle an escape from his discouragingly dull career, and providing imaginative escape from degraded and low environments came to define for him what literature should do.

In his *Memories and Adventures*, Doyle conjoins in close sequence sections on his encounter with Dr. Bell, his poverty as a student, his medical observation of the lowly, and the awakening of his literary appetite as a means of escape or "adventure." Each of these "memories" in some way reflects on his medical story of the impoverished and neglected old specimen, Corporal Brewster. Then, just after his report of the beginnings of his writing career, Doyle describes the death of his aged father, an artist, a tall man, elegant, from whom Doyle had grown distant, and who died in a convalescent home in 1893, the year before *Waterloo* was staged. An image of his father was surely one aspect of the *life* that tall, elegant Henry Irving was meant to realize for Doyle, who must have felt some guilt over the fact that the only treatment he provided his father was fictional. Irving's skill in depicting age would provide the naturalistic effect—an actualization of Doyle's life story—but at the same time Irving's idealist tendency would answer and fulfill Doyle's desire for an imaginative and financial escape from those conditions. The corporal escapes the grim circumstances of his corporeal life among the lowly by spiritually rejoining his regiment and his "Dook" in the afterlife, exhibiting at the moment of his transcendence a phenomenon that can be accounted for medically, in which he returns in memory to the story of his life—a short story, as it happens. The new father figure thus created makes contact with the heroic past and thereby provides for Doyle an imaginary hereditary lineage, a literary destiny for him to live out. The natural yet sublime leap into the supernatural, such as Brewster makes, into contact with the dead, was a subject that would fascinate Doyle in his involvement with spiritualism throughout his later years. Doyle presses the limits of naturalistic representation to show that, even under the new standards of scientific exactitude, something remains of the old miracles. Something remains of what legendary fathers might have been, what military leadership and British dominance could have been. And Henry Irving was the man who could stand for all that.

Zola calls the stage the last frontier available for the naturalist to conquer, "the last fortress of conventionality," because of the influence of its massed audience. However, the stage also operates with a radically different mechanism from literature: "It is not necessary to carry descriptions to the stage;

they are found there naturally."[27] In illustration of this fact, he discusses
scenery and costumes, which of course convey much information but require no description. But Zola devotes little attention to the actor, who, he
assumes, "naturally" carries out the analytic task of the physiologist/au-
thor. Zola prescribes avoidance of histrionic poses and extravagant gestures, but offers no sense that he regards the actor as an artist capable of
making an analytical interpretation. Irving, on the other hand, believed
acting could provide such interpretation. He often defended the social benefit of the theatre as a place where an audience could gain insight into the
workings of character, not the typical example of character but the extraordinarily clear and resonant case, lucidly realized by the actor. On the other
hand, he agreed with the French actor Constant Coquelin, who wrote in
1887:

> "Naturalism" on the stage is a mistake. In the first place the public
> won't have it. It always resents the exhibition of revolting hideous-
> ness, of pitiless and naked realities. People do not come to the theatre
> for that sort of thing. . . .
> Just as I would not allow any departure from truth on the plea of
> picturesque effects, so I would not permit a representation of com-
> monplace or horrible things on the pretext of reality. I am always on
> the side of nature, and against naturalism.[28]

The notion that a certain category of the natural might taint theatrical representation is expressed by both actors as an aesthetic problem, as a threat
to beauty and the ideal. However, a distaste for the commonplace might
easily translate into a rejection of the commoner, and a disdain for the trivial or ugly into a revulsion against the lowly. The only acceptable purpose
for the low is to set off the high, to bring into relief all that is noble. And
yet, neither saw the purpose of his acting as the creation of idealized types.
Irving often echoed the attitude of John Ruskin, very much the pre-
Raphaelite position, which works as a simultaneous rejection of French
naturalism and "Purism" (idealization of life): "Great art accepts Nature as
she is, but directs the eyes and thoughts to what is most perfect in her."[29]
Irving saw the issue in national as well as personal terms and in 1891 expressed himself in words that provide an excellent gloss on his portrayal of
Brewster:

> [T]o merely reproduce things vile and squalid and mean is a debase-
> ment of Art. There is apt to be such a tendency in an age of peace,

and men should carefully watch its manifestations. A morose and hopeless dissatisfaction is not a part of a true national life. This is hopeful and earnest, and, if need be, militant. . . . Life, with all its pains and sorrows, is a beautiful and a precious gift; and the actor's Art is to reproduce this beautiful thing, giving due emphasis to those royal virtues and those stormy passions which sway the destinies of men. Thus the lesson given by long experience—by the certain punishment of ill-doing—and by the rewards that follow on bravery, forbearance, and self-sacrifice, are on the mimic stage conveyed to men. And thus every actor who is more than a mere machine, and who has an ideal of any kind, has a duty which lies beyond the scope of his personal ambition.[30]

The "lesson given by long experience" in *Waterloo,* might even be construed as the lesson of this very passage. Brewster's endorsement of the "royal virtues," so clearly "beyond the scope of his personal ambition," holds sway over the "stormy passions" of the gathered audience, demonstrating the way to a "true national life" that is "hopeful and earnest, and, if need be, militant." This ideological system runs beautifully until a critic impertinently insists the actor is, perhaps, no more than "a mere machine."

A few critics, particularly Americans, called Irving's impersonation of Brewster anything but picturesque. A Boston critic, while acknowledging that the performance was full of Irving's "peculiar sweetness of feeling, his contagious sympathy with what is pure, noble, and good," nevertheless said it was entirely spoiled by "a repulsive hideousness of make-up and a minute scrupulousness in sparing the spectator and listener no single item of the unlovely side of extreme old age, such as one cannot but call sensational."[31] Another Boston reviewer, while declaring that he liked the play as well as anybody, called Irving's impersonation an artistic mistake despite its skill:

> "A Story of Waterloo" is an entirely romantic and pathetic little sketch; Irving's impersonation is of the crassest, the most painfully elaborate realism. It brings all the ghastliness and physical dishonor of extreme old age ruthlessly into the foreground; and this, too, in a way that is revolting. The essentially genial, but upon the whole rather slender, thread of romantic sentiment that runs through the little piece cannot bear the strain of this load of realistic hideousness.[32]

Both these reviewers seem to have in mind a conventional stage representation of the old man, lighter in weight, less insistent on the grain of nature. As the first reviewer writes, using the same term as the latter, "It would have been so easy to act the part on other and more genial lines!" For both, the pathos of the play has seemingly less to do with the plight of an aged man than with the conventionally beautiful demise of a clown figure.

Whether genial or hideous, Irving's portrayal of Brewster had necessarily a layer of elaboration on its surface in the makeup and whatever else would be required to add thirty years to the actor's figure. The twenty or so drawings that survive to show Irving's "make-up" present a considerable range of styles, but almost all give the impression of a younger man in the guise of an old man. Most would be taken at once, without question, as illustrations of an actor rather than "life" drawings by Herkomer or Brown. In other words, there is caricature and staging in virtually all of the pictures of this production. Shaw once observed in a comparison of Irving and Ellen Terry: "The few and insignificant attempts that were made to caricature her were hopeless misfires, whereas caricatures alone could give a truthful impression of Irving."[33] Two pictures only seem to be recognizably Irving, resembling the man one sees in photographs. One is by Bernard Partridge, an actor and former member of the Lyceum company, who, as Stoker explains, was the only artist freely allowed to enter the theatre at any time to sketch. He also "filled in the faces" in other artist's illustrations for use in the souvenir programs.[34] His realist style of drawing Irving came to be well known, and in each picture the face and frame of Irving can be seen within the makeup. His drawing of Brewster (Fig. 5) strongly conveys the effect of age, as well as the aspect of Irving, without caricature and with a minimum of theatricality. The other drawing that clearly represents Irving is, ironically, a satirical cartoon that appeared in *Punch* (Fig. 10), where one might expect a comically distorted portrayal. The juxtaposition of his figure with the cartoon of Mr. Punch has a dislocating effect, which perhaps suggests the effect of hyperreality conveyed by Irving's performances.

Most drawings of *Waterloo* attempt to illustrate Irving's detailed rendering of the weakness and debility of old age. They show his tears at the loss of his pipe or his dismay at the "breaking" of the gun. A few prefer to show his one moment of revivified strength. In his two versions of this moment, Arthur Rackham cannot seem to recall which arm it was that Irving raised upon shouting his defiant line (Fig. 1 & frontispiece). These two are among the more exacting in their depictions of scenic and costuming details, but they are not at all successful in conveying the emotional thrust of that mo ment. Irving's heroic pose looks ridiculous, like a ham actor's. Balliol Salmon shows Brewster raising *both* arms in a pose that is still more ridiculous, as if he has just finished a softshoe dance. Finally, the caricaturist for the *Pall Mall Budget* shows a terrifying, mad figure in an extreme pose, which in fact strongly (and perhaps self-consciously) recalls Partridge's drawing of Irving as Mephistopheles (Figs. 8 & 9). It is a deliberately outrageous portrayal, a good-natured mockery.[35]

Thus, no effective picture of the climactic moment of this play survives. This is the moment that breaks violently from the picturesque in a sudden return to an older, more overstated style of heroic acting—from genre painting to the sublime. It is also the moment that ends the scene, interrupting its lifelike continuum with a deathlike blow. The magnified and concentrated quality of the moment (and its violence) appears in vivid contrast to the subtle and dispersed effects (and weakness) of the preceding "sketch" of character. It is hard enough to accommodate this stylistic contrast in the forty-five or so minutes of the performance, forty-four of which go to the sketch. A. B. Walkley's review of the play, which does not so much as mention the concluding moment, points out the difference in Irving's stylistic emphasis in this work: "Studies of senility we have had from Mr. Irving before—in 'Lear,' for instance, and in 'Louis XI.'—but never so complete a study as this, I think. They were 'in the grand manner,' this is in the minute."[36] No photographs survive of Irving's Brewster, despite the fact that most, if not all, of his successful later roles were featured in photographic portraits (over the objections of Irving, who was reported to have said, "If the public wants to see me, let them come to the theatre.")[37] Here, though, is a case where the camera would tend to reveal too much minute detail in the makeup itself. Better to rely upon the slight distortion of gas light in a crowded theatre and an artist caught up in those feelings. Shaw, of course, saw through that veil of illusion, declaring, "There is a make-up in it, and a little cheap and simple mimicry which Mr. Irving does indifferently because he is neither apt nor observant as a mimic of doddering old men."

If *Waterloo* was in some way an experiment, a test case, in search of the new trend, then its results, however triumphant in the specific, must have been unsettling in the general. In response to the change of taste, Irving turned from romantic revivals in the later years of his career, toward the well-made and comparatively realistic historical dramas of Sardou and at one point, unsuccessfully, attempted a modern subject. But Irving's style as actor was not suited to "texture," to subordination of himself within a

FIGURE 8. Henry Irving as Corp. Brewster, from a drawing by Frederick Henry Linton Jehne Townsend. (*Pall Mall Budget*, 27 September 1894) (Courtesy of the Garrick Club)

FIGURE 9. Henry Irving as Mephistopheles, from a drawing by Bernard Partridge, souvenir program of *Faust*, ca. 1885. (Private collection)

situation. As his career came to a close, he depended more and more on a few proven titles, one of which was *Waterloo*. One can imagine the sad subtext Irving might have assigned to Corporal Brewster's comments on the modern ways of younger folk. After examining the sergeant's carbine, he says, "Ah! it won't come up to Brown Bess. When there's work to be done you mark my words and see if they don't come back to Brown Bess." His famous pronouncement—"That wouldn't ha' done for the Dook. The Dook would ha' had a word there"—seems almost a comment on the dramaturgy of the world in which he finds himself. And every night that he played this piece, he rehearsed at the end of the play his own mustering up. Over and over again, he came back to Brown Bess, a sensational death, the device that was surefire.

Perhaps, indeed, Shaw struck a nerve at the end of his review of *Waterloo,* when he asked, "What, I wonder, must Mr Irving . . . feel when he finds this pitiful little handful of hackneyed stage tricks received exactly as if they were a crowning instance of his most difficult and finest art?" How that, above all in Shaw's review, must have stung. Alfred Darbyshire recalls speaking with Irving one evening in December of 1905 (clearly an error on Darbyshire's part, as Irving had then been dead two months). Darbyshire had given enthusiastic praise to his Corporal Brewster in a speech at a social gathering, and Irving later told him, "My friend, you think too highly of 'Waterloo'; there cannot be in it what you say."[38] William Winter, too, recalls that Irving "disliked" the role and explained, "Old age is dreadfully selfish, and this old man is utterly so."[39]

A WELLINGTON (STREET) MEMORIAL.

GENERAL OPINION (MR. PUNCH) PRESENTS THE MEDAL OF THE
HIGHEST ORDER OF HISTRIONIC MERIT TO HENRY IRVING IN
RECOGNITION OF DISTINGUISHED SERVICE AS *CORPORAL GREGORY
BREWSTER* IN THE ACTION OF CONAN DOYLE'S "STORY OF WATERLOO."

FIGURE 10. Cartoon from *Punch*, 18 May 1895 (Courtesy of the Garrick Club)

It was a most faithful, realistic study, an exact portrait of a quite ordinary piece of
outworn humanity. Yet it had a universal reference, and subtly and sweetly raised the
virtues of patriotism and obedience, vindicated the nobility of common everyday instinctive duty, and reconciled us to patient, poverty-stricken old age.

Henry Arthur Jones, *The Shadow
of Henry Irving* (1931)

CHAPTER V

HISTORIES OF WATERLOO I: "ALL THAT A SOLDIER SEES"

> It was Napoleon, I believe, who said that there is only one figure in rhetoric of serious importance, namely, repetition. The thing affirmed comes by repetition to fix itself in the mind in such a way that it is accepted in the end as a demonstrated truth.
>
> Gustave Le Bon, *The Crowd,* p. 142

It seems likely that Conan Doyle took his subject for the 1891 story, "A Straggler of '15," from a book called *Waterloo Letters,* a compilation of hitherto unpublished letters, penciled notes, and such, written by officers of the Waterloo campaign, with explanatory notes, diagrams, maps, etc., published in 1891. Several such volumes appeared around this time, perhaps, like this one, in commemoration of the seventy-fifth anniversary of the battle, certainly as a gesture to solidify or amplify the diverse testimony offered by the hundreds of personal memoirs that had been published. The outpouring of memoirs had ceased with the deaths of the remaining participants in the battle, and now, along with the continuing efforts toward synthesizing the history, came the posthumous evidence, with the force of deathbed testimony.

In one letter, Captain Horace Seymour of the 60th Rifles wrote:

> Late in the day of the 18th, I was called to by some Officers of the 3rd Guards defending Hougoumont, to use my best endeavours to send them musket ammunition. Soon afterwards I fell in with a private of the Waggon Train in charge of a tumbril on the crest of the position. I merely pointed out to him where he was wanted, when he gallantly started his horses, and drove straight down the hill to the Farm, to the gate of which I saw him arrive. He must have lost his horses, as there was a severe fire kept on him. I feel convinced to that man's service the Guards owe their ammunition.[1]

The anecdote lacks several features of fine battlefield mythography; above all, its final sentence builds ludicrously to an anticlimax. What claim could be more self-evident? The private's anonymity also creates a demand. Acclamation asks for a name. This is nothing but a sketch, tracing only one contour of the incident, but it has trajectory, a gestural intensity, leading from "the crest of the position . . . straight down the hill to the Farm." Doyle's innovation was to take this hero through the "severe fire" and the burning hedge, to the definite point where the conviction might be established that to his service the Guards owed the *whole* battle, pivotal point of the war. By completing the chain of cause and effect, Doyle brings the soldier's name to light, gives him individuality and a fate—to live on.

Doyle had a strong appetite for Napoleonic literature. Much of his literary career was spent writing historical adventure tales, and Waterloo in particular was the setting for several of his stories. Each pronounces something of the difficulty of recapturing that distant scene; too much has changed, the heroes are dead. It is only by the agency of sudden and surprising representative anecdotes that the imaginative gulf can be crossed. Doyle's strategy, hardly original, was to identify and pursue the soldier who is suddenly swept into heroic action by the circumstances of the battlefield.

The Great Shadow, which appeared in 1892, tells the story of the battle from "the very centre of the nineteenth century," in the voice of Jack Calder, a greying survivor, who might be taken for a younger version of Corporal Brewster. He states that he looks back upon his past as one who has "lived in a time when the thoughts and the ways of men were as different as though it were another planet from this." Indeed, he disclaims responsibility for an accurate narration of the history of the battle and declares that he has learned more about the battle from what he has read than what he saw, "for how much could I see with a comrade on either side, and a great white cloud-bank at the very end of my firelock?"[2] The scenes of humor and pathos that are open to this soldier at his close range, the wounds given and received, will "tell" the true story, which is one of fate or force propelling soldiers. Hesketh Pearson imagines Doyle writing the book "with all the gusto of one who savors slaughter from a comfortable distance."[3] The distance that Doyle prefers is that of the anecdote related above, where a sketch might be filled in with a few details, showing a soldier stepping forward from the mass into a distinct identity.

The description of Hougoumont in Doyle's novel provides a good example of the sort of heroic detail to which he was drawn:

The farm that they called Hougoumont was down in front of us, and all morning we could see that a terrible fight was going on there, for the walls and the windows and the orchard hedges were all flame and smoke, and there rose such shrieking and crying from it as I never heard before. It was half burned down, and shattered with balls, and ten thousand men were hammering at the gates, but four hundred guardsmen held it in the morning and two hundred held it in the evening, and no French foot was ever set within its threshold. But how they fought, those Frenchmen! Their lives were no more to them than the mud under their feet. There was one—I can see him now— a stoutish, ruddy man on a crutch. He hobbled up alone in a lull of the firing to the side gate of Hougoumont, and he beat upon it, screaming to his men to come after him. For five minutes he stood there, strolling about in front of the gun-barrels which spared him, but at last a Brunswick skirmisher in the orchard flicked out his brains with a rifle-shot. And he was only one of many, for all day, when they did not come in masses they came in twos and threes, with as brave a face as if the whole army were at their heels.[4]

This story is also reminiscent of a true incident of Hougoumont, a story often told in stirring terms. During an intense period of fighting, a young French officer grabbed an axe and led a group of soldiers in an assault on the massive north gate of Hougoumont. A breach of this gate, the very same gate through which Brewster would bring his powder, could well have meant loss of the château and its strategic position on the battlefield. Two English guardsmen, a lieutenant-colonel and a sergeant, valiantly managed to close the gate, a deed the Duke of Wellington later acclaimed in these terms: "The success of the battle of Waterloo turned upon the clos-ing of the gates of Hougoumont." The body of the French officer was found after the battle with the axe still in his hand: "Long afterwards the imprint of bloody hands upon the gate-post and timbers told the tale of the frantic disappointment and passion of the assailants, which became fiercer as the cries of the hunted Frenchmen still within the yard became gradually si-lenced in death."[5] In this case, a story that history records in terms of proper names, a story of officers, even gentlemen of noble warrior ancestry, has become generalized by Doyle into an anonymous, even humorous, an-ecdote. But this story, like Brewster's, emphasizes the synecdochal signif-icance of Hougoumont stories, a point made clear in Victor Hugo's telling of the tale: "This corner of earth, could he [Napoleon] but have seized it, would perhaps have given him the world likewise."[6]

Doyle's narrator conceives of the war as "an old story how a third of the grown folk of our country took up arms" against a man who had the Fates behind him ("He had always won") and fear of whom "hung like a black shadow over all Europe." The miraculous ending to this story was that "[t]here was still to be a land of free thinking and free speaking in Europe."[7] The jingoism of *The Great Shadow* combines with a never entirely concealed awe of Napoleon himself. There is, of course, a great deal of admiration of Wellington, the Iron Duke, whom Tennyson was to call the "great World-victor's victor," the very type of English hero, but there is also a constant ambivalence, a sense that Napoleon and the French soldiers make the better story.[8] Doyle wrote of the character of Napoleon in his unsuccessful 1896 novel, *Uncle Bernac:* "I was still unable to determine whether I was dealing with a great hero or with a great scoundrel. Of the adjective only could I be sure."[9]

This ambivalence resurfaces in the *Adventures of Gerard,* Doyle's most popular Napoleonic stories, which appeared over the next decade. Here his rather ridiculous hero is a French soldier who both despises and admires Napoleon. Again and again, Gerard happens to be in the right place at the right time to play the hero in extraordinary incidents of the wars, driven by loyalties and necessities he cannot define. He comes into contact with Napoleon repeatedly, and he identifies this leader as an important emotional force, but the chaos introduced by the continuous flow of accidents makes it obvious that no simple causality is at work. Indeed, a note of puzzlement runs through these "long-winded stories of an old broken soldier," as if the narrator seeks to find in them some mystery that might explain his position in relation to the history of which he was part. He hopes the reader will see through his "dim eyes something of the sparkle and splendour of those great days," and that he will have recovered "some shadow of those men whose tread shook the earth."[10]

His last adventure begins with an awareness of his imminent end, similar to Corporal Brewster's, after the time when the others, at least the great ones and all but about fifty of his fellow Hussars, "have ridden round that dark turning and passed into the beyond." His attitude is the familiar sort of noble resignation: "I have played my part in my time. The time has passed. I must pass also. Nay, dear friends, do not look sad, for what can be happier than a life completed in honour and made beautiful with friendship and love? And yet it is solemn also." Storytelling does not seem to figure at all into this conventional assessment of his "part" in his time, but at this late hour, he, like Brewster, rises to offer one final burst of recollection, "more than a tale—it is a great historical secret." The story culminates as Gerard, on a bold journey to St. Helena, arrives in time to see the body of Napoleon on his deathbed, and on his face "a gentleness of expression which I had never seen in life." He concludes the tale, and the series of tales, with a declaration of the hope he holds for the power of his own historical narration:

> Treasure it in your minds and pass it on to your children, for the memory of a great age is the most precious treasure that a nation can possess. As the tree is nurtured by its own cast leaves, so it is these dead men and vanished days which may bring out another blossoming of heroes, of rulers, and of sages. I go to Gascony, but my words stay here in your memory, and long after Etienne Gerard is forgotten a heart may be warmed or a spirit braced by some faint echo of the words that he has spoken. Gentlemen, an old soldier salutes you and bids you farewell.[11]

Gerard asks his reader to accept these tales as true testimony of a valiant heritage, as elements of a collective consciousness, in the hope that they might generate a resurgence, a transcendence. What is it, if anything, in these fictions that can occupy the space of memory, serving as history?

Doyle took pride in his research into "Napoleonic days," and especially his "military detail," which had been praised by a famous war correspondent.[12] In a comment on Doyle's historical fiction, Pearson suggests that Doyle wrote best when he "forgot the notes he had taken from the books he had read on the period with which he was dealing, and let himself rip": "Then the martial man seized the pen, and the book came to life; only to die again when the soldier in him, who had such a profound respect for the scholar, recalled his period and handed back the pen to the fellow who had so laboriously studied it."[13] The book came to life in forgetting, rose to vivid action in the figure of "martial man," warrior of the pen, then died in memory, when the respectful soldier, man of the ranks, "recalled" the laborious scholar of military detail. Doyle gets it all wrong, according to Pearson, as does Gerard, in his notion that it is, in any simple sense, memory that stirs the reader. Gerard has faith in his recollections, Doyle in his researches, as the source of a power that might touch the reader, even the reader of a future time. Pearson is doubtful. A certain sort of remembered past is deadly to a book; a writer wants to "forget the notes" in order to bring his book to life. But memory discloses both life and death, as Corporal Brewster demonstrates. From his past comes the lineament of an an-

ecdote that stirs, that might blossom into a new generation of heroes and
echo into the hearts and spirits of the future, as Gerard predicts, as well as
the "military detail" that stifles the hero by creating the full landscape of
circumstance within which the seizure of the "pen" is an indifferent act.
Brewster's history unfolds two sorts of memory: his pride in "writing" a
good heroic story and his terror at facing death. The play shows that the
two are inextricably combined, though the former almost entirely over-
shadows the latter.

One could say that Brewster's "story" is an allegory about dramatizing
such historically inspired literature. The dry document hangs on the wall
over the fireplace, intriguing, perhaps, but essentially a memorial, marking
something dead and simulating its stillness, its completion, its dignity. The
researcher must begin here. Then come the recollections, disappointingly
humble and quaint, far from contact with the heroic conduct honored by
the document. And then these subside, as the old men grow weary of recollection and fall asleep. Suddenly, through some mysterious surge of
imagination, the subject comes alive: "The martial man seized the pen [or
'let himself rip'], and the book came to life." The instauration of the past
occurs in this moment of reinscription, which is also a dramatic reenact-
ment. The final curtain achieved, the "period" recalled, the living (enacted)
memory returns to death and to those who have "so laboriously studied it."

In September of 1897, the dramatic critic of the *Chicago Times-Herald,*
Lyman Beecher Glover, made a discovery that might shed a different light
on the origins of Doyle's play. Glover came upon a copy of Dion Boucicault's one-act play from 1844 called *The Old Guard* (a rewritten version
of Boucicault's first play), and, struck by its many similarities to *A Story
of Waterloo,* called it "at least a strange coincidence" and "another case of
minds running in the same channel." Glover manages to express and re-
press his suspicions in the same sentence when he writes, "The idea is
inconceivable that the big-hearted, brilliant author of 'The White Company' [Doyle] would descend to petty theft."[14] The irony is compounded
when one considers that the idea might have been taken from a writer who
was notorious as "the most impudent plagiarist in the world" (as Louis
Moreau Gottschalk called Boucicault).[15] The several points of intersection
between these two short plays are worth observing.

Both plays feature an aged survivor of the Napoleonic wars, in Boucicault's case a corporal of Napoleon's Imperial Guard. Corporal Havresack,

a feeble and impoverished Frenchman now living in Kensington, is aided
by a young woman named Melanie, niece of a General Lefebre, who died
in the corporal's arms years before. Melanie believes herself to be the corporal's daughter. Two men have fallen in love with this beautiful woman
from afar. One is the general's son, Henry Lefebre, now an English officer.
The other is Lord Beauville, Lefebre's guardian, who had been a captive
under General Lefebre and had eventually married Isabel Lefebre, a
woman of unspecified relation to the general's family. When the wars
ended, Beauville left his wife behind. His wife died after giving birth to a
daughter, who turns out to be Melanie, the corporal's companion. Lord
Beauville, who does not recognize his long-abandoned child, plots to take
advantage of her before his ward has a chance to obtain her hand honorably.
His scheme is foiled, though, by the old man who persistently reminisces
in broken English about the war and his devotion to Napoleon. When
young Lefebre arrives in his uniform, the corporal springs quickly to attention and then has to be helped into a chair. He tells the pitiful and heroic
tale of his old general's death, at the climax of which he shows his cross of
the Legion of Honor and then recognizes the son of the general by a similar
cross inherited from the young man's father, which was pierced by the fatal
bullet. Joyously he brings out one million francs he has been keeping for
the lost heir. Young Lefebre proposes to Melanie and then leaves to make
arrangements, at which point Lord Beauville makes an attempt to abduct
her and is halted only by the frantic efforts of the feeble old man, who
rushes out wildly with his musket. As the corporal nears death, young Lefebre reenters and calls out the name of his guardian, which triggers the
final recognition:

> [CORPORAL] HAV[RESACK].   [*Recognises Beauville.*] Ha! 'tis he,
> indeed!—Beauville, you remember me?—Havresack, the witness of
> your marriage!
>   LORD B[EAUVILLE].   Can it be?
>   HAV[RESACK].   Husband of Isabel Lefebre—now is my re-
> venge—Melanie—here—here—look on this girl whom you would
> destroy—she is your own child—ha!
>
> [*He sinks on the ground.*]
>
>   MEL[ANIE].   Hush!
>   HAV[RESACK].   [*Very faintly.*] Melanie, where are you? I cannot
> see—your hand—how cold it is—what is this darkness?—Hush?
> what's that? a drum? Aha!—again—to the attack—now! now!—al-

lons, mes braves!—a tramp, and the rumble of the guns—they
come—allons—Napoleon, look at us!—Now, up—en avant,
charge!—Vive l'Empereur!—Vive!—vive—Napol—

[*Dies.*]

THE END.[16]

Doyle might have had several chances to see this play, since it had remained a popular work in the repertoire of English and American actors,
especially provincial players, for much of the remainder of the century.
Colonel H. L. Bateman, manager of the Lyceum Theatre during Irving's
early years as a starring actor in London, had performed the piece in America up to the year of his departure for England, though there is no record of
his presenting the piece at the Lyceum. Even so, it is likely that Irving
would have known this play.

The point, however, is that both authors have identified and exploited a
mechanism to obtain a particular histrionic effect, having to do with the
comic and tragic dimensions of an old man's loyalties to a distant past.
Shaw called this Doyle's "exploitation of the ready-made pathos of old
age," and indeed this aspect of the character of Corporal Brewster was defined well before Corporal Havresack and is a staple of the melodrama, the
infirm old man who *would* do right but is incapable, for whom the possibility of heroism remains in the past. The old man strives to defend the
virtue of the heroine, typically his daughter or granddaughter, but the
forces of villainy (often an alter ego of the father figure) run too strong,
until the hero at last emerges and with his newly acquired excellence res-
cues the young woman into a marriage. Melodrama affirms the sanctity and
purity of marriage by intimating its unspeakable alternative, rape and/or
incest. The old man's physical incapacity to defend the heroine throws emphasis on his ability to speak. Typically, he is the one to tell the story of the
buried past, as well as to hurl imprecations at the villain and call loudly
upon God and the law for intercession. His death often provides the necessary moment of pathos before the hero's final victory.

Boucicault has followed this pattern closely, drawing added attention to
his old man's speaking ability by the device of his comically broken English. He is the good but impotent father figure who has providentially
taken the place of the incestuous father, and his death answers the discovery of a fit husband/hero for the young woman. Doyle, on the other hand,
has surgically removed the sexual plot, indeed virtually all of the melodra-

matic apparatus except the character of the old man. Brewster can ably attest to the remote past, to the hidden springs from which heroism might arise. He can invoke the powers of God and the law, thus affirming their efficacy. His death, though, does not respond to the rise of a heroic agent within the scene or the appearance of a fit husband for the heroine. Instead, Doyle seems to imply that the new species of hero/husband must arise from the audience upon the death of his old man. And rise they do—to applaud.

Melodrama bears only a generalized relation to history. The past is a reservoir of energy because it holds the information that is vital in order to rescue the endangered present, and the old man, as bearer of this knowledge, occupies a nearly central position. Ultimately, however, the present is all that matters, defeating the evil and marrying the good. The old man, for all his knowing of the past, typically proves impotent without the actuating capacity of the young hero. Those who would insist on the information, the history, align themselves with such ineffectuality. The present is when the martial man seizes the pen and lets it rip; freedom is achieved in that newness. And yet the strong plots come out of those long-unresolved situations from the past, which have, in fact, brought about the differentiation of good and evil. So a certain attention to history cannot be avoided in the framing of such a story. On the other hand, the historian finds it difficult, if not impossible, to avoid the tendency to construct such melodramas in reporting on the past. Doyle brings history and melodrama into complex and unsettled relation in *Waterloo,* which is constructed somewhere between a historical document and a plagiarized (and archetypal) play. This conceptual breach (and the various heroic sallies into it by both Doyle and Irving) must be explored.

Walter Benjamin, in his essay "The Storyteller," draws a distinction between the historian, who is bound to explain or interpret his material, and the medieval chronicler, who can "content himself with displaying [happenings] as models of the course of the world." The modern novelist and storyteller replicate much of this distinction, each bearing memory, "the epic faculty *par excellence,*" but to different ends, the former toward accounting for the "meaning of life" and the latter toward an encounter with oneself. Benjamin asserts that the two functions were bound together in the ancient epic but became separate in the later, differentiated forms of epic. The novelist drives toward a "perpetuating remembrance," which incorpo-

rates an interpretation, while the storyteller works with "short-lived reminiscences," a web of stories that always generate more stories, so that the
whole process can be the occasion of a discovery of community, of contact
with other stories: "The first is dedicated to *one* hero, *one* odyssey, *one*
battle; the second, to *many* diffuse occurrences." The novelist has come to
the fore under the influence of the "form of communication" known as
information—nearby, verifiable facts, such as "military details,"—while
the storyteller has always relied on "intelligence coming from afar," in
other words, distant truths which can only be known by all the stories that
tell of them. [17] As a novelist, Doyle pays respect to his role as an informant
of the reader, but occasionally, as the storyteller Gerard, he "lets himself
rip," forgets his particularizing, approximating notes, and tells his stories,
as if to locate a distant, though perhaps imminent, community of heroes,
or at least to touch those who might need bracing by the "faint echo of the
words that he has spoken."

Doyle stands at a remove from Gerard's solemn wishes, an ironic com-
plement to this old, distant, reminiscent, even opposed (French) teller. Jack
Calder (of *The Great Shadow*) also enunciates the difference between historian (novelist) and chronicler (storyteller). On the one hand, he acknowledges his debt to the informative historian, or, as in Pearson's description
of Doyle, the soldier who has handed over the pen to the laborious scholar,
and, on the other hand, he defines the different sort of story he can tell:
"But of my own knowledge I can only speak of what we saw during that
long day in the rifts of smoke and the lulls of the firing, and it's just of that
that I will tell you." [18] His account of the fighting at Hougoumont is
wrapped around a brief statement of the historian's facts, but it comes alive
in the briefly delineated sketch of the Frenchman on a crutch, "strolling
about in front of the gun-barrels," until a skirmisher "flicked out his
brains." Such details have nothing to do with the scholar's information
about Waterloo; it is surely in such features that Pearson imagined Doyle's
historical texts coming to life.

The metaphor of coming to life is incorporated in a difficult but important formulation by Benjamin, which illuminates Doyle's representation of
Corporal Brewster's Waterloo: "The value of information does not survive
the moment in which it was new. It lives only at that moment; it has to
surrender to it completely and explain itself to it without losing any time.
A story is different. It does not expend itself. It preserves and concentrates
its strength and is capable of releasing it even after a long time." [19] A story
comes to life because it is different from or goes beyond information; it

survives the moment in which it is new, and, like the seed buried in the Egyptian tomb, can germinate long years afterward. Brewster lives with the registered and recorded version of his deed, the yellowed newspaper clipping that hangs over the fireplace. The newspaper is a principal promoter of that form of communication Benjamin calls information, and this clipping, as a bearer of information, empties of significance—dies—with its appearance. The article is called "A heroic deed," but the specific action it reports is the presentation of a special medal to the corporal in commemoration of his deed. A citation is incorporated into the article, in which his action is described, ending with a call for Brewster to live long to treasure his medal and to recall, not the deed itself, but the reception of "this tribute to his valour from the hands of the first gentleman of the realm." In fact, in telling of his role in the battle, Brewster dwells on the details of the conferring of the medal, his remark to the prince regent and the subsequent laughter (at his expense). (" 'The ridgement is proud of ye,' says he. 'And I'm proud o' the ridgement,' say I. 'And a damned good answer, too,' says he to Lord Hill, and they both bust out a laughin'.") The citation takes the place of the action. He is to recall the tribute and the medal, while the deed itself recedes within their frame. But the "story" of Waterloo is capable of releasing its strength even after a long time, when Brewster achieves a long distance in time from his past, when the story can come like intelligence from afar.

Brewster had exceeded the demands of routine service, which was anonymous conformity to his role in the comprehensive strategy. He had bravely defied death at a time when the lives of many others depended on him. One had died in the effort to bring the powder through the burning hedge. Brewster luckily lived on to be named and singled out of the crowd for honor. Those who inscribe the text of history registered his name, not those of the others, as part of the official history. Benjamin writes: "In the crowd that which is below a person comes in contact with what holds sway above him."[20] Brewster effects this sort of contact between the mass of anonymous soldiers and the "first gentleman of the realm." Brewster enters as a subject into a "higher" sort of story, of the heroic genre, but his story is carefully circumscribed by the official history of the deed. In a sense, what makes the deed heroic is its entry into print, in the genre of heroic literature.

Sixty-six years later, the whole crowd, above and below, has passed away, "from Colonel Byng right down to the drummer boys." Brewster has again been singled out, in a way that recalls by analogy his heroic deed.

Again he has been visited by the military hierarchy, though at a lower level. The sergeant and colonel have heard his name and come to certify his presence or affirm his existence:

> COLONEL.   Is this Gregory Brewster's?
> CORPORAL.   Yes, sir. That's my name.
> COLONEL.   Then you are the man I came to see.
> CORPORAL.   Who was that, sir?
> COLONEL.   Gregory Brewster was his name.
> CORPORAL.   I am the man, sir.
> COLONEL.   And you are the same Brewster, as I understand, whose name is on the roll of the Scots Guards as having been present at the battle of Waterloo?
> CORPORAL.   The same Brewster, sir, though they used to call it the 3rd Guards in my day. It was a fine ridgement, sir, and they only want me now to make up a full muster.[21]

The tributes he receives in these latter days—a clay pipe, some tobacco, a bit of cash—are not on a level with the citation he received earlier, but then neither is his information. He reenacts the battle vaguely with his pill bottles and such, recalls his loss of three crowns to a dead comrade, and repetitiously recounts the anecdote of his reply to the regent. That story, indeed his whole character, does not conform to the heroic figure he is supposed to represent, and as he was the butt of gently mocking laughter then, so is he now. Through a quirk of fate, this common soldier has become author and subject of a heroic tale. This story was lost when, in effect, Brewster handed back the pen to the historical mechanism, when his deed was absorbed into the information of a citation, when he became a name and a tribute and a medal.

The storyteller's sort of memory, reminiscence, gives way to the novelist's or historian's "perpetuating remembrance." The commissioned officers, as it were, commit his act to memory, to commemoration, by displacing it onto the honor he receives. The death of Brewster is foreshadowed in this embedding or burial of his story in that citation. Seemingly all he does in his life is carry out the order, contained within the citation, to live long, to treasure his medal, etc. That *is* his life. Brewster's resistance to this alienating historical process is clearly represented in his defiance of death at the end of the play. Benjamin writes:

> It is . . . characteristic that not only a man's knowledge or wisdom, but above all his real life—and this is the stuff that stories are made

of—first assumes transmissible form at the moment of his death. Just as a sequence of images is set in motion inside a man as his life comes to an end—unfolding the views of himself under which he has encountered himself without being aware of it—suddenly in his expressions and looks the unforgettable emerges and imparts to everything that concerned him that authority which even the poorest wretch in dying possesses for the living around him. This authority is at the very source of the story.[22]

The "unforgettable" that emerges from Brewster at the close of this play, at his figurative and literal final curtain, is in the form of a quotation from memory of his words on seizing the reins of the tumbril: "The Guards need powder, and, by God, they shall have it!" The tribute and medal were personal honors conferred on him, but now the audience hears directly of his impulse to bring firepower to his comrades. They suddenly see his service from the perspective of his equals, not his superiors.

This is a play about a storyteller of one resonant tale, a tale of contact with a community, and his storytelling has been delimited by his insertion into a historical order, which has had the effect of cutting his existence down to a mere token of life. The novel, Benjamin argues, in its insistence on identifying the "meaning" of a life, represents all characters to memory in the form of "perpetuating remembrance." Concerning this process, Benjamin writes: "A man . . . who died at thirty-five will appear to *remembrance* at every point in his life as a man who dies at the age of thirty-five."[23] Brewster appears as a man who dies at eighty-nine, having lived but two moments. His death certifies the former moment; all else that we see or hear about might be regarded as mere time-serving. But this is not a novel. It is a play about a man who has been given existence without life, whose life has been given a meaning without a purpose. Brewster has little in the way of "real life"; he is the merest corner of a corner of a fully existent person. He is little more than the occasion for a death, and death is what gives his life a meaning.

What is that meaning? On one level it has to do with the service due to superiors, the validation of an attitude toward the past, certification of the historical process itself. A military victory is remembered as a treasure to be honored and protected, as the sum of innumerable acts of duty commemorated by a historical process that honors the chain of command, and finally as certain extraordinary acts of duty marked out for singular notice by such authorities as the prince regent. As a short story, in Benjamin's terms more a novel than a story, this is about the sum of it. Beyond these simple functions, Benjamin suggests another dimension of significance in concluding his discussion of the novel in "The Storyteller": "The novel is significant, therefore, not because it presents someone else's fate to us, perhaps didactically, but because this stranger's fate by virtue of the flame which consumes it yields us the warmth which we never draw from our own fate. What draws the reader to the novel is the hope of warming his shivering life with a death he reads about." [24] But in the theatre an audience might seek shared experience, which is the aim of the storyteller, instead of isolation, which is the condition of the reader of novels. And the actor who animates the sketch of a man who appears at every point in his life as a man who dies at the age of eighty-nine is thought to be able to fill in the "real life" omitted in the novel. Perhaps, when Henry Irving has "let himself rip" and has "seized the pen," then Doyle's short story can come "to life" and, instead of a cold and alienated reader, there might be a communion of souls.

Irving was said to have performed a miracle in bringing Doyle's "dramatic sketch" to life. One witness to the scene wrote, "Every one at a distance at once knew and was interested in the old corporal." [25] A storyteller had drawn the community together. Shaw claimed its "life" was an illusion (or delusion) of the crowd, an optical trick produced by Doyle's use of the mechanical tricks of creating an emotional effect and by his endorsement of common sentiments. At the end of his review, Shaw regrets the demise of the "Gallery of Illustration," a midcentury entertainment, which offered inspirational dioramas for communal enjoyment. [26] This would have been the place for *Waterloo*. Shaw would prefer to see a theatre like the Lyceum turned to "literary" purposes, where, one can imagine, the isolated "reader," set stolidly apart from the pack, as Shaw must have been, would take a shivering, distant interest.

> Well might the great Napoleon say, we trafficked in every thing; but he was little aware that to "a nation of shopkeepers," he might have added, of showkeepers.
>
> *Letter to the Examiner,*
> 7 March 1824

Beginning in 1815, Napoleon himself figured as one of the more popular subjects of London exhibitions during the nineteenth century; direct from Waterloo, his battle-scarred horse, Marengo, went on display at the Waterloo Rooms on Pall Mall. Nearby, a Waterloo Museum featured a large

painting of the battle and an assortment of weapons and armor. A variety
of other commemorative, illustrative, and reliquary shows followed. But
the London Museum in Piccadilly topped them all with Napoleon's battlefield carriage, two of his horses, *and* his wounded coachman to tell the
story, along with his camp bed, "two leather bottles . . . and a cake of
Windsor soap." A Cruikshank cartoon shows "A Swarm of English
Bees"—a portion of the estimated ten thousand visitors a day—in an enthusiastic rush to see these tokens of recent history. The carriage was later
purchased by Madame Tussaud's and displayed in "The Shrine of Napoleon," where Doyle would have seen it on his visit to the Wax Works (on
Baker Street) as a boy of fifteen.[27] Doyle's biographer, Charles Higham,
recurs several times to this visit as an occasion that awakened Doyle's romantic, and particularly militaristic, imagination: "Indeed, he was fasci-
nated throughout his life by the mystery of this unheroic, potbellied figure,
who looked like a French schoolmaster and controlled the destiny of em-
pires."[28] History here comes framed by exhibition, commodified as the
stuff of spectacle, and, in turn, it becomes the frame for another sort of
fiction, the historical novel and drama. But how does one determine the
truth behind this show, the real Napoleon within the carriage? Or, more to
the point for Doyle, how does one articulate the dubious historical categories of fact and fiction within a novel sort of adventure that trades on the
past?

Doyle very likely would also have seen at some time, perhaps on the
same London excursion, one of the scale-model representations of the
battle of Waterloo in London. One of these was built in the 1830s by Lieutenant William Siborne, author of the standard history of Waterloo, who
himself just missed fighting in the battle, having enlisted under Wellington
a few weeks afterwards. The model was on display throughout the nineteenth century. Here, again, the theatrical limitations of a packaged entertainment distort the purpose of historical recording. This man who missed
being eyewitness to history sought retroactively to fix it in permanent, visible, static form. Wellington himself was the one to contend that this strategy of exhibition corrupted the task of recording. He refused to visit the
display because he had learned "that the Model would not give an accurate
Representation of the Position of the Troops of either or of both the Armies
at any particular period of the Day. . . . I was unwilling to give any Sanc-
tion to the truth of such a representation in this Model, which must have
resulted from my visiting it, without protesting against such erroneous representation."[29] Wellington opposed all attempts to represent Waterloo,

whether literary or historical, arguing: "The history of the battle is not unlike the history of a ball! Some individuals may recollect all the little events of which the great result is the battle lost or won; but no individual can recollect the order in which, or the exact moment at which, they occurred, which makes all the difference as to their value or importance."[30] Like the histories of legendary figures, battlefield histories are notoriously difficult to construct in a way that leaves them free of hypothetical solutions, creative interpretations, or mythic distortions. Having surveyed a scale model of Waterloo from an aerial perspective, the young Doyle might have wondered how it would feel to be in that landscape, among the "upwards of 50,000 Figures," but in his research he would discover the labyrinth of historical narrative within which that experience is contained.[31] Like his character Jack Calder, he would discover that returning to the scene of Waterloo was more about reading books—or going to the theatre—than about anything else.

During that same visit to London in 1874, Doyle first visited the Lyceum Theatre, where he saw Henry Irving in *Hamlet*. "The play has continued three months," he wrote to his mother, "yet every night the house is crammed to suffocation by people wishing to see Irving act."[32] On that occasion and during his university years, when he was a regular in the gallery of the Lyceum, Doyle might have recognized the correlation between the organized crowd on a battlefield and in a theatre. The problem of representation is critical in both contexts. By analogy, David Howarth, in the introduction to his military history of Waterloo, describes one problem the theatre historian faces: "Of course, what a general does in a battle is more important than what a soldier does, or what he feels or thinks; but the deeds and thoughts of soldiers have a special interest, because they sometimes illuminate the mystery of military life. The mystery is this: what makes a man, who joins an army and puts on a more or less exotic kind of dress, behave on the word of command entirely unlike himself, but like a ferocious animal?"[33] Theatre history records in some fashion the remarkable actions of the great actor, but the "deeds and thoughts" of audiences have, too, a "special interest" and illuminate a mystery. What makes an audience member, who puts on a more or less exotic kind of dress and enters a theatre, behave on the word of command (or the command of words) entirely unlike himself, sympathizing utterly with imaginative figments or becoming one with a willful and impulsive crowd?

Histories of theatrical events, like histories of battle, are most often told from an authorized or privileged vantage point, specifically the perspective of the officers (actors, authors, critics)—those who impose order on the event. But certain events seem to demand an alternative perspective, from the point of view of the mass upon whom the event has been imposed, such as Howarth undertakes for the battle of Waterloo. *Waterloo* was, in theatre history, such an event, both because of its utilization of the crowd, discussed earlier, and because of its representation of such an alternative historian in Brewster, who came from that mass. That both Doyle and Irving brought a superior or commissioned perspective to this noncommissioned soldier's story gives the work a deceptive and ironic twist, as an object lesson in both political and theatrical history, which are, indeed, more actively in dialogue with one another than this apparent coincidence might suggest.

In fact, Waterloo has been a kind of test case for the methods of military history. Many sorts of account have been written, and each has been carefully measured against the other. In the years following the battle, a number of English versions in heroic style were published, all rather distorted. One historian of this period defended his method in terms that make clear the dramatizing function of historical writing: "It is the business of the historian . . . to bring the exploits of the hero into broad daylight . . . the multitude must be told where to stop and wonder and to make them do so, the historian must have recourse to all the power of words."[34] Quite an opposite approach was taken by Byron in the third canto of *Childe Harold's Pilgrimage,* which was written and published one year after the battle. This poem set a standard for "all the power of words" in the depiction of Waterloo and its heroic and antiheroic occasions, and it remains the great literary treatment of Waterloo in English. Byron's way of telling the multitude "where to stop and wonder and to make them do so" was, of course, to scorn them entirely and make it seem that the experience of the heroic, its obscure and evanescent essence, comes only to souls highly susceptible.

He comes to focus on the heroic deed of Major Howard of the Tenth Hussars, Byron's kinsman. Howard was ordered to lead his soldiers on a charge against a French infantry regiment. He saw that the action was hopeless, but led the charge bravely nevertheless, fell, and was killed by a man in the French ranks who beat his brains out. His story was told often in the histories as an example of honorable conduct among officers. For Harold, this story signifies something quite different. He stands beneath a tree that grows at the place where Howard fell, observes the recovered landscape, green and full of life, and thinks about the "ghastly gap" in life that has been left by this death and by the thousands of deaths of which this one is typical. No forgetfulness will ever erase the fact of their deaths, and fame can do little to ease the "fever of vain longing." "Millions of tongues" record the battle, and the words will be echoed in future generations: "And this is much, and all which will not pass away." The permanent record stands, such as it is, and it employs the terms of glory—this much is a confirmation of the heroicizing historian's impulse. But Byron portrays the survivors (who recall and record the history) in stark and frightening terms, which might show the timeworn character of Corporal Brewster in another light:

> They mourn, but smile at length; and, smiling, mourn:
> The tree will wither long before it fall;
> The hull drives on, though mast and sail be torn;
> The roof-tree sinks, but moulders on the hall
> In massy hoariness; the ruined wall
> Stands when its wind-worn battlements are gone;
> The bars survive the captive they enthral;
> The day drags through though storms keep out the sun;
> And thus the heart will break, yet brokenly live on:
>
> Even as a broken mirror, which the glass
> In every fragment multiplies; and makes
> A thousand images of one that was,
> The same, and still the more, the more it breaks;
> And thus the heart will do which not forsakes,
> Living in shattered guise, and still, and cold,
> And bloodless, with its sleepless sorrow aches,
> Yet withers on till all without is old,
> Showing no visible sign, for such things are untold.[35]

This Byronic alternative to the heroic can be discerned in the final moment of *Waterloo*. Harold's vision is partly to be found in the solitude of Corporal Brewster within his memory, staring into the "ghastly gap" in the landscape, the opportunity to die that existed there. He charged toward that opportunity valiantly, and yet it remains as a blind spot in the scene he sees "afore me, every time I shuts my eyes." As a "broken mirror" he reflects the silent, broken-hearted attentions of the audience gathered to witness another heroic end—every night at eight forty-five or so. Byron's "Waterloo" segment from *Childe Harold* was also one of Irving's pieces for "readings and recitals."[36]

The next wave of Waterloo accounts brought a variety of technical analyses of strategic and tactical questions, written by participants. Several
attempts were made to synthesize these analyses and to give a comprehensive picture of the battle; foremost among these was Siborne's two-volume
1844 history, which David Howarth has called "the most detailed, authoritative and boring account of a battle ever written."[37] This response is odd
since in fact this study contains some remarkable detail about the actions
of soldiers in the fighting. Siborne's soldiers are pictured in discrete, aggre-
gate units and are anonymous, referred to by name of regiment or by the
commanding officer, but this is the range at which a certain structure of
events, a causal chain, appears. The fighting at Hougoumont poses some
difficulty for Siborne (and for many other writers) because here, for the
most part, the English and allied soldiers did not fight on open terrain but
rather from concealed positions and more as skirmishers than as coherent
units. The following is an excerpt from Siborne's account of the struggle
for Hougoumont late in the day, when Corporal Brewster might have
brought the much-needed ammunition:

> The flank companies of the guards, within the walls and buildings,
> held at defiance every attempt of their assailants to dislodge them
> from their cover. By this time, all the outhouses were on fire, with
> the exception of those that fronted the wood. The roof and upper
> story of the château had fallen in, and flames continued bursting
> forth on all sides with the greatest fury. The heat had become so
> intense as to produce upon the men whose duty brought them within
> its influence, a feeling of suffocation; while the frequently emitted
> volumes of thick smoke gave an indistinctness to every object around
> them. Yet so admirable was the system of defence, so perfect were
> the discipline and the order, maintained throughout this trying scene,
> by the devoted garrison, that the enemy completely failed in forcing
> an opening at any one point. . . . The French *tirailleurs,* pushing
> forward in pursuit, were staggered by the sudden and vigorous fire
> opened upon them by the troops within the eastern garden-wall; and
> the 3rd guards having, in the mean time, been reinforced by the 2nd
> line battalion and the light companies of du Plat's brigade, drove the
> enemy back to the front hedge of the orchard.[38]

The corporal's bold deed occupies a hidden space within this description.
But it does not register on the indicator of just what historic drama was
unfolding here. How does one fit this magnified detail of a timely charge

with an ammunition wagon, and the grandniece's, "It was as much as to say that uncle won the battle," into the entirely different scale of Siborne's orderly succession of movements among second-line battalions and brigades denominated by the officer in command? The anecdote becomes a story and then a play, and so it takes one small aspect of the "drama" of the battle onto the stage. Where the author—the commander with a bird's-eye view—controls the naturalism of the narrative, the performer takes charge on the stage.

Siborne is consistently self-conscious about his dramatization of the battle as a particular sort of spectacle intended for a particular sort of theatrical effect, as in these summary statements following his description of the first grand attack:

> Thus terminated one of the grandest scenes which distinguished the mighty drama enacted on the ever-memorable plains of Waterloo; a scene presenting in bold relief, genuine British valour crowned with resplendent triumph; a scene, which should be indelibly impressed upon the minds as well of living British warriors, as of their successors in ages yet unborn. Britons! before other scenes are disclosed to your view, take one retrospective glance at this glorious, this instructive spectacle.

> Honour, imperishable honour, to every British soldier engaged in that never-to-be-forgotten fight! When Britain again puts forth her strength in battle, may her sovereign's guards inherit the same heroic spirit which animated those of George, Prince Regent, and inspire them with the desire to maintain in all their pristine purity and freshness the laurels transmitted to them from the field of Waterloo.[39]

Between these two passages, Siborne presents the reader with the promised "retrospective glance," retelling the story he has just told at great length, using a new set of terms, stripped of all names of companies and commanders. For four pages, he runs together precise sequences and points of decision into a vivid painting of the action, full of dynamic contrasts. Siborne calls on the reader to *see* the action, which he presents, not for factual instruction, not with the aim of comprehensive understanding, but in terms of whatever is most stirring—eye-catching movements and thrilling deeds. Motion is the matter:

> See! the struggle is but a moment doubtful . . . men and horses reel and stagger to the earth—gaps open out in the line—numbers are

backing out—others are fairly turning round—their whole line now
bends, and breaks asunder into fragments—in the next moment they
appear, as if by a miracle, to be swept from off the crest of the position, and being closely and hotly pursued by the victors, the whole
rushing down the other side of the ridge, are snatched from your
view. Your attention is now irresistibly drawn to . . . .[40]

Intense involvement of the reader through imaginative participation in this
action might well encourage a wholehearted participation on those future
occasions when Britain "again puts forth her strength in battle."

Corporal Brewster, too, "tells" two sorts of story about the battle. One
of these is derived from retrospective narrations; he knows where the reserves and guns were positioned, where the Prussians made their advance.
He "sees" the whole battle as if he had obtained a bird's-eye view, but his
telling of the story is little more than a quotation of reconstructed textbook
narratives, a replication of the historian's map. Brewster assumes an implicit passivity in this view; battle is being in a position, under command.
The other sort of story surges up through the years with a different kind
of vividness or immediacy; it has to do with the leap out of formation and
into action. This story is the moment from his own past that is quoted and
reenacted.

History might have more than one reason, more than one rhetoric, Siborne seems to imply, and if the one seems, so to speak, deadly, then the
other is necessary in order to vivify. The purpose of commemoration is not
served by granite slabs alone, or by a newspaper clipping; an active engagement with the community must be part of the process. Historical commemoration and theatrical representation are congruent in this respect. In
A Story of Waterloo, a neglected commemorative text comes to the surface
as a theatrical work; it meets its audience face to face. But the battle had
all along had its place within the theatrical vocabulary of England. One
might even say that Doyle's work, which takes the act of commemoration
as its subject, operates within an ironic self-consciousness that the aging of
the story of Waterloo has to do with the passing of a sort of theatre.

Siborne's accentuated tableau might be compared to the various panoramas of the battle that were on display in his day, such as the one shown
at Burford's Panorama in Leicester Square in 1820 (which Wellington attended, willingly, and which was revived at his death). Panoramas were
vast paintings on a cylindrical (or at least a broad curving) canvas, made to
surround and absorb the spectator in some great scene. Though naturally

inclined to show fixed moments of time, some panoramas did incorporate successive phases of action. The diorama, invented in 1822 by Daguerre, also used the principle of enfolding the audience but incorporated devices to allow alterations in the scene, as with the passing of time, first with tricks of lighting and later by actually changing the image. These devices were used, more often than not, either to show distant settings or to realize historic moments, and the battles of the Napoleonic wars, especially Waterloo, were popular subjects. In fact, one writer commented in 1824 that there had been "so many daubs of this national 'set-to,' that people . . . would now almost as soon wish to be in such a battle itself, as to visit representations of it."[41] In 1852, coinciding with the death of Wellington, a "Grand National and Historical Diorama, Illustrating the Wellington Campaigns, in India, Portugal, and Spain; Concluding with the Battle of Waterloo" opened at the very Gallery of Illustration that Shaw mentions at the end of his *Waterloo* review.[42]

Funerals themselves were like public dioramas and Wellington's was a prime example. In a letter to his cousin, fourteen-year-old John Henry Brodribb (later called Henry Irving) records that he attended the funeral of Wellington, whom he called "one of the most illustrious statesmen, & the greatest warrior the world ever produced."[43] In addition to the diorama mentioned above, Irving could have visited a "Magnificent Shrine of Memorial" in honor of Wellington at Madame Tussaud's and a variety of other funerary rites of a theatrical nature.[44] Novelty and sheer scenic wonder surely drove much of the interest in this form, but the documentary function—making the factual visible—also figured in, and not just as a means of placating those who would criticize purposeless entertainments. One writer commended a diorama of "the wars of Wellington and Napoleon [which] are now commemorated and in part made intelligible to the public by the dexterous brush of the theatrical scene-painter."[45] Here we have a theatrical form that is in part redeemed by serving the purpose of instruction and gratifying an interest in historical self-consciousness. The situation is quite the reverse, it would seem, in Siborne. The interesting thing there is that he sees fit to interrupt or vary his authoritative document with a less authoritative, deliberately scenic and theatrical representation.

Siborne's latter version of the battle implies an all-seeing narrator, but it brings out the limitations in the perspective open to the reader—the change of focus, the obstructions within the landscape. Siborne sweeps the reader down from the sky and onto the battlefield in this way, engaging the reader's emotions. The romantic (or, better, melodramatic) rhetoric of this second narrative stands in contrast to the dry, analytical rhetoric of the first. Both seem determined largely to honor (or flatter) the ruling powers of England, but in different ways. The one attends to the named and titled officers, preeminently the "Chief," while the other takes up the role of the mass, the natural force of thousands who (appear to) pronounce loyalty to their commanders by executing their orders, who (appear to) give substance and shape to the artful will of those powers by moving across the landscape in lines that give pictorial focus to that will, and in this way reaffirm its authority. The one version attends solely to the history within the frame, the heroic attainments of leaders in command, soldiers in conformity. The other conjoins the masses of commanding and obedient warriors with the mass of readers who are urged to follow along, bonding the two by means of all the stories that might be told. The one attends to actors, while the other involves audience. This alternation of rhetorical modes is well known to the theatre historian.

The military historian John Keegan, in *The Face of Battle,* assesses the formidable difficulties facing the historian of battle. Who, after all, could ever see a battle from all sides, given the vast scale, the noise and smoke and sheer danger? Who could know all the decisions that had been made or put off, the orders sent out or lost, executed or misinterpreted, the myriad circumstances of fifty thousand or more living soldiers and others dead? The traditional battle piece, of which Siborne's is a good example, stands back from the field at a certain distance, from which position an idealized pattern can be observed. It portrays the movement of soldiers in blocks, as if each individual in the group participates simultaneously and equally. Collective imagery of a diagrammatic quality (lines, squares) is used for the fighters, in such a way as to fit precisely within the mapped topographic details. The traditional battle piece gives a clear cause-and-effect structure to the action, like the movement of game pieces. As Keegan observes, the dead and wounded are physically absent from such descriptions; they are counted at the end, but they seem to "dematerialize as soon as struck down."[46] Also characteristically omitted are references to the less picturesque of human emotions common on a battlefield—terror, revulsion, self-concern.

Waterloo was the occasion for some change in this pattern of military history. In his attempt to tell the story from "the soldier's ground-level, smoke-shrouded point of view," Howarth observes that the Napoleonic wars were the first in which large numbers of soldiers were literate and could offer written versions of their experiences. He notes the disparity between the source material for his book and that for the other military histories: "These soldiers' stories have nothing to say about strategy and not very much about tactics, and so they are only sparsely used, on the whole, in the critical histories. But some of them give very clear impressions of the tiny part of a battle which is all that a soldier sees."[47] This, what might be called naturalistic, approach to military history was one that fed directly into the novel, and Waterloo was often the topic for this sort of novelistic treatment.

Émile Erckmann and Alexandre Chatrian wrote a popular historical novel about the Napoleonic campaigns of 1813–15 and a sequel, entitled *Waterloo,* during the 1860s. Both were narrated by a young French conscript who is careful to spell out the limits of his personal knowledge. Standing before the ruins of Hougoumont the day after the battle, he says:

> I did not see this with my own eyes, but some veterans gave me an account of the attack on this farm; it was called Hougoumont.
> One must be exact in speaking of such a battle, the things seen with one's own eyes are the principal, and we can say:
> "I saw them, but the other accounts I had from men incapable of falsehood or deception."
>
> I have often heard the veterans repeat the order of battle given by Napoleon. The corps of Reille was on the left of the road opposite Hougoumont, [etc.]. . . . That was all that I understood, for when they began to talk of the movements of eleven columns, of the distance which they deployed, and when they named the generals one after another, it seemed to me as if they were talking of something which I had never seen.
> I like better therefore to tell you simply what I saw and remember myself.[48]

He thus gives an account that aims not at historical reconstruction or even at adventure but at the human experience of being a soldier, the emotions, the doubts, the very things that are elided in the traditional battle piece. As in the above passage, the narrator of such an account distinguishes clearly the testimony of his own experience from the received accounts, all of which tend to tell the story from the angle of the named and titled hierarchy.

The editor of an edition of the book that came out during World War I praised Erckmann and Chatrian for, among other things, "the generous sympathy with which they depict the lowly, for the respect they endeavour to inculcate for every form of labour, and for the robust faith they show in the unceasing progress of mankind."[49] The conscript's egalitarian ideas about the purpose of his participation in these wars are conditioned by a friend in his village, an old revolutionist who begins to doubt that Napoleon is truly a defender of republican values. Both this man and the young conscript are dubious at best about Napoleon's return from Elba, and by the end they agree that "the Rights of Man are annihilated." But they trust in the reawakening, through instruction, of the impulse to liberty, equality, and justice, and looking back from some unidentified later point in time, the conscript affirms that this prediction has proven true: "To-day the people are sovereign!"[50] The implicit point is that Waterloo was in its own way a revolutionary stage for the people; at this moment they began to take control of the representation of history, to tell their own story. The common soldier emerges from anonymity, from obscurity, from the background, to tell "all that a soldier sees." This naturalistic approach to military history obviously influenced Doyle, and indeed *The Great Shadow* might well be read as an imitation of Erckmann-Chatrian's *Waterloo*.

Stendhal, in *The Charterhouse of Parma,* offers a historical novel of sorts, which makes of Waterloo a nearly chaotic series of fragmented personal events, radically unknowable in terms of larger structures. Stendhal makes Waterloo a topic of the antiheroic tradition, which Shaw will take up at the end of the century. Both examine the haphazard junction between vague ideals and dimly perceived reality in the formation of history. Stendhal hilariously mocks his young, romantic would-be hero, Fabrizio, who wanders through a labyrinth of misdirections, pressing blindly toward the object of his desire, which is true contact with the heroic. He has resolved that he must die or win victory beside Napoleon. Through the smoke and mud, and at a disappointing distance, Fabrizio manages to obtain only the most limited impression of the battle of Waterloo, so limited that he must ask a nearby soldier if it is, in fact, a battle at all. He is not an exception in this regard; no one in this world seems to have a sure sense of his role, active or passive, in the battle. His notion of what a battle is and how one conducts oneself in war is formed by military literature, especially of a romantic sort, but he finds remarkably and disappointingly little literature on the battlefield. His relentless drive toward the most alluring point in his tiny field of vision is a search for an ideal piece of literature, at once history and epic, and it continually turns up nothing better than quaint characters, genre pictures, chaotic and accidental actions. But he accumulates by happenstance a story that is, perforce, a history of the battle of Waterloo, however oblique. This story (or history of sorts) takes its shape from the desire to recover a past in the present, to realize in life, and then in the story of that life, a historic deed.

Desire is an inevitable component of historical awareness, as much a factor in "all that a soldier sees" as smoke, noise, liquor, fear. Desire can also lead, as Fabrizio finds, to a dangerous exposure of the self; he suffers as a result of being associated with Bonapartists. The object of desire, in this case a mythic image of Napoleon coupled with a vague sense of the republican values associated with the Revolution, has been put in place in the past and is nostalgically recalled in the onrush toward the realization of that desire. Fulfillment lies always in a future in which the significance of that object will have changed. Each story of Waterloo appropriates some imperfectly apprehended aspect of what that event signified, and each attempts to articulate that point of view while taking account of the prospect that lies ahead. For Siborne, the history of Waterloo is a way of validating English supremacy and redeeming the dead. For Brewster, a return to a story of Waterloo is a way of encountering his own death. For Doyle, Waterloo stories are historic sites where he can fight to reconcile science and art, or "Memories and Adventures," or mechanism and spiritualism. For Irving, A Story of Waterloo has to do with the old theatre against the new drama, the Napoleonic hero against the populist entertainer, and so on. For Bram Stoker, the story of A Story of Waterloo is a miracle in a saint's life. Each of these stories is a history of Waterloo, an instauration of some dispersed trace of the past, feeding the present desire and founding the future.

Victor Hugo, whose father was a general in the Imperial armies, came to the battlefield of Waterloo in 1861 to complete Les Misérables, his epic story of the transcendence or redemption of history, "the progress from evil to good, . . . from nothingness to God." [51] There he wrote a massive digression for the beginning of the second volume of his novel, some eighty pages describing the battle, beginning with the fighting at Hougoumont, and presenting his analysis of the significance of its conclusion. These nineteen chapters have only a tangential relationship to his plot, but, to use Victor Brombert's phrase, they form a "spiritual gateway" to the book. [52] Hugo confidently seizes history, the calamity of which must, he believes, soon cease. He predicts that destiny will grant deliverance from the strife that has marked the nineteenth century and will open onto a twentieth century that will be happy. He describes his book, which reveals the course of this historical transformation, as itself a realization of the change: "The starting-point is matter, the terminus the soul; the hydra at the beginning, the angel at the end."[53] Hugo sets his stage to prepare for this angelic presence, using the matter of history to announce the apotheosis of humankind at the end. On an epic scale, Hugo produces the sort of affirmation of the good, accomplished through a marvelous transformation, that melodramas produced more crudely night after night on the stage.

Brombert argues that in *Les Misérables* Waterloo takes on symbolic significance as an expression of the fateful/fatal process initiated by the Revolution: "The apocalypse of Waterloo foreshadows the end of violence in history, and, better still, of history as violence."[54] Waterloo was not the center of his story but the "porch," because when one enters the story with the battle as a preliminary, the individual destinies of his characters must be seen in the context of historical epochs, and their trials and tribulations must be seen against a background of the struggle and agony of thousands of soldiers on the battlefield. His melodrama thus assumes an epic dimension and a universality. The ghastly scene of a battlefield strewn with the bodies of dead and wounded, as well as scavengers, with which his digression concludes, gives a vivid sense of the nadir of human degradation and contrasts sharply with the glorious final scene in which the hero is transfigured into Christ.

Doyle's *Waterloo* articulates a different historical progression from the same point of origin. Following that frightening but, from an Englishman's perspective, glorious moment of victory, life has returned to normal, and the intervening years have brought changes, but no grand fulfillment. The scavengers are still on the field. Brewster has fallen out of step with this "progress," has not changed, and resists all signs of change. Nevertheless, he remains imprisoned in a present of which he no longer feels a part, in a body that no longer represents him, in a life that he will endure until he is "called." In the meantime he fixes on the ever more distant moment in the past when, he recalls, he was entirely present, entirely in possession of himself, and engaged in the process of historical change. Perhaps, in effect, he did lose his life in that battle because he has been dead to life ever since. He is another sort of casualty, and his story, too, can be projected against that ghastly battlefield in Hugo. His life, such as it is, depends on the story that connects him, albeit tenuously, to the moment when he was fully alive and present and self-possessed. History—only history—gives his life meaning. Then, at the moment of his death, comes the lightning flash, the volcanic upheaval of the past into the present. His momentary contact with his memory, across the gap of blank, intervening years occurs at the moment when he faces a new set of blank years in the uncertain future of death itself. He can only face that future in the image of his past— he will rejoin his comrades and fight the Battle of Armageddon. To parody the Brombert quotation above, "The apotheosis of *Waterloo* reflects upon the origin of violence in history, and, better still, of history as violence." It is a lost presence he fights for, lost in history, and lost by the action of history, at the moment of his death. Yet a belief in the redemptive power of history stirs him on.

Shaw, however, rejects that basically romantic attitude toward time. For him, the past has no greater significance than as disparate material with which to form a future. He is less interested in momentary self-possession or illumination than in creating an endurable life. Memory does not haunt him; the task of self-creation does. The romantic preoccupation with the past and with the desire to realize a fully occupied present, with the time of origin and the traditions that give the illusion of a return to origins, all struck Shaw as dangerously seductive and beside the point. For him, the important issue is making strong choices in the present in order to shape the future. He saw no reason why one cannot create the world anew by taking charge of the present, ignoring the past as anything more than a distraction that is easily sidestepped. During the 1890s, when Shaw began to confront the present theatre in its actuality, he discovered how difficult it is to overturn that romantic attitude, which is, more than a distraction, a positive obstruction to the effort to create the theatre anew. *Waterloo* was perhaps a hard lesson for him, as it showed that an old man, fixed on the past, never really dies. He revives night after night, and an audience always gathers to care for him and attend to his story.

CHAPTER VI

HISTORIES OF WATERLOO II: "NAPOLEON IN THE MIDST OF HIS ARMY"

Another aspect of *Waterloo*'s integration into history has to do with its inscription into the moment of its production. Control over this aspect was more in the hands of Irving than of Doyle. Indeed, it is the issue of control that sets the terms for the play's participation in the historical unfolding of the late-Victorian era. Irving's authorization and management of the work, and self-presentation within it, reveal much about the situation of its politics.

Irving had, as usual, chosen a propitious moment to produce his new play. Several months earlier the chief columnist of the *Dramatic Review* had led off his "Gossiping and Critical Notes" as follows:

> We are a nation of heroes! The blood of hosts upon hosts of British warriors courses through our veins, and when the spirit moves us to deeds of martial glory let the fiery foreigner ter-emble! Were we not at Waterloo? Toured we not to Trafalgar? And haven't we been making matters bad for the mad Matabeles—knocking daylight, in fact, into the Darkest Africans? Are our doughty deeds of daring to go unrecorded? No, a thousand times no!—or, at least, not while the brave Nelson-Wellington-Last Shot Godfrey is alive to tell the story, or while a later Leyton has strength to warble "Waterloo."
>
> An epidemic of martial madness, so to speak, would seem to have broken out at the halls lately. Not that it has been altogether unexpected, for British braggadocio ballads of the "Who-dares-this-pair-of-boots-misplace-must-meet-Bombastes-face-to-face" description have been growing into favour with the more demonstrative portion of music-hall assemblies for some time past. The demand being noticeable to the ever-watchful entertainments caterer or caterers we get the supply—and a satisfying supply too. . . .
>
> In the refrain of a song which, commencing with the incident of

the ball at Brussels, more or less graphically describes the details of
the battle, Mr. Leyton [as Wellington] tells us how "At Waterloo, at
Waterloo, Fighting for England's fame, A soldier brave and fearless,
Spread far and wide his name; Against the tyrant's army, He made a
splendid stand, And overthrew Napoleon, The terror of the land."
That there is nothing very stirring or very inspiriting about these
rhyming lines can readily be seen when they are simply chronicled
in cold print, but wedded to a catchy sort of melody, with a bang or
two on the big drum thrown in, and sung with vigour by the Welling-
tonian wocalist (as Sam Weller would say), they go with what is
known as a whiz.[1]

A few weeks later, the same columnist noted a continuing spread of music-
hall items in "the spirit of patriotism, or jingoism, or bombastism, or
'cock-o'-the-walkism'" among "descriptive vocalists," including a "Nel-
son" expressing his conviction "that it would be better for England if some
of the ways and some of the days—(those dear delightful days of old of
which we read so very much about, but of course have never, never seen)—
would come back to the land again." Also among these "militant attractions" which were "stirring the hearts of buoyant and boyish Britishers"
was a production called "Heroes of Waterloo," featuring "Wellington and
his old foe Napoleon doing a friendly duettising turn outside a joint-stock
tent."[2] Irving's oblique entry into this trend was not above a "bang or two
on the big drum." Several critics mentioned the stirring overture that had
been composed for the play by Meredith Ball, a medley of military airs
titled "Rank and File," and the passing of the military band in the course of
the play also had a marked effect. Gordon Craig noted, "This is what called
up the tears."[3]

The *Times* review of the 1894 Bristol premiere of *A Story of Waterloo*
stated that it "invites comparison with Southey's poem of 'The Battle of
Blenheim,' but Corporal Brewster has a touch of Jingoism not recognizable
in the veteran Kaspar."[4] Jingoism as such was a new phenomenon in
1881—the year of the play's setting—the term deriving from the refrain of
a music-hall song that was taken up by chauvinistic elements on the British
political scene. "The Jingo is the aggregation of the bully. An individual
may be a bully; but, in order to create Jingoism, there must be a crowd,"
commented *The Gentleman's Magazine* in 1881.[5] The reviewer for the
Bristol *Mercury* is more explicit about the currency of this "touch of Jingoism" in 1894 and, indeed, considers it part of the originality of Doyle's
play: "Studies of soldier life, patriotic tributes as it were to the veterans of

TWO GREAT ACTORS.

Mr. Disraeli.—I came round to congratulate you on the unprecedented run of *Hamlet.*
Mr. Henry Irving.—Thank you very much; I hope your social drama at St. Stephen's will also have a prosperous time.
Mr. Disraeli.—The *Arabian Nights* were a thousand and one; I shall double that, and more. Shall I tell you my secret ? [*Dialogue interrupted by Call-boy.*]

FIGURE 11. Cartoon by Alfred Bryan [1879]. (Courtesy of Harvard Theatre Collection)

Had Disraeli the Younger drifted from literature to the foot-lights, and had Henry Brodribb [Irving] strayed from the schoolroom into politics, I daresay that neither our political nor our theatrical history would be very different from what it is—except in the matter of dates.

Max Beerbohm, "Henry Irving,"
Saturday Review, 21 Oct. 1905

the Great Army, are by no means unknown upon the French stage, but the
English avoid sentiment. Mr Rudyard Kipling, however, has begun to
teach us that we ought to regard Tommy Atkins as possessing heroic qualities, and the success of Mr Hayden Coffin's latest song shows that the
British public has a warm corner in its heart for its private soldier."[6] Another Bristol paper pointed to the lesson of the play: "[Brewster] is a
hero—one of those old warriors who have plenty of disciples in the ranks
now, a member of a phalanx which will never diminish in numbers as long
as Great Britain can class itself as one of the dominant Powers of the
world."[7]

Midway through the play, the sergeant tells Corporal Brewster:

> SERG[EANT].   [*Hotly.*] By the Lord, sir, they need some change
> out in South Africa now. I see by this morning's paper that the Gov-
> ernment has knuckled under to these here Boers. They are hot about
> it in the non-com. mess, I can tell you, sir.
>   CORP[ORAL].   Eh! eh! by Jemini, it wouldn't ha' done for the
> Dook! the Dook would ha' had a word to say.

Indeed, one might hypothesize that Doyle had set his play in 1881 specifically in order to make historical reference to Prime Minister Gladstone's
vacillation with the Boers and the eventual conflict at Majuba. This exchange was certainly used in performances during the first few years of its
production but was eliminated around the turn of the century, at the height
of the Boer War. A 1902 review in a London newspaper says, "The allusion
. . . may have been all right when the play was produced some six years
since, but it will be a long time before it can be restored."[8] The passage
might have been cut two years earlier, in response to a newspaper story that
complained, "But it is really deplorable that our leading actor should so far
forget his historical sense and his feeling for artistic canons as to introduce
into the piece references to the Boer war. He cannot mean us to believe that
the corporal is 105 or 110 years old, which would have to be the case if the
date of the piece were the present day." A draft of Irving's reply survives in
which he writes, "The 'Dook would have a word to say' on the subject of
the introduction of a gag concerning the Boer war into Dr. Conan Doyle's
little play of Waterloo. No gag has been introduced & I [sure didn't?] forget
that Dr. Conan Doyle's play was written . . . long ago."[9] The passage does
not appear in the earliest published version of the play (1907) or in any
later edition, but it does surely figure in opinions of the play during its early

years. Even without the passage, the more general political impact of the play is unmistakable, as the columnist for *The Sketch* in 1900, at the height of the war, reveals in calling the play a "wonderful study of the dying hero who represents the traditions which, fortunately, despite the views of croakers, our soldiers of to-day are gallantly fulfilling." [10]

Over the years, *Waterloo* was played on numerous special occasions, at a variety of benefits, and once before the king and the kaiser at Sandringham. In 1897, during the jubilee celebrations and "with Royal Assent," Irving invited two thousand colonial troops to the Lyceum, where, with the visiting premiers and princes of the empire, he performed *Waterloo,* which a critic termed "surely the most appropriate choice possible for a military audience." [11] The fife and drum band of the Guards accompanied the marching soldiers to the theatre. Higher officers were assigned seats in the stalls, and the dignitaries received boxes, while the rank and file, with their "picturesquely contrasting uniforms and piquantly diverse facial hues," marched directly into the pit and gallery. Colonial Secretary Joseph Chamberlain, the former near-socialist reformer, turned champion of the new imperialism, occupied a stage box. Irving was greeted with a roar of welcome on his first entrance, and then point after point of the performance "touched his martial auditors to the quick." One writer recalled, "The scene that followed the death of Corporal Brewster, closing the performance, was one such as has seldom, if ever, been equalled. The whole audience rose and a roar of enthusiastic cheering swept through the building, swords were drawn and waved in air, and amid it all Sir Henry stood—a striking figure—bowing his acknowledgements." [12] The "[t]empestuous cheers" that met Irving at the curtain call alternated with calls for "three cheers for Mr. Chamberlain." Irving spoke:

> Ladies and Gentlemen, or, rather, let me say, my dear comrades, I cannot tell you what a delight, honour, and privilege it is for me to receive you here to-day. I hope that centuries hence our children will still hold very dear to them the spirit which has given the opportunity for our meeting—the spirit of love and devotion for our Queen and our country, for that great nation which you typify as its strength and power, and for that sweet and gracious lady, our Queen, for whom your swords will flash and our hearts will pray. I thank you with all my heart for your welcome, and from one and all of us behind this curtain I give cordial greeting to one and all in front. [13]

At that point, a "murmur of applause suddenly swelled into another roar, and no other words were spoken. . . . Cheering again and again, the remarkable audience gradually dwindled away, to carry the memory of the occasion to every quarter of the world." [14] Bram Stoker also remarks the "veritable ecstasy of loyal passion," and sums up the quality that helped make this play a triumph in its time: "It sounded the note of the unity of the Empire which was then in celebration." [15] This event is an excellent example of a sort of dialectic that operated frequently at the Lyceum. Through the plane of the proscenium arch, spectacle magnifies spectacle. Here, the upsurge of a common soldier's past glory mirrors in a most flattering way the "loyal passion" of the colonial armies, so that each, in a sense, offers a spectacle of supremacy for the other. The confusion in the terms of the discourse—between Napoleon's imperialism and Chamberlain's—receives no examination. Brewster is "the dying hero," as the critic says, "who represents the traditions which . . . our soldiers of to-day are gallantly fulfilling." And Irving, who represents Brewster, one who breaks from the ranks in heroic honor, stands opposite to Chamberlain, who represents the empire, which calls on the ranks for its unity.

It was three weeks after the Lyceum premiere of *Waterloo* that Irving received notice that the queen would confer knighthood on him. Irving had long campaigned for the honoring of the theatrical art as the equivalent of the other arts, including the conferral of titles on its more distinguished leaders. The idea of knighthood for Irving himself went back to 1883 when Gladstone proposed the idea. Upon inquiry, it was found that Irving would not be inclined to accept it because "there was a fellowship among actors of a company that would be impaired by any elevation of one member over another; that his strength as a manager and power as an actor lay far more in the suffrages of the plain folk in the pit than in the patronage, however lofty, of great people; that he knew instinctively that large numbers of these same plain folk would be offended at their simple Henry Irving accepting decorations of a titular kind." [16] Word of this offer must have been leaked; a cartoon of the period shows the queen knighting Irving over the caption, "Why Not?" [17] Over the years, in his effort to have theatre recognized as a respectable art, he appears to have changed his mind about the possible disruption to the rank-and-file comradery of the profession. Just four months before the announcement, Irving had addressed the Royal Institution of Great Britain in these words:

Official recognition of anything worthy is a good, or at least a useful thing. It is a part, and an important part, of the economy of the State; if it is not, of what use are titles and distinctions, names, ribbons, badges, offices, in fact the titular and sumptuary ways of distinction? Systems and courts, titles and offices, have all their part in a complex and organised civilisation, and no man and no calling is particularly pleased at being compelled to remain outside a closed door.[18]

Stoker, who probably wrote this and most of Irving's other speeches, claims that the very lack of official recognition of this particular art was taken as proof that it was no art at all.[19] Shaw, on the other hand, while conceding that the theatre was entitled to official honor, not to mention state patronage, was not above pointing out what he saw as Irving's effort to force recognition, writing a column entitled "Why Not Sir Henry Irving?" in the second month of his reviewing, soon after Irving gave his speech.[20] Stoker, without mentioning Shaw's name, reproaches him for his attempt "to destroy all the claim of gracious courtesy—of the spontaneous kindness from which high favour springs."[21] "Gracious courtesy" cannot always, without prodding, fulfill its systematic role in "a complex and organised civilization." Ellen Terry, in a letter to Shaw, offers her analysis of the situation, an analysis that makes clear the problem faced by one who, like Irving, self-consciously adopts the role of Representative Man: "H. I. did not 'demand' the knighting for *himself*. But he resented the followers of his calling being left out in the cold."[22]

Irving's problem after the conferral of the honor was, like Gregory Brewster's, a matter of how to live up to, live through, or live beyond the title conferred on him. As leader of the profession, he wanted to exert his power in inspired ways, as a hero, without losing contact with the people who formed his audience and who ultimately constituted his power by their willing patronage of him. He had several ways in which to make a spectacle of his loyalty to the people. For instance, he was noted for his ready assistance to disaster victims, hard-luck cases, and, especially, to the downtrodden of the acting profession, through charitable funds that he organized and sustained and through personal efforts. He sympathetically hired numerous bit players or stage hands—out of work, down at the heels—at decent salaries, and this had something of the effect of making the Lyceum a dream vision of English monarchy, with its benevolent king and queen, its hard-working middle class, and a well-fed and grateful underclass, all marshaled to serve the world according to a great tradition.

Critics, of course, charged that his spendthrift habits were designed to buy devotion. On the other hand, one finds remarkably little jealousy of his position, even among rival managers, and to the average player he was a hero. (Little, if any, contradictory testimony can be found; the unanimity of opinion is impressive.) Those aspects of privilege that he did enjoy— membership in private clubs, particularly the Garrick, honorary degrees, and the patronage of royalty and nobility—he used to the benefit of his friends. He had always insisted on equal type size for all actors in his Lyceum programs. After receiving his knighthood, this did not change. He was listed as simply Henry Irving, without the "Sir" (though also without the customary "Mr."). In his own time, at any rate, Irving was the actor-manager most successful at holding together the often opposed interests contained in the two parts of that title.

> Mr. Irving in the Lyceum is but the microcosm: Mr. Gladstone in England is the macrocosm. The parallel is close in every respect except that of magnitude. Mr. Irving is deservedly so popular as an artist that it is unpopular to deny that he is a connoisseur in literature as well. And Mr. Gladstone, too, is so popular as an artist that it is unpopular to deny that he is a great political thinker as well. Yet Mr. Irving's mutilation of *Lear* is so atrocious that a bookstall keeper would blush to father it; and the version of *Faust* which he produced cannot be recalled without a shiver by readers of Goethe. And Mr. Gladstone's essays as a political thinker have all to be carefully ignored lest the exposure of their absurdity should make the critic too odious.
>
> G. Bernard Shaw, "What Mr. Gladstone
> Ought to Do," p. 276

In his political associations, Irving was said to be "naturally more attracted to" the Conservative Disraeli than the Liberal Gladstone.[23] Stoker tells of Irving's meetings with the former and adds, "He admired, of course, [Disraeli's] power and courage and address; but it was, I think, the Actor that was in the man that appealed to him."[24] Gordon Craig, who insisted, "H. I. had no politics," makes the comparison in terms of style.[25] He quotes a biographer of Disraeli who became convinced that Irving had adopted his manner from the prime minister, and then offers his own analysis:

> Gladstone and Salvini roll their words out, they stride, they glare very grandly and are spacious: you want to look and listen to them.

Disraeli and Irving do something quite different. They glide, they are terribly self-possessed, their eyes dart flame: you *have* to look and listen to them whether you want to or no. Rhetoric is for whoever likes to use it—not for Disraeli or Irving. "He will say something fine" is what listeners would murmur to themselves in the presence of Gladstone or of Salvini—and fine it was. But the same listeners, when watching Disraeli or Irving, would not know where they were, who exactly this being in front of them could be, and would think to themselves: "What will he say—what will he do now?"[26]

An Alfred Bryan cartoon of the period (fig. 11) shows Disraeli and Irving backstage, congratulating each other on the success of their very different roles. It is entitled "Two Great Actors." But Disraeli died in 1881, and continuing association with the seat of power was as crucial to Irving for his paragraphs of publicity as was the prime minister's continuing association with the leading actor of the English stage, for the idealization and ennoblement of his political role. Gladstone became a regular backstage visitor at the Lyceum and later had a chair kept just for him in the wings to hear the performance better. That began in 1881, the year in which *Waterloo* is set and the year in which Gladstone was said to have fumbled the confrontation with the Boers. Stoker believes that Gladstone often visited as a "relief of change from fact to fancy" following some important event in what Craig calls "that Theatre Royal, the House of Commons."[27] In 1883, a cartoon appeared called "Farewell! The Apotheosis of Irving," showing Gladstone and the foreign secretary weeping at the feet of a laurel-wreathed Irving as he leaves on his first American tour.[28] Irving's American tours were certainly on a scale with British imperialistic ventures; they brought complete productions, with enormous casts and vast scenery, to a large number of cities, and they returned with unprecedented revenues. But the interchange of imagery between the prime minister and the "Governor" of the Lyceum can only be completed with the sight of Gladstone in his chair in the Opposite Prompt corner of the stage. The stage men had rigged up a crimson velvet canopy, and they wore their Sunday clothes; all hats came off when he entered. Two men were deputed to insure that the roller curtain would not hit him on its descent. Here was another attraction the Lyceum might offer: "The public seemed to take a delight in seeing him at the theatre, and he appeared to take a delight in coming." He made it a practice to come to the theatre early, to sit behind the scenes, to fit into the mechanism, and Stoker praises this in fitting terms: "This is the true spirit in which to enjoy the play. No one who has ever sat in eager expectation can forget the imaginative forcefulness of that acre of green baize which

hid all the delightful mysteries of the stage. It was in itself a sort of introduction to wonderland, making all the seeming that came after as if quick-
ened into reality."[29] On one occasion, Clement Scott watched a performance from Gladstone's backstage chair and felt himself going mad with
an overwhelming compulsion to walk out upon the stage. Ellen Terry told
him that Gladstone, too, had experienced this lure onto the stage of symbolic power, where he imagined himself making a speech.[30] He was eighty-
six and recently out of power when *Waterloo* appeared on that stage. He
was eighty-nine, the age of Corporal Brewster, when he died. His death
was marked as "the end of an era" as much as Queen Victoria's a few years
later and, on the other side of that permeable and reflexive proscenium
arch, Henry Irving's a few years after that. G. M. Trevelyan, in his *History
of England,* sums up the achievement of "The Grand Old Man" in the following words: "He did more than any other man to adapt the machinery of
the British State and the habits of British politicians to modern democratic
conditions, without a total loss of the best standards of the older world."[31]
Adapt the terms to the "microcosm" that Shaw refers to at the head of this
section (omitting Shaw's cynical disdain), and a similar claim might be
made for "the Antique," Henry Irving.

> An interpreter of Napoleon explains Napoleon, after a fash-
> ion. But the interpreter remains to be explained; and . . .
> he may be the harder of the two.
>
> Albert Leon Guérard, *Reflections on
> the Napoleonic Legend,* p. 256

Waterloo obliquely refers to Napoleon, the superman whom legend called
"a poet in action," a "professor of energy," but he is referred to by name
only once. Sergeant McDonald calls him "Napoleon Boneypart," and that
quaint detail says much. Doyle's "low" play reflects this "height" only indirectly, reflected in the defiant eyes of Brewster at the very end. Napoleon,
however, was present still more on the Lyceum stage by way of the actor
who infuses Brewster with the vigor and authority to rise up and command
crowds. Irving interprets the controversial legacy of this Great Man in his
construction of the English hero within the society of the 1890s. Shaw, as
the resistant force, and Craig, as the reactionary, participate as well in that
representative battle. Here, an aesthetic conflict, discussed earlier, echoes
a conflict over the "style" of *political representation* within art.

    If the battle of Waterloo may be said to represent the downfall of the last titanic hero, Napoleon, when the soaring eagle came to earth (as Victor Hugo, among others, likes to suggest), then *A Story of Waterloo* seems a nostalgic inversion of that moment. In the play, earthbound mortal suddenly soars to a sublime height, apotheosizing the hero. This moment seems to sweep aside the "naturalistic" text that led up to it, discounting the significance of all that heavily textured, highly detailed realization. The ordinary milieu of this common soldier suddenly gives way to a reincarnation of the Napoleonic hero. Napoleon, who is said to have taken advice from Talma himself on how to enact the role of emperor, is reported to have said, in words that seem to comment directly on this aesthetic (read "political") struggle: "In life there is much that is unworthy which in art should be omitted; much of doubt and vacillation; and all should disappear in the representation of the hero. *We should see him as a statue in which the weakness and the tremors of the flesh are no longer perceptible.*" [32] These words are quoted in Gordon Craig's "The Actor and the Über-Marionette," where they are used in defense of the idea that "photographic and weak actuality" should be banished from the stage:

> Do away with the real tree, do away with the reality of delivery, do away with the reality of action, and you tend towards the doing away with the actor. This is what must come to pass in time, and I like to see the managers supporting the idea already. Do away with the actor, and you do away with the means by which a debased stage-realism is produced and flourishes. No longer would there be a living figure to confuse us into connecting actuality and art; no longer a living figure in which the weakness and tremors of the flesh were perceptible. [33]

The death of Corporal Brewster relieves the stage of its "weakness and tremors" and recurs to an earlier moment of glory. It might therefore be seen as simultaneously effecting (in Napoleon's terms) a mystical return to the fallen heroic past and (in Craig's terms) a leap forward into an idealized future theatricality.

Throughout his writings, Craig describes Irving as the forerunner of the actor of the future, who anticipated the pure ideas toward which Craig would aim. This has at various times seemed paradoxical to students of Craig's work—Irving's great cause was to show that acting is an art, and Craig became notorious for insisting that it was not. Craig saw in Irving a supreme command of all aspects of a production and an ability to give unity and focus (if not idea) to a work. These, of course, are qualities of a great manager. But Craig also thoroughly respected Irving's qualities as actor, his self-mastery, technical accomplishment, and deliberate manner of controlling audience response. Two obstacles had stood in the way of his attaining the ideal. The first was the conventionality of the expectations held by the audience and critics. He would have to find a way to break free of those restraints in order to become the embodiment of pure artistic will. And yet Craig counts the adoration and enthusiasm of Irving's audiences as important measures of his stature; indeed, he can find no better comparison (in 1931) than the enthusiasm evoked by Mussolini. Craig envisions the artist of the theatre (and Irving as its precursor) as an individual of great power, acting boldly and decisively but maintaining strict order, and holding sway over a crowd. This artist does not make contact with the crowd, does not flatter or condescend, but by his art improves the crowd, ennobles them, in a sense, even as he throws them into the shadow.

The second obstacle, more a threat, to Irving's attainment of Craig's ideal of the artist of the future was the "Realistic Theatre," which "drags back a curtain and exposes to our view an agitated caricature of Man and his Life, a figure gross in its attitude and hideous to look upon": "Photographic and Phonographic Realism injure the minds of the people. They thrust upon them a grotesque and inaccurate representation of the outward and visible life—with the divine essence—the spirit—the beauty of life left out." The danger of "this false-witnessing Realism" is the "restlessness" it stirs up, because "Realism contains the seeds of Revolt." Craig dates this impulse in art to 1789, when art itself became "a threat against the well-ordered life of the Citizen."[34] He envisions himself leading the campaign for freedom of the theatre and away from realistic subversion. For the most part, Irving stood firm against the fearful influx of ugliness, against minute examination of the small and hopeless particles of life, and he kept down the restlessness in his crowd. In an essay on "The Old School of Acting," Craig found this way of describing Irving's acting:

> I then told him [Salvini] that we in England were in a sense a race of policemen. The policeman is typical of the English race. This probably is an exaggeration, but it sketches the picture, especially for Italian comprehension, and serves to explain how Irving, with his scientific movements, his scientific play of voice, was interpreting that type—man as policeman, a passionate man expressing no passions, the man who quietly controls multitudes and says little, and has no expression on his face; and that to do this was the best that could be done in England so far as acting went.[35]

This authoritarian image of Irving suggests that what led Craig to grant that Irving, the actor, might nevertheless be seen as an artist was his restrictive will that minimized *acting* (in a general sense) in himself, his company, and his audience. His acting was, in a larger sense, management. Craig's marginal annotations within his books on Irving show that he delighted in evidence of the financial supremacy of the Lyceum, and he is fond of telling anecdotes that show the Chief in total command of the theatre. Craig's artist, Craig's Irving, was an absolutist ruler. He was, in a twisted sense, like the very adversary who had made the Corporal's heroic deed count for anything at all. As Craig, and others, put it, "Irving in his theatre was what Napoleon was in the midst of his army." [36]

From another point of view, Irving, like Napoleon, had scorned idealistic concern for the future, and had taken up little except the raw energy of the revolution that was afoot. In 1798, Napoleon wrote to his brother Joseph: "There is nothing left for me but to become really and completely selfish." [37] In her memoir, Ellen Terry found a comparable term for Irving: "He was an egotist—an egotist of the great type, *never* 'a mean egotist', as he was once slanderously described—and all his faults sprang from egotism, which is in one sense, after all, only another name for greatness." [38] Craig was similarly fussy about defining this quality:

> His will was all that mattered at the Lyceum Theatre. The man who wills the rest of mankind to do as he wishes, is a selfish man— with or without personal interest, benefiting much or not at all. I object to calling a spade anything but a spade—but I object more to finding a spade something to apologize for. So the word "selfish" must stand. But let no *farceur* who hides a far greater and a far meaner selfishness under a breezy manner, attempt to make out that Irving was meanly selfish or arrogantly selfish. So devoted was Irving to our stage, that he really was innocently selfish. [39]

Here, as elsewhere in Craig's writings where he is discussing whether Irving has been slandered, Shaw's name can be assumed to be at the head of the list of victimizers. Shaw was only slightly more aware than Craig of the irony of his accusing someone of egotism. Still, his public and private writings on Irving are filled with references to the "certain egotistical intensity" of "His Immensity." [40] Pearson, in his authorized (if not co-authored) biography of Shaw, offers this assessment: "Irving was a queer person: he was interested in nothing but his work and nobody but himself. Thus he was strangely ignorant about people and things, ignorant even about Irving, for he was too self-absorbed to objectify himself."[41] In his review, Shaw rails against Doyle's play and its "vulgar conception of the battle of Waterloo as a stand-up street fight between an Englishman and a Frenchman, a conception infinitely less respectable than that which led Byron to exclaim, when he heard of Napoleon's defeat, 'I'm damned sorry.'" What more respectable construction, one is tempted to ask, might a Byron have put on the struggle of self-important wills at the battle of *Waterloo?*

Laurence Irving strives to make the point that Irving and Shaw "were, in fact, allies marching towards the same objective," which is generally described as the creation of an intellectual audience for theatre. He continues with his military metaphor: "Instead, Shaw, as he advanced, wasted his ammunition by taking pot shots at his fellow-campaigner, while Irving was unable to recognize his friend through the smoke of his own discharge."[42] In his marginal annotations to this passage, Craig assumes a distance from these foes. He writes: "Very roughly stated their objective was—each *himself.*" He then comments on his own note, placing the word "SELF" in a box and adding the words, "not the truth about the theatre—not the deepest truth—opportunists both of them."[43] Shaw made no headway with Irving; neither, for that matter, did Craig. And Irving was in desperate straits within a few years, out of control of his theatre, then out of the Lyceum completely, in "exile" on tour in the provinces and America, and then dead on Friday the thirteenth in Bradford.

Victor Hugo calls Waterloo "the hinge of the nineteenth century," when "the perspective of the human race was changed." Hugo had seen Napoleon, had seen Napoleon *disappear,* and had himself undertaken to represent the great age that was brought about in that disappearance. The pathway to the "true genius" who was Napoleon is obscured by the very process Hugo carries out. He participates in the paradoxical legend-making process that was turning Napoleon, a tyrant, into the idol of liberals. Legend sometimes overwrites history, turning the Great Man into his opposite, and turning his opposition into an image of himself. Gregory Brewster responds dialectically to Napoleon by a somewhat similar process.

On another level, Shaw observed the legend-making process in action, transforming a man he took to be a craftsman of average intelligence, self-serving and manipulative in theatrical management, and not so much a great actor as a skillful stage technician, into a man who was idolized as an artist of exceptional intellectual power, altruistic and high-minded in the-

atrical management, and a natural genius as an actor. But Shaw then established his own legend of Irving, for reasons that resembled Hugo's idea
that "the disappearance of the great man was necessary for the advent of
the great age."[44] The downfall of this tyrant of the English stage foretold
for Shaw the coming of a great age of drama. With the dramatic revolution,
the stage would no longer be ruled by its most conspicuous figure, the
leading actor, but would theoretically express new values, which one might
regard as republican values—power to the disenfranchised playwright, the
alienated director, the supporting actors, with prestige shared among the
entire company. Shaw wanted to show that Irving's popularity was falsely
established, and he proposed to reform the theatre so that it might rest on
progressive and intellectually sound principles.

And yet, of course, it was not as simple a conflict as that, and the very
struggle to achieve his ends transformed Shaw's cause. Albert Leon Guérard, in his study of the Napoleonic legends, put it this way: "In order to
conquer Napoleon, his opponents had to become, like Napoleon himself,
sovereigns 'by the will of the people' as well as 'by the grace of God.' "[45]
Shaw became, like Irving, an autocrat, a dominating personality in his productions, indeed a writer whose fierce cleverness sometimes took the place
of intelligence. In place of Irving's admittedly pretentious efforts toward
high art, in which it must be remembered he almost never lost sight of the
importance of appealing to the widest possible audience, from cab drivers
to royalty, from scholars to the uneducated, Shaw produced a sort of theatre
that selected its audience narrowly, concentrating on an intellectual elite.
Irving made a career of embodying Great Men, dressing his personal magnetism in the guise of approved cultural values. On the other hand, it is
clear from many discussions of his acting that audiences found him intriguing as much for a dark, secret, subversive side of his personality, as if he
always showed the latent possibility of deviation from those values. Shaw
picked up this latent Mephistophelian aspect of his nemesis and transformed it into his own devilishness, a deliberate intractibility that served
the purpose of causing specific discomforts in his audience but lacked the
magnetic quality of Irving's secret self because it was so self-conscious.

Irving brought indisputable changes to the theatre in its situation within
the society and in its representation of the interests of the public. His conception of his leadership, his standing in the forefront, had to do with his
elevation of the profession from a degraded condition, even as recently as
Diderot's day, when, he wrote, actors "were not only devoid of sensibility
on the stage; they had not a particle of sentiment in private life."[46] His drive

was to bring dignity, and even the possibility of true nobility, to the common player. He practiced a similar strategy on the theatrical public. However, Craig, Ellen Terry, and others recall Irving's behind-the-scenes defiance of the public, his canny manipulation of his "army of followers." Craig takes pleasure in these recollections, but he also recalls with regret that at the end of his career Irving had been obliged to cheapen himself by appealing to the public with trash, and even "to some extent helped to make this trash popular, for he could not prevent it."[47] Napoleon was no republican at heart, Hugo argues, and Craig says the same of Irving. They were both servants to historical imperatives. Nevertheless, the people, "that food for powder, so fond of the gunners, sought him," and Irving, too, came to be deified and to symbolize at once bygone greatness and future possibilities. Waterloo, the battle and the play, was the turning point in the careers of both Napoleon and Irving, a moment when, in the reign of splendid materialism or naturalism, the idealism that had given them power cheapened into an ideology inconsistent with what they had symbolized. "Bonaparte, victor at Waterloo," Hugo writes, "did not harmonize with the law of the nineteenth century."[48] Irving was victorious at *Waterloo*, but it could be said that his victory did not harmonize with the law of the dawning twentieth century. One might even say that his victory at *Waterloo* was in fact a loss.

CHAPTER VII

MEN OF DESTINY

His hold upon *me* is that he is INTERESTING no matter
how he behaves. I think he must be put down among the
"Greats," and that *that* is his only fault. He is Great. Con-
stantine, Nero, Caesar, Charlemagne, Peter, Napoleon, all
"Great," all selfish, all, but all INTERESTING. Interesting,
but terrors in the family.

Ellen Terry, "About H. I.," *Memoirs,* p. 271

Six days after attending the Lyceum opening of *Waterloo,* on 10 May
1895, the day before his review would appear, Shaw sat in Regent's Park
and began *The Man of Destiny,* later subtitled "A Fictitious Paragraph of
History."[1] A few months later, on 8 August, he told Janet Achurch: "I keep
fiddling at the little one act thing . . . with Napoleon in it, of all people. I
will finish it anyhow, as I want to see whether I can write a good curtain
raiser. Forbes Robertson ought to play Napoleon in order to forestall Irving
in 'Madame Sans Gêne.' It is a perfectly idiotic play—or rather scene—
but good acting, especially if the woman is a good comedian and very
fascinating."[2] Whether Shaw's curtain raiser came about as in any sense a
response to Doyle's can never be established, as Stanley Weintraub points
out, but this work became the field on which the grand battle between
Shaw and Irving was fought, and *Waterloo* represents the pivotal opening
skirmish, the Hougoumont.[3] *The Man of Destiny* is not one of Shaw's more
high-minded works—he would continue often to disparage it, as above,
and eventually to dismiss it as entirely insignificant. He would also boast
of it during the first two years but mainly in order to promote it as an
entertainment. His description of it as a "commercial traveller's sample"
tells much about his evaluation of the piece.[4] It is the first play he would
write as a member of the theatrical industry of London, though his position
as drama critic would certainly define the outermost margin of that business. There is much in the way he handled this play, and spoke of it, that
suggests he was trying to "play the market." His comment on Irving in

Sardou's *Madame Sans-Gêne* is based on inside information, because Irving officially announced the piece a few weeks later, at the end of his season.[5] The famous French actress Gabrielle Réjane had made her first appearance in London in that play on 23 June 1894. She brought the production back the following summer, and on 8 July Shaw attended:

> I have never seen a French play of which I understood less; and that, for me, is saying a good deal. Many of the sallies of Réjane which provoke the loudest laughter are just those which escape me. Napoleon is an inscrutable person, as becomes the Man of Destiny. . . . Surely the twenty minutes or so of amusement contained in the play might be purchased a little more cheaply than by the endurance of a huge mock historic melodrama which never for a moment produces the faintest conviction. . . . Of course I admire the ingenuity with which Sardou carries out his principle of combining the maximum of expenditure and idle chatter with the minimum of drama.[6]

London experienced a particularly heavy influx of French drama that summer, Sardou especially, which provoked Shaw to coin the term "Sardoodledom" for that sort of clever drama. He despised such dramas' mechanical plots, their substitution of sensational effect for true emotion, their efforts to achieve realism through elaborate sets and incorporation of the minutiae of ordinary life ("[t]he postal arrangements, the telegraphic arrangements, the police arrangements"). All this was, for him, the worst of theatrical frippery: "To see that curtain go up again and again only to disclose a bewildering profusion of everything that has no business in a play, was an experience for which nothing could quite prepare me."[7] That he should then start in on a play based on amorous intrigues, mistaken identities, and letters that must not be opened appears suspiciously like a sellout. That his play should also take the very historical premise favored by Sardou for Réjane—Napoleon and a fictitious, strong woman, a Strange Lady, who gets the better of him—makes it seem that Shaw was deliberately posing himself a challenge.

Perhaps that challenge was to do the well-made play better, give it some intellectual substance. Gordon Craig argues instead that Scribe, father of the well-made play, and Shaw were a pair, linked by their cleverness, their unreality, and "the gift of the gab, the slick capacity to write apace without bothering about anything further." Neither Shaw nor Scribe "was at all backward in haggling for the spoils of war," and the fact that Irving never produced a play by either one can be taken as evidence that "you could not

FIGURE 12. "Mr. George Bernard Shaw at the Rehearsal of his Play [*Arms and the Man*] at the Avenue Theatre," from a drawing by Bernard Partridge [1894]. (Courtesy of Harvard Theatre Collection)

You don't get opportunities every day of being what is called a real hero. You don't find battles ready for you in which to win Victoria Crosses. You may have no opportunity at all: and the result is that, not having an actual opportunity of being a real soldier, you have to pretend to be a soldier; so you develop your personality, you give yourself the air of a soldier. You wear your hair, or sometimes do, of a length at which heroes were supposed to have worn it at whatever particular period it happens to be; and you pose before your fellow-creatures, you utter heroic sentiments. If you are in a difficulty as to improvising the heroic sentiments, you may possibly get another person to do it for you, and learn them off by heart; in which case you invent the dramatic author—you invent me, in fact.

Bernard Shaw, "Bernard Shaw Talks about Actors and Acting" (1929)
Shaw on Theatre

buy him."[8] This argument grows shaky when one considers that Irving did produce three plays by Sardou, Scribe's prodigious successor; however, the notion that Shaw's writing was akin to the French well-made play bears closer study. Martin Meisel, in his masterful *Shaw and the Nineteenth-Century Theatre,* offers such a study, and he takes note of the fact that at one point Shaw mentions that he had agreed to do an operatic version of *Madame Sans-Gêne* "if I had time, which I never had (time meaning will)."[9] While he despised Sardoodledom in print, Shaw could not help admiring the superior craftsmanship of French works in comparison with the ruck of new English writing, and perhaps, too, he felt drawn to these works for the successful assault they had been making on the dull establishment of English theatre. Ibsen, by comparison, was making little headway.

Perhaps the challenge Shaw was attempting to meet in *The Man of Destiny* was, after years of disappointment, simply to obtain a commercial production at any cost. His mention of Johnston Forbes-Robertson in the letter to Achurch might imply that he saw a commercial opportunity there, and by the way perhaps teases her with the possibility of a role or, in any case, a production for the reorganized Independent Theatre that she and her husband would run with Shaw's assistance. A week later, Shaw reports to her that the play "progresses very slowly, and grows more ridiculous from page to page. The fun of it to me is that the character is not Napoleon at all, but Mansfield."[10] Richard Mansfield had, of course, been the well-known actor-manager who, taking on the unproduced *Arms and the Man* in 1894 and making a popular success of it in America, produced Shaw's first commercially successful enterprise in the theatre. Shaw had since then sent him *Candida,* hoping to repeat the success, but Mansfield replied in April with a vehement letter, calling the play "three long acts of talk—talk—talk—no matter how clever that talk is—it is talk—talk—talk":

> If you think a bustling—striving—hustling—pushing—stirring American audience will sit out calmly two hours of deliberate talk you are mistaken—and I'm not to be sacrificed to their just vengeance.
> . . . All the world is crying out for deeds—for action! When I step upon the stage I want to act—I'm willing to talk a little to oblige a man like you—but I must act—and hugging my ankles for three mortal hours won't satisfy me in this regard. . . . Shaw—if you will write for me a strong, hearty—earnest—noble—genuine play—I'll play it. Plays used to be written for *actors*—actors who could stir and thrill—and that is what I want now—because I can do that—the

world is tired of theories and arguments and philosophy and morbid sentiment. . . .

You'll have to write a play that a *man* can play and about a woman that heroes fought for and a bit of ribbon that a knight tied to his lance.[11]

Shaw had to respond dismissively to this rejection/demand/appeal. It would take a writer like Doyle to fill those requirements. But, for all that, Mansfield remained a significant figure for Shaw, if for no other reason than for the very forthright admixture of opportunism and idealism, the one blind to the other, that is demonstrated in his letter. *Arms and the Man* had utilized that quality, and *The Man of Destiny* would also. Then, too, having had a taste of commercial success with Mansfield, and receiving these instructions, it was quite obvious that in this new play, his first to center on a heroic and historical character and a scheming bully to boot, the image of Mansfield would figure prominently.

When Shaw next writes to Achurch, he has finished a draft of the play and says it is "in the style of Arms & The Man rather," referring, no doubt, to its revisionary attitude toward military heroism as well as to its paradoxical dialogue, its burlesque of romantic expectations. Mansfield is mentioned in connection with plans for a production. A week later, Shaw has "filled in" most of the stage business, "of the good old Napoleonic kind," and, liking what he sees, especially the "good comedy part" for the Strange Lady, he begins to "build the usual air castle in the way of theatrical business."[12] In regard to casting the Strange Lady, he says that he had never seen Achurch in the role while writing it, and then admits that he had not written it for or from anyone in particular: "It is a pure fantasy." He confirms this several years later in a letter to William Archer, identifying sources for many of his characters, and calling the Strange Lady "only a confection."[13] He discusses several leading actors for the role of Napoleon, but the principal question, as he conceives it, is where to find "an actor who will be excited instead of revolted at the idea of anticipating Irving."[14] Three of the more prominent actor-managers are dismissed quickly as unlikely to "brave etiquette" and to go head to head with Irving in the same character. Shaw knows that, as a commercial property, the work is a direct challenge to the lord of theatrical business.

In another sense of "theatrical business," he also enters into a dialectic with Irving, that is, in terms of the movements or actions of his actors, the "business of the good old Napoleonic kind." In November, his correspondence with Ellen Terry begins in earnest. He expresses exasperation over the idea of her playing Madame Sans-Gêne when he has just finished a work that would offer her a better part opposite the same old hero. Terry took the bait and demanded to read the play, which was duly sent. Shaw then contrived to make her jealously eager to claim the part, while at the same time sending signals that this is only the curtain raiser, that he has more substantial works to be proud of and to promote. He calls this work "not one of my great plays, you must know . . . only a display of my knowledge of stage tricks." Nevertheless, the play interested her, and she soon revealed that "H. I. quite loves it, and will do it finely." Feeling this tug on the line, Shaw restrained himself from pulling in too quickly, insisting that his only intention had been to impress her with his cleverness and that in any case there were several other commercial possibilities for its production, including Mansfield. Still, he concedes a production by Irving would be ideal (though later in the same letter he declares he would have to teach them how to act it). Having so easily succeeded in entering the Lyceum Theatre by the side door, he set about at once to obtain a passkey. He announces that as a critic he would have to insist on being paid royalties on actual performances, instead of just selling his play, since otherwise he might be bribed by a manager who would simply put his play on the shelf. He comments on the controlled wildness of his letter: "You will detect at a glance the adroit mixture of flattery and business in this letter. I am eager for business—keen on it—because it will be an excuse for more flattery— because I can gratify my desire to talk nonsense to you under cover of filling my pockets. I *must* attach myself to you somehow: let me therefore do it as a matter of business. Gold, be thou my idol henceforth!"[15] "Flattery" (or better, "desire") and "business" infuse his attachment to the royal couple of the Lyceum Theatre.

As in most modern monarchies, the loyalty of a citizen exacts a cost on the rulers as much as it places a duty on the subject, and in Shaw's case the cost to Irving was validation of the New Drama. Unfortunately for Shaw, the duty of the subject was patience with the Old Theatre. The flattery was paid to Terry, and it gained her favor. The play would give her a flashy part, at a time when she was less than ever favored by Irving with good roles. What a good counterpart to *Waterloo* the play would make—the one for him to shine in, the other for her. Perhaps Irving acknowledged to himself that the Sardou play was no great thing, and given its elaborate empire sets, would be an expensive opportunity to play Napoleon. In any case, Irving could lose little by paying the usual indulgence to this nasty critic, according to the standard practice of the day. But a moment's acquiescence, a mere nod of the head to Terry, would, in effect, give credit to Shaw and the New Drama, because the former was peculiarly resistant to greed and other unexamined areas of typical human weakness, and the latter was in fact the only practical alternative to the encroaching French realism, which, as a matter of fact, would never suit Irving. The more sophisticated tastes of the audience Irving had helped bring into the theatre tended to rule against the melodramatic revivals that he alternated with his Shakespearean productions. The trend in these sophisticated circles was toward French plays and the dramas of Oscar Wilde, Henry Arthur Jones, and especially Arthur Wing Pinero (who had once acted in Irving's company). Based on social convention, drawing-room manners, urbane dialogue, well-ordered romantic plots, these plays did not suit Irving's naturally extravagant style. Shaw had promoted this movement and had, he claims, begun writing plays in order to certify that the New Drama was not, in fact, "a figment of the revolutionary imagination."[16] At first glance, Shaw's early plays do appear to fit right into this disturbing trend, but upon further reflection they can be seen to fulfill deeper revolutionary motives, ones not merely aesthetic and still more disturbing. On the other hand, given that it at least had a historical setting and a heroic main character (one would suppose), and furthermore since it was short, *The Man of Destiny* might well have appeared to Irving the best of a bad lot. Finally, when Shaw had proclaimed at the end of his *Waterloo* review that such plays "are not the business of fine actors and first-class theatres," that is a charge that a conscientious leader of the profession must take seriously, even when it stings personally.

For some combination of reasons, the nod was given to Terry, word relayed to Shaw, and then the only defense for Irving against this assault on his empire, this first sign of winter, was denial and procrastination. Terry sent word that it might be two years before a production could be mounted. Shaw reacted instantly and vehemently, suspecting the worst of Irving, perhaps because he had already glimpsed his own venality. The play would look worse and worse to him from this time forward, more and more a token of his unacknowledged willingness to sell out to an unworthy art. It was now a "trumpery toy," "flimsy stuff," reflecting a moment of weakness: "I hate the play already now that my Strange Lady has faded away into the unreal Future. There is no Future: there is only the Present."[17] This lady had begun as a "pure fantasy," and then had been filled with Ellen Terry (his description of the character in the play would be rec-

ognized as a word-portrait of her), and in the process he had engaged her
in the indulgence of his desire, coded in terms of love, which was largely
a desire for some power in the theatre (her desire was in many ways similar).[18] He gets her to insist upon the Present, exerting all her influence on
Irving, on his (and her) behalf, by threatening her with loss of love (i.e.,
of the play). As he fills her image into the business of the Strange Lady, he
must as a matter of course fill Irving's into the business of Napoleon, which
is perhaps a difficult thing, as it means giving much that is himself to Irving, who was his antithesis. Later, Shaw would insist on the notion, expressed earlier, that the part was pure Mansfield, that Irving was not in it at
all. In a letter to Mansfield in September 1897, toward the conclusion of
this whole messy affair, Shaw wrote:

> I was much hurt by your contemptuous refusal of "A Man of Des-
> tiny," not because I think it one of my masterpieces, but because
> Napoleon is nobody else but Richard Mansfield himself. I studied
> the character from you, and then read up Napoleon and found that I
> had got him exactly right. . . . But you will never get over your dif-
> ficulties until you become the master and not the slave of your pro-
> fession. Look at me, enviable man that I am: I act the real part of
> Bernard Shaw, and get you or anyone else stagestruck enough, to
> dress up as Bluntschli or any other of my figments and fakements. It
> is as an organizer of the theatre that you really interest me; and here
> I find you paralysed by the ridiculous condition that the drama must
> always be a Mansfield exhibition.[19]

For a year and a half before this letter was written, however, Shaw had
exercised much imagination in an effort to negotiate an agreement with the
other, similarly "paralysed" organizer of the theatre, Sir Henry Irving.
Throughout this period, Shaw played the one egotist against the other, reminding Irving (through Terry) that Mansfield was someone "who burns to
contest his supremacy."[20]

Irving, meanwhile, had to negotiate some agreement between himself
and these two possible Napoleons, Sardou's and Shaw's. Neither made
even a moment's appearance on a battlefield; both were overshadowed by
women characters. Both plays, in fact, concentrated on the subject of marriage and the jealousy of rival lovers. Both also turned on the discovery of
incriminating evidence that would possibly show the woman's betrayal of
the Emperor. In Shaw, the evidence is a letter, and in Sardou a letter is also
a key element of the plot. Shaw's plot, like Sardou's, involves some intri-

cacy (not to be mistaken for serious complexity), but its interest lies in the brilliantly combative characters, Napoleon and a "Strange Lady," reminiscent in many ways of Shaw and his associates, including Ellen Terry.

General Napoleon hears that his despatches from Paris have been stolen from his lieutenant by the ruse of a young man, seemingly an Austrian spy. When a lady who has just arrived at the inn enters the room, the lieutenant in disbelief identifies *her* as the undisguised spy. Napoleon demands the return of the despatches, but she begs him to let her retain just one private letter, a stolen letter not addressed to him. She claims first that he has no right to read the letter, later that for his own sake (and hers) he must not read it, hinting that it might compromise his wife. If he believes this story and opens the letter, he proves that he is suspicious and jealous and, in short, vulnerable to scandal. To do so would be to lose face before this formidable confidante of his wife. On the other hand, he cannot be certain she is not, in fact, a clever spy trying to keep him from receiving valuable intelligence. Sensing that she has gained the upper hand, she now presses the letter on him, as if purely to prove his weakness. To be thought weak, especially by such an extraordinary woman, is anathema to him. His ploy is to call back the lieutenant and berate him for failing to deliver the despatches. The man must find the spy, whom he now believes to be the lady's twin brother, or face severe consequences. The lady must then decide whether to be the cause of his dishonor or concede the general's victory over her. She counters this strategy by telling the lieutenant that *she* will deliver the spy. She returns in the disguise of the young man and mysteriously shows that the despatches are concealed in Napoleon's coat. The innkeeper and lieutenant think her a witch, and all agree that the despatches should be burnt. The Lady appears to have won this master competition of confidence games, and, as a final jab, again gives him leave to read the letter. But just then Napoleon claims that he has already read it, on the sly. (Or is this just another deceptive twist?) Finally, the truth of the situation (not to mention the contents of the letter) can never be known, and both are beside the point. She pays homage to him as "a man who is not afraid to be mean and selfish," and he pays similar homage to her at great length, attributing her fortitude to her ancestral English blood:

> You wanted some letters that belonged to me. You have spent the morning in stealing them—yes, stealing them, by highway robbery. And you have spent the afternoon in putting me in the wrong about them—in assuming that it was *I* who wanted to steal your letters—

in explaining that it all came about through my meanness and selfish-
ness, and your goodness, your devotion, your self-sacrifice. That's
English.

Having seen each other through to the core, they stand together in the
moonlight, a perfect (though adulterous) couple, watching the letter burn,
as the curtain "steals down and hides them." [21]

The play is, in essence, a brief romantic comedy of intrigue, and also a
"harlequinade," as Shaw described it, alternating punch and counterpunch,
ruse and counterruse. Drawing on William M. Sloane's *Life of Napoleon
Bonaparte,* which was being serialized at the time in the *Century Magazine,* it intersects with history in an admirably precise fashion. [22] Shaw ordered from the publisher a copy of the early installments just after completing the first draft; his revisions reflect information gathered from this
reading. In general, however, he takes a certain pride in writing the play,
as he puts it, "[o]ut of the vacacitude of the densest historical and geo-
graphical ignorance," relying upon historical research only to decorate with
a few factual details what his intuition has told him. [23] By the time he writes
his next historical play, *Caesar and Cleopatra,* in 1898, he seems to have
developed this approach into a method of historical dramaturgy: "[History]
is only a dramatisation of events. . . . I never worry myself about historical details until the play is done; human nature is very much the same
always and everywhere. And when I go over my play to put the details
right I find there is surprisingly little to alter. . . . You see, I know human
nature. Given Caesar, and a certain set of circumstances, I know what
would happen, and when I have finished the play you will find I have written history." [24] *The Man of Destiny* offers, then, some insight into the historical Napoleon, but by the same token, the insight is not specific to that
point of history but instead concerns that which is "very much the same
always and everywhere." Charles A. Berst makes an interesting case for
the play as an exploration of modes of theatricality in social behavior, but
finally it does little more than jest with this theme. The play is a curtain
raiser, just as Shaw had intended, swollen out of proportion by infusions
of marvelously clever speech—and little of substance. The play's figurative and literal participation in the lives of Shaw, Terry, and Irving is what
makes it important.

Love letters, in fact, were causing Irving a great deal of anxiety, and
perhaps some jealousy, too. Shaw was writing a series of entrancing letters
to Terry, flattering her self-esteem with praise for her every quality, char-

acterizing himself as a superman and an ideal lover, and disparaging Irving as her selfish exploiter. She eagerly absorbed his attentions, perhaps seeing in him a capable successor to Irving, who was showing signs of age and was, some said, neglectful of her interests. It was not that Irving was a cad—he paid her better than any actress, possibly better than any woman in England, and her association with him assured her a position of high honor—but Shaw was, on paper, as supreme as was Irving on the stage and, like his Napoleon, "not afraid to be mean and selfish." Terry and Shaw did not meet at all for several years, during which time they wrote several hundred letters. When they finally met, the correspondence died. Of course, by then, she could be of little use to him, as Irving had lost his supremacy, and she was well past her prime. But Terry was far too astute to be a dupe to his flattery and conniving. The correspondence has dramatic tension because she wishes and demands something more from him than a good role or two. This woman, who was revered for her sympathetic stage presence—that airy and undefinable quality—managed, in this correspondence, to project herself into written prose that, in its extraordinary vividness, almost matched Shaw's. And in Shaw she had an interlocutor who could reflect this defined and determinate aspect of herself more truthfully than anyone else. Moreover, she could return the favor in her letters to Shaw, flattering him with her attentions, ennobling his concerns, and often setting him straight.

Irving idealized Terry; Shaw realized her. (Neither quite succeeded.) Her work with Irving was like the "good acting play," while her correspondence with Shaw was the "literary play," as Shaw defines the terms parenthetically in his review of *Waterloo:* "A 'literary play,' I should explain, is a play that the actors have to act, in opposition to the 'acting play,' which acts them." Irving gave Terry little or no direction in her acting and placed few demands on her (a good acting play "requires from the performers no qualifications beyond a plausible appearance and a little experience and address in stage business"). Shaw, on the other hand, would supply her with a part in which he would tell her everything she would need to do. This sort of mastery, complementary to his idolatry, was his way with her. In a series of letters in 1896, he gave her detailed instructions on performing Imogen in *Cymbeline*, though he disparages the play ("as dead *dramatically* as a doornail"). Another time he offered to teach her the role of Candida without her opening the book, "dinning the part into your head until you pick it up as one picks up a tune by ear."[25] Whether this would prove an actual liberation in comparison with the parts Irving was supplying her, many of which did indeed require little more than her beautiful and beloved presence, is hard to determine, but the contrast with Lyceum practice was striking. The plays Irving chose during his later years tended increasingly to center on him, with more marginal roles for her. *Waterloo* was such a "good acting play" *for Irving* that all it required of her was her absence! (The role of the grandniece was hardly suitable for Terry. Still, she wrote to an American friend, "We are all well, & have some fine new plays— 'Waterloo' is too wonderfully done to describe & *a great favourite of mine* is Don Quixote"; she also had no part in the latter piece.)[26] There were several reasons for the change. For one thing, the contrast in their styles and personalities made it difficult to find works that would suit them both. Near the end of his life, Gordon Craig wrote a concise (and for present purposes felicitous) description of this contrast: " 'Inspiration is but a calculation made with rapidity.' It is reported that Napoleon made the statement, and the genius of Ellen Terry was always rapid and rich. Irving's way was deliberate and nothing rash or chance-like."[27] Others suggested that calculation was not part of her mechanism, that her inspiration came instead from an impulsive nature and a bright, nervy manner. In Craig's analysis, one can detect the often-repeated point that they operated at different speeds, which sometimes had the effect of catching her up in waiting for her cues. Then, too, her memory, never good, was growing more spotty, and long roles were difficult for her to learn. Of her difficulties in learning Imogen, Shaw writes, "Unless you really want to say the things a character in a play says, your soul is not interested, and without that sort of interest memory is *impossible*." On another occasion, he sympathized with her in the "galley slavery" of learning a part, saying he would rather write a thousand plays: "Imagine learning live emotion—live thought— from dead matter—linen rag and printer's ink."[28] Shaw here seems to conceive of the actor as an originating presence who must submit her voice to the task of representation. In the best case, when fully interested in the play, the actor can speak from the soul, from live emotion.

This view of theatre as live emotion transcending the literal seems to run contrary to Shaw's practice in writing the "literary play." The inserted directions and commands in his scripts take control of every aspect of a character's manner, mood, and gesture; the playwright attempts to step into the acting. He describes a character's behavior as a novelist would, taking note not just of the voluntary actions but also of (presumably) involuntary responses. In describing the first entrance of the Strange Lady, Shaw investigates her behavior to the point of indelicacy: "One can see that she is blushing all over her body."[29] Of course, such passages aim toward the reader of the published play more than the actor, and Shaw was quite purposeful about doing that, but his letters to Achurch show that he saw it as his responsibility to "fill in the business." The stage directions did not trouble Terry, so far as is known, but she did register a different sort of problem with his text, and his response indicates that he invested a good deal more belief in the power of his "linen rag and printer's ink" than one might think. In September 1896, she wrote: "One word about the little play. . . . If you let the little man [Mansfield] play it, it will be of little count, for he's rather clever, but not enough clever. In the first place he'd play it as it is, uncut, and Lord help you both then! For, although I love every word of it, it is too long in certain places to *play-act* as it now stands. All well, as it stands, to read, but not to play-act."[30] His reply tells much about the ongoing conflict between Shaw and Irving, and between literary and acting plays:

> I have no objection whatever to an intelligent cutting out of the dead & false bits of Shakspere. But when you propose to cut *me,* I am paralysed at your sacrilegious audacity. I always cut myself to the bone, reading the thing over and over until I have discovered the bits that can't be made to playact anyhow. *All* of Napoleon can be done, if only the right touch is found. If a single comma is omitted, that will be because the actor has been beaten by the author. And I always like to beat the actor, and to beat the public, *a little:* it is the only way to keep screwing up the standard. I own I have certain misgivings about H. I. as Napoleon. Swift, brusque brute force, concentrated self assertion and the power of letting the electricity discharge itself in the meaning of the line, instead of in the look & tone of the stage figure, are all just what he has not got. His slowness, his growing habit of avoiding his part and slipping in an imaginative conception of his own *between* the lines (which made such a frightful wreck of "Lear"), all of which are part of his extraordinary insensibility to literature, are all reasons why he should avoid me, though his feeling for fine execution, and his dignity & depth of sentiment, are reasons why I should *not* avoid him.[31]

By Shaw's own admission, his text should "beat the actor . . . *a little*," asking for slightly more than the actor can supply. The actor, in failing to execute *all* of the text, falls short of Shaw's genius. But then, Shaw points out what makes Irving wrong for his play, and it shows that, conversely,

Irving has a way of beating the author, by "avoiding his part and slipping in an imaginative conception of his own *between* the lines." In other words, Shaw out-acts the actor, while Irving out-writes the writer.

Shaw returns constantly to Irving's "extraordinary insensibility to literature," by which he usually means his disrespect for the playwright as originator and prime mover of the theatrical art. Irving would certainly have disagreed with this characterization of him, citing his devotion to the cause of returning Shakespeare (including some of the less well-known works) to the repertoire. He had assisted in the publication of an eight-volume, annotated edition of *The Henry Irving Shakespeare,* along with Shakespearean scholars Furnivall and Furness. He had also performed three new plays by Tennyson, but indeed a number of his successes were in adaptations of literary classics dealt out by hack writers (e.g., *Faust, Olivia, King Arthur, Don Quixote*). In any case, Shaw asserted, Irving believed a play was "a length of stuff necessary to his appearance on the stage." [32] Shaw, too, would take exception to the claim that he himself was insensible to the art of acting, but, as he narrates it, his ideas about acting were undergoing a transition at this time. In 1896, he wrote in his *Saturday Review* column, "The mystery-man who takes me in is not the doctor nor the lawyer, but the actor. In this column I have prated again and again of the mission of the theatre, the art of the actor, of his labor, his skill, his knowledge, his importance as a civilizing agent, his function as a spiritual doctor." He does not deny the attainment of remarkable skills through long training. Like the concert pianist or the expert laborer at a mill, the actor "is actually doing things that would be miracles if done by an untrained man." "Potentially," therefore, acting is an artistic profession. However, he continues, "An actor might know all this, and yet, for want of the power to interpret an author's text and invent the appropriate physical expression for it, never, without coaching, get beyond Rosencrantz or Seyton." He announces that he has been cleared of his delusion. Actors perform no miracles, but instead—to use the phrase from his *Waterloo* review—it is all "an illusion produced by the machinery of a 'good acting play.'" He concludes: "We have no actors: we have only authors, and not many of them." [33]

It could be said, therefore, that each had made encroachments on the art of the other. Irving's Shakespeare, on the one hand, and his *Waterloo* (and similar projects), on the other, make inroads on Shaw's domain by allowing him to appropriate the writer's effects as his own. The aura of Shakespeare complements Irving's own sanctified personality; *Waterloo,* as the very type of the "good acting play," dignifies his "avoiding his part" and makes his "imaginative conception of his own [slipped in] *between* the lines" seem a masterpiece of original creation. Shaw's *Man of Destiny* made incursions on the actor's art, and these must be examined next. The conflict between the two could be conceived as a struggle for dominance over the disputed zone in between, that portion of a script known as stage directions.

In his book on Irving, Craig barked angrily about this play that Shaw had attempted to foist upon Irving, tricking his mother into collusion. His accusation was based entirely on the wording of Shaw's stage directions. "Irving rejected the play," writes Craig, "because, by putting in all the stage-directions (most of them taken from things he had seen Irving do), Shaw positively bored Irving—as was to be expected." Craig says it is acceptable for a dramatist to show off in this manner as a dramatist (for "Suburbia's wife") but Shaw had done so "as a performer," meaning he had usurped control over the area an actor would know best, nonverbal actions. Furthermore, Shaw had stolen his bits of business from the customary ways of the very "exceptional actor of genius" whom he was attempting to instruct. The business of Napoleon marking his map with bits of grape skin taken from his mouth, for example, "is precisely the sort of thing Irving did," and similarly with Ellen Terry's business. He had insulted their talents by adding self-evident adverbial instructions, such as "impatiently," to each line, so as to insure "that his play will be properly acted by these two puppets of his, in the safe, old-fashioned way which he adores." The setting, Craig proclaims, is 1870–80; the way of clearing the table is 1875; even the Strange Lady's all-over blush is 1895 Eleanora Duse. To "ape the actor in this mannerless way" strikes Craig as odd, because it comes from a writer "who wanted to bring Irving flush with the coming twentieth century."[34]

Craig's annoyance with Shaw over this imposition of directions on puppetlike actors sounds rather odd coming from someone whose ambitions for the twentieth century had to do with making the director the sole artist of the theatre, with actors who would perform like ideal marionettes. The notion that Shaw's business is hackneyed, if not actually copied, cuts deeper. In an interview (with Golding Bright, Shaw's private link to the press since the late 1890s) following the publication of Craig's book, Shaw saw no reason to be ashamed that he had learned his business "in the theatre instead of in the air." He said the directions were intended mainly for amateur performers and that Irving's "elaborate strokes" of business were not copied because they "would have been of no use to any other actor."[35]

There is no question, however, that Shaw is working with a self-conscious theatricality in this play, a theatricality derived from its subject and anticipating its targeted performers.

During the time of his negotiation with Irving, Shaw was preparing the two volumes of *Plays, Pleasant and Unpleasant,* which eventually included this play. He adhered rigorously to his own rules about the preparation of a reader's edition of a play, avoiding all reference to the stage and its equipment and instead describing everything as a novelist would: "A dramatist's business is to make the reader forget the stage and the actor forget the audience, not to remind them of both at every turn. . . . Every such reminder is a betrayal in art and a solecism in manners."[36] The stage directions often include literary excursions and effects which could not be staged directly, but they nevertheless indicate how Shaw thought the imaginative experience of his play should be shaped. A certain sarcastic tone, a point of background information, or a literary reference in the stage direction might signal the actor how to engage the audience's attention.

They also reach for pictorial effects. The setting of the play is an inn at Tavazzano, in northern Italy, on 12 May 1796 (ninety-nine years, almost to the day, before when Shaw started writing the play), two days after the battle at Lodi, when Napoleon was a general, aged twenty-seven. An entry in Shaw's diary for March 1894 indicates that he saw an exhibition of François Flameng's paintings of Napoleon, including one that Stanley Weintraub notes Shaw appears to have copied in his opening stage direction.[37] "Le Petit Caporal" sits at a table strewn with dishes, books, and papers; he is intent on studying his map in preparation for future maneuvers. Flameng and Shaw choose to depict the hero by way of the genre painting, to show the aspect of his life that brings him into contact with matter-of-fact reality. It is hard to imagine that the public would have recognized this description as a literalization of a painting, but the genre is quickly apparent. The multiplication of details about this commonplace setting, juxtaposed against the legendary character, forms the first comic effect of the play, a joke that is sustained throughout.

His "literary play" thus aims for the condition of literature and picture in the theatre, forming another of what Martin Meisel calls "coordinates," instances of the narrative, pictorial, and theatrical arts crossing over into one another. In its subject matter, also, *The Man of Destiny* responds to this typically nineteenth-century opening of the boundaries between the arts. In *Realizations,* Meisel provides an analysis of Napoleon as a subject of profuse narrative, pictorial, and dramatic figurations. The theatre's drive to represent him as a great subject of "history as spectacle" was centered in France, but England joined in the trend, especially in the season of 1831. Meisel gives a useful summary of what followed:

> All in all, the Napoleonic season was a mixed success in England, and though battle spectacle and military drama remained a staple of the popular theater through the century, its heroes were more likely to be named Dick than Napoleon, Marlborough, or Cromwell; and its scene was more likely to be the present-day Crimea or garrison India than either Agincourt or Waterloo. The Great Man as an embodiment of the national *gloire,* the notion of history as an expression of the masterful will, appealed very little to the English audience; and during this great imperialist and expansionist age, even the splendid revivals of *Henry V* (by Macready and Charles Kean) were innocent of such interpretation. Rather, the interest in historical figures was overwhelmingly private and domestic.[38]

Corporal Brewster clearly participates in this trend, offering a private and domestic perspective on a heroic ordinary man, yet with a present-day setting that points to a glorious past when "the notion of history as an expression of the masterful will" was tested. Shaw's play, on the other hand, returns directly to the quintessential embodiment of that notion. His Napoleon is relatively young, not yet utterly dominant, but at the point of discovering the potential for a man of absolute will and theatrical instincts. Shaw's purpose in violating the pattern that Meisel describes is, in part, to make an heretical spectacle of that violation. He would impose upon the audience (the Lyceum audience, he hoped) the idea that he expresses in his opening stage direction: "Indeed, it is even now impossible to live in England without sometimes feeling how much that country lost in not being conquered by him as well as by Julius Caesar."[39]

The play shows Napoleon's will at a moment before it attains absolute dominance in the world's eyes. His forceful actions are, Shaw insists, driven by practical necessity, simple expediency, and skillful manipulations—"academic militarism or Viennese drawing-roomism"—and are not expressive of "heroic miracles," as the world's romanticists would suppose. The "romanticists of a hundred years later" will, therefore, find it hard to credit "the little scene now in question," which shows Napoleon meeting a test of his will and securing an early, hard-fought victory over the English, in the form of the Strange Lady. He proves that a hardheaded, practical sensibility can win over even the most powerful and canny idealism. To this extent, Shaw opens the casing of the Carlylean Great Man theory of history to show the machinery within. The Lyceum audience, whom Irving had led on a romantic return to several of the Great Men of history—Wolsey, Becket, Arthur—were not likely to appreciate this sort of unflattering qualitative analysis. Doyle's *Waterloo* had adopted the customary strategy of tapping nationalist feeling, showing military heroism from the point of view of Dick (to use Meisel's term). The matter-of-fact circumstances of the great figures of history had never greatly concerned Irving or his audience; those characters were of use chiefly as outsized embodiments of heroic ideals. Irving had indeed put Cromwell on the Lyceum stage, but as a supporting player who is seen from the perspective of his Charles I, in a play grossly distorted from historical fact because of Irving's insistence that the audience must sympathize with the king.[40] History was, for Irving, the occasion for a celebration of authorized sentiments.

Finally, though, Shaw's play has less to do with the past than with a "present-day Crimea," a private and domestic battle with public consequences, that was going on at the Lyceum Theatre itself. In effect, Irving had sought to show himself (as Brewster) without his trappings, in humble quarters—without all the obvious machinery—in order to show that not he, but some greater destiny, rooted deep in the past, ruled the sentiments of the Lyceum audience and popular thought. Shaw had blown the whistle on that fraud and in his play had shown the same figure in his true light— not an old and dying concept, but a young and growing one, not a passive participant in the fate that brought glory to him, but a clever manipulator of his own destiny, greedily seizing his laurels, not a Great Man but an actor-manager. In Shaw's long opening stage direction he gives a wry analysis of Napoleon's success, an analysis that might cynically be applied to Irving himself (just as it has often been applied to Shaw): "He is imaginative without illusions, and creative without religion, loyalty, patriotism or any of the common ideals. Not that he is incapable of these ideals: on the contrary, he has swallowed them all in his boyhood, and now, having a keen dramatic faculty, is extremely clever at playing upon them by the arts of the actor and stage manager."[41] Of course, Irving was taken almost universally as the genuine embodiment of those ideals, but occasional glimpses of another character behind the curtain come through. Gordon Craig, for example, wrote the following on the endpapers of his copy of the Laurence Irving biography:

H I says in Public
    This noble person—
    this grand building—
        etc.
    (cheers)
aside he says to Loveday or E T
    "a silly fool"
    "a wretched hovel."
This I dislike in H. I.

———

My one criticism of him.[42]

When Shaw's Napoleon launches into his diatribe about English arrogance, Shaw's stage direction indicates that he begins in a manner reminiscent of Talma, the great tragedian from whom Napoleon is said to have taken lessons in theatrical self-presentation, and the authority Irving quotes most often on acting. In an 1894 essay, Shaw had written: "Napoleon, called on, as a man who had won battles, to cast himself for Emperor, grasped the realities of the situation, and, instead of imitating the ideal Caesar or Charlemagne, took lessons from Talma."[43] That a world leader should require the methods of an actor in order to exert full influence strikes Shaw as no curious anomaly but as a pervasive *and* not entirely ominous fact, as he states in his preface to the volume in which *The Man of Destiny* was published:

> Public and private life become daily more theatrical: the modern Emperor is "the leading man" on the stage of his country; all great newspapers are now edited dramatically; the records of our law courts show that the spread of dramatic consciousness is affecting personal conduct to an unprecedented extent, and affecting it by no means for the worse, except in so far as the dramatic education of the persons concerned has been romantic: that is, spurious, cheap and vulgar.[44]

The case of Irving proved to Shaw the dangers of a romantic and conventionally idealistic theatricality, perpetuating sentimental lies; bad theatre of that sort could be pernicious.

Shaw could see that a man of Irving's powers would be a Napoleon in any case. Sardou's Napoleon would simply perpetuate the dangerous romanticism and leave Shaw as one angry voice in the crowd. If Irving were to play Shaw's Napoleon, however, participating in Shaw's analysis of the very phenomenon of which he is a leading example, he might at least appear to awaken to a self-consciousness. He might seem to expose the machinery behind his mystique, the "mean and selfish" foundation that makes a conqueror. It would, in addition, give the illusion that Shaw had become emperor of the Lyceum, that Shaw had become leading man and would now write his column *from the stage*. Near the end of the play, Napoleon discovers that the Strange Lady, whose grandfather was an Englishman, had an Irish grandmother. Imagine the Englishman Irving, governor of the English stage and chief of the acting profession and his army of admirers, considering how to say the Irishman Shaw's line: "An English army led by an Irish general: that might be a match for a French army led by an Italian general."[45] The possibility was there. Irving can hardly be blamed for letting it pass. As one writer put it some years later, "Irving had no mind to make up as Shaw."[46]

Ellen Terry noted, "It was not *Napoleon* who interested Henry Irving, but *Napoleon for his purpose*—two very different things."[47] The selection of Sardou's *Madame Sans-Gêne* was an odd one "for his purpose" because the role of Napoleon is distinctly secondary, is seen only in a domestic context, and is not terribly interesting, but he set his old friend (and former dramatic critic) J. Comyns Carr to work on the translation. Carr had earlier written *King Arthur* to Irving's specifications. When Shaw's *"Napoleon for his purpose"* came along, Irving might have been tempted by the stronger role, the more vivid dialogue, and so on, but he would miss the scenic opportunities afforded by Sardou. After a prologue set in the laundry of Madame Sans-Gêne in 1792, Napoleon is first seen in the salon of his palace at Compiègne in 1811. He is seated at a table piled high with books—the hard-working Napoleon in a domestic scene, not unlike the opening of Shaw's play, except that the room "was a vast one with pillars and pilasters which carried the eye upward from the floor."[48] He is surrounded by servants and aides, all big men, and the point of all this grandeur is to play a trick on the audience's perception and make them believe that tall, lean Henry Irving was short, squat Napoleon. In Shaw's setting, intentionally intimate and humble, the trick might not have worked. Furthermore, Irving would not have had the opportunity, as he did with Sardou, of giving his audience a dazzling spectacle—impressive uniforms, furniture, wigs— while employing the whole huge cast of Lyceum regulars. After his lush and populous *King Arthur* (designed by Burne-Jones) and his *Cymbeline* (designed by Alma-Tadema), and many earlier such spectacles, his audience had come to expect splendor. Shaw's five-character one-act would remind them of nothing so much as *Waterloo,* an incongruous setting for the magnificent Napoleon.

To be sure, Sardou takes an ironic approach to the opulence of his play. The plot concerns a romantic intrigue among the arriviste "nobility" who surround Napoleon. "You can't grow a new nobility in a day," says the title character. (One can only wonder whether the newly knighted Irving attended to the irony in this theme.) The laundress had been a hero at the battle of Fleurus and had been mentioned in the order of the day. Since then, she has risen to prominence by marrying a duke, who is now an important figure in Napoleon's court, but she has not left her common manners behind and does not hold her tongue when it comes to reminding them of the great cause that has given them their positions: "All honour, I say, to those who, starting from the foot of the ladder, have climbed to the top. And how? Why, by their own right arm, and by the sword that has served their country! That's what makes them glory in being the sons of the Revolution, which picked them from the gutter and made them what they are to-day." Still, Napoleon has decided that this woman is bringing disgrace to him and must be divorced from her husband. He comes jealously to suspect that a royalist ambassador, a count, who has long been a friend of Madame Sans-Gêne, is involved in an affair with his wife. Sans-Gêne attempts to protect her friend, exposing herself to the emperor's reprisal, until the count is caught, at which point she contrives to show that the empress is entirely innocent. Napoleon cannot help admiring this resourceful and principled woman, and he rescinds the order for her divorce. His debt to her, happily now repaid, goes beyond her reminding him of the humanitarian and altruistic ideals for which they fought. He also owes a twenty-year-old laundry bill. As Napoleon says, in a phrase that just about sums up the idea and effect of this play, "The past gives zest to the present."[49] Indeed, the same might be said of the play's dramaturgy; of which William Archer would write, "It exemplifies in high perfection the technique of sixty years ago, and is therefore, so to speak, a timely anachronism." Archer and most of the other critics were appreciative of the production, but not on the score of any advance in playwriting. As Archer put it, "Sardou alone, of living men, could have written that deadly last act, in which the worst methods of Monsieur Scribe are resurrected in all their ruthless unreality."[50] (Though the production was popular, Irving perhaps took a lesson from Archer at the end of the season, when he presented only the first three acts of the play, along with *A Story of Waterloo*.)

Long before he began the work of mounting Sardou's play, Irving was sufficiently tempted by Shaw's more ambitious, though slight, drama, and in July 1896 he offered him supposedly the same terms as Doyle had accepted for *Waterloo*, which meant outright purchase of the copyright. Shaw would receive fifty pounds per year, starting in 1897, calculated at three pounds per performance, so that performances beyond sixteen per year would be compensated at that sum.[51] Doyle happens to recall being given one hundred pounds in payment for purchase of the copyright and, in addition, Irving, "with his characteristic largeness in money matters," sent him a guinea for each performance.[52] (By the time of Irving's 1904 summer provincial tour, this figure had increased by a shilling. The one-hundred-pound figure might be inflated, as Doyle shows signs of resentment at the "good bargain" Irving had gotten.)[53] Shaw, however, had from the start insisted on payment by royalty only and guaranteed performances, so as to prevent having his play wind up on Irving's shelf, "a play cemetery."[54] He also maintained that Irving had adopted this fee structure because he was reluctant to open the books of the Lyceum for a royalty calculation.[55] Shaw was suspicious from the start that Irving was attempting to bribe the critic, which he says had become by the nineties "a routine so pleasant and friendly that actor managers did it as a sort of ritual; and there was no feeling of anything improper about it." Shaw claims he had had that sort of thing from other actor-managers, and yet he allows that "Irving's case was different."[56] Irving controlled his critics by favoring them with his attention, inviting them to banquets, and so on. Shaw suspected that in this case the actor was offering to buy the play to keep it out of the hands of rival managers, and perhaps also to grant the wish of Ellen Terry.

Irving could make no promises about performances, and so he and Shaw remained at a standoff for a time, with Terry as the linking party. Shaw, however, understood that Irving had first claim to his play and could even have it for free if he would agree to produce a play by Ibsen. Meanwhile, in a similarly aggressive way, Irving went ahead with his plans for *Madame Sans-Gêne*, which he announced at the opening night of *Cymbeline* (with Shaw in the audience) for the spring of 1897. Since Shaw's play had been tentatively announced in the trade papers for production at the Lyceum, Irving's decision in favor of the *other* Napoleon play was calculated to embarrass him, or at the least to suggest he should have little hope for a speedy production. Then Shaw wrote a typically caustic review of *Cymbeline*, saying, "The truth is that [Irving] has never in his life conceived or interpreted the characters of any author except himself."[57] On the day this review appeared, Shaw met personally with Irving for the first and only time to discover whether, indeed, he had any intention of taking on Shaw's Napoleon. When Irving made only indefinite promises, Shaw had little choice except to submit. He redoubled his assault on Terry, beginning with his report on their meeting: "I liked Henry, though he is without exception absolutely the stupidest man I ever met—simply no brains—nothing but character & temperament." He repeatedly attacked Sardou's play and Irving, and took advantage of her loyal affection for him—mimicking the plot of Sardou's play, with Irving as Napoleon, Terry as the laundress, and Shaw as the subversive element, the disloyal ambassador from an "other" country. All along, he was writing new plays (*Candida, You Never Can Tell,* and beginning *The Devil's Disciple*), plays he valued far more highly than his "baby comedietta," *The Man of Destiny.*[58] But the bit of leverage he had secured beneath Irving, and the competition for Terry's love, magnified the play's importance.

As the opening of *Madame Sans-Gêne* approached, Shaw openly expressed his frustration at being left out (and the Lyceum staff did their best to keep him out by withholding his tickets) and at the same time a redoubled determination to get in, by "a hatchet and revolver plied by myself" if necessary.[59] He made clear progress with Terry; she expressed to him her dislike of Sardou's play, though her reason for hating it ("Words—words—words!") would not match Shaw's. Indeed, she made a confession that might have told Shaw that, for all her fervent proclamations, she was still far from being his own: "I think I'm a little handicapped by knowing you wont like me in it, because I cant get it out of my head. The vulgarity I shall go for is the vulgarity (?) of BRUTAL NATURALNESS, for the more I read the part the more I love the woman."[60] On opening night his impatience with his pen, as a device to secure his wishes, becomes legible: "Oh play *me*, Ellen, *me*, ME, ME, ME, ME, ME, not Sardou or another."[61] His ordinarily small, mechanical handwriting grows larger with every "ME." At the prospect of losing her to his nemesis Irving and to a vulgar character, one quite opposite to his cultivated, enlightened, and far from brutal Strange Lady, Shaw becomes peevish, prey to an unforeseen "BRUTAL NATURALNESS" of his own.

Yet Shaw's pen is also his weapon against Irving: "I am impatient for

Saturday's revenge." [62] His review gives five times more space to Terry than to Irving. "Sardou's Napoleon is rather better than Madame Tussaud's, and that is all that can be said for it," he writes.

> He is nothing but the jealous husband of a thousand fashionable dramas, talking Buonapartiana. Sir Henry Irving seizes the opportunity to shew what can be done with an empty part by an old stage hand. The result is that he produces the illusion of the Emperor behind the part: one takes it for granted that his abstinence from any adequately Napoleonic deeds and utterances is a matter of pure forbearance on his part. It is an amusingly crafty bit of business, and reminds one pleasantly of the days before Shakespear was let loose on Sir Henry Irving's talent. [63]

In other words, it seems Sardou's play is an "acting play," but bad in contrast to Doyle's "good." Doyle had no particular character to delineate; Brewster was to be a typical sort. Sardou manages only to create another typical sort. Both, however, are chiefly intended to gain an emotional effect through an engaging plot. Doyle's plot is so simple and, in Shaw's view, so well-formed, that one hardly notices his effort. The play seems to stand back while Irving displays his supposed skills at making a sketch come to life. Sardou's play is a bit more complex, Irving's role less central, but here, too, the point seems to be the opportunity for a bravura display of skills (for both Irving and Terry). Sardou's Napoleon is a figure (like a wax model) in whom an audience can with some effort choose to believe, attributing some quality of reality to what is, after all, a fake. Irving manages by the tricks of "an old stage hand" to trigger that belief to the extent of producing an illusion, as if one were seeing the real thing, and this is done in spite of the play as it is written, "behind the part."

How this is done is analyzed in a densely compacted statement, flickering with contradictions, which at once gives credit to Irving and takes it back: "One takes it for granted that his abstinence from any adequately Napoleonic deeds and utterances is a matter of pure forbearance on his part." This sentence is an ambush for Lyceum followers. Shaw has given the actor credit for his stage wisdom, "old" though it might be, and he has seemed to commend "Sir" Henry Irving's transcendent powers, though the title was not used in the program, and though he has just insisted that the part was not a hard thing to transcend. Now, he ironically adopts the supercilious tone of the devoted Irvingite and the gentleman's club "one"—"one takes it for granted"—in order to mock them. As Napoleon is an "empty"

MADAME SANS-GÊNE AND NAPOLEON.
Drawn by Alfred Bryan.

FIGURE 13. Alfred Bryan cartoon of *Mme. Sans-Gêne,* 1897. (Courtesy of Harvard Theater Collection)

Sir Henry—you should not play Napoleon. Wellington perhaps—but not Napoleon.

Edward, Prince of Wales, on the
opening night of *Madame Sans-Gêne,* quoted in
Laurence Irving, *Henry Irving*

part, Irving has presumably been doing what Shaw had accused him of in his letter to Terry, quoted above: "slipping in an imaginative conception of his own *between* the lines."[64] Here, though, he lauds Irving for something different, "abstinence" and "forbearance," which have opposite moral connotations, the one evoking indulgence, the other, mercy. The actor's restraint has, in this case, kept him from doing anything "adequately" Napoleonic. Added up, this praise might have the effect of insinuating that Irving's performance was inadequate, that his "pure forbearance" was an illusion produced by drunken incapability, that "the illusion of the Emperor behind the part" is no more than an effect of his imperious nature and his command of the loyalty of his unthinking followers. That goes too far, of course, and can be denied to the last syllable, but one can easily see how a Gordon Craig or a Clement Scott or Irving himself might come habitually to suspect the worst of Shaw on the basis of such a double-dealing criticism.

Irving represents for Shaw an emblem of vested authority; he symbolizes the power that is assigned by the unthinking crowd to an idea, which upon further inspection turns out to be no more than the principle of conformity itself. In his letter to Terry, just before his review appeared, Shaw reiterates his grudging admiration for Irving's "making a part out of nothing." He calls it "a Gladstonian sort of performance," and compares his hand gestures to those of the French Socialist leader Jean Jaurès. Irving's emperor reflected all the characteristics of political authority, including the capacity to be taken in by one's own illusion. Irving as authority rules absolutely over his Lyceum and over each production in which he appears, and even imperially exerts an authorial sort of control over such territory as this inadequate French play, *writing in* the interest between the lines. At the same time, Irving embodies the complementary side of authority, the compliant, dutiful role of old stage hand who knows how to give what is required of him, *acting* on assignment. This aspect is visible in his Napoleon, too, much as the emperor is visible in Corporal Brewster. The very fact that Napoleon is a subsidiary role points to the deferral of power, Irving's submission of himself to encompassing forces. The implied dualism of writer/master/emperor and actor/slave/Brewster is, of course, seriously insufficient; each is a manifestation of the other and, as with an optical illusion, but a shift of the glance is necessary to make the figure change from the one to the other. Willing submission to dominance, as well as willing domination of the submissive, can be detected in both. Shaw can take no comfort whatever in the spectacle of Irving. As a figure of unthink-

ing compliance to his audience, his tradition, and his times, and of blind
conformity to imposed ideas, he would offend Shaw; Shaw registered his
offense by *isolating* himself as a critic. On the other hand, as the man in
command of the theatrical mechanism in England, Irving was a prime obstacle to Shaw, a formidable opponent, and a symbol of the authoritarian
means by which such a position is held. Shaw dealt with his anxiety about
this specter of what he might like to become by creating within his column
as extensive a picture as possible of the community of right-minded people
of which he felt himself a part, and *associating* himself with them. When
addressing himself to Irving's productions, Shaw makes his critical column
a mirror image of the Lyceum. Ultimately, his primary attempt to make
more than a merely reflective contact with that theatre—*The Man of Destiny*—was not up to the level of this dialectic, but for the time being he had
no better hope, and so he pursued it.

Ellen Terry remained steadfast by Irving's side. She made a comment in
her diary about Irving's performance that nicely indicates the complex relation between actor and "the part" in a play of this sort: "It seems to me
some nights as if I were watching Napoleon trying to imitate H. I., and I
find myself immensely interested and amused in the watchings."[65] She, of
course, knew the other Napoleon, the one trying to imitate Shaw, and never
stopped insisting that Irving should do that play as well. But it was at this
time that Irving lost all patience with this importuning critic/dramatist.
Some four months earlier, Irving had opened his revival of *Richard III* to
generally strong reviews, though some suggested that he himself had suffered from opening-night nerves, allowing overlong pauses, for example.
Shaw's review appeared (to Irving's associates) to insinuate that he had
been drunk during the performance. As it happened, Irving did later that
night trip on the stairs and injure his leg as he returned home, necessitating
the cancellation of further performances. While Irving recovered, Herman
Vezin took his place in the cast of Terry's showpiece, *Olivia*, and Shaw
took the occasion to compare their performances, to Irving's disadvantage.
He voiced his grievance with Irving clearly:

> I purposely force the comparison between the two treatments because
> it is a typical one. The history of the Lyceum, with its twenty years'
> steady cultivation of the actor as a personal force, and its utter ne-
> glect of the drama, is the history of the English stage during that

period. Those twenty years have raised the social status of the theatrical profession, and culminated in the official recognition of our
chief actor as the peer of the president of the Royal Academy, and the
figure-heads of the other arts. And now I, being a dramatist and not
an actor, want to know when the drama is to have its turn.[66]

The extent of Irving's jealousy and annoyance can be measured by a scene
Shaw described in a letter to Terry: "After the play [*Olivia*] I wrote you a
note begging you to let me come round and kiss you just once; but Stoker,
whom I asked to deliver it, said that he had sworn to H. I. to prevent my
communicating with you in any way if he could, and that the note should
only reach you over his dead body. So I tore it up and crept weeping
home."[67]

These assaults on Irving's citadel did not lead to an immediate upheaval,
but shortly after Shaw's review of *Madame Sans-Gêne*, he received a note
from Stoker saying Irving had changed his mind about *The Man of Destiny*,
and Shaw was free to take it elsewhere. (Stoker is an agent in many of the
tactical maneuvers relating to Shaw; perhaps he supplemented Irving's
hardheadedness with a personal antagonism toward his fellow Dublinite.)
Terry insisted it was the comparison of Irving and Vezin in *Olivia*, Shaw
that it was the guilty construction put upon his review of *Richard III*, and
it might even have been the slighting and condescending review of Irving's
Napoleon, but whatever the reason, Irving at last lost patience. When Shaw
wrote to Irving to deny haughtily that there had been any accusation of
drunkenness in his review, Irving responded in kind, saying, "I never read
a criticism of yours in my life. I have read lots of your droll, amusing,
irrelevant and sometimes impertinent pages, but criticism containing judgment and sympathy I have never seen by your pen."[68] Shaw declared to
Terry that he was ecstatic—he had been "spoiling for a row"—while Irving
gave her vague excuses for his anger.[69] She found that he was "ashamed"
in her presence, and she felt "strangely powerfully sorry for him" (like the
Strange Lady!), and, in short, the bond of trust and affection between them
was suddenly in question. She had never taken much interest in journalistic
criticism of the theatre, having no illusions that it was anything more than
a publicity device, and Irving's feelings on this occasion baffled her: "For
the life of me I cannot realize how it feels, the *pain* for a thing of the kind."
The pain in this case had certainly to do with Irving's growing awareness
that Shaw was a conqueror—a general now, an emperor-to-be. Terry had
been the intermediary, receiving the love of both to make up (from Shaw's

letters and Irving's presence on stage) a sufficiency out of two inadequate parts, and now she felt guilt for her inadequacy to them. Her chief desire, she told Shaw, was that Irving play his Napoleon. Perhaps this was because in that figure she might glimpse the whole conquering hero of her heart, a synthesis of the two. Also, in the role of the Strange Lady she might stand up to Irving at last as an equal, if not dominant, partner. Her words to Irving ("I just long for you to play a REAL Napoleon—and here it is!") suggest that she did not appreciate that he had already glimpsed a "REAL Napoleon" in Shaw. Finally, her analysis of the conflict seems to have demurely ignored the possibility that Irving was jealous of Shaw, because that, in her view, would imply that *she* was the prize sought by both. That the prize might have to do with professional rivalry, even dominance of the English stage, seems not to have concerned her seriously. Shaw insisted it was personal jealousy over her that was at issue. Her response is a characteristic misreading, which proves her unwillingness to accept either jealousy as a cause or professional rivalry as an excuse: "H. is not jealous of me. I remember he once said: 'The best proof of my love for you is that I am not jealous of you.' (Of course you understand he meant 'jealous of the public liking me!') He astounded me by saying that. As if one *could* be jealous of such a paltry having! As if one *could* do anything but give and give if one had even a little bit of true love!" [70]

The paltry having of public esteem was, indeed, worth fighting over, as would soon be proved. The Lyceum staff made quick use of their network of connections in the press to disfavor Shaw. In the trade paper *The Era,* on the same page with a typical paragraph of Lyceum publicity (Sardou gave Irving a green malachite and ormolu inkstand of the Empire period in appreciation of Sir Henry's fine production), the following paragraph appeared:

> The danger of crediting as accurate any unsubstantiated rumour respecting things theatrical was shown by the statements confidently made in many papers a short time since that Sir Henry Irving had accepted a play by Mr Bernard Shaw entitled *A Man of Destiny* [sic]. This information was copied in many quarters, and various comments were made upon it. It turns out that Sir Henry had done nothing of the kind. He had merely read the piece, and has now returned the manuscript to the author. [71]

Another version had it that Irving had sent "a handsome compliment and a present" along with the returned script. [72] In response to Shaw's disgruntlement, Irving sent a letter, most of it likely drafted by L. F. Austin or Bram Stoker, the "literary henchmen":

> Your irritation is to me most refreshing.
>
> It has been so long your habit to worry the helpless that there is a certain amount of satisfaction in witnessing your own vexation & bewilderment.
>
> Your irrelevant beastlinesses have become so much a part of yourself, that, I believe, you have really lost the consciousness of vulgarity.
>
> You who are so callous to the feelings of others will readily forgive me for addressing you so frankly.
>
> I don't know anything about the paragraphs which I return. For all I know, they have emanated from your own fertile brain—for you have accused yourself at times with such unconsidered trifles. . . .
>
> Bram Stoker wrote to you concerning your admirable little play, that I should not be able to produce it—but on second thought, I think I shall, if I see any way to give it a fair run. If I cannot do that & should it be in my power only to play it for a night or two—I shall return it—if you persist in [——ing?] it back—then beg! . . .
>
> If Mansfield & I were to go into partnership now, we ought to do well, being so highly recommended!
>
> You see what a weathercock I am & how I believe in the philosophy that only a fool remains ever in the same mind.
>
> Who knows? There may be hope for all.
>
> I should be glad to meet you at any time—but as to answering your letters—this is the only answer.[73]

Irving read this letter to Terry before sending it, and she tells Shaw she "screamed with laughter," advising him that the more high-handed sections were not written by Irving: "This, of course, you understand since you are not a born fool." On the other hand, she would remind Shaw that he is "an amateur on the subject of conduction of a theatre," and that he was foolish to be so hotheaded over what did not appear to her to be a hopeless cause.[74]

But where Irving, the actor, had publicists who exploited the press in the usual ways, Shaw, the writer and political orator, could command the printed word with dazzling skill. He let his friend and correspondent on the *Weekly Sun,* Golding Bright, know that soon he would tell the story of his play and promised it would be "quite as amusing as a Lyceum performance of the play would have been."[75] As Shaw well knew, the New Drama demanded a New Theatre, and as the press had become an inseparable part of the theatre, fully an element in the spectacle because of its power to shape expectations, the press would have to be comandeered in the cause. Shaw's method of obtaining such control was direct—to write brilliant interviews of himself. (He is quite insistent that Irving never wrote a word of his own orotund speeches, his "elaborately sarcastic" letters, and so on, leaving the words to be turned out by his publicity machine, while at the same time Shaw himself could not trust the public discourse to handle his words properly, and so insisted on exercising literary control over his presence in the public eye.)[76] The guiding principle of his interview on *The Man of Destiny* is stated in his cover letter to Bright: "The most fatal character to appear before the public in is that of a man with a grievance." His self-interview casts the divergence of opinion on the affair (almost all of which represented the matter from Irving's side) as a matter of whether the writer "ran anti-Ibsen-wards or the reverse." He rates himself as "this most modern of the moderns, high priest to Ibsen and contemner of Shakespeare, [who] had gained admission to the shrine of the Lyceum, sacred to the memory of 'W. S.'" He calls the play "a trumpery little one-act play of mine," which Irving, "whose literary judgment is his weak point, enormously overrated."[77] He defuses the grievance by downgrading the play and construing its rejection in terms of specific practical matters on the one hand and general resistance to the Ibsenist revolution on the other. He indeed lets Irving off easy, except for casting him as something of a liar and a fool. But Shaw, no doubt, also appeared something of a fool in the public eye, for the abuse he must heap on his own play, for his rationalization of its rejection, and for his nagging insistence on the cause of Ibsen against such foes as the "good old anti-Ibsenite grandmother, The Era," which had so stingingly mocked his situation in the first place.

The spirit of contrariety (easily mistaken for mockery) was, of course, Shaw's mainstay; it was also his self-indulgence, and would nearly always in his career make the writer more visible than the writing. His construction of "Ibsenism" got confused in the public understanding, not to mention Shaw's understanding, because of the emphasis he placed on contrariety, on abusive public address, as qualities of Ibsen's plays. Outraging the public, creating an outcry, was part of the program of a pioneering drama, Shaw reasoned; he sought to be one of those who, like the Ibsen of his *Quintessence*, "tramples on ideals, profanes what was sacred, sanctifies what was infamous." Philistine critics, such as Clement Scott, whose notorious hysterical response to the "almost putrid indecorum" of Ibsen occupies Shaw's attention through the first three chapters of that book, set up

a humorless defense of the high moral purpose of the English stage against
the assault of these invaders, and this defense was seen as one with the
more general cause of elevating the stage from its degraded social, aesthetic, and intellectual state. Scott, whose cause was as much the latter as
the former, and Irving, who lent his hand to the anti-Ibsenist cause, sought
always to insure that the drama would be regarded as a *serious* art. It remained to Shaw to profane this cause, by demonstrating the folly of its
seriousness, and the profound quality of its lightness. By self-consciously
submitting himself to the ridicule of the unselfconsciously empowered, he
set them up for self-destruction. With contrary humor, he exposed the
sanctimonious air surrounding the holy ideals of the stage (the cult of
Shakespeare is only the most famous of his targets), counting on the fact
that not all would see the joke. The key would be for the public then to see
those resisters (the Scotts and Irvings) for what they *were*—ideological
machines—rather than for what they claimed to believe: "And if any man
does not understand, and cannot foresee the harvest, what can he do but
cry out in all sincerity against such destruction, until at last we come to
know the cry of the blind like any other street cry, and to bear with it as an
honest cry, albeit a false alarm."[78] At the same time, Shaw risked under-
mining his cause when his witty attack came to seem impelled by petty or
personal motives.

Irving had spotted Shaw's threat to the stage at least from the time of the
appearance of the *Quintessence,* in 1891. At a banquet in Liverpool, Irving
said:

> I have lately read in the polite language of the writer of a book
> about what is called Ibsenism, that our finished actors and actresses
> cannot play Ibsen because they are ignoramuses. I thought that some
> of our younger actresses had played Ibsen rather well, though this, it
> seems, is because they are novices in art but experienced in what is
> called the political and social movement. Outside this mysterious
> movement you find "inevitably sentimental actresses" we are told,
> who are quite good enough for Shakespeare but not educated enough
> for Ibsen. I understand from this authority that one of the qualifica-
> tions for playing Ibsen is to have no fear of making yourself "acutely
> ridiculous" and I can easily believe that this exponent of Ibsen is not
> troubled by that kind of trepidation.[79]

Shaw had indeed doubted the capacity of conventional English actors to
undertake Ibsen, because the "whole point of an Ibsen play lies in the ex-

posure of the very conventions upon which are based those by which the actor is ridden." The stage conventions that catalog characters as villains or heroes, that count on actors to deliver unambiguous performances, and that do not acknowledge the possibility of ironic depictions cannot be suitable for Ibsen's plays. Ibsen's mockery of his *characters* for their conventional ways leads an audience to give an antithetical response, laughing at the actor playing a serious part, sympathizing with the apparent fool. For a conventional actor, the laughter is particularly hard because "it is derision, than which nothing is more terrible to those whose livelihood depends on public approbation." The actor-manager especially, who must be sensitive to signs of approbation, and who conventionally takes the most serious of characters, would be likely to fear appearing "acutely ridiculous sometimes at the very climax of [his] most deeply felt passages," and would resist Ibsen.[80]

But Shaw has also another object of attack in his *Quintessence*. He writes about the conventional ways of English dramatic critics, their complicity in the commercial mechanism of production. They become personally involved with the artists—as friends or friends of friends, as enemies or enemies of enemies. They act on prejudice; they bow to pressure from editors and advertisers; they take favors or bribes; they honor sacred cows. They are not realists. Shaw developed his critical ethic out of these observations, rejecting the customary corrupt ways of the profession, but on the last point—realism—he would never quite meet his own standards, any more than he would ever write a play quite like Ibsen's. Shaw continues:

> In short, the law is against straightforward criticism at the very points where it is most needed; and though it is true that an ingenious and witty writer can make any artist or performance acutely ridiculous in the eyes of ingenious and witty people without laying himself open to an action, and indeed with every appearance of good-humoured indulgence, such applications of wit and ingenuity do criticism no good; whilst in any case they offer no remedy to the plain critic writing for plain readers.[81]

It is no accident that Ibsen's plays, in Shaw's view, call for an actor willing to appear "acutely ridiculous" and that a Shavian sort of criticism can have exactly the same effect (in the eyes of those of a common ingenious and witty bent). In his criticism, Shaw takes conventional artists and performances and places them in the context of the whole English stage, making of the latter one great Shavian-Ibsen play, with himself as an authorial, ironic presence. Deeply "serious" plays can thus be made to seem "acutely ridiculous," sharp and dangerous to the eye, while marginal works and artists—amateur performances, experimental productions, provincial actors—can be made to define the central tradition.

Those who resist Ibsen's plays (and Shaw's criticism as well), he says, are the blind who make a cry, albeit an honest one, in the street. On the other hand, Shaw's outcry too reveals a blindness, an ignoring of his own conclusion that "such applications of wit and ingenuity do criticism no good." Aside from the added notion that such criticisms do not answer the needs of "plain readers," they do not properly serve even the "ingenious and witty" because they do not meet Shaw's own standards of independence and realism. They advocate, they promote himself, they rile for the sake of riling—they do not always answer the call for careful analysis of what is at hand, but instead appropriate the theatricality of the subject for the staging of a different drama, one that typically features Shaw as a sort of actor-manager. In 1891, Shaw expressed his doubts about that sort of critical writing. From January 1895 through May 1898, he nonetheless tasted its possibilities.

Realism was not, finally, what Shaw would claim for his writings. Indeed, his prefaces to collections of his reviews, and his other notes on the subject, largely apologize for the purposeful distortions they contain. But on the issue of independence from commercial influence, he was always insistent. Therefore, when the Lyceum staff made public the rejection of *The Man of Destiny,* even hinting that some compensation had been made to the author for the favor of submitting his (unworthy) work, Shaw was vexed. He was not alone in observing the monopolistic practices of the Lyceum, particularly its peculiar ability to command the press. Toward the end of May 1897, an article by Philip Amory appeared in a new magazine called *The Comet* ("A Magazine of Free Opinion") which charged Irving with conspiracy even more directly than Shaw himself, and with less of an "appearance of good-humoured indulgence." Amory charged that Irving was using his stranglehold to thwart the career of Wilson Barrett:

> Something like a stroke of moral paralysis has stricken English histrionic art ever since the great, the only Sir Henry Irving became the fashion. Very little can be done—very few new advances can be made, seldom can a younger or more promising actor have a real chance—so long as the shrewd actor-manager of the Lyceum Theatre retains his hold on popular favor, and has Clement Scott as his body-guard and Boswell. One of the most extraordinary things in our

modern English social and fashionable life is this fetish-worship of a man who is, artistically speaking, by no means worthy of such excessive adulation. It was "worked up," of course, in the first instance; and now it is "kept up" by the united efforts of three men in three different branches of labour,—socially by Sir Henry himself, critically by Clement Scott, financially by Mr. Bram Stoker. These three individuals, like Dumas' "Trois Mousquetaires," have resolved to "keep the boards"; and they have succeeded in England as they never could possibly have succeeded in any other country, because, of all publics in the world, the British public is the most guileless and most good-natured. A French or an Italian audience would not stand either the walk or the talk of the great Henry,—but an English audience has that excessive kindness which generally accompanies total ignorance of the matter in consideration, and sits and stares, blandly, resignedly and sleepily, where less patient peoples would rise, stamp, howl, and insist on pulling down the stage curtain.

This mocking diatribe continues for pages, utilizing an elaborate conceit of Mr. and Mrs. John Bull in conversation with an unnamed critic who claims reviewers are denied the privilege of their own feelings and are made to serve Irving's will, under threat from their editors who "dance to the Lyceum piping." The critic muses on what would happen if Mr. Bull, having been apprised of this conspiracy against Wilson Barrett and other rivals, should go to Clement Scott and tell him, "in that particularly plain and forcible manner of his, that he doesn't believe in him or his falsetto criticisms any longer," and that he knows about those critics who attend Irving's "suppers on the stage" and "produce their criticisms on the succulent memory of that same booze and guzzle." The Bulls come to recognize the hoax they have been a party to, "pretending" to admire him while ignoring his obvious faults. Such is Irving's delusive hold on the public that his acting can be lauded as melodramatic, an "epithet of opprobrium flung at all aspirants for the highest histrionic honours *except* Irving." On the other hand, they acknowledge, "Wilson Barrett is worth ten Irvings: he speaks like a man, walks like a man, and *is* a man. By-the-bye, the critics find fault with him for that. I wonder why? They object to his manliness. They call it 'affectation.' " Shaw is mentioned as one who opposed the trend and praised Barrett, but how vexing for him to read what follows:

I don't know whether he's of the same mind now, for I believe Irving has offered to buy a play of him. That's a well-known "pleasant manner" of Sir Henry's, you know,—or so people say. When he finds any critic or author who is of a doubtful mind, he says, "God bless you, my boy!" or something of that sort, and suggests his writing a play for him. Of course the poor devil jumps at the idea, and while he is writing the said play, he naturally cannot criticise his possible future patron. D'ye see? Clever, isn't it?"

Finally, with the cry, "*I will have those back-stairs pulled down!*" they set off for the theatres, with "their wholesome round faces . . . full of serious and absorbed interest. They evidently mean business." [82]

To be serious, to mean business—these are the lessons of the author's facetious dramatization. The serious, business-minded critic will see the "acutely ridiculous" aspect of Irving's melodramatic manner and will expose it as such, and the relatively coarse tone of sarcasm suggests how that criticism would sound. Criticism should operate as a scourge in order that manly, unaffected actors like Wilson Barrett get proper respect. Shaw ruefully remarked this article in a letter to Terry, adding, "Oh my head! I must away to my stall of torment, unconsoled." [83] He could take no comfort in recognizing many of his own ideas dressed in this policeman's uniform, utterly unselfconscious and unironic. One vague notion of seriousness and business can be easily substituted for another, and that makes a revolution of sorts, but hardly the sort of insurrection that Shaw was mounting. Terry responded that she had seen the *Comet* article: "Heavens what common, what vulgar stuff! But no harm done to Henry since they didnt *praise* him. My poor Henry! That at least was spared him." [84]

In the competition for honorable praise, Irving's struggle was to grow more and more desperate. He had too strong a business sense to ignore the growing appetite for modern-dress, realistic plays, but his production of *The Medicine Man* in 1898, the only true example of such a work in his later career, proved a failure, not the least because Ellen Terry took offense at her unworthy part. On the other hand, his grandiose production of his son's historical drama *Peter the Great* also failed to go, giving Shaw a welcome moment to gloat, in a letter to Terry, "I see that Peter is coming off, and that H. I. is going to fall back on that silly old Story of Waterloo as a first piece to The Bells. This is heaven's vengeance on him for assassinating the Strange Lady." [85] The main victory Shaw could relish from the Napoleonic battles was that Terry now sporadically took his view of Irving, complaining often about the poor parts she was receiving. The conflict over Shaw's play was not the final or even the critical factor in bringing about

Irving's downfall, but it helps define what Irving would soon come to realize was a losing battle. In a few years the union of Terry and Irving was severed: Terry was unceremoniously left to her own devices, Irving was nearly broke and losing the Lyceum to a limited partnership, and Shaw was the ascending star.

In the meantime, however, there was more torment without consolation, more headache for the upstart. The victory the playwright was to seize from the actor would not come without a full measure of pain; the theatre, still under the sway of the latter, kicked against the pricks. Two months after the Lyceum rejected it, *The Man of Destiny* was produced for a few performances at a theatre in Croydon to secure its stage rights. Shaw was unenthusiastic about its possibilities from the start: "*All* plays are thrown away on the stage. . . . Words cannot express my indifference to all this external business at Croydon." Here he faced the practical struggle of how to carry off a "literary play" with a group of experienced but conventional actors. The production satisfied no one, proved nothing, least of all to Shaw: "Picture to yourself the worst you ever feared for it; raise that worst to nightmare absurdity and horror; multiply it by ten; and then imagine even that result ruined by an attack of utter panic on the part of the company in which each made the other's speeches when he (or she) could think of anything to say at all, and then you will have some faint guess of what it was like." Shaw's two personae met uneasily on the occasion—"an agonizing experience for the author, . . . but an intensely interesting one for the critic."[86] He later recalled that the other critics on hand had gone "to the verge of downright mendacity" in their uncertainly appreciative reviews (showing there can be more than one sort of back-stair conspiracy).[87]

William Archer, however, had not pulled his punches, declaring that Shaw's play "represents nothing, illustrates nothing, typifies nothing, caricatures nothing," and then offering Shaw a sample of his own merciless assault in the following interrogation: "Now, frankly, my dear Shaw, if Mr. G. R. Sims had introduced such a piece of mechanical and meaningless claptrap into an Adelphi melodrama, what would the *Saturday Review* have said? And why should that in G. B. S. be a stroke of genius which in G. R. S. would be flat idiocy? And, taking it all in all, *is* this a play of which your critical intelligence can approve?"[88] In fact, the critic in Shaw had to acknowledge that his play had not properly engaged its actors or its audience, that there was something baffling to them about it. It came down to the fact that neither group knew what to do with the personality of G. B. S. / Bernard Shaw, which figures so prominently in all his writings. He claimed the actors had been incapable "of getting on terms of real intimacy and enjoyment with my stuff." To play Shaw one must love him, it seems, or at least participate in the buoyant self-confidence that is so manifest in his works. The audience was also cowed by his personality, which was most obtrusive as a literary fact, a formidable presence in the great quantities of perfectly ordered language, as Ellen Terry had foreseen. As Shaw put it:

> There was something insane & ghastly about the business; for since the dialogue does not consist of obvious jokes (which must either come off or be perceptibly muffed) but has, apart from its comedy, as continuous a grammatical sense as any blue-book, it sounded at once serious and inexplicable, like a dream-play. Fortunately the audience was humble in its agony, and mutely respected Napoleon for saying things it could not understand. It would even make a mouselike attempt to shew its appreciation now & then; but each time it shrunk back lest it should be taking seriously something that was perhaps one of my dazzling jokes.[89]

It seems that a continuous "grammatical sense" can act as a wall, screening the audience from their customary participation in familiar scenes of comedy or seriousness. Shaw's "dialogue" has a disconcerting way of leaving the audience out—that is, the audience untutored in the "literary play." Shaw had, in his *Waterloo* review, defined the term as "a play that the actors have to act, as opposed to the 'acting play,' which acts them," and he might have added, a play the audience have to read, in opposition to the 'acting play,' which reads them. In practice, Shaw's dual personality is an inscribed literary fact, which might be described as an overwriting, a writing beyond the confines of the curtain, joining directly with the critical writing (or "reading") that it requires for its completion. Shaw's famous prefaces literalize this overwriting, this interfusion of personae. They are Shaw's equivalent for, on the one hand, Irving's profusely and intensely detailed acting and, on the other hand, his dominance of the whole theatrical mechanism, including his management of the Lyceum, of the press, and of the audience. Ronald Peacock has observed that "the only proper way of judging [Shaw's] work finally is one that takes account of the unity of preface and play."[90] Although this is misleadingly overstated with regard to Shaw's later plays, it rings true for the early work, when the attempt to carve out a new theatre, as expressed in the prefaces, had almost as much to do with the plays' finding their audience as their productions did. When *The Man of Destiny* was published, however, along with three other plays, in *Plays Pleasant,* the preface to the volume brushed over the play in a few dismissive sentences. Here was a play whose playwright (Shaw) stubbornly refused to meet face to face with its critic (Shaw), having had his head turned by an actor (Irving) or perhaps by the abstract possibility of an ideal actor (Shaw) who could dominate the public directly from the stage by force of personality, inscribing his opinions and effects onto the audience just as he had as a critic.

Much as *Waterloo* had, from a certain point of view, rebounded against Irving, tempting him into a success he was not entirely willing to enjoy as his own, so *The Man of Destiny* rebounded against Shaw, leading him into a failure of which he was for once unwilling to boast. Failure, while frustrating, had been Shaw's proof of true achievement, evidence of predicted blindness on the part of the managers. This had the effect of drawing attention to his "impossibilist" cause, creating an audience *outside* the existing theatre. But with his Napoleonic play, he had drawn into the hypothetical cast the icon of theatrical success, Henry Irving, and furthermore, he had gone far toward placing his unmediated personality upon the stage, becoming in effect an actor in his own "good acting play." Eric Bentley, in his essential book on Shaw, remarks this problem in the play. Referring to Shaw's description of Napoleon in the opening stage direction, Bentley argues that Shaw has infused something of himself: "When Shaw insists on making his hero so like himself, the character has more reality in the stage direction than in the play."[91] The stage direction in general is an ambiguous region of a dramatic text, often as much in the hands of the actor or manager as the playwright. One might imagine the direction as either the site of rapprochement between writer and actor, or the zone of belligerent encroachment. Shaw insistently occupies the stage direction describing Napoleon, obtruding his personality and denying entry to the actor. Several writers believed that this was the case in all of Shaw's plays, as the following comment suggests: "A monologue is not a play, entertaining though it might be, and in the cast of Mr. Shaw's plays there is only—Mr. Shaw."[92] Shaw denied this accusation without discounting the fact of his dominant presence: "All my characters are 'Shaws.' But to say that they are all self-portraits is silly. It is what every bad critic said forty years ago. You must not be yourself overwhelmed by my style."[93] Bentley disagrees with Shaw in the single case of *The Man of Destiny,* which does overwhelm by its style, its flood of ink from the pen. Shaw's stylus inscribed a new line for others to follow, making the question clear: "Were they coming my way or staying in the old grooves?" He saw himself as the author "who had to cut his own way into [the theatre of the nineteenth century] at the point of the pen," and in this play his insistence on his own way was barely masked.[94] Toward the end of his life, Archer wrote that what was needed in Shaw's play was that he "should blue-pencil his personality!"[95] The inscribed personality in his plays—the writer *on* the stage—drastically limits the freedom of other voices, different creators, and so threatens to suspend the drama. Bentley acutely defines the escape that Shaw found from this problem in most of his other plays: "Another way of using one's own personality is to make of it the measuring-rod for what is *not* oneself: one can measure *difference* with it as well as likeness."[96] The measure of opposition or difference makes his plays dramas rather than the sermons that so many of his early critics accused him of writing. Shaw took a lesson in articulating difference dramatically during his four years of writing dramatic criticism, and especially so by repeatedly setting his personality opposite to the ultimate theatrical personality of the day, Henry Irving.

CHAPTER VIII

PERSONALITY

While Shaw advanced his sociological theory of Irving's success, preferring to derive his analysis from the submission of the audience rather than the dominance of the actor, most other critics and commentators set forth a psychological or even mystical theory, whether they chose to disparage his abilities or to laud them. Their debates turned on the use of the term "personality," which referred mainly to the distinguishing or strong features of an actor, the individuality that could not be suppressed entirely in impersonating a character.[1] Of course, physical and temperamental qualities figure into the personality, but unconscious elements do as well, and they are by definition beyond the artificial control of the actor. Critics often sought to define the personality of an actor by describing physical and temperamental attributes, but in the case of a great actor, those unconscious qualities were often what seemed to put the unique stamp on a performance. The great actor appears in a variety of roles, demonstrating versatility with all that can be controlled, and yet there remains an unchanging quality that can be studied again and again, over many years. The exercise of defining this mysterious or hidden self of a prominent actor necessarily leads the observer into a sort of psychoanalysis. But in the case of the most powerful performers, their personalities might be said to inscribe themselves on the audience, unifying the impressions of the crowd, even shaping the self-image of a generation of theatregoers.

The history of the Lyceum Theatre and Irving in the years following *Waterloo* and the Napoleon controversy is the story of his personality's growing more pronounced and more out of step with the mainstream of theatrical art in London. Irving's commercial and artistic disasters outnumbered his successes during these final years, and yet still a large and faithful following attached themselves to him. As more than one writer observed, his audience was by no means composed entirely of nostalgic old playgoers. Shortly before Irving died, his former assistant, L. F. Austin, wrote: "The younger generation had knocked at the doors in a sense quite different from that of Ibsen's famous saying. They had come in thousands,

not to tell the old actor that his day was done, that his methods were outworn, that he must yield his sceptre to another, but to swear fealty to him,
to crown him with fresh laurels, to thunder his praises with passionate
emotion."² His greatness would, it was felt, prove immortal. Ten years of
a dying actor dying almost every night in some disguise on the stage prepared the audience to receive him into the immortality of honored memory.

The challenge, especially when the faults of his personality became increasingly obvious in bad plays, was to reconcile his greatness with those
faults. This was accomplished largely by hypothesizing a sublime internal
Irving, at odds with the external, and hidden from the view of impertinent
upstarts and inhumane critics. Sir John Martin-Harvey, for many years a
member of the Lyceum company before going on to a distinguished career
of his own, introduces the crucial term "mind" in his analysis of Irving's
personality:

> I suppose no actor can altogether escape from his mannerisms any
> more than he can escape from his mental limitations. Physical limi-
> tations are rarely a serious disability. Indeed, as our friend of the
> *Manchester Umpire* wrote: "The mannerisms of the actor are as the
> handling of the painter," but they must be largely controlled or they
> will obtrude themselves to such an extent that we become bored with
> the intrusion of a personal habit which, when we are confronted with
> a character on the stage or an aspect of nature in a painting, becomes
> an impertinence. In his moments of excitement and passion these
> peculiarities of Irving did steal forth, but his mind, *his mind,* his
> conception, were so determinedly apparent, that we thrust them out
> of our vision, and if we were old Lyceum devotees, we got so used
> to them that they no longer were obtrusions.³

In the same context, he offers a marvelous description of Irving making an
entrance that shows at once the transformative property of the stage mechanism and the exercise of this mental power:

> I hope I shall not be misunderstood. Irving had a greater knowl-
> edge of the elements of his art than any actor I have ever met or seen.
> It was only an intractable husk which *sometimes* obscured the perfect
> expression of it. I have seen him walk loosely and naturally toward
> the wing from which he was going to make an entrance, and sud-
> denly his cue having been given, a strange metamorphosis has come
> over him. His limbs and neck have stiffened, he has struck the boards
> of the stage with a preliminary stamp, tripped and plodded his stride

through the entrance and emerged upon the audience, conscious for the moment, no doubt, of this unpliable muscular system, but determined that his audience shall observe his mind and not his gait—and he triumphed![4]

Since *Waterloo* was a drama of an "intractable husk" of a man, it gave his audience a perfect opportunity to observe and meditate on this mental/ physical split in Irving and on his magical ability to secure the victory of mind over matter. His performance revealed a character who cannot perform physically, whose life is reduced to a spiritual preparation for death. Irving invested this physical mimicry with the qualities of his personality, which included the effect of profound dignity, of humble authority, of intellectuality, and of a mysterious reservoir of spirituality, but all of these had to come through the "husk" of his physicality. The final moment of the play would seem a great release of the pure personality, freed in death.

The author of an 1897 book on acting (with prefatory endorsement by Irving) argues that the highest achievement in acting comes from superior artificial control of voice, gesture, thoughts, and so on, in concert with "the actor's indestructible, insuppressible individuality, making itself felt by means which lie outside of art and come direct from nature," and furthermore, that "the great actor is generally a great individuality."[5] The implication is that the great actor must draw from nature a superior personality, including unconscious effects. Just what the author might have meant by "insuppressible individuality" bears closer examination. It seems to suggest something like what the romantics felt to be the site of creativity, a susceptible impulse center for the production of art. In this view, each artist bears a distinctive internality or self from which the expression would spring, as if by a spiritual or inspirational process. This embedded genius gave the individual poet or artist his or her unique style. On the other hand, Freud's discussion of the "insuppressable individuality"—the unconscious—would argue that psychic trauma and unsatisfied desire might be structural elements of this self. The actor of the 1890s might have intuited the tension between these divergent concepts since performance entails an artistic production, founded in sensitivity and aimed at a distinctive style, but focused upon the stresses of unusual and often traumatized characters.

Some writers on acting sought to give the term a mystical aura, implying that it was hardly different from the creative temperament of writers and painters. Others insisted that the personality was not entirely inherent and involuntary but was more or less equivalent to character in the moral sense, requiring careful training, such as is prescribed in the following passage, written in the mid-1880s:

> Physical peculiarities, however largely they may have contributed to the artist's celebrity, must be kept within the bounds of appropriateness, and the actor's intellectual bias must be subordinated to such sentiments as seem likely to be entertained by a majority of the audience. So far as the question of *physical* personality goes it is a matter of taste and judgment; but the *mental* personality is far deeper in its source, and more important in its influence. Eye speaking to eye, and ear to ear, involve trivial issues compared with the momentous conversation of soul with soul.[6]

The same writer calls for cultivation of "ethical personality," without which the actor will fail to discern the moral nature of the dramatic character and so prove out of harmony with the audience.

Each of these connotations played a part in the discussion of Henry Irving's personality. The playwright Hall Caine, who made efforts to write a play for Irving during his later years, regarded Irving's personality as an impediment. Caine wrote that Irving had indeed "created a character and assumed it for himself." That character was so powerful and *sui generis* that Irving was unable to "sink" it into a role, especially as he got older and still more peculiar and famous, so that finally "it was only possible for him to play parts that contained something of himself."[7] One might say that Irving, through the force of his willful personality, had broached the limits of acting, had begun creating character independently (and in defiance) of the writer, much as Shaw had broached the limits of playwriting and, by imposing his personality on his plays, had willfully preempted the role of actor. *Waterloo* and *The Man of Destiny* are perhaps the moments of maximum interpenetration of enemy lines, when each fights most strenuously to co-opt the other. Both fail in this respect, but both also announce that there must heretofore be a different sort of dialogue between the writer and actor.

Irving's process of drawing an audience to him by the dominance of his distant personality was appreciatively noted by Oscar Wilde, in his "The

Soul of Man Under Socialism" (written after hearing Shaw speak at a Fabian meeting):

> With his marvellous and vivid personality, with a style that has really a true colour-element in it, with his extraordinary power, not over mere mimicry but over imaginative and intellectual creation, Mr. Irving, had his sole object been to give the public what they wanted, could have produced the commonest plays in the commonest manner, and made as much success and money as a man could possibly desire. But his object was not that. His object was to realise his own perfection as an artist, under certain conditions, and in certain forms of Art. At first he appealed to the few: now he has educated the many. He has created in the public both taste and temperament. The public appreciate his artistic success immensely. I often wonder, however, whether the public understand that that success is entirely due to the fact that he did not accept their standard, but realised his own.[8]

This was written in 1891, before the last phase of Irving's career had begun. Wilde suggests that Irving's personality, although instrumental in his success, is incidental to his artistic quest. His magnetism could have been used to cheaper ends, but instead Irving placed his artistic aspirations foremost. He trained the audience to accept his own standard of art, which Wilde defined as intensely individualistic and entirely unconcerned with popular opinion: *"The work of art is to dominate the spectator: the spectator is not to dominate the work of art."* What's more, since personality is an expression of individuality, art should be an expression of personality. The attitude of the public toward such a work ought to be receptive, honoring the individualism of the artist. At the same time, he says, *"the public should try to make itself artistic."*[9]

Both Shaw and Wilde stand in awe of Irving's domination, and both see in Irving's personality some reflection of their own, including a deep longing for authority. Shaw recognized in Wilde at once a double and an opposite. Unlike Shaw, Wilde was ready to adore, admire, appreciate—and to flatter. Gordon Craig recalled: "To be kind was why he flattered—but woe to any fool who *accepted* the flattery. It was the ancient Irish power to charm: the desire to give pleasure. A great-hearted being."[10] Shaw's recollection was different: "His Irish charm, potent with Englishmen, did not exist for me; and on the whole it may be claimed for him that he got no regard from me that he did not earn."[11] Wilde admired and flattered Irving, and adored Ellen Terry; in them he saw some intimation of the ideal in stage art. And Irving, perhaps, *was* foolish enough to accept this flattering estimation. It might be said that Irving had shaped much of his theatrical career around the need of audiences for an object to flatter. Flattery by its nature allows for self-congratulation, and the Lyceum Theatre was a place where audiences could depend on that sort of pleasure, at least. It was precisely this aspect of the Lyceum that most annoyed Shaw. On the other hand, both Shaw and Wilde believed that literature would come to dominate the future of the arts, and both created a sort of theatre that, as Nina Auerbach has put it, "laughed at heroes and imperial boasts." [12] Craig finally could not forgive either Shaw or Wilde for making "a jest of the stage." [13] Shaw, of course, especially admired that very quality in Wilde.

In the early 1890s, Wilde wrote of the disadvantage of actors when compared with puppets, since the latter have no personalities. He points out that puppets are utterly docile and mindless, and so present no challenge to the author. Puppets "have no private lives" and so behave properly in public, whereas actors must work with an "accidental personality" which, according to their school, they must either exaggerate or suppress. [14] Irving was, as Wilde recognized, an actor who had both to exaggerate and suppress his personality. Its obvious faults hindered his effort to perform classics and to institute acting as an art. So, Wilde praised Irving's Hamlet in 1885 because his awkward personality had been "replaced by exquisite grace of gesture and clear precision of word." [15] On the other hand, Irving relied on his strength of personality to entrance the audience in works where an effect of actuality, beyond the compass of a puppet, was required, such as in *Waterloo*. Wilde, of course, obtained an effect of artificiality by the manifestation of his own personality, as did Shaw. Wilde was to be no puppet, but would exaggerate his unique characteristics upon the world stage, suppressing only one crucial portion of his private life. Frank Harris points out that, like Wilde, Shaw adopted the method of making himself known by writing about himself as often as possible, at the slightest invitation. Shaw, too, exaggerated his personality, even beyond Wilde, because he had no need to suppress the sexual nature of his private life. He exposed himself thoroughly, and yet it became a question whether the nature that was thus uncovered was in fact human. Was the public Shaw some sort of highly advanced puppet, or a machine—heartless, as some accused? (There were not many writers, especially ones as egotistical as Gordon Craig, who would be likely to call Shaw a "great-hearted being.")

The question of the mechanism of their personalities (and Irving's too) turns on the intersections each was able to create between the dramatic

stage and the stage at large, i.e., his celebrity. Late in his life, Shaw recalled a story Wilde had told him one day when they chanced to meet at a
military exhibition in Chelsea, of all places, an elaborate anecdote of a man
whose innovations in the mechanism of the theatre brought ruin to him:

> Oscar's . . . story was of a young man who invented a theatre stall
> which economized space by ingenious contrivances which were all
> described. A friend of his invited twenty millionaires to meet him at
> dinner so that he might interest them in the invention. The young
> man convinced them completely by his demonstration of the saving
> in a theatre holding, in ordinary seats, six hundred people, leaving
> them eager and ready to make his fortune. Unfortunately he went on
> to calculate the annual savings in all the theatres of the world; then in
> all the churches of the world; then in all the legislatures; estimating
> finally the incidental and moral and religious effects of the invention
> until at the end of an hour he had estimated a profit of several thou-
> sand millions: the climax of course being that the millionaires folded
> their tents and silently stole away, leaving the ruined inventor a
> marked man for life.[16]

Here is a story that, by curious accident, comes to seem an oblique tale of
the man who had always remembered it, as well as the man who initially
told it. Both Shaw and Wilde had invented, as it were, a clever new way to
get people into the theatre, and both proclaimed their "ingenious contriv-
ances which were all described." Then, oblivious to the fact that the world
might think they were offering too much of a good thing, they extended the
application of their new drama to the churches and legislatures, predicting
also the moral and religious effect to be anticipated. Their invention had to
do with extending the application of theatricality beyond the stage proper,
observing it in all facets of life, and conducting themselves as leading players, actors of strong personality, on that world stage. Wilde overextended
himself by presuming that his superior powers as a "performer" gave him
full authority over the play. Then the actual sources of power backed away
from him in horror, "leaving the ruined inventor a marked man for life."
Shaw played a safer game. In a sense he never invested himself in his
invention. His "G. B. S." remained on the market as a novelty or toy,
which the millionaires watched warily. Occasionally one or another would
silently steal away, but more often they let him run until the key in his back
stopped turning. Irving, by contrast, could keep the millionaires happy because his "invention" implied no ultimate extension beyond the theatre it-

self. While the mystery of both Shaw's and Wilde's personalities seemed, in different ways, to touch on the unnatural, the mystery of Irving's personality had more to do with his cultivation of the very authorities that define the natural, the official cultures of state, church, and art. His was a theatre where the stalls might safely be crowded.

A remarkable analysis of Irving's personality was given by Max Beerbohm, in his 1905 obituary column in the *Saturday Review,* where he writes, "As an actor, and as a manager, he had his faults; and these faults were obvious. But as a personality he was flawless—armed at all points in an impenetrable and darkly-gleaming armour of his own design." After itemizing some of Irving's limitations as a performer, Beerbohm argues that they are of secondary importance and that Irving's prime appeal was not "to a sense of obvious beauty" but "to a sense of strange, delicate, almost mystical and unearthly beauty." Then he proposes the intriguing idea that audiences were routinely deluded even in their devotion:

> Irving's presence dominated even those who could not be enchanted by it. His magnetism was intense, and unceasing. What exactly magnetism is, I do not know. It may be an exhalation of the soul, or it may be a purely physical thing. . . . I only know that Irving possessed this gift of magnetism in a supreme degree. And I conjecture that to it, rather than to the quality of his genius, which was a thing to be really appreciated only by the few, was due the unparalleled sway that he had over the many.[17]

Beerbohm posits a series of dualities in this analysis: the actor (flawed) and the personality (flawless); the beauty of excellent acting (ordinary) and the beauty of Irving's acting (unearthly); the bulk of the audience (mainly or even exclusively dominated by his magnetism) and the few (enchanted by his genius). The sum of this is that Beerbohm acknowledges a difference between personality and magnetism, because the latter can be effective even with those who do not realize the true quality of the former. As a critic, Beerbohm cannot disregard the lapses from ordinary standards, but these faults, which, he says, prevented "the cruder members of the audience" from seeing Irving's true quality, have not inhibited him from appreciating the flawless personality. Its "impenetrable and darkly-gleaming armour" prevents him from knowing what lies inside, but its flawlessness rebuffs all criticism. In a way, his personality *is* the ideal of beauty. By means of its mysterious magnetism, it holds sway over all—the ideal absorbs all wishes for an ideal. Only the few, however, can suspend judgment on the obvious faults and appreciate that Irving's difference in itself represents beauty, that his extraordinary personality itself is a real work of art, of which the magnetism (the evocation of the ideal) is a secondary effect.

At any rate, that appears to be the situation as Beerbohm (one of the few, of course) views it, and the reader is made to understand that any other response is vulgar. Who could disagree? Arthur Symons, a few years later, echoed Beerbohm's terms: "Irving was an incomparable orchid, a thing beautiful, lonely, and not quite normal."[18] His abnormality set him at a distance from the many, as a spectacle of difference, and from that unique position he glorified the ordinary, unanimous response, giving each member of the audience a sense that his difference stood for their desire. In this way, perhaps, he dignified the common ideals of his audience by making each individual feel a part of the elect who share his "rare" sense of beauty, however difficult that may have been to define. The "cruder members of the audience," who found him ridiculous, thus could not attack him without assaulting the ineffable ideals of the many. In this light, a production like *Waterloo* might be seen as a direct challenge to his detractors and a confirmation of his authority to define the terms within his theatre.

Many observers vaguely attributed supernatural significance to Irving's personality. In his 1930 book on the theory of acting, Lane Crauford admitted, "Personality is such an intangible element that it may not be too abstract to conceive it as being some electrical force": "A fair understanding of the word 'personality' is to be obtained by terming it 'mental magnetism.' With players of strong personality it is as if they had some hypnotic power over the audience. In Irving we had a most illuminating instance of the power of personality in the art of the player. Mental magnetism was personified in him. He had the 'hypnotic eye.' "[19] Nearly every writer on Irving remarked this forcible personality, using terms like "mysterious fascination," "personal magnetism," "dynamic force."[20] One reviewer of his Louis XI in the mid-1880s described "that picturesque mystery of manner through which his magnetism plays, like the lightning in the cloud," and of the same production another wrote, "That first look, the first sentence he spoke, were the magnetic shock which made the whole audience his at once. A more potent impression of personal force we have never received. . . . What struck fire at once was behind all these; the

strong will . . . flashed out upon the audience with all-subduing force."[21]
The American journalist Amy Leslie outdoes all others in her lengthy discourse on Irving's "stage personality," demonstrating along the way an extraordinary personality of her own:

> He has cast a singular glamour over obvious faults, and his potent
> magnetism and intelligent forces make all things in Irving shine as
> though they were right. . . . He is devoured with a flame of con-
> scious power, is quickened with the light of genius and shrinks from
> assimilation or envelopment. . . . His personality is so distinguished
> and lovable, his genius, brain, and equipoise so far towering above
> any other actor in England or in England's history, that the distinction
> bestowed upon him by his Queen was simply an honor his affection-
> ate public would have given him were it within the power of publics
> to decorate rather than applaud. . . . The Satanic touch inseparable
> from the Irving personality is a grotesque contradiction to the great
> actor's impulse and his disposition. . . . A wonderful smolder of
> magnetism lies in his face. . . . Henry Irving's genius in its expres-
> sion, its dominion, and its terrific conquests is like unto the glory of
> the four winds. . . . He is equipped with a personal magnetism act-
> ing like an explosive upon the even temper of the hours, and there is
> an unacknowledged but undeniable flutter of the minor elements
> when this gentle indicative asserts his temperamental authority
> among a people.[22]

Underlying this baroque masterpiece of idolatry, which grants Irving the
utmost of belief, are several contradictions. On the one hand, there is the
miracle of his all-embracing heart ("the lowliest, the most fatuous, the superb, and the foolish all find tolerance") and the correlative affection he
receives from all and sundry. On the other hand, there are glimpses of the
potential danger of his immense power—its combustible, deviant, and inhuman aspects. One can appreciate something of the psychological background of this magnetic effect when Leslie calls him "kind in a cold, monumental way" and attributes this (quite gruesomely) to "the paternal
instinct developed to an inexhaustibly embracing degree."[23]

Others took a far more skeptical attitude toward Irving's personality.
One observer claimed that he lacked the power to move listeners on the
stage: "His intensity hypnotised me, but I was awed by his weirdness and
strangeness rather than moved by the emotional appeal of his acting.
Everything helped this magnetic power—Irving's strange voice, fantastic
bearing, ascetic face, and curious, compelling eyes."[24] Shaw also em-

ployed this terminology in his assault on Irving: "The condition in which he works is a somnambulistic one: he hypnotises himself into a sort of dreamy energy, and is intoxicated by the humming of his words in his nose." [25] Here Shaw pictures Irving subjecting himself to his own mental magnetism, which is imagined as a physiological process (with yet another reference to intoxication), but this "dreamy energy" presumably captivates his audience in his brainless spell. Words are no more than a sensation in his nose. The submissive "sleep" of the hypnotic subject—indeed, the very idea of suggestibility—were what horrified Shaw most about what he saw in the London theatres.

Gordon Craig chose similar terms in his analysis of Irving's personality, but with quite a different reading of his attitude. He narrates an anecdote of Irving's early career, in which the actor and two colleagues reenacted the supernatural demonstrations of two American "spiritualists," with Irving mockingly portraying the "doctor" who was enlisted to give the display some credibility. Later, a theatrical manager ordered him to perform this unmasking as a commercial entertainment. For refusing to do so, Irving lost his job. Craig's interpretation of this incident must be quoted at length:

> But the secret is simple. Irving was one of the first actors thoroughly to understand the public . . . but thoroughly. A thrill, to be taken in comfort, was what they asked for, was it? Then they should have it. Irving, being fond of the mysterious, had not watched the Davenport brothers mystifying England for nothing; and when, in a moment of youthful fun, he had appeared on the Manchester stage and announced that he would unmask those Davenport brothers, he was within an ace of ruining his career. Having shown how the Davenport brothers did their little trick, he went home to his lodgings, and slowly there dawned an expression on his face . . . a very strange expression. This expression dawned slowly, as he recalled the gaping faces of the sturdy spectators he had that day seen watching him unveil a mystery.
>
> He had not a very great opinion of the public. The booing and the hissing it had subjected him to had taught him that it was an unreasonable animal—a nervous animal, given to kicking if you showed it a good serious play with very fine playing and without any barn-storming. After all, it was Barry Sullivan at his worst that the unreasoning, unreasonable public loved most.
>
> "But I cannot barn-storm," said Henry Irving to himself. "Besides, I will not. Suppose . . . suppose I mesmerise 'em. That's an idea. Kemble? . . . Kemble was too noble with 'em. Edmund Kean?

. . . a ruthless assault! I am not Kean—more like Kemble, perhaps, but er-r—Kemble—too noble—too noble. Garrick? too long ago—silks and satins—and a damn small city—coffee houses—powder and patches—another age. But Mesmer . . . Mesmer never went on the stage. Joseph Balsamo . . . Cagliostro. Suppose we put *him* on now?" Saying which, Henry Irving with decision went off to bed.

The next morning—the next week—the next years—allowing his mind to rehearse once more the tricks of the Davenport brothers, he saw clearly how gullible was a public which had been allowed to fall in love with itself—and coming by easy stages to the far more profound thoughts of Mesmer, and to the most surprising powers of Cagliostro, and perceiving that he possessed something of these powers too—he made up his mind, and the Rubicon was passed.

These powers of mesmerism he developed in himself to an astonishing degree, and if only a few actors of to-day would develop a modicum of the dangerous faculty, I think it would greatly increase the enjoyment of those evenings which at present we are forced to pass without too much happiness, in the theatre. We should then perhaps, feel something . . . be attracted.[26]

The effects obtainable under hypnotic trance engaged the attentions of scientists and practitioners (spiritualists and showmen) almost equally during the nineteenth century. Demonstrations were so widespread and so often discussed in newspapers and books that nearly everyone might be expected to possess a mental image of a subject under the psychic control of an operator. By the middle of the century, the whole image cluster associated with such invisible powers came to be applied to descriptions of acting—"mesmerizing," "hypnotic," "electrifying," "magnetizing," "galvanizing." Actors had a related reason to explore hypnosis, as one modern writer has pointed out: "From the beginning, mesmerists were struck by their subjects' ability to display emotions and to enact roles with astonishing perfection, utmost apparent sincerity, and, it seemed to them, with more skill than experienced actors."[27]

A flood of "how to" manuals on hypnotism (as well as on acting) hit the market around the middle of the century and again around the turn of the century. These offered enticing "keys" to the particular sorts of power available to an adept.[28] Following the first influx of books, which were often distinctly spiritualistic, Christian authorities set about attacking the more extravagant claims made by these practitioners, whose occult theories certainly represented a threat to church dogma. Civic authorities also viewed them warily, especially when they demonstrated their powers in public. Laurence Irving tells the story of Irving, in his late teens, being mesmerized by his friend, Henry Palmer, who had a decidedly romantic, if not heretical, imagination. Though Irving had earlier undergone an ecstatic conversion experience, much to the relief of his aunt and guardian, who had worried over his impulses toward playacting, little more is heard of his association with Christianity thereafter.[29] Indeed, Craig might have figured these stories, too, into the Faustian scene quoted above.

With the receding of the more outlandish (and likely fraudulent) demonstrations, and the increase of the popularly scientific and practical shows and writings, the curse was, to some degree, taken off hypnotism. Similarly, the traditional prejudice against actors, based in part on the notion that this little-understood art of simulation might represent a threat to a stratified society, began to give way as the profession policed itself against abuses, the wildness and childishness and libertinism that had long been part of the public image of actors. Also, the writings on both hypnosis and acting took on the aura of scientific inquiry as a way of improving their public images. These changes were reflected in the newer publications (magazines, souvenir books, autobiographies, and so on), though it is always important to bear in mind that in both professions the writings were a secondary effect of a practical discipline—a discipline of performance. The power of the hypnotist was discussed less often in terms of electromagnetic forces, invisible fluids, or psychic rays and more often in terms of willpower, the controlling mind, and suggestion. It was not that understanding of the true nature of hypnotic phenomena was advancing to any great degree; in fact, the hypnotic literature of the turn of the century represented techniques that had been well-known for decades. Only the packaging had changed, bringing a respectable exterior without losing the old allure. Many works responded to public fears that hypnotism could be used to criminal or sexually deviant ends with assertions that it was impossible to override a subject's higher moral sense. Nevertheless, the practical literature traded on the enticing project that hypnotic techniques could heighten a man's personal power. (Women, especially young women, were reputed to be the best subjects.)

Textbooks on acting also tended more often to address the art in terms of practical methods, professional customs, technical advice. Some of this literature was cautionary, advising against a hasty decision to go on the stage, but even these works inevitably acknowledged that the stage holds mysterious enticements, including access to an incomparable sort of personal power. Mrs. Alec-Tweedie's *Behind the Footlights* (1904), for example, takes as its mission the project of dissuading boys and girls, especially the latter, from careers on the stage:

> There may still be a few youthful people in the world who believe the streets of London are paved with gold—and there are certainly numbers of boys and girls who think the stage is strewn with pearls and diamonds. All the traditions of the theatre are founded in mystery and exaggeration; perhaps it is as well, for too much realism destroys illusion.
> Boys and girls dream great dreams—they fancy themselves leading actors and actresses, in imagination they dine off gold, wear jewels, laces, and furs, hear the applause of the multitude—and are happy. But all this, as said, is in their dreams, and dreams only last for seconds, while life lasts for years.[30]

The likelihood of a life of poverty, obscurity, promiscuity, divorce, alcoholism, and failure then is demonstrated in numerous ways, including, in the last chapter, "A Fantasy Founded on Fact," an appalling story of a chorus girl ruined by a deceiving man. She winds up dead of "mental shock," and there the book ends. On the other hand, this book also offers (as an inducement to read it in the first place, one would imagine) numerous wonderful anecdotes and impressive pictures of the great figures of the contemporary London stage. She sketches out the circumstances of stage life, the customs of auditions and rehearsals and stage practice, in part to take away the glamour that usually surrounds everything theatrical but also to represent the institution for what it is. Meanwhile, however, the book makes use of the familiar mystery terms, as in the following: "Who in the latter end of the nineteenth century did not weep with Miss Terry?—who did not laugh with her well-nigh to tears? A great personality, a wondrous charm of voice and manner, a magnetic influence on all her surroundings— all these are possessed by Ellen Terry."[31] Needless to say, the author makes no mention of Terry's several marriages or her illegitimate children. With her high salary, Terry could afford to live well and escape all association with nefarious ways. As Tracy Davis has ably shown, the influence to which women were dangerously subject in the theatrical profession was sexual exploitation.[32] Thus, as in hypnotic practice, the theatre opened the possibility of a male operator's using his power to take advantage of or even prostitute women, if only indirectly by allowing such a pitifully inadequate salary as was still customary for the chorine toward the turn of the century.

Terry, however, was in no danger of such exploitation and, the passage above implies, could even use her accumulated prestige to become an operator herself, exercising magnetic influence, always, of course, benevolently.

Alec-Tweedie reserves her most reverential prose for Irving, making, of course, no remark on his broken marriage either. She calls attention to his dignified public speeches, his financial largesse, his executive control, his rise from humble origins through hard work, and his austere physical presence—in short, everything that links him to the archetypal man of business. Concerning his acting, she quotes his disapproval of the fact that, as an actor, "in my youth I was associated in the public mind with all sorts of bad characters, housebreakers, blacklegs, thieves, and assassins."[33] Of course, he never entirely escaped this association, playing *The Bells* and *Louis XI* into the last year of his life, and he took on new "bad characters" throughout his career. An intriguing story is told of Irving's opinion on the impersonation of evil character, from late in his career, probably around 1900:

> He had in his desk a modern play on murder, and he often showed some desire to enact the hero, who had been falsely imprisoned as a murderer in the first act, and was liberated to become one in the following act, when he discovered his wife had been driven by hunger into the hands of a "bully," threatening the happiness of his daughter, and driving his son into bright red Socialism.
>
> I was much in favour of this when he read it to me, and regretted his unalterable decision that he was too old to present such sordid pictures. He inclined then exclusively to sweetness and to light.[34]

The temptation to play the vice figure, even in a situation such as this, where the heroic frame is clearly retained, seems driven by almost a sexual urge. At the start of Shaw's column on *Waterloo,* which began with a review of Irving's Don Quixote, Shaw introduced a primitive theory of repression, taken from a fellow Fabian and master of scandalous paradox, to account for Irving's choice of these roles: "It was Mr Grant Allen, I think, who familiarized us with the fact that all attempts to sustain our conduct at a higher level than is natural to us produce violent reactions." The theory is that Irving had had to dignify himself so enormously for the roles of Wolsey, Becket, Lear, and King Arthur, that a "terrific reaction" had to result in his playing of the buffoonish Don Quixote and quaint Brewster.[35]

A similar surfacing of repressed desire might account for his impulse toward the vice figure—to taste the sordid delights of masculine personality after so long preaching celibacy, so to speak. Indeed, one recent commentator has argued that "the Lyceum, during the last three decades of the nineteenth century, was a place to which you could take your family, and yet its atmosphere was almost licentious, certainly neurotic, possibly subversive."[36] Certainly it is true that the literature on the profession of acting, even on its high priest Irving, could not avoid the fact that even the noblest drama necessarily puts an actor in contact with the more mysterious and nefarious sources of human behavior—madness, evil, dissolution. The actor who would faithfully represent these psychological conditions must in some way experience them, however provisionally. In one of his high-minded speeches, Irving describes the experience of the actor, in regard both to the exploration of self in character and to the engagement of an audience, using terms that express an almost sexual satisfaction:

> A player of any standing must at various times have sounded the gamut of human sensibility from the lowest note to the top of its compass. He must have banqueted often on curious food for thought as he meditated on the subtle relations created between himself and his audiences. . . . How engrossing the fascination of those thousands of steady eyes, and sound sympathies, and beating hearts which an actor confronts, with the confidence of friendship and cooperation as he steps upon the stage to work out in action his long-pent comprehension of a noble masterpiece! How rapturous the satisfaction of abandoning himself, in such a presence and with such sympathisers, to his author's grandest flights of thought and noblest bursts of emotional inspiration![37]

Indeed, use of the conventional mystery terms in late nineteenth-century discussion of acting—"personality," "magnetism," etc.—often suggests that the mystery has something to do with sexuality, especially dominant (and violent) male sexuality. Take Mrs. Alec-Tweedie's description of the "prominent characteristics" of Irving, printed opposite a photographic portrait in profile, which highlights his jutting chin, protruding eyebrows, and long nose: "If there ever was a case of striking individuality on the stage it is surely to be found in Henry Irving. People often ask if it is a good thing for the exponents of the dramatic profession to possess a strong personality. It is often voiced that it is bad for a part to have the prominent characteristics of the actor noticeable, and yet at the same time there is no doubt about it, it is the men and women of marked character who are successful upon the stage."[38] "Marked character," indeed. Irving's close friend during his final seven or eight years, Elizabeth Aria, wrote a memoir of their intimacy that gives a vivid portrait of his offstage personality. Without in the least implying that there had been anything sexual in their relationship, she nevertheless conveys something of the attractive fascination he inspired. When she came to know him after seeing *Waterloo,* her idolatry of him became a rush of idealized feeling (her book is called *My Sentimental Self*) which he entirely absorbed as his due. Although she is otherwise often shrewd and sarcastic in her judgments on people, when it comes to Irving, she cannot find sufficiently orotund phrases to express her overflow of feeling. This platitudinous language is all very proper but, compounded with desire, it becomes voluptuous: "I felt ever when listening to him, on or off the boards, his morally elevating tendency, his possession of the highest ideals, and the true aestheticism which was his with an artistic intellectual completeness."[39] The utter utterness of this sort of writing reflects the mystery at the heart of an actor's magnetic personality. (In a marginal note, Craig wrote, "I should say a rather dangerous woman.")[40]

When it came to Irving idolatry, the great poet of this sort of sentimental gush was, of course, Clement Scott, and it is no accident that Mrs. Aria was "by no means impervious . . . to his personal charm" as well.[41] Scott effused over the sanctioned ideal image of Irving and Terry, constantly declaring their moral elevation of the stage, but in 1897 he also underwent a "terrific reaction." In an interview, he spun out his real suspicions about the sordid aspect of the theatre, the danger that women, "who have so unhealthy a craving for matters theatrical," faced in the profession: "It is nearly impossible for a woman to remain pure who adopts the stage as a profession. Everything is against her. The freedom of life, of speech, of gesture, which is the rule behind the curtain, renders it almost impossible for a woman to preserve that simplicity of manner which is after all her greatest charm. The whole life is artificial and unnatural to the last degree, and, therefore, an unhealthy life to live."[42] An enormous outcry from the profession resulted in Scott's resignation from the *Daily Telegraph.* His editor considered the interview to be a direct attack on Irving, and pleaded only that he did not believe Scott had been "master of himself physically or mentally" at the time.[43] So blind was Scott to the investment of his own desires in the theatre, and so ready was he to conform his rhetoric to the high moral tone typical of Victorian antitheatricalists, that he even tells of his astonishment "that any man should calmly endure that his wife should become an actress," calling that man "a fool or knave."[44] Just at this time his own wife was making efforts to go on the stage. As Max Beerbohm wrote some time later of Scott ("a personality, a definite and unmistakeable personality"): "It is a common trick of the man who knows he is not so good as he should be to drown the accusations of his conscience by accusing other men of naughtiness."[45] Scott had become mesmerized by his own rhetoric, thus losing sight of the gap between his idealized expectations of the theatre and his more base reasons for indulgence in it, much as Irving had become transfixed by his own exalted image, thus losing touch with the sort of acting for which he was suited. Both men were, in effect, led to a repudiation of a substantial portion of what they were in order to answer the demands of cultural imperatives they helped implement. Neither, however, was immune to the influence of personality, not even his own. The psychological rule behind this sort of self-abnegation was being worked out in the hypnotic literature, where, in 1892, one might read that the mesmerist *"hypnotizes himself by the same act by which he mesmerizes the subject,"* which means his "threshold of consciousness" is also displaced, leaving him equally subject to suggestive influence.[46]

In this vaguely understood realm of "personality," with its clashing mystical, moral, and psychosexual elements, yet another example of a creator mesmerized by his own creation to the point of self-destruction is the indispensable commentator on Irving, Bram Stoker. Half a year before the Clement Scott controversy, in the midst of the *Man of Destiny* controversy, Stoker's famous novel *Dracula, or The Un-Dead* was published, with its vampire—domineering, attractive, mesmerizing, fatal—whom many have said might have been modeled on Henry Irving. Shaw certainly regarded Irving's exploitation of Terry and other actors in the company as a kind of bloodsucking. Stoker, however, never gave any indication he shared Shaw's point of view and, if anything, was inclined to regard Shaw (or Ibsen) as the threat to womanhood. Indeed, the whole novel might fancifully be read as an allegory of the defense put up by a band of decent fellows, such as Irving, Stoker, and Scott, against the invasion of the Ibsenist drama. Those plays were thought to hypnotize the audience with their obsessive attention to matters of blood and sex and corruption itself. Even a pure soul like Mina / Ellen Terry might be susceptible to such entrancements, nearly becoming a bride of the vampire. On the other hand, some say that Irving had sucked the blood from Stoker, relying on his absolute devotion to the Lyceum and its chief for over a quarter of a century without returning an equal measure of affection or credit. Irving made use of Stoker's literary skills for his own speeches and letters but gave little encouragement to his independent career as a novelist. Ellen Terry recalled Stoker's hourly association with Irving but questioned whether even he really knew the man: "I believe myself that [Irving] never wholly trusted his friends, and never admitted them to his intimacy, although they thought he did, which was the same thing to *them*."[47] Stoker's great-nephew and biographer, Daniel Farson, tells the painful story of a hastily arranged stage reading of a dramatic version of *Dracula* (to secure copyright protection) at the Lyceum on 18 May 1897. Irving is said to have listened in for a moment, then turned to go. Someone asked him what he thought: "'*Dreadful!*' came the devastating reply, projected with such resonance that it filled the theatre."[48]

Stoker made no acknowledgment whatsoever of the sexual themes in his book, concerning which one modern psychoanalytic interpreter has written, "from a Freudian standpoint—and from no other does the story really make sense. It is a vast polymorph perverse bisexual oral-anal genital sado-masochistic timeless orgy."[49] Dracula is an embodiment of sexual danger, the death wish that perhaps circulates around every lustful impulse. Stoker knew personally the sublime powers of seduction in such a dominant personality, perhaps even felt that he, too, had been used by this figure, but received little satisfaction for his own desires for power. Stoker's relationship with his wife, who married him on the eve of his becoming Henry Irving's acting-manager, was unsatisfactory. His work at the Lyceum consumed night and day, and furthermore she appears to have rejected Stoker from her bed at an early stage. At the theatre, Stoker joined in the sublimated love of Ellen Terry, later writing of her, "She has to the full in her nature whatever quality it is that corresponds to what we call 'virility' in a man."[50] Stoker observed her "marriage" to Irving up close and knew that it was Irving, in large measure, who empowered her, just as in Stoker's novel, according to Nina Auerbach, "Lucy and Mina, the vampire's brides, acquire metamorphic powers that are at once infernal and celestial."[51] When it comes to explaining the cessation of their partnership, when Terry was "set free" from the Lyceum, Stoker recalls the confusion created, saying that "Curiosity began to search for causes, and her handmaid Gossip proclaimed what she alleged to be them."[52] This is the only acknowledgment (if so it be) of any hint that Stoker suspected an act of infidelity or betrayal of Irving, in Terry's association with Shaw. Long after Stoker's real marriage had failed (as Irving's had, also with a woman who had no appreciation of the enticements of the theatre), he watched this ideal marriage fail. He might have thought of the 1898 fire that burned the Lyceum sets, which were inadequately insured (whose fault was that?), thus forcibly restricting the repertoire. He might have thought of the business affairs at the Lyceum, which he had always run in the spirit of Irving's impulsive generosity, suddenly faltering in a new era. He might have reflected on a play, this one by Bernard Shaw, tossed by Irving onto his desk, much as Doyle's play had been. *The Man of Destiny,* indeed. No miracle lay in that, but instead a sign that the Un-Dead writer was at hand.

In 1908, in the midst of a public controversy over the censorship powers of the Lord Chamberlain, prompted in large part by Shaw's plays and his ongoing, fervent campaign against the censor, Stoker testified on behalf of censorship and also published an article on the subject. The latter is a strange document, so bound up in its elevated syntax as to be almost unintelligible but fueled by a vehement repulsion against the "startling fact of decadence" in fiction and drama. Writers who "deal with what they call 'problems' "—those Ibsenites, once again—have catered to the base appetites of audiences. But the author of *Dracula* is still more specific about the threat represented by those works that have "crucified Christ afresh": "A close analysis will show that the only emotions which in the long run harm are those arising from sex impulses." The most depraved of these writings, he says, "deal not merely with natural misdoing based on human weakness, frailty, or passions of the senses, but with vices so flagitious, so opposed to even the decencies of nature in its crudest and lowest forms, that the poignancy of moral disgust is lost in horror." [53] Here is the stern aspect of repression, astonishing from one who had conceived Count Dracula, not to mention his quintessentially weird final novel, *The Lair of the White Worm* (1911). Daniel Farson adds the final, gruesome twist in this story. It seems Stoker died of syphilis, which he may have contracted from French prostitutes as early as the 1890s. Farson cites medical testimony to show that this might account for the apparent decline in Stoker's business acumen, his growing unreliability, the peculiar tone of his reminiscences of Irving, and the undercurrent of self-flagellation in his article on censorship. Irving, Stoker, Scott, all might be seen as loveless victims of a system created to satisfy an audience's desire for a display of idealized masculinity—the exposed personality of priestly men. This sublimating mechanism seems to have served public longings, interestingly both masculine and feminine. But the celibacy (or purity) enforced upon its operators took its toll, and periodically they would each "go Fantee," as Shaw puts it: "Was there not a certain African divine, the Reverend Mr Creedy, who tamed the barbarian within him and lived the higher life of the Caledonian Road for a while, only to end by 'going Fantee' with a vengeance?"[54] Of course, Shaw and Terry, both of whom had a complex relation to celibacy on other grounds, to some extent stood apart from this holy fiction and laughed.

Public fascination with the hypnotist's potentially diabolical domination of a subject culminated with the publication of *Trilby* in 1894 and its dramatization the following year. Both were enormously popular. Shaw, in his review of the latter, praised the novel as entertaining, humane, even enlightened, but he does not like what happens to the work when it is turned into dramatic literature. The adapter (an American) took George du Maurier's well-known story of a young singer ruthlessly held under the hypnotic dominance of the insidious music teacher, Svengali, and reshaped it to clarify (some would say, correct) its moral character and to place the evil cad, played in London by Beerbohm Tree, more at the center of attention. Shaw's campaign against Tree, whom he regarded as no more than an indifferent character actor and entirely unsuited for literary plays, was at least as venomous as his campaign against Irving. And here he found the actor-manager Tree playing a domineering, hypnotizing character and "spreading himself intolerably over the whole play with nothing fresh to add to the first five minutes of him." Shaw assigns most of the blame to the adapter, but it is no wonder that, when it came to appraising the performances, he would write: "As to Mr Tree, I should no more dream of complimenting him on the Svengali business than Sir Henry Irving on A Hero [sic] of Waterloo."[55]

Indeed, half a year after his *Waterloo* review, one can detect that the same nerve had been touched: "Trilby is the very thing for the English stage at present. No need to act or create character: nothing to do but make up after Mr du Maurier's familiar and largely popular drawings, and be applauded before uttering a word as dear old Taffy, or the Laird, or darling Trilby, or horrid Svengali."[56] Predictably, Clement Scott took an opposite position on the production, preferring the word "caricaturist" to "character actor" in reference to the more sensational roles of both Tree and Irving. He argues that du Maurier had caricatured Svengali, and Tree, "with the pictures before him, followed suit." After all, such a fiend would not have been possible in real life: "But art permits these things. The stage must be a magnifying glass, not a diminishing one. Absolute fidelity to nature, 'accurate realism' as it is called, is scarcely possible, nor would it be good art if it were."[57] The magnified effect to which Shaw objected most strongly was the death scene of Svengali, just at the beginning of Trilby's London premiere at Drury Lane. As she is about to sing, she suddenly loses her powers, cannot recall where she is or what she is doing. The spell is broken, and it is soon discovered that Svengali is dead. The death itself is not even described in the book. On the stage, though, Tree died spectacularly, chillingly, in a way that invited comparison with Irving's death scene in *The Bells*. That death had also come as an act of divine retribution; Mathias's bad conscience finally executes him for the murder of a Polish Jew after a dream in which he is forced by a hypnotist to expose his guilt before a judge. (Of that death scene, Terry would write: "He did really almost die—he imagined death with such horrible intensity.")[58]

The play was, of course, enormously popular, confirming Shaw in his belief that these character actors, these actor-managers, these Svengalis, held the theatre—its creators, its critics, its public—in hypnotic thrall, blinding them to all progressive ideas. Their caricatured portrayals, each a vehicle for crowd domination, for enhancement of their own prestige, differ from his strong characterizations, such as his Napoleon, presumably according to some gradation of realism or verisimilitude, but there are other ways to qualify the difference. Bertolt Brecht expressed admiration for Shaw, based on his anticipation of the anti-Aristotelian, confrontational sort of dramaturgy that Brecht espoused—plays that contain the framework for their own analysis.[59] Shaw's characters exhibit the intellectual and verbal powers of extraordinary individuals, and starting with Napoleon they often coincide with significant historical figures, but in every case they account for themselves in what they say. If they regularly manifest an unusual personality, they do so in words, not in manner or makeup or magic. In effect, they leave behind a document (having begun as a playscript), and in written form they can be examined. They inscribe themselves into the stage space, and they can rely upon the permanence of the written record to carry their point of view into the future, indeed to influence the future. The playwright's personality can thus become political in a way that the actor's cannot. Scott quotes a pronouncement made by Tree a few years after *Trilby*, a defense of his particular line of histrionic art, which reveals an anxiety about the uses to which the stage could be put in the hands of a dangerous author. The unnamed individual to whom these words are addressed is not hard to identify:

How narrow-minded must a man be who thinks that it is inartistic for
me to present dramas that amuse and may not elevate one exactly
into the seventh heaven of ecstatic aestheticism! "'Ism" my friend!
Think of that vile ending to so many inoffensive and otherwise useful
words!

The world of art is full of "'Isms." As though art itself were not
cosmopolitan and all embracing! Art knows no rule, no restrictions;
it is elastic and benevolent. It has, or should have, no prejudices. It
cannot move in a groove.[60]

Svengali is a Polish Jew, a hypnotist, and also an artist of sorts, creating
pure beauty through the voice of his protégé. Du Maurier seems to have
based the character of Trilby in part on his memory of Ellen Terry during
her first marriage, to the painter George Watts. He saw her then, a very
young and beautiful woman in the midst of a circle of artists—not an artist
herself but a body in whom they envisioned their aesthetic ideals. Trilby,
an artist's model, is regarded similarly at the beginning of the novel, and
then she is taken away by Svengali, who is convinced he can implant in her
by his mesmeric means the ability to become "the apotheosis of voice and
virtuosity." He succeeds to the extent that "no such magnificent or seductive apparition has ever been seen before or since on any stage or plat-
form—not even Miss Ellen Terry as the priestess of Artemis in the late
laureate's play *The Cup*."[61] Ellen Terry, too, passed from the paternalistic
care of the devoted artists, for whom she was foremost an image, into the
control of a still more comprehensively dominating figure on whose stage
she became a universally beloved performer. But by the mid-1890s, when
the novel was published and the play opened, Terry was losing her powers.
Her memory was seen more often to fail on the stage, and her beauty was
fading. Irving had suffered no sudden fit of apoplexy, as did Svengali, but
he was aging, and her loss of power mirrored his. After Svengali's death,
Trilby's former admirer and friend, Little Billee, more recently an ardent
admirer from the midst of her crowded audiences, who thinks only to rescue her from her abductor, has her brought back to his house. Like Shaw's,
that house was in Fitzroy Square. The rescue comes too late, however, and
when she dies Svengali's name is on her lips: Irving . . . Irving . . . Irving.

Dorothea Baird, who played Trilby, was an actress of little experience,
about whom du Maurier nevertheless said, "No acting will be wanted; for
here *is* Trilby!"[62] She soon thereafter married Henry Brodribb Irving, Irving's eldest son, who along with his brother Laurence had recently disappointed his mother (and his father) by turning from an Oxford training and

prospects for a career in the law to go on the stage. One recent scholar
makes the quite reasonable error of thinking that H. B., known as Harry,
took the role of Little Billee, opposite his fiancée—the replica of Irving
bound in a chaste relationship with the replica of Terry.[63] In fact, he was
just at that time preparing to play his first Hamlet, the role in which his
father had first captured acclaim as a Shakespearean. The young performers—the heirs—were assembling to take the places of their elders. In
1897, Shaw seriously suggested to Terry that H. B. Irving and Dorothea
Baird, along with her children, Gordon and Edy Craig, start a "Next Generation" theatre and go on a worldwide tour.[64] The children would carry the
torch, and Shaw trusted that its light would be after his own mind, but
these gifted children of the greats never cut themselves entirely free. They
were all ultimately drawn back to the legacy of the parents, especially of
the man whom his sons called "The Antique."[65] After Irving's death, H. B.
Irving drew a great deal of attention for his revivals of several of his father's
roles, capitalizing on a streak of nostalgia in the Edwardian audience but
also making use of a deeply felt kinship to his father's sensibility. He
played such outmoded roles as Louis XI, Charles I, Mathias (in *The Bells*),
and Corporal Gregory Brewster.[66] Of the last role, Conan Doyle wrote:
"Henry Irving the son carried on the part and played it, in my opinion,
better than the father. I can well remember the flush of pleasure on his face
when I uttered the word "better" and how he seized my hand. I have no
doubt it was trying for his great powers to be continually belittled by their
measurement with those of his giant father, to whom he bore so remarkable
a physical resemblance."[67] It should be noted that H. B. Irving's performances of *Waterloo* took place, as Shaw had recommended, in a music hall.

To continue the train of associations for a bit, consider the following. The
only Shaw play in which, after all their scheming, Ellen Terry actually did
appear was his melodrama of imperialism, *Captain Brassbound's Conversion,* which Shaw had written specifically for her, "a deserving actress employed in a subordinate capacity by an Ogre at one of our leading theatres."[68] She, however, found herself in the awkward position of being
reluctant to betray the Ogre but also finding herself in a more and more
vaguely defined and tenuous situation at the Lyceum. Shaw, of course, had
tried to get Irving to produce the play, predictably with little success. Irving
balked at royalty demands and at any cooperation with Shaw, but he allowed Terry to give a copyright performance at the Lyceum, which she did

opposite his younger son Laurence Irving's Brassbound, in 1899. The next year plans were made to perform the play privately under the auspices of the Stage Society. When Terry continued to hesitate, Shaw had to find someone else. With great reluctance, he did so. Terry attended the opening night, briefly meeting Shaw backstage for the first time after all those years, all those letters. Abruptly, their correspondence ceased and was not resumed for over a year and then only sporadically. The charm or "spell," as he called it, was broken. She had disappointed his hopes, and perhaps up close he saw through his glorified dream vision of her. Eventually, in 1906, the year after her Ogre or Svengali, Irving, had died, she did play Shaw's Lady Cicely, but by then she was nearly sixty and prey to illness. The production was, on the whole, unsuccessful.

During his deliberations over casting the earlier production, Shaw briefly had hopes that H. B. Irving would recommend Dorothea Baird, his wife—"Mrs H.(Tril)B. I."—but he had to admit that he could not see her in the role. Writing in defense of the play's stage-worthiness a few years later, Shaw implied that the role of Lady Cicely was designed for an actress, like Terry, well beyond her youth, or, as he put it, "too old to stand the competition of pretty young women side by side with her on the stage." [69] A new wave of actors was overtaking the old, and Shaw was, of course, all for encouraging the change. The future represented a threat to Irving, though, and Terry, whose wagon was hitched to Irving's star had also to feel anxious about being displaced. Though he always urged her to continue with him (in part just to keep her name in the bill), Irving found it increasingly difficult to find plays to suit his personality as well as hers, and meanwhile he had lost exclusive control of the Lyceum, so they faced separation. Then, as Shaw later described it, "Meanwhile the star of Beerbohm Tree had risen in London. No actor less like Irving could be conceived, but he too had personality and overwhelming singleness of purpose, and the new theatre (Her Majesty's) he had built on the site of one of the great London opera-houses had supplanted the Lyceum as the centre of theatrical fashion." [70] A year or so after Tree had made a hit in Trilby, just after this new theatre had opened, Irving came upon Tree, "beaming self-satisfaction, avid of gratulation," and remarked, "Hullo, Tree! Doing anything?" [71]

Irving's more direct response to Tree's Svengali, however, had been to commission a new play. Laurence Irving reported that Irving had asked for "a Monte Cristo story in modern dress"—a man of wealth gaining a just revenge. [72] At a time when Tree and others were coining money, while Irving's own financial status was becoming precarious—*Madame Sans-Gêne* had done reasonably well, but *Cymbeline* and his son Laurence's *Peter the Great* had been commercial failures—such a plot might have reflected a desire for vindication. He offered this commission to H. D. Traill, an old-school academic book reviewer and editorialist on the *Daily Telegraph* (Clement Scott's newspaper), who proposed a collaboration with another writer, Robert Hichens, Shaw's successor as musical critic on *The World*. The latter recounted a different and still stranger story of this curious turn in Irving's career:

> At supper I sat beside him, and of course the proposed scheme was discussed. Having been for a winter to Egypt, with Mr. Traill's agreement I suggested to Irving that we might write a big drama for him laid in the time of the Pharaohs. He listened in silence, and with apparent attention, to all we both had to say on this subject, and when we had finished, jerked out: "Ha! Very fine! Very tremendous! But I, ha!, want a modern play." As modern plays were never given at the Lyceum Theatre, Mr. Traill and I were, to put it flatly, flabbergasted. "With an unusual part for me," continued Irving. "And Miss Terry?" said Mr. Traill. Irving made a slight gesture, as if waving someone away. "You can find something for her. Ha! But the character for me must be something strange. Occult perhaps. That's the word, oc-cult! Why not a doctor now? I could play the part of a doctor—couldn't I?" [73]

Thus was Irving's only true coat-and-trouser production (excepting *Waterloo,* which was a special case) set in motion, the play which came to be known as *The Medicine Man,* featuring Irving as "a scientific inquirer who, to the outer world, and in other people's drawing-rooms, should be merely a brain specialist or what not, but secretly, in his consulting-room, is a cold-blooded experimentalist using his patients in the spirit in which a vivisector uses his rabbits." [74] This doctor, a man almost fanatically committed to science, studies the power of hypnotism, but a long-buried emotion twists him into abusing his powers for evil ends. *Punch* was not alone in suspecting that Irving had himself been hypnotized into presenting such a silly play. [75]

Shaw, in his very last review of a play in *The Saturday Review,* allowed that the play reflected the worst literary disrespect for the drama. The play showed Irving at last so thoroughly hypnotized by his own ego, so perfectly in love with his own role, that he had become blind to reality, unaware that his audience and even his own company seemed at last to see the actor at a critical distance. No whispers of admiration are reported among the audience; instead, he records another sort of running commentary on the performance—the signs he detects of Terry's barely veiled dissatisfaction with the work: "When, after some transcendently idiotic speech that not even her art could give any sort of plausibility to, she looked desperately at us all with an expression that meant 'Dont blame me: *I* didnt write it,' we only recognized a touch of nature without interpreting it, and were ravished."[76] As he knew from her letters, she loathed the play and particularly resented the fact that Irving had made so little provision for her part, giving her no direction while he fussed over his own business. Later in his reminiscence of Irving's commissioning of the play, Hichens recalls asking Irving what sort of character Ellen Terry should have. Irving replied, "Contrast! That's the chief thing. A complete contrast to my role. They like her. The public likes her. But this play is for me."[77] Her role was that of a young society maiden, daughter of a woman who went mad and died and whom the doctor once loved. He plots revenge against the man she married by using his hypnotic powers to drive his daughter mad, and thus makes her enact the symptoms of her mother's affliction. In effect, as more than one critic pointed out, he had her play Ophelia, the role in which Ellen Terry had begun her partnership with Irving twenty years earlier. Another one of the doctor's subjects, however, a brutish East End dockworker, comes to her defense and, although the doctor has by then repented of his vile intentions and sent the young woman home, throttles him. Shaw particularly resented this representation of the working class, blaming the author, "to whom the life of the poor is a tragi-comic phantasmagoria with a good deal of poker and black eye in it."[78] So Henry Irving, a man almost fanatically committed to the ideals of his art, studies the powers of hypnotic acting, but long-buried love, now surfacing as jealousy, twists him into abusing his art toward unworthy ends. He seeks revenge for the loss of his beloved 1878 Ophelia by willfully imposing on his 1898 Ellen Terry a role that badly suits her, dominating her by his magnetic powers, but then a loutish and ignoble critic, misinterpreting the situation, climbs onto the stage and brings him down.

FIGURE 14. Henry Irving in 1899. Photograph by Histed. (Courtesy of Harvard Theatre Collection)

Meantime, do not forget that the very nearest approach that has ever been to the ideal actor, with his brain commanding his nature, has been Henry Irving. There are many books which tell you about him, and the best of all the books is his face. Procure all the pictures, photographs, drawings, you can of him, and try to read what is there. To begin with you will find a mask, and the significance of this is most important. I think you will find it difficult to say when you look on the face, that it betrays the weaknesses which may have been in the nature. Try and conceive for yourself that face in movement—movement which was ever under the powerful control of the mind. Can you not see the mouth being made to move by the brain, and that same movement which is called expression creating a thought as definite as the line of a draughtsman does on a piece of paper or as a chord does in music? Cannot you see the slow turning of those eyes and the enlargement of them? These two movements alone contained so great a lesson for the future of the art of the theatre, pointed out so clearly the right use of expression as opposed to the wrong use, that it is amazing to me that many people have not seen more clearly what the future must be. I should say that the face of Irving was the connecting link between that spasmodic and ridiculous expression of the human face as used by the theatres of the last few centuries, and the masks which will be used in place of the human face in the near future.

Gordon Craig, *On the Art of the Theatre*

CHAPTER IX

IRVING'S GHOST

A *Story of Waterloo* receives relatively little mention in Gordon Craig's books and essays, despite the fact that he returns frequently to Irving as his subject. One reference to Corporal Brewster includes him in a list to show the diversity of Irving's roles; another curiously suggests that perhaps Irving's unspoken opinion of the acting of Eleanora Duse manifested itself in his performance of Brewster.[1] These references seem to suggest that Craig did not see in this piece any threatening shades of the Realistic Theatre closing in upon Irving, a scenario that was his favorite in explaining the close of Irving's career. Like most others, he seems to have regarded the piece as yet another of Irving's triumphs. But a passage in his *Index to the Story of My Days,* commenting on his attending the first night of *Waterloo* in London, obliquely suggests that a glimpse of death might have been visible to him on the stage that night: "I was in the stalls. At the time I felt no great sadness at not being in my place on the stage of the Lyceum Theatre. It is only now that regrets come along. Youth *won't* be sad if it can help it—and so youth is held to be cruel and thoughtless. But youth is right to resist grief—for if not, youth would shrivel—sometimes does (Keats)—and die."[2] Craig was in his early twenties on that first night, in his eighties (Brewster's age) when this reminiscence was written and published. The mythic material of *Waterloo* filters into his memoir. A moment of early victory over grief and the prospect of death, here surges back through the old man's memory and touches him with sadness. His resistance to the onrush of death has weakened, shriveled, over time, and now, presumably, he would will himself back there, "in my place on the stage."

What place was there for him in *Waterloo?* As a juvenile lead in the company, he might have played the sergeant, a good supporting role first taken by Fuller Mellish, later by Lionel Belmore. Sergeant McDonald, like Craig, has advanced faster and more easily in the ranks than the old man. This says times have changed, but a common sense of duty to the Third Guards—the theatre—binds them together. They share a tradition. The sergeant shows proper respect for the old man, helps to show him at his best, but his eye is on the grandniece, whom he will no doubt marry in some realm where unimportant subplots resolve themselves. Among other factors, a powerful sexual attraction to women drew Craig away from the sanctified Lyceum and into several marriages. He was playing the artist-lover Cavaradossi in *Tosca* at the time of the Lyceum opening of *Waterloo;* his second child was born the day after. Craig spent one day with the mother and baby before returning to his company to play the man whose absence kills a woman. Brewster remains, unconcerned with women, on duty in his house. Marriage entails duty, as does the theatre, and Irving never wavered in his commitment to the latter. Craig always demonstrated insubordination to both.

Craig was right to see little reward in the supporting roles of *Waterloo*. On the other hand, the place he regrets having lost might more generally have been that of the inheritor of Irving's mantle. The nonexistent role he might have played would be the son Corporal Brewster never had, the man who might one day mingle with the first gentleman of the realm. Family is a marginal concern to Brewster; he speaks only of a brother. Brewster had no "place on the stage" for a son. Irving, too, was married to his career. Before walking out on his wife, he had two sons. Both became actors, both died young. Both were struggling to make a mark as actors in provincial companies at the time of the *Waterloo* opening. Later, one of them, Laurence, played the role of the colonel, an advancement in rank on the strength of his name. There *could* have been a place for Craig, too, on the set of *Waterloo* and other plays of this period. He was accounted one of the more promising young actors of his day, one of those who might one day command the stage as Irving had, but Craig was not one to wait for a place to which his claim was uncertain. He had, on Terry's account, pressed his advantage to the limit, pulling rank to secure a position for himself, and then had decided that the necessity of showing deference to Irving was too onerous. He turned from the Lyceum company to act elsewhere, then turned from acting itself and from a place in the tradition, in order to find some new home in the art of the theatre, ideally a new theatre for no actors at all.

Craig was Ellen Terry's second illegitimate child. His real father, E. W. Godwin, was out of the house by the time he was three. Irving's "marriage" to Ellen Terry seems to have been a bond that fulfilled the requirements for continued success of the Lyceum Theatre, and little if anything more, but by this bond he became as close to a father as Craig ever had.[3] In his delimited but exalted role, Irving could provide Craig the example of an utterly dominant force in theatrical art, a force that flows from a place *on the stage,* but Craig did not want to be an actor. He wanted a place of his own from which he could exert a similar force (the place that would later be called the director's), and it was that sort of theatre he set out to create. Looking back, though, he perhaps felt some regret—regret that he had not seized the opportunity for the actor's power, for a certain kind of charge into the heart of the crowd. *Waterloo* constitutes just one grain in the complex picture of Craig, a mere flicker of memory within an *aperçu,* and yet, from an apocalyptic point of view, that play, as an emblem of his absence from the Lyceum and from acting, represented a "heroic" opportunity that he might have taken but had not. Looking back as an old man he seems to wonder whether his decision at that early stage was a good one, or indeed whether there was to be any heroism in his chosen mission at all.

Later in the same memoir, Craig speculates that if he had not abandoned acting, Irving, London, he would have met the fate of Chatterton—suicide at seventeen. He then offers this consolatory assessment of his career, pointedly associating himself in *King Lear* with the fool, not Irving's king: "For although I have swayed in the wind for more than eighty years of life, by bending to the wind I have prevailed for fifty-two years with my dream for the Theatre. In my heart the dear Theatre as it is, in my soul the Theatre as it shall be. The wind was after all the wind of Heaven, all the barking of dogs was drowned by the grand howling of the winds. I sway still—and abide the coming of time."[4] Counting back those fifty-two years from the year the memoir was published, one arrives at 1905, the year of Irving's death and the year after Craig left England for Isadora Duncan and soaring aspirations. Those are the years in which he persevered with his ideal, locked though it might be, as a memory and as an anticipation of what would be, within his heart and soul. In effect, he might be said to look back upon the memory of Irving in *Waterloo* as the time when he lost his stiffness to the wind, which is a resistance that can lead to death, as it did for Irving. At that early point, he gave up on the inheritance he might have received from Irving, an actor's career in an actor's theatre, and instead took up the legacy of his father, a tradition of running away, of being remembered for his absence. If Irving was like Lear, who raised his fist to the storm, Godwin was in Craig's mind closer to the distant and inscrutable god who stirred the winds. Godwin died in 1886 at the age of fifty-three, when Craig was just fourteen and had no memory of ever having seen him. Four years later, his mother wrote to her son, "But there was no one like him, none—A man born long before his time—Of extraor-

dinary gifts, and of comprehensive genius—Until lately you have had so
little understanding of the world, I have not been able to speak with you
of many things but when you come back we must have some nice long
quiet talks—and you will *understand, and feel,* I am sure."[5] This call to
faith in a shadowy god suggests how unknowable was the legacy Craig
would inherit and transmute into his theatre. It was borne as a dream, or
as a feeling, passed on by his mother, who, several months earlier, had
written to Clement Scott: "With a *woman,* it is the *Father of her children* who lives for her in the middle of her heart—the holy of holies."[6]
There in the middle of his mother's heart was the sacred, inaccessible
figure who would become, through a dream, the mysterious force of this
theatre.

Edward Anthony Craig, in his biography of his father, quotes the extraordinary text of an actual dream Craig had of his father, some time between 1901 and 1903, as recorded in a notebook. He has a vision of a man
whom he knows as his father, though he has never seen him, a sad man,
floating on a calm sea, his eyes raining colored tears. As Craig approaches,
feeling torturous pains, the vision suddenly disappears and he is on the
stage of a huge theatre, crowded with "thousands and thousands of gods
and goddesses": "And I looked into the great audience once more in search
of something . . . and there I found a smile for which I had waited, it
seemed ten thousand years—Into it I fell and knew nothing more but heard
two voices whisper 'My Son'—and felt four arms laid over my shoulders—."[7] The father—"holy of holies"—thus takes his place within the
theatre that resides within his heart for the next fifty or sixty years. The
four arms laid over his shoulders might be those of Godwin and Terry, or
perhaps of Godwin and Irving, since the place from which he looks out
upon his theatre in the dream is the place of the actor. The long-awaited
smile must be Godwin's; Irving's place would not be among the audience,
and Terry's smile he never lacked. Into this smile he fell—he did not jump.
He is the reed in the wind here. The paternal gesture of arms over the
shoulder, and the phrase "My Son," suggest that in this ending Craig finds
himself caught between two fathers. The fall into the smile in the audience
tells at least in which direction he will move.

In a reminiscence of 1894, he wrote that he had been talking in his
sleep, saying, *"Acting is a great art—I must go on acting, and be a great
artist!"* This night-thought, so clearly an expression of the influence of
Irving, Craig deemed a result of an "impediment" in his development: "The
'impediment' came from the union and separation of E. T. and E. W. G.

For my father might—would—have taught me what I had to discover for myself. The 'impediment' was in my bones, in my blood, which cried out vaguely that an artist is . . . well, not what an actor is."[8] The union of E. T. and E. W. G. had brought the mother's instinct for acting to him, and the separation of the two had deprived the same child of his father's artistic instinct, some amalgam of his visual sense, his aesthetic sensibility, and his general character, which would include his impulse to abandon the woman/actor (Terry). Terry defines the actor, and Godwin the something other that is an artist. Craig had lost the latter in the separation, lost all but what was hidden in the middle of his mother's heart, the impress of art that had made her exceptional. The actor in this equation becomes identified with the feminine. The example of his mother tells him that the actor is the subject—subject to the manager (Irving), subject to the critic/playwright (Shaw), and subject to the artist (Watts, Godwin, Craig himself). The substitution into this failed marriage of a surrogate father, the great actor who would abandon his wife rather than his beloved profession, confuses the issue for Craig. Irving also creates the impediment. By, in effect, playing the role of the father, Irving is the man who gives authority to the actor—he is, in himself, subject and object, the artist who "marries" the actor, the man who incorporates the idealized woman. But Craig could not overcome what was in his bones and blood, an impulse to use his stage and to use his women (or femininity itself) differently, more according to the example of Godwin. He would leave women and illegitimate children across Europe, and he would develop a theatre of idealized architectural effect. Craig knew so little, in fact, about Godwin that he had to invent a new idea of a theatre to associate with him. This was a theatre not based on actors, so that Craig could define for himself his opposition to his mother and Irving.

In an interview in 1930, Shaw offered his opinion of Craig's turn away from the Lyceum toward some shadowy and remote ideal. He takes offense at what Craig would do with plays in his theatre, echoing his own outcries against Irving, and then, remarkably, he takes offense at Craig's negligent way with actors, almost as if to voice the outcry he imagines Irving would make. The abusive purpose to which Craig would turn the theatre—making pictures—is the one he might have derived from his allegiance to Godwin. In the course of his venomous statement, Shaw unselfconsciously reflects on his own arabesques at the "doors of the theatre":

> If ever there was a spoilt child in artistic Europe, that child was Teddy Craig. The doors of the theatre were far wider open to him

than to anyone else. He had only to come in as the others did, and do his job, and know his place, and accept the theatre with all its desperate vicissitudes and poverties and inadequacies and impossibilities as the rest of us did, and the way would have been clear before him for all the talent he possessed. But that was not what he wanted. He wanted a theatre to play with, as Irving played with the Lyceum; a theatre in which he could frame his pictures in the proscenium, and cut the play to pieces to suit them, and forbid the actors to do anything that could distract the attention of the audience from his pictures.

Such theatres are not to be had; that is not what a theatre is for.[9]

The obvious scheme that can be derived from this analysis is that Shaw worked for plays, Craig for pictures, and Irving for actors. The implied equilateral triangle, however, does not precisely match the oppositional configuration among these three figures. Craig became obsessed—haunted—by the mythic figure of Irving, the betrayed father, and sought to speak on his behalf against the evil adversary, Shaw, who was, of course, Craig's rival for Terry in this Oedipal melodrama. Craig published his hagiographic memoir of Irving in 1930, and it is filled with charges against Shaw. Shaw immediately responded in the interview in *The Observer* quoted above. Craig shot back with a letter to that publication, saying "Mr. Bernard Shaw has ever been the sincere enemy of English art and artists," and sarcastically begged the reader to remember that Shaw is a "foreigner," an Irishman, and therefore, "entitled to our sufferance." He concludes: "Mr. Shaw would destroy everything that is worth while in England. His Irish motives may be noble—I cannot say—but had an Englishman written as he has done of Irving, we should have called him a liar, and there an end. Mr. Shaw, being our guest, the most we can say is that in this he is not like his better self—and, in short, is rather unwomanly."[10] In reply, Shaw called this "such a perfect gem of Craigery that it leaves me speechless." In answer to Craig's charge, Shaw writes, "I am not a refugee here: I am a conqueror," adding, "Mr. Craig is the last of the rebels. I should be sorry to see him surrender." Soon thereafter, the Shaw-Terry correspondence was published, with Shaw's contentious preface and commentary, giving his most polished and definitive assessment of Irving and the Lyceum. This brought more letters and interviews. Craig answered with *Ellen Terry and Her Secret Self*, an extraordinary recasting of the whole mythic constellation of Irving-Terry-Shaw, in which Shaw is compared to "a very large, malicious, poke-nose old woman, meddling with persons and things about which he knew not much, and with an idle and vindictive tongue quite fussily spreading falsehoods about them up and down the street." [11]

Craig's device is often to suggest that Shaw is attacking the honored dead. Shaw's response is always to accept the role of spoiler but to remind the reader of the utter propriety of his truth-telling: "To many people I am a repellent person with an odious character. One of my professions is the profession of critic, a sort of literary gangster whose business it is to put my victims on the spot; and the more skillfully and accurately I do it the less they like it." He stresses his seniority over Craig, his appreciation of the circumstances that made the younger man's attitude (or even "psychosis") understandable. If Craig portrays himself as a "thwarted genius," well, "No doubt that began at home, when he was up against the all-conquering mother and her faithful lieutenant, the strong-willed sister." His final word on the reason for Craig's agitation indirectly credits Irving: "I wounded that sacred thing, a boy's idolatry of the first great actor he ever saw." [12]

Shaw is the one who, in Craig's eyes, tampers with the deserved immortality of Irving, disgracing his grave. Irving would have been ninety-two in 1930, but instead had fought the good fight and passed at sixty-seven. Both Shaw and Craig would live into their nineties, when last musters are called. For Craig especially, the conflict between Irving and Shaw that erupted in the Lyceum Theatre in the mid-1890s came to seem an apocalyptic battle to which he belatedly sought to return. He was at the time a low-ranking officer on the field who was in full retreat, just when the final fight was beginning and the ammunition starting to run out. Instead of rushing in with the powder, though, he was in the stalls, smiling, feeling no regret about his defection. In effect, the battle of *Waterloo* (or the greater conflict it betokened) is revised in the 1930s when Craig, fighting for the "Dook" who is now but a ghost, at last stands in against the Napoleonic or Mephistophelian adversary. The ghost of Irving figures in both Craig's and Shaw's later careers, for Shaw as a sign of the principle of death, for Craig as a sign of the principle of life. Craig works for the immortality of his memory or effect, Shaw for its transience.

After that early confrontation, Shaw found the doors of the theatre increasingly wide open for him, and, in retrospect, he casually includes himself among those who did his job and knew his place and accepted the theatre "with all its desperate vicissitudes," etc. Shaw blends in with the rank and file in this reminiscence; at the time, his profile was hardly so low.

In an 1896 letter to Terry, he makes no secret of his impetuosity, which he contrives to instill in her: "Next week is nothing to me or to anyone else: Napoleon might have won the battle of Waterloo a week later. . . . Tonight will never come again: your enemy, *his* enemy, will be there in the stalls; and woe betide the Lyceum and its traditions & reputation if you do for Cymbeline what he did for Lear!"[13] What Irving had failed to do for Lear was *execute*. Shaw deeply desired a chance to test his own executive abilities in the theatre, but, confined to the lowly role of critic, he could be no more than executioner. In due time, Shaw won the opportunity to take command of the theatre with his plays. Craig, on the other hand, had ruined his chances by being impossibly demanding and idealistic at some times and by bending to the wind instead of taking charge at others. In self-imposed exile in Italy, and later in France, Craig could be no more than the artist whose pictures and ideas were "good to steal from," as Shaw puts it, stealing the phrase from Craig.[14] His books on Irving and Terry obsessively carry him back to the troubled period of his own origins, the time of "union and separation": of Terry and Godwin, Terry and Irving, Irving and Craig. In the foreword to his last such work, *Index to the Story of My Days,* he writes:

> And will they be "memoirs"? Memoirs are—what? Books made up—sat down to and written at a sitting, even in two months, six months. That is certainly what many a man's "memoirs" amount to. But what precisely are memoirs—are they not remembrances? and do not these float up in fragmentary filaments?—yes, with an effort—up they float, out of one's whole being. When the mind is at rest and the heart beats evenly and in great quiet and at unexpected moments—first this thought, then that—a little vision of a place— of two persons—or even an imagined reconstructed group . . . say Father, Mother and one child, Edy, and I as yet unborn. How see that? Is it a memory? If so, my blood and bone of which I was made do this conjuring. Yes, this can be a scrap in a memoir. This blood, bone, feeling, can serve as a most faithful dictionary to which my brain turns. Every day, maybe, for some moments; but not long, laborious puzzling about it all. Catching the thought as it plays in me.
>
> Only this way, so far as I can see, can true memoirs be recorded, and vivid, living ones.[15]

The fragmentary filaments float up out of the whole being of the retired, old man, leading him back to scenes of an earlier existence. Memoirs become "vivid, living," and "true" not by "laborious puzzling" but through a conjuring of blood and bone; the dead past comes forward at their call. Blood and bone were also part of his "impediment," which told him that an actor was no artist, contrary to what his surrogate father, Irving, would insist. A memoir that attends to "unexpected moments" of recollection can summon up the dead.

In conversation with his biographer, Archibald Henderson, Shaw once said, "Art, like life, has to renew itself by returning repeatedly to its childhood and burying its dead." [16] Craig's attitude differs completely; his dead must live on in idealized immortality, purified of reality, of death. The great figures of the past—Irving, Terry, Godwin, Salvini, Duse, and many others—brought forward into his continuing company, will, he seems to think, help to raise him from his own imperfect state. Coy allusion to his own defects, in contrast to the superior qualities of these great figures, makes for a kind of self-effacement that nevertheless keeps him in the picture. In effect, he gives the stage to these "actors"—most of them are actors, in fact—while he controls the *mise en scène*. He begins the prologue to his *Henry Irving* with a testament to its failure, and at once conjures the dead to life: "Henry Irving was born in 1838 and died in 1905. The book I wanted to write on this very remarkable being, I wanted to be perfect. This is far from perfect, still it is the best that I can do. I hear from afar the quiet, dear voice of my old master, ever critical and kind, saying: 'Hmm— it's a pity the young man's best is so bad!'" Just what makes the book imperfect he does not say. Instead he explains that, though he is well over fifty, in fact just ten or so years younger than Irving when he died, he "is now as he was then," still the "young man" in his affection for his master, and that he has "never known of, or seen, or heard, a greater actor than was Irving." Of this statement he declares, "This first crow as challenge, and as salute to the sun." Perfection is his subject (the sun); imperfect, his approach (a crow, a challenge). God is in His Heaven, the disciples are faithful on earth, the family is at peace: such is always the melodramatic pretext. Always, too, a discordant note is struck in the opening scene; an unexpected adversary is spotted. He follows up his image of a crow to the sun:

> I hear, from all the hill-tops, answers coming back from other reckless fellows who strut up and down their own runs, crying: "Cock-a-doodle-doo! We too have seen the sun!"
> Well, then, we are all agreed. The sun's the sun. Our opinion is

our opinion, and what is more, we have in us a certain something spoiling for a fight about it all.

We are not concerned with any of those fellows who would like to argue the point. We have no time to wait until their talk has driven the sun down and plunged us all in the dark.

We are concerned with the other thing—the sun rising, the curtain rising, the excitement which lies in the words: "I am going to see Irving in *The Bells!*" . . .

So that is why I abandon myself to the old joy, and here throw all self-conscious logic and egoism to the wind and become once more spectator and whole-hearted admirer of this exceptional actor, Irving.[17]

The discordant note comes from the imperfect author, whom Shaw would soon call "a spoilt child." This young man is "spoiling for a fight" with those unenlightened fellows who doubt the sun. He insists he is "not concerned" with their petty arguments—surely they will not enter *this* house, and just as surely they do. Like the typical melodrama *naif,* he throws open the door and invites them to enter. He also quotes, with seeming approval, Irving's son's statement: "I wish they wouldn't make such a white-winged angel of father. He was never that." Then he confesses: "Not to make him out to be a saint is easier said than done, and, for the life of me, I can't make him out to be anything else."[18] Craig's imperfection is that he will break the rules, do what should not be done. He will take time with the cavilers, put on "the white wings of sentimentality," play the antagonist, and see that it all comes out right in the end. His subjects' lives are his show, and the happy ending is his effect. Craig knows the value of imperfections, the effect of reality they give to a representation. They make a life seem lifelike. By making a point of his own queer tastes, self-indulgence, and contradictory impulses, he takes the curse off his idolatry. Alternatively, by idolizing his personal gods and goddesses, he makes his impish ways seem sympathetic. In the foreword to his *Index,* he writes:

> I am eighty-five. This is just the age when one can look into one-self and consider one's defects—that is to say, if one has any—for, indeed, the doubt is permissible; are there not a tremendous number of men who have no defects at all? If you doubt me, ask them, and you will hear what you will hear. And take a glance at some of the autobiographies of the old, the middle-aged and the young men who have lived to write their memoirs, and see how perfect most of them have been. Should they have written no memoirs, get their biogra-

pher's account, or some such books about them, and I think you will find it difficult to attribute any defects to any of them.[19]

This combination of disarming honesty and sarcasm, all in the cause of a forthright self-assertion, recalls a similar mixture that often appears in the writings of an unlikely parallel—Bernard Shaw. On the other hand, Shaw is probably foremost among the unnamed targets of Craig's attack in this passage. He would be included among those who had written no autobiography as such but had contrived numerous ways to tell his own story, or to have a reporter or biographer tell the story in Shaw's own words, and in most cases with an air of perfectly ingenuous self-justification. As suggested by his response to Craig's letter to *The Observer,* Shaw writes as a "conqueror," Craig as a "rebel." On the other hand, Craig has always the spiritualist's answer to the skeptic. Shaw would of course be blind to the miracle of Irving because he is subject to intellectual preconceptions, and at stake for him in his skepticism are all his causes: rationalism, atheism, socialism. Craig, on the other hand, readily calls a miracle a miracle, and a saint a saint.

But the contrasts between Shaw and Craig can be emphasized too much. In fact, both men were subject to preconceptions, both prone to extraordinary enthusiasms, both brilliantly illuminative, and both unfair in love and war. Both, on that level, were like Irving. It is no wonder, then, that they misapprehended each other so completely, jealous of each other as they must have been. A letter from Max Beerbohm to Shaw in 1948 brilliantly analyzes one of Shaw's misperceptions of Craig: "You allow that his writing has 'cleverness and subtlety.' There never, however, was a less clever or less subtle fellow than Craig. The qualities that his writing has, and has from the outset had, are a lovely freshness and vivacity and luminousness; 'magic is about'—with a lot of nonsense, and much artlessness, and sudden splendid beams of wisdom and rightness. Cleverness never is there, believe me, nor subtlety." Cleverness and subtlety are, of course, to be found abundantly in Shaw, as Craig (and Irving, too) frequently pointed out, but those are the *little* virtues that can be credited to an author. Wisdom, rightness, freshness, vivacity, luminousness: those are grander qualities, credited to Craig. Beerbohm goes on in the same evenhanded letter to bring Irving into the equation:

> You hold that "the Lyceum, that little hell of ignorance and egoism, aborted" the soul of Craig. I should have supposed rather that (despite his great and in-many-ways right veneration for Irving) the

Lyceum acted just as a spring-board for his leap into the void and in quest of an Ideal Theatre. (If you imagine, as you imply, that he is an egoist in his work or in his mind, let me assure you that you might just as well say that Blake—whose work and mind his somewhat resembles—was egoistic.)

Below this, he adds the note: "And why *shouldn't* you say so? What *wouldn't* you say to make somebody sit up?" Beerbohm then comes to the crux of the difference between the two: "That an essentially poetic person should not begin to be faintly understood by a quintessentially prosaic personage, is only to be expected."[20] Given the great prose dramas of the Norwegian playwright whose quintessence he had represented, Shaw could not take offense at this distinction. And the isolated, lonely-as-a-cloud Craig, his heart set upon a theatre of *one* creator, would be inclined to accept the designation of lyric artist of the theatre. Victor Hugo sketches the chiasmus:

Dramatic poetry admits prose; lyric poetry excludes it . . .
Lyric genius: to be one's self. Dramatic genius: to be others.[21]

Craig had sought to turn Irving into an earlier incarnation of himself, a precursor who affirms all that he will lyrically embody. Shaw, on the other hand, felt that he had comprehended all that Irving sought to be and could make use of Irving's otherness for the purposes of his dramatic poetry. Both, however, took hold of an incomplete Irving, Shaw failing to appreciate his genius at being himself, and Craig failing to accept his genius at being others. Each of them was, no doubt, drawn to Irving by the counterpart, the dimly perceived, but unreachable, quality—for Shaw the lyric, for Craig the dramatic. One might also say that Shaw had failed to appreciate the fact that in so strongly asserting himself, flaunting his personality, Irving came thereby to represent the crowd and, in effect, to dramatize their interests, sacrificing himself to their demands. Craig had failed to perceive that, in adapting himself to the tastes of the crowd, Irving had consolidated a singular identity of unprecedented magnitude in theatrical celebrity, embodying in that way an ideal of the artist, not unrelated to his own romantic quest—a man not altogether apart from the crowd, but distinctly above it.

Shaw finally needed Irving dead to populate the stage with many others, not replicas of the unitary one. Irving, and the example of Irving, would always get in the way of his dialectical conception of the stage. For him,

Irving would remain a ghost—of romanticism, of idealism—who would haunt England as a present danger even after his death. Through sheer diligence, Shaw was, at his best, able to write this ghost off the stage, writing against its insistent presence, but the specter of Irving would always hover nearby, reminding the writer, the reader, the actor, the audience, of the possibility of ultimate control. The death of Brewster was, for Shaw, the ominous sign that the hero dead stands for more than the living being. It would be Shaw's life's work to keep attention on the living being, rather than on any idealized death.

Craig needed to fill the stage with his own presence in some impressive way, but without being an actor. He sought to be the all-encompassing, omnipresent artistic force on the stage without subjecting himself to public scrutiny or any convenience of the crowd. The ghostly figure of the absent Irving—the actor supremely there and not there—was just what Craig needed for his ideal theatre. Irving's existence as a bodiless memory of magnetic power approximated the theoretical actor in Craig's scheme, the actor present only in effect and not in person. Late in his life, Craig described in an intriguing, though somewhat garbled, letter the sort of theatre in which such a ghost might walk:

> If I had a Theatre—I would allow no one behind the scenes there—there I too would somehow vanish—I would be a ghost & as partners in the haunting fellow-ghosts i.e. I suppose we call them workers. All silent—I think it has not yet been even dreamed this silent workshop of ghosts for in *doing* i.e. *acting* what need of words—a nod is as good as a wink etc.
>
> I think a stagework produced in utter silence might be really WORTH while.[22]

This grandiose vision of a monumental theatre, occupied by silent, inhuman presences—essentially an antitheatrical theatre—would have no place for the playwright, of course, and would even transcend many of the substantial qualities of actors, such as identity, voice, and life itself. He had speculated on such an idea even at a much earlier stage of his career. In "The Actor and the Über-Marionette" (1906), he had postulated a theatre that would be the antithesis of the theatre of impersonation, of realism, of life itself:

> This flesh-and-blood life, lovely as it is to us all, is for me not a thing made to search into, or to give out again to the world, even conven-

FIGURE 15. Edward Gordon Craig, ca. 1960. Photograph by Arnold Rood. (Courtesy of Arnold Rood and the Geraldine Womack and Norman D. Philbrick Library of Dramatic Literature and Theatre History). Compare Fig. 7.

tionalized. I think that my aim shall rather be to catch some far-off glimpse of that spirit which we call Death—to recall beautiful things from the imaginary world; they say they are cold, these dead things, I do not know—they often seem warmer and more living than that which parades as life. Shades—spirits seem to me to be more beautiful, and filled with more vitality than men and women; cities of men and women packed with pettiness, creatures inhuman, secret, coldest cold, hardest humanity. For, looking too long upon life, may one not find all this to be not the beautiful, nor the mysterious, nor the tragic, but the dull, the melodramatic, and the silly. . . . And from such things which lack the sun of life it is not possible to draw inspiration. But from that mysterious, joyous, and superbly complete life which is called Death—that life of shadow and of unknown shapes, where all cannot be blackness and fog as is supposed, but vivid colour, vivid light, sharp-cut form; and which one finds peopled with strange, fierce and solemn figures, pretty figures and calm figures, and those figures impelled to some wondrous harmony of movement—all this is something more than a mere matter of fact.[23]

In his designs and ambitions for the theatre, Craig sought to recover the light from the darkness and bring relief to the ongoing catastrophe, which is the present, the life of life. He turned from the potentiality of the stage, which demands the making of new life, to a morbid fixation on the ashes of its past, a return to the dead fathers.

Craig's transfiguration from creator to historian comes about, in part, from a growing concern for the mechanisms and simulacra that produce apparently miraculous effects. He studied closely the machines of theatre, practical and political, and came to know more exactly the difference between the cheap wonders and what he remembered as the true marvels or revelations of the metaphysical space. Sunlight poured down on the "glorious red boards" of the Lyceum stage, even on foggy days, he recalled, adding, "These board are gone. How could a nation let them go? Not only sentiment but logic should have preserved them intact." Presumably, if the boards had been saved, so might the sunlight. But they were not, and now from the perspective of many years later, when progress has perfected the technology of making miracles, and when life itself might be made upon the stage, Craig regrets that in the process the sunlight has been lost. That old metaphysical space—the theocentric world theatre, with its Great Chain of Being—has disappeared. This was the place where the godly light of the sun shone and where transcendence seemed to occur, if one did

not look too closely at the mechanisms and subhuman agents in the shadow
that made it happen:

> Above and around these boards hung innumerable cords—some
> taut, lashed to cleats, others hung loose over our heads, coming we
> knew not from where . . . we knew vaguely, of course, but we didn't
> enquire further—we actors don't bother very much what they do up
> there or down under, or at the side—for the centre of the clearing is
> ours—let the gnomes, the stage carpenters, scene-shifters and their
> masters, burrow and climb and look like elves and monkeys in the
> forest—we are the Gods of the place. Occasionally one of these fur-
> tive creatures would roam from a dark corner into the full glare of the
> rehearsal sunlight, looking white-faced and worried—but we hardly
> noted their existence, and never knew their names.
>
> Their chiefs we knew—Arnott, Jimmy, Allen, Fillery and a few
> more—but, poor brutes, they soon disappeared into the shadows—
> there, we supposed, to grub for acorns. [24]

Death was beautiful in this hierarchic space. On the other hand, Craig discovers as he grows older, its beauty was the effect of the final curtain, the
scenic and metaphoric encoding of a transcendental view of death, and no
more. With attention to the machine, by way of historical inquiry, Craig
would come to grips with the illusion of this metaphysics:

> Another corner of the Lyceum Theatre which now no longer looks
> its old self is the O. P. corner, or opposite prompt. There, night after
> night, stood a very tall and muscular man, whose name I am sorry to
> have forgotten, and whose task was to control the guide-rope which
> held in place the immense roller of the curtain as it slapped its way
> down its forty-feet drop. . . .
>
> The roller on such a curtain would be distinctly heavy. Two thick
> ropes which wound themselves round each end of the roller as it de-
> scended unwound themselves as it was pulled up—counterweights
> raised it, and a big wheel worked by two men lowered it. I believe
> this was the action, though I cannot be positive. . . .
>
> You could time it so well—it came under more perfect control,
> somehow, than any other curtain ever has done; its descent could be
> rapid or lingering—its slight thud as it touched the stage lent a cer-
> tain finality to the scene, as a full stop does to a sentence. [25]

"What more could be desired," Craig asks, "but why is Mr. Allen forgotten, except by a few?" [26] Mr. Allen is forgotten for a reason not unlike the

reason Gregory Brewster is forgotten. They both might serve as reminders that the notion of death as a final curtain to be transcended by a heroic actor who does not die is perhaps no more than a mechanical illusion. The historian who determines to remember Mr. Allen or Corporal Brewster is likely to find that the "beautiful . . . the mysterious . . . the tragic" of that metaphysical world view suddenly seem "the dull, the melodramatic, and the silly." That was certainly what Shaw had seen at *Waterloo,* insisting upon the mechanical metaphor, but Craig remained confident that something else was there on Irving's stage, too, in addition to the clever devices, some spirit within the machine. By looking into darkness and death itself, he hoped to recover that spark. He had stood in the flood of sunlight on that stage, alongside Irving himself, the actor who played his father. In a dream, he had looked out from that stage into the shadows and seen his real father, somewhere amid the "innumerable cords," which are the tensions of historical contingency and determination. As the theatre shone more and more light upon life upon the stage, he retreated into the shadows, among the shades, not to grub for acorns, but to know death. Somewhere in the past, he thought to find presence, origin, truth, beauty, light, in contrast to the tawdry imitations of these things available in the present. This was his quest as a historian. Walter Benjamin writes:

> This is how one pictures the angel of history. His face is turned toward the past. Where we perceive a chain of events, he sees one single catastrophe which keeps piling wreckage upon wreckage and hurls it in front of his feet. The angel would like to stay, awaken the dead, and make whole what has been smashed. But a storm is blowing from Paradise; it has got caught in his wings with such violence that the angel can no longer close them. This storm irresistibly propels him into the future to which his back is turned, while the pile of debris before him grows skyward. This storm is what we call progress.[27]

On the bright stage of the past, between the dark wings, the noble, angelic, ideal effect was felt, the effect of annunciation, of spirit. The curtain rose upon that dream scene and revealed the actor who brought that message across to the crowd. Concealed in the wings were the obscure laborers who worked the machine, made the spirit appear to appear. Hands on one rope made the curtain rise. Hands on another made it slowly fall. The past grows dark and remote behind that falling curtain.

Near the end of Craig's *Henry Irving,* the author describes himself writ-

ing the book's conclusion, when suddenly the ghost of Irving stood before
him: "You must not think I exaggerate. I was alone; the wind, 'tis true, was
howling down the valley outside my house—how it howwwled!—yet all
was cosy and well-lit in my room—nothing dusky, nothing weird: yet
there—there stood Irving." The spirit soon comes to the point:

> "I know what it is you have written," he went on. "These papers
> here, my boy—very excellent—highly flattering too, I'm sure—do
> a great deal of good." He broke off abruptly . . . "What do you intend
> to call the book?"
> "Well, sir, I thought to call it *'On Henry Irving.'*"
> There was a long pause: Irving took a few steps in the direction of
> the south wall of my room, and said: "Why not *'On George Bernard
> Shaw'?"*
> This slightly embarrassed me, for I thought I had been devoting
> myself entirely to one subject—that is to say, to Irving—and I felt
> as small as I always had done thirty odd years ago, when he was
> speaking.
> "But there is so little about Mr. Shaw in this book. . . ."
> "Dam sight too much," said Irving, wheeling round noiselessly
> and in a flash, and looking precisely as he used to look when he held
> four thousand people silent: even if a zany should have run across the
> stage, making grimaces, still he would have held them silent; there-
> fore, I would ask you to be silent now.

Craig's writing should command the authority of its subject, after all, because he is an agent of Irving's transcendence, and "Irving off the earth is
more extraordinary still than Irving on the stage." This "white-winged
angel," after a time, allows that it is perhaps necessary to counter the influence of Shaw, observing that he has taught dramatic critics to "hold the
Theatre in contempt": " 'But you, my dear Ted, always loved the Theatre:
I have watched you, and I know it. I think, too, you have always loved the
actor. But the actors seem to have . . . er . . .'—a slight movement of the
hand—another faint motion—a pause—'vanished.' "[28] No one to stand at
the final curtain. No one to fall. No one to act. How dearly would Craig
love to be the heroic historian, the redeemer and subduer, described by
Benjamin: "In every era the attempt must be made to wrest tradition away
from a conformism that is about to overpower it. The Messiah comes not
only as the redeemer, he comes as the subduer of Antichrist. Only that
historian will have the gift of fanning the spark of hope in the past who is

firmly convinced that *even the dead* will not be safe from the enemy if he wins. And this enemy has not ceased to be victorious."²⁹ But at the cock's crow, the actor turns away from him: " 'Well, good-bye,' he said—that gentle motion with his hand—and, 'Good-bye . . . Good-bye.' "³⁰ So ends the book. Finally, Craig's Irving will not face the light of day with him, remaining instead a figure of his night thoughts. Craig prefers mystification, the convenient darkness of the wings that allows him to create the effect of a heroic transcendence of human limits, even of death. Irving was an actor at home on the brightly lit stage, but Craig's Irving resides in the characteristic half-light of the historical text, caught somewhere between miracle and nature. As Craig grew more and more fed up with his present struggle in the theatre, he turned to staging the past in historical writing, and in this "theatre" Irving appears as gloriously as ever.³¹ Craig's concern in this work, as in his theories, was with the paradisiacal future—how the battle of Armageddon will be fought by all the dead heroes. But Irving turns away from the morning, away from the future, since there are other battles to be fought, critical battles, battles that have to do with redeeming tradition. True to form, Irving seems dubious of the value of Craig's literary attack on the upstart Shaw. The weapon of choice for Irving would be the stage—acting. Then again, Craig seems to be the only one who fully suspects that this Shaw might be the ultimate threat to a redeemed history, might indeed be the Antichrist. Craig, who had betrayed Irving once with his denial of acting as an art, would dearly love to become his Peter or Paul, and found the church (theatre) that would stave off such assaults till the end of time. Craig writes in a different context in the same book, "This perhaps sounds strange to you—especially to you who may be reading this in 1979, when surely all of us who saw Irving will be dead and gone. But it is the truth; Irving's immense success for thirty years was designed on a very small piece of paper, with space to hold just two words—*'Henry Irving'* . . . that stood for concentrated inspiration."³² Craig sought to substitute for the thirty-year paper another of his own, called *Henry Irving*, testament of a church founded upon rock (the word), not sand (the performance), and headed with his own three-word name—a place where the "virgin" Nelly and her bridegroom/son (i.e. the Irving/Craig lineage) might reign without fear of the brimstone critic.

This perhaps sounds strange to you—especially to you who may be reading this in 1993, when Mr. Craig is forgotten, except by a few.

FIGURE 16. Henry Irving in 1904. Photograph by William Crooke. (Courtesy of Harvard Theatre Collection)

CHAPTER X

"THEY COULD NOT SHOUT THAT CURTAIN UP"

> "That raising of the curtain, as it were," said one of his
> player comrades; "the introductory march, the distant es-
> corting of the procession with a vocal chant, the dim clois-
> ters rather imagined than seen, the slow oncoming of the
> cortege, the music growing louder, the initiatory appear-
> ance of the Christian symbol carried before the officiating
> priest, the bier with its floral tributes borne aloft—it was
> one of those scenes that a stage-manager dreams of."
>
> Joseph Hatton, "Sir Henry Irving," p. 992

Irving decided to leave *Waterloo* out of his final provincial tour, in 1905.
Its place in the repertoire, on a double bill with *The Bells,* meant two
stressful roles—two deaths—in one evening. Some years earlier, during a
prolonged attack of the lung disease that eventually killed him, Irving lan-
guished in his rooms under the care of his faithful dresser, Walter Collinson, who attended him every day for over twenty-five years. Stoker came
to visit one day and found Walter in tears:

> When I asked him the cause—for I feared it was death—he said
> through his sobs:
> "He is like Gregory Brewster!"—the old soldier in *Waterloo.* . . .
> Poor Walter's description was sadly accurate.[1]

During his final year, he gave many signs, in public and in private, that he
saw himself as a man "the sands of whose life are running fast," and so the
role of Brewster rang all too true.[2] Maude Fealy played the role of Nora at
the end and later recalled that every time the sergeant spoke the line, "He
isn't long for this world, is he, miss?" Irving would mutter, "That's true!
That's true!"[3]

His friend, Percy Fitzgerald, later his biographer and memorialist, re-

called those last few years: "And thus as the days went by he felt the liga-
tures coiling tighter about his heart. Each night worn and sinking, he must
have returned spent and exhausted. The same old weary routine—'The
Bells,' 'Brewster,' Shylock and Becket—'Backet' as he would call it—
who could stand the wearing grind of that stage machinery going on from
eight till eleven? And this—all this for a poor frail being such as he was!"[4]
He played Brewster for the last time at a benefit matinee, on 15 June 1905,
his last appearance in London. At that performance, as so often before, the
stage machinery ground on. On a signal from Mr. J. H. Allen, prompter
and stage manager, or some other stage manager, equally forgotten, the
great roller curtain of the Lyceum Theatre began to descend. A man's
hands on a rope reversed the balance between curtain and counterweight at
the slow, steady speed that perfectly mimicked human recognition of the
fact of an old man's death. Two thick ropes wound themselves round the
roller, and, under most perfect control, the lingering descent of the curtain
continued until there was a slight thud as it touched the stage. (And that
slight thud can be felt to this day; Gordon Craig, as historian, relays its
impact. So, too, does St. John Ervine, who wrote, "Even now, three decades after I saw the last one, I can hear the thud with which it rolled down
on a tense scene."[5] The hands on the rope paused briefly before reversing
the balance once again for the curtain call. The rhythm of the curtain was
in those hands, anonymous, compliant hands of the machine, moving in
the shadowy wings.

Waterloo demands a *slow* curtain, perhaps not the rhythm Irving fore-
saw for himself. Ellen Terry recalls once asking him, " 'And the end. . . .
How would you like that to come?' 'How would I like that to come?' He
repeated my question lightly, yet meditatively too. Then he was silent for
some thirty seconds before he snapped his fingers—the action again before
the words. 'Like that!' "[6]

And so, his plans for the Farewell Tour were to play Shylock, *Becket,*
Louis XI, and *The Bells* until he dropped, dying "in harness," as he wished.
In each of his final roles, excepting Shylock, the play would conclude with
the image of his death. Finally, though, the strain of *The Bells,* dying a
gruesome death of self-recrimination, proved too much, and he took the
suggestion of the company to have the sets of that play sent back to London. Stoker says that *he* was the one who gave the order, before consulting
Irving, but Irving acquiesced and seemed relieved. That was the day before
his death. Stoker says he "seemed tired, tired; tired not for an hour but for
a lifetime."[7]

On the last of last nights on his Farewell Tour, in the city of Bradford, he played Tennyson's Becket, whose curtain line, "Through night to light, into Thy Hands, O Lord, into Thy Hands!" became his last words on a stage. Within an hour he was dead in the lobby of a hotel, his head in the lap of his weeping dresser, Walter. A member of the company recalled his final performance:

> His acting in the death scene was terribly realistic, and when he fell I thought he would never rise. All that week the stage hands had been obliged to lift him after the death of Becket, so that he could respond to the enthusiastic applause at the end of the play. They would put him on his feet while the curtain was down, and when it rose he would be standing there waiting to bow his acknowledgment of the nightly ovation. That night when they lifted him to his feet he seemed dazed. Turning to the prompt corner, he said to Mr. Loveday, the stage manager:
> "What now?"
> "You take the curtain, sir," was the reply.[8]

A stately funeral, burial in the Abbey, wax death mask made, tributary poems and black-framed eulogies published: these and other ritual deeds were performed to give proper significance or, indeed, staging to his death:

> No need of pity—died the hero still;
>   Strong & triumphant till the last brave breath.
> Fronting the battle, heart & soul & will.
>   He died the Splendid Death.
>
> With crash of music & the noise of Fame,
>   The pulses throbbing & the great mind keen—
> He pass'd amid the shouting of his name,
>   Into the quiet Unseen,
>
> "Into Thy Hands"—thus straightway to his King—
>   To render up the mighty talents given;
> And they shall have their thousandfold who bring
>   Such into Heaven.[9]

The solemn atmosphere was punctured only by a controversy over Shaw's words of commemoration, published in a Viennese newspaper. Shaw had written, "The truth is, Irving was interested in nothing but himself; and the self in which he was interested was an imaginary self in an imaginary world. He lived in a dream." This got mangled by translators into, "He was a narrow minded egoist, devoid of culture, and living on the dream of his own greatness."[10] In this way, even in the grand, final metadrama of Irving's career, his passage into the hands of God, Shaw provides a burst of laughter, of anticonventional enormity, at the whole, superegoistic pretense of the thing—an impulse of the id, deviated through Freud's Vienna into the English ego.

As much as anything else, Irving's death, in all its phases, was a journalistic event. Ten years earlier, not long before the Lyceum premiere of *Waterloo,* an editorial in the *Dramatic World* announced confidently, "Irving to Retire":

> Did men know the awful, weary, tedious, reverential anxiety of power, glory and renown, they would believe that bliss found its resting-bower there; they would never crave for fame; their hunger and thirst for notoriety would cease; they would falter ere they accepted the crown of glorification, for verily it is a coronet which many a famous hero has laid aside, has thrown down in order to pass from wild tumult into heavenly peace; and the latest man, the latest king, the latest grand life that is to, in the near future, pass away from the clarion of publicity to the solitude of hermitage is no other than the ruler of the English stage, HENRY IRVING. Doubtless a cynical laugh will go round, and, coolly, people this statement will attempt to deride, but nevertheless it is absolutely true that Mr. Henry Irving has determined, probably at the termination of the London season following the tragedian's return from America, to retire permanently into private life. That this sorrowful, lamentable, and equally sudden intelligence will wrap the whole universe up in surprise there can be no doubt. Even the Lyceum lessee himself will doubtless, as yet, not desire to give credence to our report, but the DRAMATIC WORLD has received the information not from an ordinary source but direct from one of the most authentic, reliable and truthful channels. Every precaution has been taken; every most careful investigation made; no time or trouble has been spared, and, therefore, the public may except [*sic*] it as a positive fact that the date is, alas! not far distant when the monarch of the stage will leave the histrionic field of glory and will, like Mr. Gladstone, cease to be the leader of a magnificent and mighty institution; an institution to which he has devoted his past life; a life utilised in the interests of Art and which has assisted to raise the latter to a pedestal from which it can never fall. God bless Irving! should be the cry of the nation.[11]

This announcement was, of course, wrong. The editorialist, however, shows that the immortalizing process had begun much earlier, and Irving's performance as Corporal Brewster suggests his compliance in the process of idealizing death. In the curtain call to Doyle's play, he could honor the crowd's wish and rise from the dead. Popular acclaim had brought another of Doyle's somewhat remote heroes back from the dead. Sherlock Holmes, apparently dead at the Reichenbach Falls at the conclusion of one story, comes back whole and strong in another when the public refuses to accept his end. Such is the force of public will. Doyle and Irving played upon the immortalizing will of the crowd; the crowd insists death can be overcome, at the curtain call if not before.

The work of the actor's obituarist is to confirm that the process does not end at the final curtain call. Thus, Talcott Williams, writing for the *Atlantic Monthly,* uses terms that are shared by many: "Through all the history of our English stage, these two [Irving and Ellen Terry] will together pass in the long flight of a great art, shadowy but real,—two that ever play together on that stage where a perpetual audience watches the manifold drama of the past." [12] One of the tasks of the obituarist is to sum things up, to find the words that can go public in place of the life. It is impossible, perhaps, for the words engraved in stone to stand for the departed spirit, but sometimes those words charge through the burning hedge and stir the willingness to believe. The words of the anonymous obituarist for the *Times Literary Supplement* spell the end and the beginning (of this life and this book) as well as any words can:

> To-day the dust that was Henry Irving is enshrined at Westminster. Henceforth he is a name, a tradition, a legend. Like all who, in Buffon's phrase, *parlent au corps par le corps,* the stage-player, if our eyes cannot see him nor our ears hear him, is as nothing. We may dispute among ourselves over his exact rank, and ransack our dictionaries for names to call him by; but just what the actor was, just what he did for us who saw and heard him, we cannot create again by words. What remains of Betterton? A few pages of Steele and Colley Cibber. What of Edmund Kean? An essay or two of Hazlitt. But these are mere printed signs; not the warm, pulsing, radiating forces that were Betterton and Kean. To read of dead actors, when all is said, is to learn nothing more than that our forefathers were pleased; it is not to share their pleasure. It will be—it is already— thus with Henry Irving. Catalogues of plays and characters, dates of this and that occurrence, reams of comment—what have all these to do with the thrills of pleasure we have had from the actual presence

of the living man? This, the eternal commonplace of all acting, is peculiarly true of such acting as Henry Irving's. The player of ductile, fluid temperament, who sinks himself in his part, who is a born mime—as Diderot said of Garrick, *naturellement singe*—is never so utter a loss as the player whose virtue is his own peculiar personality. The finest thing—not seldom the only fine thing—in any stage-character of Irving's was Irving himself. And so it is an effort for us to recall the details of his playing—how he emphasized this, with what gesture or "business" he illustrated that—but what the man was, in his totality, as he stood there before us, we can still feel in every fibre of our being.[13]

What the next generation remembered of Irving's productions was less the play than the picture, less the minute detail than the grand display, less the "flesh-and-blood life" of realistically depicted characters than the superhuman figure of Irving, powerfully present and repeatedly dying. Death figured larger than life in the final phase of his career, especially when the outright failures began to overtake the successes. Accounted unsuccessful were *King Lear* (1892), *Don Quixote* (1895), *Peter the Great* (1898), *The Medicine Man* (1898), *Coriolanus* (1901), and *Dante* (1903); and enjoying only qualified or limited success were *Cymbeline* (1896), *Richard III* (1896), *Madame Sans-Gêne* (1897), and *Robespierre* (1899). Disasters, such as the injury to his knee in 1896 and the burning of his stock of scenery in 1898, further complicated his final years, bringing him near bankruptcy, and forcing him to sell off his absolute authority over the Lyceum. Finally he was reduced to the grueling series of revivals of past successes, plays ever more out-of-date, leaving him dead (or nearly so) upon the stage at the last. As one contemporary put it, "He allowed himself to be driven, like a willing horse, to death."[14] St. John Ervine tells a pathetic story of these years: "Henry Irving, already a knight, and still faithful to the gasjets, left the Lyceum and became, to all intents and purposes, a touring actor. He was still our leading actor, and still a noble and impressive figure on the stage, but his day was dwindling. A morning came when he received a blow to his pride. The manager of a music-hall offered him an engagement to act in a sketch! The old man turned his face to the wall and wept. This, he said, was the end."[15] Craig, looking back on Irving's theatre, his chief model of an artistic theatre, as well as of paternal influence, had good reason to see it as a theatre of death, in stark contrast to the "life" school of the prose Ibsen and the early Shaw. William Archer, from another point of view, closer to Shaw's, compared the Lyceum to a sarcophagus, by which he meant the sort of institution that encloses and per-petuates the past without reference to the present or future.[16]

Throughout these years of decline, Irving performed *Waterloo*, which might be seen as a great trope on the end of his career and of his era: the old and infirm soldier abides by his stock of outdated wisdom and fond memories in a meager dwelling, until at the point of extremity he rises heroically to inspire the general heart and is met by a rush of feeling, fol-lowed by wild applause. The concentration of this moment is remarkable: one moment of romantic soaring—a promise of powder for the charge that brings freedom—one explosive *coup de théâtre,* brings the curtain slowly down. Each closing of the curtain on this scene anticipated the collapse of the Lyceum machine and the demise of the ghost who gave it spirit. That is the fact of death in the theatre; curtains close forever, and the crowd is left without focus, without spirit, still at heart. The most strenuous dem-onstrations and full-throated cries cannot restore the hero. Feelings without vent mount into nostalgia, which is a sickness, an aching to return, to go home, to regress. The past toward which this nostalgia is directed appears in idealized form, as a dream of satisfaction. The heart bears this sentiment alone, and the dream gives it convenient labels aligning it with privilege and power: titles, virtues, values. That is a killing version of contentment, self-pity in the name of high ideals.

A splendid commentary on the legend that was Irving can be found in Victor Hugo's appraisal of the legend that was Napoleon:

> Man had been at once aggrandized and lessened by Napoleon; idealism, in this reign of splendid materialism, received the strange name of ideology. It was a grave imprudence of a man to ridicule the future, but the people, that food for powder, so fond of the gunners, sought him. "Where is he? What is he doing?" "Napoleon is dead," said a passer-by to an invalid of Marengo and Waterloo. "He dead!" the soldier exclaimed; "much you know about him!" Imaginations deified this man overthrown. Europe after Waterloo was dark, for some enormous gap was long left unfilled after the disappearance of Napoleon.[17]

Napoleon was, as Hugo and Le Bon suggest, a figure better represented by his absence than his presence, more potent as a memory than as a living agent. Alive, he was subject to the grim machine that gave him power, while dead he soared free of those contingencies as an abstract force, a symbolic fulfillment. Irving's Lyceum was another sort of machine, one that gave the illusion of a regenerated presence, a renewed and intensified

life, and a death that sits well in memory. Especially toward the end of his
career, the Lyceum became a place for Irving to become better than life in
death. This extreme sort of metonymy, representing presence through absence, operates in *Waterloo,* where the loyal soldier's death calls up the
whole edifice of English values which modernism would steadily undermine.

Freud, in his *Beyond the Pleasure Principle,* speculates on the nature of
that instinct, which he calls the death instinct, opposite to the pleasure-
seeking life instinct. The work is occasioned in part by an inquiry into the
dreams of soldiers afflicted with war neuroses—dreams in which the veteran fulfills an unconscious wish by returning to the scene of the trauma
and reliving again and again the painful or frightening circumstances. This
"repetition compulsion," he argues, can be seen in the games of children
who play with the loss of a desired object, such as a toy, as well as in the
"play" of adults in the theatre when they subject themselves to tragic emotions as a form of entertainment. Beyond the "pleasure principle," which
had been proposed for the earlier dream theory, Freud saw that another sort
of principle or instinct might be at work, more in line with the masochistic
tendencies of the ego. From his observations, he constructs a more comprehensive theory of instincts, which posits that all instinct is directed toward the restoration of an earlier state of things, including the inanimate
state of nonexistence that precedes life:

> It would be in contradiction to the conservative nature of the instincts
> if the goal of life were a state of things which had never yet been
> attained. On the contrary, it must be an *old* state of things, an initial
> state from which the living entity has at one time or other departed
> and to which it is striving to return by the circuitous paths along
> which its development leads. If we are to take it as a truth that knows
> no exception that everything living dies for *internal* reasons—be-
> comes inorganic once again—then we shall be compelled to say that
> *'the aim of all life is death'* and, looking backwards, that *'inanimate
> things existed before living ones.'* [18]

Brewster is a veteran whose memory returns compulsively to an earlier
state in which a desired object—glory, heroism—was in his grasp, but
who, from another point of view, is drawn back to a trauma, a fright, which
has become concealed, literally decorated, by the citation. In his final

dream, though, the harrowing prospect of death before him penetrates all the talk of citations and pride in the regiment. His impulsive bravery cannot carry him through the burning hedge this time. It remains to the observer—the sergeant, the grandniece, the audience—to supply the belief that glorifies or decorates this man's death as a transcendence. Furthermore, the society of which that audience is a part demands constant repetition of this and other dreamlike scenes of death and transfiguration, night after night for years, in order to satisfy its instinct for restoration of an earlier order.

The theatre serves that function of enacting the repetition compulsion, opening the curtain on a dreamlike scene that must close with the descent of the curtain, withdrawal of the desired object, restoration of deathly silence. A play like *Waterloo* allows the actor to reflect the conservative instincts of the crowd and to dignify them as great virtues: nobility, heroism, individualism. The play glorifies the death instinct, which is a basic longing for an earlier quietude, by suggesting that the higher causes of duty, honor, and faith lead the soldier to his fate. In this way the crowd uses the leader/actor as a symbol who makes death seem an individual triumph rather than a common fate. The collective enthusiasm generated by the Lyceum over those many years stemmed from its effectiveness in placing the audience in the condition of the dream, not solely to satisfy their desire for pleasure but also to respond to the cultural "war neurosis" to which they were subject. Irving lived out that almost compulsive repetition of decorated death over the last ten years of his life, if one takes *Waterloo* as the inauguration of the final, instinctive, nostalgic phase of his career—the death phase:

> On the last night of this last London season (10 June 1905) Irving appeared as Corporal Brewster in Conan Doyle's A Story of Waterloo, and as Thomas Becket in Tennyson's Becket. . . . He received a wonderful ovation at the end of the performance. After he had taken an unprecedented number of calls, and made his customary speech of thanks in that manner which Max Beerbohm once likened to a Cardinal's when washing the beggarmen's feet on Holy Thursday, the fireproof curtain was lowered and the house lights turned out. But the audience remained in the theatre, and for at least twenty minutes cheered and applauded with undiminished enthusiasm. Perhaps they had a premonition that if they could not shout that curtain up, they would never see Irving again.
>
> He was told of the demonstration as he was leaving the theatre, and returned to the stage. But the staff had gone, and a stage hand

had to be fetched from a public-house nearby to raise the curtain. A London audience saw Irving for the last time in his "street clothes," and very fine he looked, I remember, in a long loose tweed overcoat, much the same colour as his abundant grey hair.

"I assure you this has taken me completely by surprise," he began. . . . [19]

A STORY OF WATERLOO
by ARTHUR CONAN DOYLE

INTRODUCTION

I have located four separate editions of this play, three privately printed
around 1893 and the fourth issued by Samuel French, Ltd., in 1907. The
manuscript might be among the papers of the Doyle estate, which are not
open to the public, but it is not mentioned in Carr's incomplete catalogue
of that collection, nor is there any mention there of the manuscript of the
short story.[1] The earliest document that refers to the play is a letter from
Irving to Stoker, dated (not in Irving's hand) 12 March 1892, making reference to dialogue that must have been carried over from the beginning of
the short story in the version of the play sent to Irving: "If you see Conan
Doyle, tell him I think it would be better to cut out the two old women at
the beginning & begin with the entrance of the girl—who keeps on, &
explains herself by soliloquy—beginning [hesitantly?] with something like
this—'Twenty six Arsenal View—this must be the house—' "[2] Three days
later, Doyle responded to Stoker:

> On looking over the little play I came to the conclusion that so long
> a monologue at the beginning might be dull, so I have altered it in a
> way which I hope that you will approve of.
>   Cutting out the two old gossips, as suggested, I make the young
> Sergeant of Artillery call in on his way to the butts, before the old
> man is down, and so the situation is explained by the dialogue be-
> tween the two. He then leaves promising to call again later in the day.
>   I think that this is the best solution but if you think not pray do not
> hesitate to say so and I can easily change it again.[3]

These are the only documents pertaining to revision of the play, other than
the three private editions, two of which bear autograph corrections. The
first (S1) is an early version, the second (S2) and third (GC) are intermedi-

ate; the fourth text (SF) is a late, published version. I will describe them in what appears to be their sequence.

1. (Designated S1)   Unmarked proof copy, titled "A Straggler of '15," and dated 14 February 1893, in the Bram Stoker Collection at the Shakespeare Centre Library, Stratford-upon-Avon. A second copy of this text is in the same collection, also unmarked except on the front and again on page nine, where it is marked "5.III.95." It bears the embossed insignia of Chiswick Press. The use of the title of the short story, as well as numerous passages that were later cut out, makes it clear that this is the earliest text of those that are available, and possibly the first printing of the work. The revisions proposed by Doyle in his letter (above) are all carried out in this text. Four lines toward the end, in which Norah redundantly points out to the sergeant the picture and clipping above the mantelpiece, might be identified as remnants of an earlier version, in which the sergeant did not appear at the beginning of the play. Doyle's tendency to lade his work with superfluous historical references (see chapter V) can be seen in this version, with references to Brewster's commanding officers and another nobleman present at the awarding of the medal. Most significantly, however, the final scene between Norah and the sergeant is much longer in this version. We learn that the sergeant feels he must stay until the old man has awakened, and he offers more consolation for Norah and praise for the corporal. He also makes more of his invitation to visit the barracks, where, he suggests, a working-class girl like Norah "is the only kind we need." While he is making this speech, a stage direction indicates that the corporal "begins to move and straighten himself in the chair, picking with his fingers at the arms."

2. (Designated S2)   An undated proof copy, different from S1, also in the Stoker Collection. This text bears numerous small autograph emendations and deletions, all seemingly in one hand, probably Doyle's. The most substantial of these revisions is the handwritten addition of the same four lines of dialogue between Norah and the sergeant as discussed above. That these lines appear in S2 in autograph might imply that this is the earlier version, but most of the differences between the two versions show S2 to be the improved version, closer to the script that was eventually published. Most of the additions in S2 are simple improvements in the pace of the dialogue and its wording: e.g., Norah calls the sergeant "noble and fine"

instead of "fine and noble." Doyle adjusts the matter of Brewster's age by
having Norah speculate on the fact that the sergeant will look like Brewster
in *sixty* years, not fifty. Brewster is eighty-nine according to the short story
(twenty-three at the time of his service at Waterloo). The sergeant, who has
had eight years' service and who appears to Brewster "full young for the
stripes," would be nearer twenty-nine than thirty-nine, hence the adjust-
ment in Norah's line. (The Samuel French edition gives Brewster's age as
seventy-six, which would make him ten at the time of the battle!) The deletions in S2 include the following: both references to the family legend that
Brewster could knock down an ox have been cut, as has the colonel's aside
on the decrepit corporal's survival of Hougoumont ("Better, surely, had he
died there").

3. *(Designated GC)* An undated proof copy, different from either of
the preceding, in the library of the Garrick Club in London. This version
bears many emendations and deletions, in at least two hands, one of which
is probably Doyle's, the other probably Irving's. This is not a prompt copy
but a revised version of S1, reflecting most, but not all, of the changes that
appear in S2. Although GC resembles S2, it contains several variations in
the wording of particular passages. The autograph revisions mark several
of the same passages for correction as S2, indicating that GC does not
follow from S2, but for some reason runs parallel. Among the similarities,
the phrase "fine and noble" is here also marked for inversion, the number
fifty is corrected to sixty as in S2, and the remark about the young Brewster
being able to knock down an ox is again marked for deletion. The opening
speech of GC is crosshatched and written out in Doyle's hand, with the
sentences rearranged and a few phrases added, such as the remark that
"Essex pigs would blush to own bacon like that." In this and other ways,
the revised text of the opening speech closely resembles the later, published
version. Someone has marked the text of the newspaper clipping, read by
the sergeant, to eliminate more of the specific historical references, such as
that Brewster was a member of Captain Haldane's flank company, but these
suggested cuts were evidently ignored or vetoed, since the phrases appear
in the published version. Several other passages are similarly marked, perhaps in an effort to reduce the play's length, but are retained in the published text. On the other hand, Doyle marks certain other passages for suggested additions, mainly interjections, such as having Norah respond, "Um
Yes . . . No . . . Yes," as Brewster ponders the fact that she traveled by

herself on a railway train. When the sergeant appears at the door for his second visit, and Norah goes to let him in, Brewster is to repeat "Where's my bottle" through their dialogue. The triviality of these additions might suggest that they are attempts to record some of the byplay that occurred during the performance. The autograph corrections in the second hand are fewer, briefer, and more difficult to decipher. Nearly all of them pertain to the corporal's lines, suggesting strongly that they are Irving's changes. He marks the script at one point for insertion of the "fine ridgement bit," and when the colonel says that the Scots Guards are all very proud of him, Irving has Brewster respond, "Ay! That's what the Regent said." This last change was taken up by the published edition, as was the revised opening speech, as noted above, but virtually none of the other, smaller changes were taken up, implying that a different copy was used in its preparation. A few of Irving's markings seem to be notes on stage business—"turns," "look at niece," "Cen[ter]"—suggesting that this might have been Irving's personal script of the play for its initial performances. Alterations in Brewster's speech, where he recreates the battle using his paregoric bottle, inhaler, and cough drops, appear to confirm this conclusion. In place of "inhaler," Irving has written "candlestick," and instead of saying "where the cough drops are," Brewster is to say, "where I puts my baccy." A marginal note says the "reserves" should be indicated by his spoon. All of this seems to respond to choices made in production. One further alteration provides solid evidence that this script was in use during the years of the play's production. The sergeant's comments on the fighting in South Africa, which appear in both other privately printed editions, are here marked for deletion, and were deleted by Irving between about 1900 and 1902. These lines do not appear in the published edition. Most of the deletions proposed in GC are ignored in the published edition; possibly they were cuts made for a later, streamlined version of the production.

   4. (Designated SF)   The Samuel French edition, published in 1907. This edition most closely resembles the printed edition text of GC with the revised opening speech. A few passages have been further altered, such as the sergeant's offer of the new pipe to Brewster and the entrance of the colonel. The stage directions have been multiplied and embellished, with ample indications of all positions and movements of actors, suggesting that the stage manager's copy might have been used. This edition contains the following scene plot:

Scene Plot

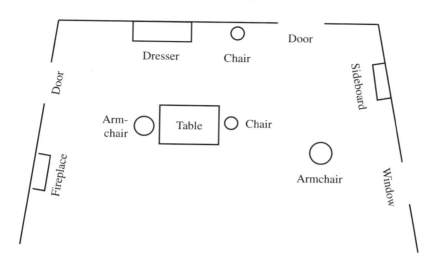

A reprint of the play appeared in *One-Act Plays of To-Day,* Second Series, selected by J. W. Marriott (London: George G. Harrap, 1925). This version follows SF almost exactly, with a few unimportant but distinct variations, possibly implying another version was used.

The text offered here follows GC because it seems to reflect most closely the state of the text at the time of its first performance. The two copies from the Stoker Collection are available at the Shakespeare Center Library, Stratford-upon-Avon, as well as in the Harvester Microform microfilm edition of the collection. I have noted some of the more significant editorial revisions of this text, along with a few variations from other versions.

A STORY OF WATERLOO

SCENE. *A front room in a small house in Woolwich. Cooking range
at fire. Above the fire a rude painting of an impossible military
man in a red coat with a bearskin. On one side a cutting from a
newspaper framed. On the other a medal, also within a frame.
Bright fire-irons, centre table, Bible on small table in window,
wooden armchair with cushion, rack holding plates, etc.*

June, 1881.

[*Curtain rising discovers the empty room; door opens, and enter
NORAH BREWSTER, a country girl, with a bundle of her effects. She looks timidly about her, and then closes the door.*

NORAH.[1]

And this is Uncle Gregory's! Why there is his portrait just above the
fire-place, the very same as we have it at home, and that must be his
medal. Oh, how strange that I should have a house to manage all to
myself! Why, it is next door to being married. I suppose that uncle
is not up yet, they said that he never was up before ten. Well, thank
goodness, that housekeeper has lit the fire before she went away.
[*Takes off her shawl and bonnet, and puts her bundle on a chair.*]
Now I do wonder where they keep everything, it's so different to
home. First I must lay the cloth. [*Opens the drawer in the dresser
until she finds it.*] Ah, here it is; but they might find him a cleaner
one. Even our Saturday cloth is cleaner than this, and it is only
Wednesday now. I'll wash it to-night. Knives and plates, and cups
and saucers. Dear, dear, what dirty folk there are in Woolwich! It
wouldn't do for the country, it wouldn't. [*Lays the table.*] How queer
to keep house for a man you have never seen. And yet, though I have
never seen him, I know quite well what sort of a man he is. I am
sure that I would know him if I met him in the street, so straight and
tall and strong, like the great soldier that he is. Now for the bacon.
Oh, my, what a cruel piece! It never came from an Essex pig, I know.
Well, there's a slice. [*Puts it in the pan and that on the fire.*] I wonder what makes the milk so blue! Now I think [*looking round*] that
all is ready for uncle when he does come down. Won't he be surprised to see me! Of course he would have had mother's letter to say

---

1. This entire speech is crossed out in GC, and the central section (Norah's
comments on the housekeeping) has been revised on the facing page in Doyle's
hand, giving a text that is nearly identical to SF. These notes refer to GC unless
otherwise stated.

I was coming, but he wouldn't think I'd be here so early. Dear old uncle! [*looking up at the picture*] don't he look grand. They must have been awful brave folk over yonder to dare to fight against him. I do hope I'll be able to make him happy. [*A knock.*] Oh, dear, dear, dear, here is someone knocking! What can I say to them? [*Knock again.*] I suppose I must see who it is. [*Unlatches the door.*]

Enter Sergeant McDONALD.

SERG. [*Saluting.*] Beg your pardon, Miss, but does Corporal Gregory Brewster live here?

NORAH. [*Timidly.*] Yes, sir.

SERG. The same who was in the Scots Guards?

NORAH. Yes, sir.

SERG. And fought in the battle of Waterloo?

NORAH. Yes, the same, sir.

SERG. Could I have a word with him, Miss?

NORAH. He's not down yet.

SERG. Ah, then, maybe I'd best look in on my way back. I'm going down to the butts, and will pass again in an hour or two.

NORAH. Very well, sir. Who shall I say came for him?

SERG. McDonald's my name—Sergeant McDonald of the Artillery. But you'll excuse my mentioning it, Miss: there was some talk down at the Gunners' barracks that the old gentleman was not looked after quite as well as might be. But I can see now that it's only foolish talk, for what more could he want than this?

NORAH. Oh, I've only just come. We heard that his housekeeper was not very good to him, and that was why my father wished me to go and do what I could.

SERG. Ah! he'll find the difference now.

NORAH. Two for uncle, and one for the pot. We were all very proud of Uncle Gregory down Leyton way.

SERG. Aye, he's been a fine man in his day. There's not many living now who can say that they have fought against Napoleon Boneypart.

NORAH. Ah! there's his medal hung up by his portrait. [*Walks over to look at it.*] Oh, I do hope that I make him comfortable.

SERG. [*Walking after her.*] He'll be hard to please if you don't do that. But what's that beside the medal?

NORAH. [*Standing on tiptoe, and craning her neck.*] Oh, it is a piece of print, and all about uncle.

SERG. Aye, it's a slip of an old paper. There's the date, August, 1815.

NORAH.   [*Turning the bacon.*] It's such small print.

SERG.   I'll read it to you. [*Clears his throat impressively.*] "A heroic deed." That's what's on the top. "On Tuesday an interesting ceremony was performed at the barracks of the third regiment of guards,
when in the presence of the Prince Regent,[2] a special medal was presented to Corporal Gregory Brewster——

NORAH.   That's him! That's uncle!

SERG.[3]   "To Corporal Gregory Brewster of Captain Haldane's
flank company, in recog—recognition of his valour in the recent
great battle. On the ever memorable 18th of June, four companies of
the third Guards and of the Coldstreams held the important farmhouse of Hugymount at the right of the British position. At a critical
period of the action these troops found themselves short of powder,
and Corporal Brewster was dispatched to the rear to hasten up the
reserve am—ammunition. The corporal returned with two tumbrils
of the Nassau division, but he found that in his absence the how—
howitzer fire of the French had ignited the hedge around the farm,
and that the passage of the carts filled with powder had become almost an impossibility. The first tumbril exploded, blowing the driver
to pieces, and his comrade, daunted by the sight, turned his horses;
but Corporal Brewster, springing into his seat, hurled the man down,
and urging the cart through the flames, succeeded in rejoining his
comrades. Long may the heroic Brewster——

NORAH.   Think of that, the heroic Brewster!

SERG.   "Live to treasure the medal which he has so bravely won,[4]
and to look back with pride to the day when, in the presence of his
comrades, he received this tribute to his valour from the hands of the
first gentleman of the realm." [*Replaces the paper.*] Well, that is
worth being proud of.

NORAH.   And we are proud of it, too.

SERG.   Well, Miss, I'm due at the butts, or I would stay to see the
old gentleman now.

NORAH.   I don't think he can be long.

SERG.   Well, he'll have turned out before I pass this way again.
My respects to you, Miss, and good morning.

2. S1 adds that "Lord Saltoun, and an assembly which comprised beauty as well
as valour" were in attendance for the ceremony.

3. Several specific references in this speech are marked for deletion but were not
deleted in SF, e.g., Captain Haldane's flank company, the Coldstreams, the Nassau
division. S1 contains still more references, such as the names of Colonels Maitland
and Byng, who were in command of the Third Guards.

4. The remainder of this speech is marked for deletion but was retained by SF.

[*Exit* Sergeant McDONALD.

NORAH.   Oh, isn't he a fine man![5] I never saw such a man as that down Leyton way. And how kind he was! Think of him reading all that to me about uncle! It was as much as to say that uncle won the battle. Well, I think the tea is made now, and——

Enter Corporal GREGORY BREWSTER, *tottering in, gaunt, bent, and doddering, with white hair and wizened face. He taps his way across the room, while* NORAH, *with her hands clasped, stares aghast first at the man, and then at his picture on the wall.*

CORP.   [*Querulously.*] I wants my rations! The cold nips me without 'em. See to my hands. [*Holds out his gnarled knuckles.*]

NORAH.   It's nigh ready. Don't you know me, grand-uncle? I'm Norah Brewster, from Essex way.

CORP.   Rum is warm, and schnapps is warm, and there's 'eat in soup, but gimme a dish of tea for chice. Eh? [*Peers at the girl.*] What did you say your name was, young woman?

NORAH.   Norah Brewster.

CORP.   You can speak out, lass. Seems to me folks' voices ain't as strong as they was.

NORAH.   I'm Norah Brewster, uncle. I'm your grand-niece, come from Essex way to live with you.

CORP.   [*Chuckling.*] You're Norah, hey? Then you'll be brother Jarge's gal likely? Lor, to think o' little Jarge havin' a gal!

NORAH.   [*Putting bacon out of dish.*] Nay, uncle. My father was the son of your brother George.

CORP.   [*Mumbles and chuckles, picking at his sleeves with his trembling hands.*] Lor, but little Jarge was a rare un! [*Draws up to the table while* NORAH *pours out the tea.*] Eh, by Jimini, there was no chousing Jarge! He's got a bull-pup o' mine that I lent him when I took the shillin'. Likely it's dead now. He didn't give it ye to bring, may-be?

NORAH.   [*Sitting at table, and glancing ever wonderingly at her companion.*] Why, grandpa, Jarge[6] has been dead this twenty years.

CORP.   [*Mumbling.*] Eh, but it were a bootiful pup—bootiful!

---

5. The remainder of this speech is marked for deletion but was retained by SF. S1 adds Norah's remark, "I feel so proud to think of a real prince speaking like that."

6. Norah appears to address Brewster as "grandpa" here, due to an erroneous comma that appears also in S2. S1 and SF correct to "grandpa Jarge," while GC is marked for the substitution of "Uncle" in place of "grandpa."

[*Drinks his tea with a loud supping noise.*] I am cold for the lack o'
my rations. Rum is good and schnapps, but I'd as lief have a dish o'
tea as either.

NORAH.   I've got two pounds o' butter and some eggs in the basket. Mother said as I was to give you her respec's and love, and that
she'd ha' sent a tin o' cream, but it might ha' turned on the way.

CORP.   [*Still eating voraciously.*] Eh, it's a middlin' goodish way.
Likely the stage left yesterday.

NORAH.   The what, uncle?

CORP.   The coach that brought ye.

NORAH.   Nay, I came by the mornin' train.

CORP.   Lor now, think o' that. The railway train, heh? you ain't
afeard o' them new-fangled things! By Jimini! to think of your
comin' by railway like that. Why, it's more than twenty mile.
[*Chuckling.*] What the world a comin' to? [*Puffs out his chest and
tries to square his shoulders.*] Eh, but I get a power o' good from my
rations!

NORAH.   Indeed, uncle, you seem a deal stronger for them.

CORP.   Aye, the food is like coals to that fire. But I'm nigh
burned out, lass, I'm nigh burned out.

NORAH.   [*Clearing the table.*] You must ha' seen a deal o' life,
uncle. It must seem a long long time to you.

CORP.   Not so very long, neither. I'm going on to ninety, but it
might ha' been yesterday that I took the bounty. And that battle, why,
by Jimini, I've not got the smell of the burned powder out o' my nose
yet. Have you read that? [*Nodding to the cutting.*]

NORAH.   Yes, uncle, and I'm sure that you must be very proud
of it.

CORP.   Ah, it was a great day for me—a great day! The Regent
he was there, and a fine body of a man too. [*Tries to stuff some tobacco into his pipe.*] He up to me and he says, "The ridgement is
proud of ye," says he. "And I'm proud o' the ridgement," says I.
"And a damned good answer, too," says he to Lord Hill, and they
both bust out a laughin'. [*Coughs and chuckles, and points up at the
mantel-piece.*]

NORAH.   What can I hand you, uncle?

CORP.   A spoonful from that bottle by the brass candlestick, my
girl! [*Drinks it.*] It's paregoric, and rare stuff to cut the phlegm. [*Norah looks out of the window.*] But what be you a peepin' out o' the
window for?

NORAH.   [*Excitedly.*] Oh, uncle, here's a regiment o' soldiers
comin' down the street with the band playing in front of them.

CORP. [*Rising and clawing his way towards the window.*] A ridgement! Heh! Where be my glasses? Lordy, I can hear the band as plain as plain. Bands don't seem to play as loud now-a-days though as they used. [*Gets to the window.*] Here they come, pioneers, drum-major, band! What be their number, lass? [*His eyes shine, and his feet and stick tap to the music.*]

NORAH. They don't seem to have no number, uncle. They've something wrote on their shoulders. Oxfordshire, I think it be.

CORP. Ah, yes. I heard as they had dropped the numbers, and given them new-fangled names. [*Shakes his head.*] That wouldn't ha' done for the Dook. The Dook would ha' had a word there. There they go, by Jimini! They're young, but they hain't forgot how to march. Blessed if I can see the light bobs though! Well, they've got the swing, aye, they have the swing. [*Gazes after them until the last files have disappeared.*]

NORAH. [*Helping him.*] Come back to your chair, uncle.

CORP. Where be that bottle again.[7] It cuts the phlegm. It's the toobes that's wrong with me. Joyce says so, and he is a clever man. I'm in his club. There's the card, paid up, under yon flat iron. [*Suddenly slapping his thigh.*] Why, darn my skin, I knew as something was amiss.

NORAH. Where, uncle.

CORP. In them soldiers. I've got it now. They'd forgot their stocks. Not one o' them had his stock on. [*Chuckles and croaks.*] It wouldn't ha' done for the Dook. No, by Jimini, the Dook would ha' had a word there.

NORAH. [*Peeping towards the door.*] Why, uncle, this is the soldier who came this morning—one of them with the blue coats and gold braid.

CORP. Eh, and what do he want? Don't stand and stare, lass, but go to the door and ask him what he wants.

[*She approaches the door, which is half open.* Sergeant Mc-DONALD of Artillery, *his carbine in his hand, steps over the threshold and salutes.*

SERG. Good day to you again, miss. Is the old gentleman to be seen now?

NORAH. Yes, sir. That's him. I'm sure he'll be very glad to see you. Uncle, here is a gentleman who wants to speak with you.

SERG. Proud to see you, sir—proud and glad, sir!

7. The following five sentences are marked for deletion but are retained by SF.

[*Steps forward, grounds his carbine and salutes*—NORAH, *half frightened half attracted, keeps her eyes on the visitor.*

CORP. [*Blinking at the* Sergeant.] Sit ye down, sergeant, sit ye down! [*Shakes his head.*] You are full young for the stripes. Lordy, it's easier to get three now, than one in my day. Gunners were old soldiers then, and the grey hairs came quicker than the three stripes.

SERG. I am eight years service, sir. McDonald is my name, Sergeant McDonald of H Battery, Southern Artillery Division. I have called as the spokesman of my mates at the Gunners' Barracks to say that we are proud to have you in the town, sir.

CORP. [*Chuckling and rubbing his hands.*] That was what the Regent said, "The ridgement is proud of you," say he. "And I am proud of the ridgement," say I. "A damned good answer, too," says he, and he and Lord Hill bust out a-laughin'.

SERG. The non-commissioned mess would be proud and honoured to see you, sir. If you could step as far you will always find a pipe o' baccy and a glass of grog awaitin' you.

CORP. [*Laughing until he coughs.*] Like to see me, would they, the dogs! Well, well, if this warm weather holds I'll drop in—it's likely that I'll drop in. My toobes is bad to-day, and I feel queer here. [*Slapping his chest.*] But you'll see me one of these days at the barracks.

SERG. Mind you ask for the non-com. mess.

CORP. Oh, lordy! Got a mess of your own, heh, just the same as the officers. Too grand for a canteen now. What is the world comin' to at all!

SERG. [*Respectfully.*] You was in the Guards, sir, wasn't you?

CORP. Yes, I am a guardsman, I am. Served in the 3rd Guards, the same they call now the Scots Guards. Lordy, sergeant, but they have all marched away, from Colonel Byng right down to the drummer boys, and here am I, a straggler—that's what I call myself, a straggler. But it ain't my fault neither, for I've never had my call, and I can't leave my post without it.

SERG. [*Shaking his head.*] Ah, well, we all have to muster up there. Won't you try my baccy, sir? [*Hands over pouch.*]

[Corporal BREWSTER *tries to fill his clay pipe, but drops it. It breaks, and he bursts into tears with the long helpless sobs of a child.*

CORP. I've broke my pipe! my pipe!

NORAH. [*Running to him and soothing him.*] Don't, uncle, oh don't! We can easy get another.

SERG.   Don't you fret sir. 'Ere's a wooden pipe with an amber mouth—you'll do me the honour to accept it from me.

CORP.   [*His smiles instantly bursting through the tears.*] Jemini! It's a fine pipe! See to my new pipe, gal! I lay that Jarge never had a pipe like this. Eh, and an amber mouth, too! [*Mumbles with it in his mouth.*] You've got your firelock there, sergeant.

SERG.   Yes, sir, I was on my way back from the butts when I looked in.

CORP.   Let me have the feel of it! Lordy, but it seems like old times to have one's hand on a musket. What's the manual, sergeant? Eh? Cock your firelock! Present your firelock! Look to your priming! Heh, sergeant! [*The breech on being pressed flies open.*] Oh, Jimini! I've broke your musket in halves.

SERG.   [*Laughing.*] That's all right, sir! You pressed on the lever and opened the breech-piece. That's where we load 'em, you know.

CORP.   Load 'em at the wrong end! Well, well, to think of it! and no ramrod neither. I've heard tell of it, but I never believed it afore.[8] Ah! it won't come up to Brown Bess. When there's work to be done you mark my words, and see if they don't come back to Brown Bess.

SERG.   [*Hotly.*] By the Lord, sir, they need some change out in South Africa now. I see by this morning's paper that the Government has knuckled under to these here Boers. They are hot about it in the non-com. mess, I can tell you, sir.

CORP.   Eh! eh! by Jemini, it wouldn't ha' done for the Dook! the Dook would ha' had a word to say.

SERG.   Ah! that would he, sir. You've spoke a true word there! God send us another like him! [*Rising.*] But I've wearied you enough for one sitting. I'll look in again, and I'll bring a comrade or two with me, if I may, for there isn't one but would be proud to have speech with you. [*Salutes.*] My respects to you, Miss.   [*Exit.*

NORAH.   Oh, Uncle, isn't he fine and noble?

CORP.   [*Mumbling.*] Too young for the stripes, gal. A sergeant of gunners should be a growed man. I don't know what we are comin' to in these days. [*Chuckling.*] But he gave me a pipe, Norah! A fine pipe with an amber mouth. I'll lay that brother Jarge never had a pipe like that.

NORAH.   [*Aside, nodding towards the door.*] To think that he will

---

8. The script is marked to be cut from here through the sergeant's "I've wearied you enough for one sitting." The passage about the Boers is taken directly from Doyle's story. See pp. 130–31 for discussion of this passage.

be like Uncle in fifty[9] years, and that Uncle was once like him.[10] He seems a very kind young man, I think. He calls me "Miss" and Uncle "sir," so polite and proper. I never saw as nice a man down Essex way.

CORP.   What are you moonin' about, gal! I want you to help me move my chair to the window, or maybe yon fancy chair will do. It's warm, and the air would hearten me if I can keep back the flies. They get owdacious in this weather and they plague me cruel.

NORAH.   I'll keep them off you, Uncle.

[He moves feebly across to where the sunshine comes in at the door, and he sits in it.

CORP.   Eh, but it's fine! It always makes me think of the glory to come. Was it to-day that parson was here?

NORAH.   No, Uncle.

CORP.   Then it was yesterday. I get the days kind o' mixed. He reads to me, the parson does.

NORAH.   But I could do that, Uncle.

CORP.   You can read too, can you? By Jimini, I never seed such a gal. You can travel by railroad and you can read. Whatever is the world comin' to? It's the Bible he reads to me.

NORAH.   *[Opening the Bible.]*[11] What part would you like to hear?

CORP.   Oh, them wars.

NORAH.   The wars!

CORP.   Aye, keep to the wars; "Give me the old testament, parson," says I, "there's more taste to it," says I. Parson, he wants to get off to something else, but it's Joshua or nothing with me. Them Israelites was good soldiers, good growed soldiers, all of 'em.

NORAH.   But, Uncle, it's all peace in the next world.

CORP.   No, it ain't, gal.

NORAH.   Oh, yes, Uncle, surely.

CORP.   *[Irritably knocking his stick on the ground.]* I tell ye it ain't, gal. I asked parson.

NORAH.   Well, what did he say?

CORP.   He said there was to be a last final fight. Why, he even gave it a name, he did. The battle of Arm—Arm—

9. The number is written in as sixty, and is so given in SF.

10. The remainder of this speech is marked for deletion but is retained in SF.

11. S1 and S2 add that she is *"leaning over the dresser with her hand on her chin."*

NORAH. Armageddon.[12]

CORP. Aye, that was the name. [*Pauses thoughtfully.*] I 'spec's the 3rd Guards will be there. And the Dook—the Dook'll have a word to say. [*Sinks back a little in his chair.*]

NORAH. What is it, Uncle? You look tired.

CORP. [*Faintly.*] Maybe I have had air enough. And I ain't strong enough to fight agin the flies.

NORAH.[13] Oh, but I will keep them off, Uncle.

CORP. They get owdacious in this weather. I'll get back to the corner. But you'll need to help me with the chair. Chairs are made heavier than they used to be.

[*Is in the act of rising when there comes a tap at the door, and* COLONEL MIDWINTER *(civilian costume) puts in his head.*

COL. Good day. Is this Gregory Brewster?[14] Then you are the man I came to see.

CORP. Who was that, sir?

COL. Gregory Brewster was his name.

CORP. I am the man, sir.

COL. And you are the same Brewster, as I understand, whose name is on the roll of the Scots Guards as having been present at the battle of Waterloo?

CORP. The same Brewster, sir, though they used to call it the 3rd Guards in my day. It was a fine ridgement, sir, and they only want me now to make up a full muster.

COL. [*Cheerily.*] Tut! tut! they'll have to wait years for that. But I thought I should like to have a word with you, for I am the Colonel of the Scots Guards.

CORP. [*Springing to his feet and saluting.*] The Colonel! God bless me! To think of it![15]

[*In his excitement he forgets his stick and totters, and would have fallen had not the* COLONEL *caught him on one side and* NORAH *on the other.*

COL. [*Leading him over to his other chair.*] Easy and steady.

CORP. [*Sitting down and panting.*] Thank ye, sir. I was near

12. Doyle's marginal note calls for "Lots of Armageddon here."

13. This line and the next are marked for deletion, but they are retained in SF.

14. Norah's response, "Yes sir," is written in the margin.

15. S1 contains the following extra dialogue at this point: "*Norah.* Hadn't the gentleman better come in, Uncle. *Corp.* Surely, sir, walk in, sir, if I may be so bold!"

gone that time. But, Lordy, why I can scarce believe it. To think of me, the corporal of the flank company, and you the colonel of the battalion! Lordy, how things do come round to be sure.

COL.[16]   Why, we are very proud of you in London. And so you are actually one of the men who held Hougoumont. [*Looks round him at the medicine bottles, etc.*] [*Aside.*] Better, surely, had he died there.

CORP.   Yes, colonel, I was at Hougoumont.

COL.   Well, I hope that you are pretty comfortable and happy.

CORP.   Thank ye, sir, I am pretty bobbish when the weather holds,[17] and the flies are not too owdacious. I have a good deal of trouble with my toobes. You wouldn't think the job it is to cut the phlegm. And I need my rations, I get cold without 'em. And my jints, they are not what they used to be.

COL.   How's the memory?

CORP.   Oh, there ain't anything amiss there. Why, sir, I could give you the name of every man in Captain Haldane's flank company.

COL.   And the battle—you remember it?

CORP.[18]   Why I sees it afore me, every time I shuts my eyes. Lordy, sir, you wouldn't hardly believe how clear it is to me. There's our line right along from the paregoric bottle to the inhaler, d'ye see! Well then, the pill box is for Hougoumont on the right, where we was, and the thimble for Le Hay Saint. That's all right, sir. [*Cocks his head and looks at it with satisfaction.*] And here are the reserves, and here were our guns and our Belgians, then here's the French, where I put my new pipe, and over here, where the cough drops are, was the Proosians a comin' up on our left flank. Jimini, but it was a glad sight to see the smoke of their guns.

COL.   And what was it that struck you most, now, in connection with the whole affair?

CORP.   I lost three half-crowns over it, I did. I shouldn't wonder

16. SF makes a muddle of the following three lines by making Brewster return to the anecdote of his response to the Prince Regent's expression of the regiment's pride in him, but doing so before the colonel says anything about the officers in London being proud of him. The intention of returning to that anecdote at this moment is indicated in the margin of GC. The colonel's aside—"Better, surely, had he died there"—appears in S1, is marked for deletion in both S2 and GC, and does not appear in SF.

17. The remainder of this speech is marked for deletion but was retained by SF.

18. Several small changes are marked in this speech, as noted in the introduction.

if I were never to get the money now. I lent him to Jabez Smith, my rear rank man at Brussels. "Grig!" says he, "I'll pay you true, only wait till pay-day." By Jimini, he was struck by a lancer at Quarter Brass, and me without a line to prove the debt. Them three half-crowns is as good as lost to me.

COL.   [*Rising and laughing.*] The officers of the Guards want you to buy yourself some little trifle which may add to your comfort. It is not from me, so you need not thank me. [*Slips a note into the old man's baccy pouch.*]

CORP.   Thank you kindly, sir. But there's one favour I'd ask you, Colonel.

COL.   Yes, my man.

CORP.   If I'm called, Colonel, you won't grudge me a flag and a firing party. I'm not a civilian, I'm a Guardsman, and I should like to think as two lines of the bear-skins would be walkin' after my coffin.

COL.   All right, my man, I'll see to it. Good-bye, good-bye. [*Corporal sinks back in his chair.*] I fear that I have tired him. Good-bye, my girl; and I hope that we may have nothing but good news from you.   [*Exit.*

NORAH.   Uncle, uncle! Yes, I suppose he is asleep. But he is so grey and thin, that he frightens me. And see the great blue veins in his hands, and his poor swollen knuckles. He that could knock an ox down, and now the flies make him cry![19] Oh, I wish I had some one to advise me, for I don't know when he is ill and when he is not.

[*Tap at the door—enter* Sergeant McDONALD.

SERG.   Good day, Miss. How is the old gentleman?

NORAH.   He's asleep, I think. But I am so frightened about him.

SERG.   [*Going over to him.*] Yes, he don't look as if he were long for this life, do he?[20] But maybe a sleep like this brings strength to him.

NORAH.   Oh, I do hope so.

SERG.   I'll tell you why I came back so quick. I told them up at the barracks that I'd given him a pipe, and the others they wanted to be in it too, so they passed round, you understand, and made up a pound of baccy. It's long cavendish, with plenty o' bite to it.

19. Most of this speech is marked for deletion, but only this sentence actually was deleted from SF.

20. In S1 the sergeant adds, "Well, he's had a good spell, but still there's many who live longer." S1 generally provides the fullest version of the scene between the sergeant and Norah; see introduction.

NORAH.   How kind of you to think of him![21]

SERG.   Do you always live with him?

NORAH.   No, I only came this morning.

SERG.   Well, you haven't taken long to get straight.

NORAH.   Oh, but I found everything in such a mess. When I have time to myself I'll soon get it nice.

SERG.   That sounds like marching orders to me.

NORAH.   Oh, how could you think so!

SERG.   You don't want me to be off then?

NORAH.   It is very kind of you to come and see uncle.[22] That's he above the mantelpiece.

SERG.   Ah! and a smart soldier, too, in his day, no doubt.

NORAH.   It was really he who won that battle. It says so in the paper.

SERG.   Think o' that, and he sitting there so quiet. Tell me, Miss, have you ever been over a barrack?

NORAH.   No, I've been on a farm all my life.

SERG.   Well, maybe, when he comes up you would come with him? I'd like to show you over.

NORAH.   I'm sure I'd like to come.

SERG.   Well, will you promise to come?

NORAH.   [*Laughing.*] You seem quite earnest about it.

SERG.   Well, maybe I am.

NORAH.   Very well, I'll promise to come.

SERG.   You'll find us rough and ready.

NORAH.   I'm sure it will be very nice.

SERG.   Not quite what young ladies are accustomed to.

NORAH.   But I am no young lady. I've worked with my hands every day that I can remember.[23]

21. In S1 the sergeant says, "Well, there's not many left like him. We ought to do whatever we can for him," and Norah replies, "I'm sure we are both very grateful." Three lines below, S1 has the sergeant volunteering to wait and see that the corporal wakes all right; Norah says, "I feel frightened of him when he is like that."

22. The following exchange, up to "Tell me, Miss . . . ," is marked for deletion and was deleted from SF. It appears in S1 and is written on the facing page for inclusion in S2. It is perhaps a remnant from an earlier version of the play, in which the sergeant does not appear at the beginning of the play to read the clipping.

23. In S1, the sergeant replies: "Ah, and that's the best sort too. That's the only kind we need in barracks. Well, you'll come up and see how you like the looks of them. [*The* Corporal *begins to move and straighten himself in the chair, picking with his fingers at the arms.*] We have some women, there, you know, all the time, and they seem happy and contented like."

CORP. [*In a loud voice.*] The Guards need powder!

CORP. [*Louder.*] The Guards need powder! [*Struggles to rise.*]

NORAH. Oh, I am so frightened.

CORP. [*Staggering to his feet, and suddenly flashing out into his old soldierly figure.*] The Guards need powder, and, by God, they shall have it! [*Falls back into the chair.* NORAH *and the* SERGEANT *rush towards him.*]

NORAH. [*Sobbing.*] Oh, tell me, sir, tell me, what do you think of him.

SERG. [*Gravely.*] I think that the 3rd Guards have a full muster now.

CURTAIN.[24]

24. SF adds the direction "SLOW," along with the information, "Time 45 minutes."

APPENDIX B

From "MR IRVING TAKES PAREGORIC" by George Bernard Shaw, *Saturday Review,* 11 May 1895. (Reprinted by permission of The Society of Authors on behalf of the Bernard Shaw Estate.)

Anyone who consults recent visitors to the Lyceum, or who seeks for information in the Press as to the merits of Mr Conan Doyle's Story of Waterloo, will in nineteen cases out of twenty learn that the piece is a trifle raised into importance by the marvellous acting of Mr Irving as Corporal Gregory Brewster. As a matter of fact, the entire effect is contrived by the author, and is due to him alone. There is absolutely no acting in it—none whatever. There is a make-up in it, and a little cheap and simple mimicry which Mr Irving does indifferently because he is neither apt nor observant as a mimic of doddering old men, and because his finely cultivated voice and diction again and again rebel against the indignity of the Corporal's squeakings and mumblings and vulgarities of pronunciation. But all the rest is an illusion produced by the machinery of "a good acting play," by which is always meant a play that requires from the performers no qualifications beyond a plausible appearance and a little experience and address in stage business. I had better make this clear by explaining the process of doing without acting as exemplified by A Story of Waterloo, in which Mr Conan Doyle has carried the art of constructing an "acting" play to such an extreme that I almost suspect him of satirically revenging himself, as a literary man, on a profession which has such a dread of "literary plays." (A "literary play," I should explain, is a play that the actors have to act, in opposition to the "acting play," which acts them.)

Before the curtain rises, you read the playbill; and the process commences at once with the suggestive effect on your imagination of "Corporal Gregory Brewster, age eighty-six, a Waterloo veteran," of "Nora Brewster, the corporal's grandniece," and of "Scene—Brewster's lodgings." By the time you have read that, your own imagination, with the author pulling the strings, has done half the work you afterwards give Mr Irving credit for. Up goes the curtain; and the lodgings are before you, with the humble breakfast table, the cheery fire, the old man's spectacles and bible, and a medal hung up in a frame over the chimney-piece. Lest you should be unobservant enough to miss the significance of all this, Miss Annie Hughes comes in with a basket of butter and bacon, ostensibly to impersonate the grandniece, really to carefully point out all these things to you, and to lead up to the entry of the hero by preparing breakfast for him. When the background is sufficiently laid in by this artifice, the drawing of the figure commences. Mr Fuller Mellish enters in the uniform of a modern military sergeant, with a breech-loading carbine. You are touched: here is the young soldier come to see the old—two figures from the Seven Ages of Man. Miss Hughes tells Mr Mellish all about Corporal Gregory. She takes down the medal, and makes him read aloud to her the press-cutting pasted beside it which describes the feat for which the medal was given. In short, the pair work at the picture of the old warrior until the very dullest dog in the audience knows what he is to see, or to imagine he sees, when the great moment comes. Thus is Brewster already created, though Mr Irving has not yet left his dressing room. At last, everything being ready, Mr Fuller Mellish is packed off so as not to divide the interest. A squeak is heard behind the scenes: it is the childish treble that once rang like a trumpet on the powder-waggon at Waterloo. Enter Mr Irving, in a dirty white wig, toothless, blear-eyed, palsied, shaky at the knees, stooping at the shoulders, incredibly aged and very poor, but respectable. He makes his way to his chair, and can only sit down, so stiff are his aged limbs, very slowly and creakily. This sitting down business is not acting: the callboy could do it; but we are so thoroughly primed by the playbill, the scene-painter, the stage-manager, Miss Hughes and Mr Mellish, that we go off in enthusiastic whispers, "What superb acting! How wonderfully he does it!" The corporal cannot recognize his grandniece at first. When he does, he asks her questions about children—children who have long gone to their graves at ripe ages. She prepares his tea: he sups it noisily and ineptly, like an infant. More whispers: "How masterly a touch of second childhood!" He gets a bronchial attack and gasps for paregoric, which Miss Hughes administers with a spoon, whilst our faces glisten with tearful smiles. "Is there another living actor who could take paregoric like that?" The sun shines through the window: the old man would fain sit there and peacefully enjoy the fragrant air and life-giving warmth of the world's summer, contrasting so pathetically with his own winter. He rises, more creakily than before, but with his faithful grandniece's arm fondly supporting him. He dodders across the stage, expressing a hope that the flies will not be too "owdacious," and sits down on another chair with his joints crying more loudly than ever for some of the oil of youth. We feel that we could watch him sitting down for ever. Hark! a band in the street without. Soldiers pass: the old war-horse snorts feebly, but complains that bands dont play so loud as they used to. The band being duly exploited for all it is worth, the bible comes into play. What he likes in it are the campaigns of Joshua and the battle of Armageddon, which the poor dear old thing can hardly pronounce, though he had it from "our clergyman." How sweet of the clergyman to humor him! Blessings on his kindly face and on his silver hair! Mr Fuller Mellish comes back with the breechloading carbine. The old man handles it; calls it a firelock; and goes crazily through his manual with it. Finally, he unlocks the breech, and as the barrel drops, believes that he has broken the weapon in two. Matters being explained, he expresses his unalterable conviction that England will have to fall back on Brown Bess when the moment for action arrives again. He takes out his pipe. It falls and is broken. He whimpers, and is petted and consoled by a present of the sergeant's beautiful pipe with "a hamber mouthpiece." Mr Fuller Mellish, becoming again superfluous, is again got rid of. Enter a haughty gentleman. It is the Colonel of the Royal Scots Guards, the corporal's old regiment. According to the well-known custom of colonels, he has called on the old pensioner to give him a five-pound note. The old man, as if electrically shocked, staggers up and desperately tries to stand for a moment at "attention" and salute his officer. He collapses, almost slain by the effort, into his chair, mumbling pathetically that he "were a'most gone that time, Colonel." "A masterstroke! who but a great actor could have executed this heart-searching movement?" The veteran returns to the fireside: once more he depicts with convincing art the state of an old man's joints. The Colonel goes; Mr Fuller Mellish comes; the old man dozes. Suddenly he springs up. "The Guards want powder; and, by God, the Guards shall have it." With these words he falls back in his chair. Mr Fuller Mellish, lest there should be any mistake about it (it is never safe to trust the intelligence of the British public), delicately informs Miss Hughes that her granduncle is dead. The curtain falls amid thunders of applause.

Every old actor into whose hands this article falls will understand perfectly from my description how the whole thing is done, and will wish that he could get such Press notices for a little hobbling and piping, and a few bits of mechanical business with a pipe, a carbine, and two chairs. The whole performance does not involve one gesture, one line, one thought outside the commonest routine of automatic stage illusion. What, I wonder, must Mr Irving, who of course knows this better than anyone else, feel when he finds this pitiful little handful of hackneyed stage tricks received exactly as if it were a crowning instance of his most difficult and finest art? No doubt he expected and intended that the public, on being touched and pleased by machinery, should imagine that they were being touched and pleased by acting. But the critics! What can he think of the analytic powers of those of us who, when an organized and successful attack is made on our emotions, are unable to discriminate between the execution done by the actor's art and that done by Mr Conan Doyle's ingenious exploitation of the ready-made pathos of old age, the ignorant and maudlin sentiment attaching to the army and "the Dook," and the vulgar conception of the battle of Waterloo as a stand-up street fight between an Englishman and a Frenchman, a conception infinitely less respectable than that which led Byron to exclaim, when he heard of Napoleon's defeat, "I'm damned sorry?"

. . . .

I hope I have not conveyed an impression that the triple bill makes a bad evening's entertainment. Though it is my steady purpose to do what I can to drive such sketches as A Story of Waterloo, with their ready-made feelings and prearranged effects, away to the music-hall, which is their proper place now that we no longer have a "Gallery of Illustration," I enjoy them, and am entirely in favor of their multiplication so long as it is understood that they are not the business of fine actors and first-class theatres.

NOTES

PREFACE

1. Bernard Shaw, *Our Theatres in the Nineties* (London: Constable, 1932), I, 113–20. This edition is a complete collection of Shaw's *Saturday Review* columns, 1895–98; the paperback edition I had been reading was *Shaw's Dramatic Criticism (1895–98),* ed. John F. Matthews (New York: Hill and Wang, 1959). Since this review is quoted very often in this book and is reprinted here as Appendix B, I have omitted all subsequent page references to it.

2. Quoted in Austin Brereton, *The Life of Henry Irving* (1908; reprint, New York: Blom, 1969), II, 216.

3. Bram Stoker, *Personal Reminiscences of Henry Irving* (London: Heinemann, 1906), I, 251.

4. Ibid., I, 29–31.

5. Quoted in Brereton, *Henry Irving,* II, 215.

6. Arthur Conan Doyle, "A Straggler of '15," in *Round the Red Lamp* (1894; reprint, Freeport, N.Y.: Books for Libraries Press, 1969), p. 39. These lines were changed or eliminated in the dramatic adaptations.

7. Arthur Conan Doyle, *Waterloo* (New York: Samuel French, 1907), p. 19. Since this short play is quoted very often and is reprinted here (in a freshly edited version) as Appendix A, I have omitted all subsequent page references to it. All quotations follow the version reprinted here, except when specified.

8. Victor Hugo, *Victor Hugo's Intellectual Autobiography (Postscriptum de Ma Vie),* trans. Lorenzo O'Rourke (New York: Funk and Wagnalls, 1907), p. 370.

9. Émile Zola, "The Novel," in *The Experimental Novel and Other Essays,* trans. Belle M. Sherman (New York: Haskell House, 1964), p. 212.

10. Walter Benjamin, "Theses on the Philosophy of History," in *Illuminations,* ed. Hannah Arendt, trans. Harry Zohn (New York: Schocken, 1969), p. 255.

11. Ibid.

I. "HAPPY THE PLAY . . ."

1. *Black and White,* I (21 March 1891), pp. 214–17; *Harper's Weekly,* 35 (21 March 1891), pp. 205–7; Arthur Conan Doyle, *Memories and Adventures* (Boston: Little, Brown, 1924), p. 113.

2. Quoted in Laurence Irving, *Henry Irving: The Actor and His World* (New York: Macmillan, 1952), p. 580.

3. Stoker, *Personal Reminiscences,* I, 264.

4. Ibid., pp. 247–48.

5. Ibid., p. 251.

6. Ibid., p. 249.

7. Doyle, *Memories*, p. 113.

8. Quoted in Hesketh Pearson, *Conan Doyle* (1943; reprint, London: White Lion, 1974), p. 146.

9. Walter Herries Pollock, *Impressions of Henry Irving* (1908; reprint, New York: Blom, 1971), p. 94–95.

10. Rev. of *A Story of Waterloo*, *Umpire* [Manchester], 9 Dec. 1894, p. 5.

11. Rev. of *A Story of Waterloo*, *North British Daily Mail* [Glasgow], 12 Nov. 1894, p. 5.

12. Rev. of *A Story of Waterloo*, *Western Daily Press*, 22 Sept. 1894, p. 5.

13. Rev. of *A Story of Waterloo*, *Daily News* [London], 22 Sept. 1894, p. 7.

14. Rev. of *A Story of Waterloo*, *Glasgow Evening News*, 12 Nov. 1894, p. 3.

15. Victor Hugo, *Les Misérables*, trans. Lascelles Wraxall (New York: Heritage, 1938), II, bk. 1, chap. 2 (p. 4). I have used many sources for information on the battle of Waterloo. A discussion of those sources will be found in chapter V.

16. Frederick Harrison, quoted in Walter E. Houghton, *The Victorian Frame of Mind, 1830–1870* (New Haven: Yale University Press, 1957), p. 309.

17. Rev. of *A Story of Waterloo*, *North British Daily Mail* [Glasgow], 12 Nov. 1894, p. 5.

18. George Arthur, *From Phelps to Gielgud* (London: Chapman and Hall, 1936), p. 81.

19. Unidentified rev. of *A Story of Waterloo* [May 1895], a scrapbook clipping in the Percy Fitzgerald Collection of material relating to Irving, Library of the Garrick Club, London, XV, p. 54.

20. Arthur, *From Phelps to Gielgud*, p. 80.

21. Alfred Darbyshire, *The Art of the Victorian Stage* (1907; reprint, New York: Blom, 1969), p. 107.

22. Alfred Ayres, *Acting and Actors, Elocution and Elocutionists* (New York: Appleton, 1894), p. 27.

23. William Archer and Robert Lowe, *The Fashionable Tragedian* (Edinburgh: Gray, 1878), p. 3.

24. William Archer, *Henry Irving, Actor and Manager* (1884; reprint, St. Clair Shores, Mich.: Scholarly Press, 1970), pp. 92, 107.

25. Quoted in Irving, preface to Denis Diderot, *The Paradox of Acting*, trans. Walter Herries Pollock [1883], published in one volume with William Archer, *Masks or Faces* [1888] (New York: Hill and Wang, 1957), p. 8.

26. Irving, preface to Diderot, *Paradox*, p. 10.

27. Quoted in Irving, preface to Diderot, *Paradox*, p. 8.

28. Max Nordau, *Paradoxes*, trans. J. R. McIlraith (London: Heinemann, 1896), p. 159.

29. Shaw, *Collected Letters, 1874–1897*, ed. Dan H. Laurence (New York: Dodd, Mead, 1965), p. 645. Hereafter referred to as *CL 1874–1897*.

30. Austin Brereton, "Mr. Henry Irving in a New Play," *The Theatre*, 1 Oct. 1894, pp. 180–81.

31. Shaw, preface to *Plays: Pleasant and Unpleasant: The Second Volume, Containing the Four Pleasant Plays* (New York: Dodd, Mead, 1940), p. xix.

32. Bernard Shaw, *Selected Non-Dramatic Writings of Bernard Shaw,* ed. Dan H. Laurence (Boston: Houghton Mifflin, 1965), p. 338.

33. Ibid., p. 324.

34. Shaw, *Sixteen Self Sketches* (London: Constable, 1949), p. 41; quoted in Michael Holroyd, *Bernard Shaw: The Search for Love, 1856–1898* (New York: Random House, 1988), p. 406.

35. See Hugh Kingsmill, *Frank Harris: A Biography* (New York: Farrar and Rinehart, 1932), p. 107.

36. Quoted in Samuel Roth, *The Private Life of Frank Harris* (New York: William Faro, 1931), p. 156.

37. Shaw, *Our Theatres,* I, 139; for an interesting challenge to Shaw's criticism, especially his *Waterloo* review, see "To George Bernard Shaw, Esq.," anonymous open letter, *The Theatre,* 1 July 1897, pp. 8–10.

38. Frank Harris, *My Life and Loves,* ed. John F. Gallagher (New York: Grove Press, 1963), p. 769.

39. Rev. of *A Story of Waterloo, Saturday Review,* 78, no. 2043 (22 Dec. 1894), pp. 679–80.

40. Quoted in Robert Brainard Pearsall, *Frank Harris* (New York: Twayne, 1970), p. 160.

41. William Archer, "Some Recent Plays," *Fortnightly Review,* n.s., 55, no. 329 (1 May 1894), p. 602. Frank Harris later recalled Archer asserting, in suspiciously similar terms, that Shaw as a dramatic critic "was a paralyzing and sterilizing force," even though Shaw had, as yet, not begun reviewing plays; see *Bernard Shaw* (New York: Simon and Schuster, 1931), p. 123.

42. Quoted in Shaw, *The Quintessence of Ibsenism,* in *Selected Non-Dramatic Writings,* p. 210.

43. Archer, "Some Recent Plays," p. 604.

44. Ibid., p. 611.

45. Ibid., p. 605.

46. Ibid., pp. 602, 612.

47. William Archer, rev. of *A Story of Waterloo, The Theatrical "World" of 1894* (London: Walter Scott, 1895), p. 344.

48. William Archer, rev. of *A Story of Waterloo, The Theatrical "World" of 1895* (London: Walter Scott, 1896), pp. 142–43.

49. Quoted in Shaw, *CL 1874–1897,* p. 428.

50. Shaw, *CL 1874–1897,* p. 429.

51. Archer, "Some Recent Plays," p. 602.

52. See Shaw, "How William Archer Impressed Bernard Shaw," *Pen Portraits and Reviews* (London: Constable, 1932), pp. 24–25.

53. Shaw, preface to *Pleasant Plays,* p. xix.

54. Shaw, "Speech as Guest of Honor at London Critics Circle Annual Luncheon, October 11, 1929," in *Shaw on Theatre,* ed. E. J. West (New York: Hill and Wang, 1958), p. 199.

55. Shaw, preface to *Our Theatres in the Nineties,* I, v.

56. Bernard Shaw, 7 Mar. 1890, *London Music in 1888–1889 as Heard by Corno di Bassetto* (London: Constable, 1937), p. 323. This and other reprints of

Shaw's review contain what seems to be a typographical error, giving "scribes" for "Scribes." I have not been able to check the text of the review in *The Star,* where it was initially published, but I have here corrected the error, since "scribes," while possible as a reading (playing on "scribes and Pharisees"), sounds unlikely.

57. Laurence Irving, *The Precarious Crust* (London: Chatto and Windus, 1971), p. 247.

58. Edward Gordon Craig, *Henry Irving* (1930; reprint, New York: Blom, 1969), pp. 17–18.

59. Shaw, "On Gordon Craig's *Henry Irving,*" in *Shaw on Theatre,* p. 203.

60. E. Gordon Craig, *The Theatre Advancing* (1947; reprint, New York: Blom, 1963), p. lxxv.

II. HEART OF THE CROWD I

1. St. John Ervine, *The Theatre in My Time* (London: Rich and Cowan, 1933), p. 94.

2. William Winter, *The Wallet of Time,* (New York: Moffat, Yard, 1913), I, 33.

3. Stoker, *Personal Reminiscences,* I, viii.

4. Rev. of *A Story of Waterloo, Bristol Mercury,* 22 Sept. 1894, p. 5; rev. of *A Story of Waterloo, Evening Times* [Glasgow], 12 Nov. 1894, p. 5.

5. Christopher St. John, *Henry Irving* (London: Green Sheaf, 1905), n. pag.

6. John Ruskin, "Of the Pathetic Fallacy," in *Modern Painters,* vol. V of *The Works of John Ruskin,* ed. E. T. Cook and Alexander Wedderburn (London: George Allen, 1904), pp. 208–9.

7. *New York Dramatic Mirror,* quoted in Benjamin McArthur, *Actors and American Culture, 1880–1920* (Philadelphia: Temple University Press, 1984), p. 186.

8. Stoker, *Personal Reminiscences,* I, 73–74.

9. Charles Hiatt, *Henry Irving: A Record and Review* (London: George Bell, 1899), p. 266.

10. Sir John Martin-Harvey, *The Autobiography of Sir John Martin-Harvey* (London: Sampson Low, Marston, n.d.), p. 337.

11. In H. A. Saintsbury and Cecil Palmer, *We Saw Him Act* (1939; reprint, New York: Blom, 1969), p. 336.

12. See Alan Hughes, *Henry Irving, Shakespearean* (Cambridge: Cambridge University Press, 1981), pp. 18, 269. The first figure represents Hughes's estimate; the other two figures are given without source. Hughes provides much worthy information on the Lyceum Theatre and company, as well as an engaging discussion of Irving's Shakespearean productions.

13. Stoker, *Personal Reminiscences,* II, 311.

14. Brereton, *Henry Irving,* II, 232.

15. William Archer, "A Plea for the Queue," *Dramatic Review,* 1, no. 12 (25 Apr. 1885), p. 196.

16. Brereton, *Henry Irving,* II, 73.

17. Quoted in Brereton, *Henry Irving*, II, 75–76.

18. Quoted in Laurence Irving, *Henry Irving*, p. 421.

19. Quoted in Brereton, *Henry Irving*, II, 232.

20. Quoted in Hesketh Pearson, *G. B. S.: A Full Length Portrait* (New York: Harper, 1942), p. 138.

21. Stoker, *Personal Reminiscences*, I, 251.

22. Rev. of *Becket* by Alfred Tennyson, *Daily Graphic* [London], 1 May 1905, p. 4.

23. Henry Irving, letters to Clement Scott, 20 Oct. 1880, 21 Sept. 1880, 26 Nov. 1881, and 21 [?] Sept. 1888, Clement Scott Collection, The Huntington Library, San Marino, California.

24. Laurence Irving, *Henry Irving*, pp. 350–51.

25. Quoted in Laurence Irving, *Henry Irving*, p. 507. Scott's letter to Irving concerning this matter can be found in the Bram Stoker Collection, the Shakespeare Centre Library, Stratford-upon-Avon.

26. Craig, *Henry Irving*, p. 23.

27. Quoted in C. Archer, *William Archer: Life, Work, and Friendships* (London: Allen and Unwin, 1931), pp. 219–20.

28. Shaw, *Our Theatres*, II, 139–140.

29. Ibid., p. 144.

30. Edward Gordon Craig, "A Note on Applause," in *The Theatre—Advancing* (Boston: Little, Brown, 1928), pp. 285–86.

31. Quoted in Laurence Irving, *Henry Irving*, p. 392.

32. Stoker, *Personal Reminiscences*, I, 74.

33. Craig, *Henry Irving*, p. 54.

34. A. B. Walkley, *More Prejudice* (London: Heinemann, 1923), pp. 78–79.

35. See "To the Audience at the Kingsway Theatre: A Personal Appeal from the Author of John Bull's Other Island," a four-page program insert, [ca. Jan.] 1913. An example is in the Geraldine Womack and Norman D. Philbrick Library of Dramatic Literature and Theatre History, Honnold Library, Claremont, California, hereafter referred to as the Philbrick Collection. See also Shaw, *Our Theatres*, I, 98.

36. Shaw, *Our Theatres*, I, 115.

37. George Gordon Byron, *Childe Harold's Pilgrimage* (canto III, stanza CXIII) in *Lord Byron: The Complete Poetical Works*, ed. Jerome J. McGann (Oxford: Oxford University Press, 1980), II, 118.

38. Shaw, *CL 1874–1897*, p. 763, 722.

39. Quoted in Archibald Henderson, *Table-Talk of G. B. S.* (1925; reprint, New York: Haskell House, 1974), p. 68.

40. Ruskin, *Works*, V, 208.

41. A. E. Wilson, *Edwardian Theatre* (London: Barker, 1951), p. 55.

42. Ruskin, *Works*, V, 209.

43. Craig, *Henry Irving*, pp. 80–81.

III. HEART OF THE CROWD II

1. William Archer, *Henry Irving*, p. 42.

2. Robert A. Nye, *The Origins of Crowd Psychology: Gustave Le Bon and the Crisis of Mass Democracy in the Third Republic*, SAGE Studies in 20th Century History, vol. II (London: SAGE Publications, 1975), p. 3.

3. Th[éodule] Ribot, *The Psychology of the Emotions* (London: Walter Scott, 1900), p. 295.

4. Gustave Le Bon, *The Crowd: A Study of the Popular Mind* (London: Unwin, 1903), pp. 5, 16.

5. F. Bartlett, quoted in Serge Moscovici, *The Age of the Crowd*, trans. J. C. Whitehouse (Cambridge: Cambridge University Press, 1985), pp. 13–14.

6. Le Bon, *Crowd*, pp. 33, 19.

7. Ibid., pp. 56, 58.

8. Guy de Maupassant, *Sur l'Eau and Other Tales*, vol. IV of *A Selection from the Writings of Guy de Maupassant* (New York: Review of Reviews, 1903), pp. 77–78, 75.

9. Rev. of *The Crowd* by Gustave Le Bon, *Athenaeum*, no. 3587 (25 July 1896), p. 124.

10. Le Bon, *Crowd*, pp. 36, 135, 134, 148.

11. Stoker, *Personal Reminiscences*, I, 259.

12. Moscovici, *Age of the Crowd*, p. 134.

13. Sigmund Freud, *Group Psychology and the Analysis of the Ego*, trans. and ed. James Strachey (New York: Norton, 1959), p. 59.

14. Le Bon, *Crowd*, p. 40.

15. Craig, *Henry Irving*, pp. 108–110.

16. Everett Dean Martin, *The Behavior of Crowds* (New York: Norton, 1920), p. 82.

17. Le Bon, *Crowd*, pp. 62–63.

18. Hiatt, *Henry Irving*, p. 262.

19. Quoted in Hiatt, *Henry Irving*, p. 262; compare a very different version of the same quotation in Laurence Irving, *Henry Irving*, p. 372.

20. Tighe Hopkins, quoted in Hiatt, *Henry Irving*, p. 263.

21. Elias Canetti, *Crowds and Power*, trans. Carol Stewart (New York: Viking, 1963), pp. 171–72.

22. Stoker, *Personal Reminiscences*, II, 155–56.

23. Le Bon, *Crowd*, pp. 36, 37–38.

24. George Henry Lewes, "Edmund Kean," in *On Actors and the Art of Acting* (Leipzig: Bernhard Tauchnitz, 1875), pp. 14–15.

IV. "A STUDY OF THE HOMELIEST REALISM"

1. Martin Meisel, *Realizations* (Princeton, N.J.: Princeton University Press, 1983), p. 404.

2. Shaw, *Our Theatres*, III, 70, 75.

3. Shaw, *CL 1874–1897*, p. 734.

4. Shaw, preface to Christopher St. John, ed., *Ellen Terry and Bernard Shaw: A Correspondence* (New York: Putnam's, 1932), p. xxv. Hereafter abbreviated as St. John, ed., *A Corr.*

5. Shaw, *Our Theatres*, III, 73, 70.

6. Shaw, preface to St. John, ed., *A Corr.* p. xx.

7. Shaw, *Our Theatres*, I, 16, 14–15.

8. Ibid., III, 74–75, 73.

9. Pollock, *Impressions*, p. 94.

10. L. F. Austin, *Points of View*, ed. Clarence Rook (London: Lane, 1906), pp. 13, 16.

11. Quoted in Meisel, *Realizations*, pp. 426, 426n.

12. Quoted in Laurence Irving, *Henry Irving*, p. 296.

13. Arthur Symons, "Sir Henry Irving," in *Plays, Acting, and Music* (New York: Dutton, 1909), pp. 54–55.

14. Clement Scott, *The Drama of Yesterday & Today* (London: Macmillan, 1899), II, 70.

15. Shaw, preface to St. John, ed., *A Corr.*, p. xxii.

16. Rev. of *A Story of Waterloo*, "Our Cantankerous Critic," *Quiz*, 15 Nov. 1894, p. 19.

17. See Meisel, "Pre-Raphaelite Drama," in *Realizations*, pp. 351–72.

18. Quoted in Meisel, *Realizations*, p. 351.

19. Meisel, *Realizations*, p. 50.

20. Quoted in "In the Provinces," *The Theatre*, 1 Nov. 1894, p. 261.

21. John Ranken Towse, *Sixty Years of the Theater* (New York: Funk and Wagnalls, 1916), pp. 307, 309.

22. Meisel, *Realizations*, p. 397. Ironically, Herkomer's later experiments in theatre were to influence Craig's ideas of a new theatre. See Edward Anthony Craig, "Gordon Craig and Hubert von Herkomer," *Theatre Research*, 10, no. 1 (1969), pp. 7–16.

23. [Clement Scott], "Mr. Irving in a New Play," rev. of *A Story of Waterloo*, *Daily Telegraph* [London], 22 Sept. 1894, p. 5.

24. Quoted in Meisel, *Realizations*, p. 400.

25. [Scott], "Mr. Irving in a New Play," p. 5.

26. Doyle, *Memories*, p. 23.

27. Zola, *The Experimental Novel*, pp. 118, 152.

28. Constant Coquelin, "Actors and Acting," in Brander Matthews, ed., *Papers on Acting* (New York: Hill and Wang, 1958), pp. 176–77.

29. Ruskin, *Modern Painters*, III, 57.

30. Henry Irving, *The Drama: Addresses* (1893; reprint, New York: Blom, 1969), pp. 163–64.

31. Rev. of *A Story of Waterloo*, *Boston Transcript*, 4 Oct. 1895.

32. Rev. of *A Story of Waterloo*, unidentified Boston newspaper, [1896], Harvard Theatre Collection clipping file, Cambridge, Mass.

33. Shaw, preface to St. John, ed., *A Corr.*, p. xxvi.

34. See Stoker, *Personal Reminiscences*, II, 86–88.

35. Fig. 5 should be compared with a signed drawing by Bernard Partridge, reprinted in Saintsbury and Palmer, eds. *We Saw Him Act,* opposite p. 334. Balliol Salmon's drawing appeared in the *Illustrated Sporting and Dramatic News* and is reproduced in J. B. Booth, *London Town* (London: T. Werner Laurie, 1929), p. 43. Other notable pictures of *Waterloo* include a drawing of a performance at Sandringham, *Shurey's Illustrated,* 22 Nov. 1902, p. 17; sketches by A. S. Boyd, *Daily Graphic* [London], 19, no. 1478 (24 Sept. 1894), p. 1; sketches by Sherie (?), *The Gentlewoman,* 29 Sept. 1894, p. 403; sketches by Forrest, *To-Day,* 26 Mar. 1898, pp. 244–45.

36. Quoted in Brereton, *Henry Irving,* II, 216.

37. Quoted in Tom Heslewood, "Relics and Memories of Irving," *Birmingham Post,* 11 Feb. 1938, p. 1.

38. Darbyshire, *Art of the Victorian Stage,* p. 107.

39. Quoted in William Winter, *Vagrant Memories* (New York: Doran, 1915), p. 291.

V. HISTORIES OF WATERLOO I

1. H. T. Siborne, ed., *Waterloo Letters* (London: Cassell, 1891), pp. 19–20.

2. A. Conan Doyle, *The Great Shadow* (New York: Harper, 1893), pp. 1, 169.

3. Hesketh Pearson, *Conan Doyle,* p. 145. Pearson's biography is marred by numerous errors of fact and exaggeration (Doyle's son called it a "fakeography"), but he writes his story with personal feeling and telling phrases. His argument that Doyle should be regarded as "the man on the street" was very controversial, but I think that viewpoint is useful for understanding the early writings. I have tried to avoid Pearson's inaccuracies in my use of his book. See John Dickson Carr, *The Life of Sir Arthur Conan Doyle* (New York: Harper, 1949) for a more reliable biography, though something of a whitewash. For a fascinating discussion of the variety of biographies of Doyle, see Jon L. Lellenberg, ed., *The Quest for Sir Arthur Conan Doyle: Thirteen Biographers in Search of a Life* (Carbondale, Ill.: Southern Illinois University Press, 1987).

4. Doyle, *Great Shadow,* pp. 173–74.

5. Edward Bruce Low, *With Napoleon at Waterloo,* ed. Mackenzie MacBride (Philadelphia: Lippincott, 1911), pp. 123, 130.

6. *Les Misérables,* quoted in Low, *With Napoleon,* p. 123.

7. Doyle, *Great Shadow,* p. 4.

8. Alfred Tennyson, "Ode on the Death of the Duke of Wellington" (1852), *The Poems of Tennyson,* ed. Christopher Ricks, 2nd ed. (Berkeley and Los Angeles: University of California Press, 1987), II, 483.

9. Quoted in Carr, *Doyle,* p. 99.

10. Sir Arthur Conan Doyle, *Adventures of Gerard* (London: John Murray and Jonathan Cape, 1976), p. 191.

11. Doyle, *Adventures,* pp. 177, 190–91.

12. Doyle, *Memories,* p. 115.

13. Pearson, *Doyle,* p. 113.

14. Quoted in "About 'A Story of Waterloo,'" unidentified clipping from Boston newspaper, dated 14 Sept. 1897, Harvard Theatre Collection clipping file.

15. Louis Moreau Gottschalk, *Notes of a Pianist,* ed. Jeanne Behrend (1881; reprint New York: Knopf, 1964), p. 87.

16. [Dion Boucicault], *The Old Guard* (New York: Samuel French, n.d.), p. 20.

17. Benjamin, *Illuminations,* pp. 96–98, 88–89.

18. Doyle, *Great Shadow,* p. 170.

19. Benjamin, *Illuminations,* p. 90.

20. Walter Benjamin, *Charles Baudelaire: A Lyric Poet in the Era of High Capitalism,* trans. Harry Zohn (London: New Left Books, 1973), p. 62.

21. Here I have quoted the Samuel French edition of Doyle, *Waterloo,* p. 15.

22. Benjamin, *Illuminations,* p. 94.

23. Benjamin, *Illuminations,* p. 100.

24. Benjamin, *Illuminations,* p. 101.

25. Percy Fitzgerald, *Sir Henry Irving* (Philadelphia: Jacobs, [1906], p. 237.

26. See Richard D. Altick, *The Shows of London* (Cambridge, Mass.: Harvard University Press, 1978), pp. 207, 479.

27. Altick, *Shows,* pp. 240–41.

28. Charles Higham, *The Adventures of Conan Doyle* (New York: Norton, 1976), p. 127.

29. Quoted in Altick, *Shows,* p. 396.

30. Quoted in John Keegan, *The Face of Battle* (New York: Penguin, 1983), p. 117.

31. Quoted in Altick, *Shows,* p. 396.

32. Quoted in Carr, *Doyle,* p. 14.

33. David Howarth, *Waterloo: Day of Battle* (New York: Atheneum, 1968), pp. vii–viii.

34. William Napier, quoted in Keegan, *Face of Battle,* p. 39.

35. Byron, *Childe Harold's Pilgrimage,* II (canto III, stanzas 31, 35, 32–33), pp. 87–89.

36. "Readings and Recitals by Henry Irving and H. J. Montague," theatrical program, Westbourne Hall, 23 Oct. 1869; a copy of this is in the Clement Scott Collection at the Huntington Library, San Marino, California.

37. Howarth, *Waterloo,* p. vii.

38. Capt. W. Siborne, *History of the War in France and Belgium, in 1815* (London: Boone, 1844), II, 118–19.

39. Ibid., II, 47, 52.

40. Ibid., II, 48.

41. Quoted in Altick, *Shows,* p. 176.

42. Altick, *Shows,* p. 479.

43. Henry Irving [John Henry Brodribb], Letter to Mrs. Wilkins, Nov. 1852, Philbrick Collection, Honnold Library, Claremont, California.

44. See Altick, *Shows,* pp. 479–80.

45. *Athenaeum,* 26 Feb. 1853, quoted in Altick, *Shows,* p. 196n.

46. Keegan, *Face of Battle,* p. 39. Keegan's writings on military history have

been of great importance in formulating the ideas in this chapter, and this book, in particular, has been important because of its fine discussion of the battle of Waterloo.

47. Howarth, *Waterloo,* p. vi.

48. Erckmann-Chatrian [Émile Erckmann and Alexandre Chatrian], *Waterloo: A Sequel to "The Conscript of 1813"* (New York: Scribner's 1903), pp. 265, 267. The same pair wrote *Le Juif Polonais,* which Leopold Lewis adapted for Henry Irving as *The Bells.*

49. Eugène Pellissier, introduction to Erckmann-Chatrian, *Waterloo* (London: Macmillan, 1924), p. xiv.

50. Erckmann-Chatrian, *Waterloo,* pp. 340, 342.

51. Hugo, *Les Misérables,* V, bk. 1, chap. 20 (p. 70). I have slightly altered the translation here.

52. Victor Brombert, *"Les Misérables:* Salvation from Below," in *Modern Critical Views: Victor Hugo,* ed. Harold Bloom (New York: Chelsea House, 1988), p. 196.

53. Hugo, *Les Misérables,* V, bk. 1, chap. 20 (p. 70).

54. Brombert, *"Les Misérables,"* p. 212.

VI. HISTORIES OF WATERLOO II

1. "The Theatres of Varieties: Gossiping and Critical Notes," *Dramatic Review,* 17, no. 499 (24 Feb. 1894), p. 124.

2. "The Theatres of Varieties: Gossiping and Critical Notes," *Dramatic Review,* 17, no. 502 (17 Mar. 1894), p. 172.

3. Craig, marginal annotations in Craig's personal copy of Brereton, *Henry Irving,* II, 216, Philbrick Collection, Honnold Library, Claremont, California.

4. Rev. of *A Story of Waterloo, Times* [London], 22 Sept. 1894, p. 6.

5. Jan. 1881, p. 46, quoted in "Jingo" (3), *Compact Edition of the Oxford English Dictionary* (Oxford: Oxford University Press, 1971), p. 1510.

6. Rev. of *A Story of Waterloo, Bristol Mercury,* 22 Sept. 1894, p. 5.

7. Rev. of *A Story of Waterloo, Bristol Times and Mirror,* 22 Sept. 1894, p. 8.

8. Rev. of *A Story of Waterloo,* unidentified clipping in the Percy Fitzgerald Collection, Library of the Garrick Club, London, XIV, 63.

9. Unidentified clipping and unsigned manuscript of Irving's reply, 20 June 1900, in the Bram Stoker Collection, Shakespeare Centre, Stratford-upon-Avon (reel 6, item 246 of microfilm edition).

10. "Theatre Gossip," *The Sketch,* 30, no. 388 (4 July 1900), p. 498.

11. Laurence Irving, *Henry Irving,* p. 607; rev. of *A Story of Waterloo, Stage,* no. 850 (1 July 1897), p. 12.

12. "Some Memories [of Henry Irving]: By London Playgoers," *Pall Mall Gazette,* 14 Oct. 1905, p. 7.

13. Rev. of *A Story of Waterloo, Stage,* no. 850 (1 July 1897), p. 12.

14. "Some Memories," *Pall Mall Gazette,* 14 Oct. 1905, p. 7.

15. Stoker, *Personal Reminiscences,* I, 252.

16. Stephen Coleridge, quoted in Laurence Irving, *Henry Irving,* p. 410.

17. Cartoon by Alfred Bryan, unidentified clipping in the Harvard Theatre Collection clipping file.

18. Quoted in Laurence Irving, *Henry Irving,* p. 573.

19. Stoker, *Personal Reminiscences,* II, 242.

20. Shaw, *Our Theatres,* I, 30–36.

21. Stoker, *Personal Reminiscences,* II, 242.

22. St. John, ed., *A Corr.,* p. 123.

23. Laurence Irving, *Henry Irving,* p. 363.

24. Stoker, *Personal Reminiscences,* II, 37.

25. Edward Gordon Craig, "Extracts from a Diary," booklet in *Edward Gordon Craig: Radio Talks* (London: Discurio, 1962), n. pag.

26. Craig, *Henry Irving,* p. 84.

27. Stoker, *Personal Reminiscences,* II, 27; Craig, *Henry Irving,* p. 84.

28. Reproduced in George Rowell, *Theatre in the Age of Irving* (Oxford: Blackwell, 1981), p. 45.

29. Stoker, *Personal Reminiscences,* II, 27, 35.

30. See Mrs. Clement Scott, *Old Days in Bohemian London: Recollections of Clement Scott* (New York: Stokes, n.d.), pp. 119–21.

31. George Macaulay Trevelyan, *History of England* (London: Longmans, Green, 1937), p. 689.

32. Quoted in Craig, *On the Art of the Theatre* (1911; reprint New York: Theatre Arts, 1956), p. 80.

33. Craig, *On the Art,* p. 81.

34. Edward Gordon Craig, *Towards a New Theatre* (London: Dent, 1913), pp. 89–90.

35. Craig, *The Theatre—Advancing,* p. 211.

36. Craig, *Henry Irving,* p. 97n.

37. Quoted in J. Christopher Herold, *The Age of Napoleon* (New York: American Heritage, 1963), p. 35.

38. Terry, *Story,* p. 94.

39. Craig, *Henry Irving,* pp. 97–98n.

40. Preface, St. John, ed., *A Corr.,* p. xx; Shaw, *CL 1874–1897,* p. 609.

41. Pearson, *G. B. S.,* p. 134.

42. Laurence Irving, *Henry Irving,* p. 572.

43. Craig, marginal annotations in Craig's personal copy of Laurence Irving, *Henry Irving,* p. 572, Philbrick Collection, Honnold Library, Claremont, California.

44. Hugo, *Les Misérables,* II, bk. 1, chap. 13 (p. 39).

45. Albert Leon Guérard, *Reflections on the Napoleonic Legend* (New York: Scribner's, 1924), p. 122.

46. Henry Irving, preface to Diderot, *The Paradox of Acting,* p. 6.

47. Craig, *Henry Irving,* p. 108.

48. Hugo, *Les Misérables,* II, bk. 1, chap. 9 (p. 29).

VII. MEN OF DESTINY

1. Bernard Shaw, *The Diaries, 1885–1897*, ed. Stanley Weintraub (University Park, Pa.: Pennsylvania State University Press, 1986), II, 1079.

2. Shaw, *CL 1874–1897*, p. 539. Stanley Weintraub corrects Dan H. Laurence's date on this letter (Shaw, *Diaries*, II, 1088).

3. Shaw, *Diaries*, II, 1079.

4. Shaw, *CL 1874–1897*, p. 572.

5. Laurence Irving, *Henry Irving*, p. 581.

6. Shaw, *Our Theatres*, I, 177.

7. Ibid., p. 133.

8. Craig, *Henry Irving*, p. 149.

9. Quoted in Martin Meisel, *Shaw and the Nineteenth-Century Theater* (Princeton, N.J.: Princeton University Press, 1963), p. 356n.

10. Shaw, *CL 1874–1897*, p. 545.

11. Quoted in Shaw, *CL 1874–1897*, pp. 523–24.

12. Shaw, *CL 1874–1897*, pp. 547, 553.

13. Shaw, *Collected Letters, 1898–1910*, ed. Dan H. Laurence (New York: Dodd, Mead, 1972), p. 34. Hereafter referred to as *CL 1898–1910*.

14. Shaw, *CL 1874–1897*, p. 553.

15. Ibid., pp. 572, 609–10.

16. Shaw, preface to *Plays Pleasant*, p. v.

17. Shaw, *CL 1874–1897*, p. 616.

18. A number of commentators on this play have fallen into the error of assuming that Shaw based the character on Terry, whereas in fact he explicitly denies this in his letters to Achurch and to Archer, quoted above. The source of the error seems to be a mistranslation, quoted by Henderson, of Shaw's statement that he had "tried to tempt [Terry] by writing into my play . . . a description of the heroine which is simply a description of Ellen Terry" (Shaw, *Pen Portraits and Reviews*, p. 170). The mistranslation stated that "the heroine is simply a delineation of Ellen Terry" (Archibald Henderson, *George Bernard Shaw: His Life and Works* [Cincinnati: Stewart and Kidd, 1911], p. 343). Charles A. Berst, in his recent article on the play, presents a good analysis of this and other biographical misconceptions about the play, along with a thorough analysis of the play itself. He discounts the importance for theatre history of this play's emergence, preferring to address its theme: "Viewed either broadly or closely, the play's action, wit, and characters all evolve through multiple modes of role-playing, including pretense, deception, posing, attitudinizing, games, bluffing, trickery, one-upping, masking and unmasking. Theatricality prevails, defining both the hero and the heroine and, perhaps even more important, the interaction of these two in turn defines theatricality as a social factor" (Charles A. Berst, *"The Man of Destiny:* Shaw, Napoleon, and the Theater of Life," in *Shaw: The Neglected Plays,* ed. Alfred Turco, Jr. [University Park, Pa.: Pennsylvania State University Press, 1986], p. 87).

19. Quoted in Holroyd, *Bernard Shaw: The Quest for Love*, p. 349, with opening phrases supplied from Shaw, *CL 1874–1897*, p. 803.

20. Shaw, *CL 1874–1897*, p. 644.

21. Shaw, *Man of Destiny*, in *Plays Pleasant*, pp. 210, 213, 215.

22. See Berst, pp. 110–116.

23. Shaw, *CL 1874–1897*, p. 552.

24. [Clarence Rook], "Mr. Shaw's Future. A Conversation," *The Academy*, 30 Apr. 1898, p. 476, quoted in J. L. Wisenthal, *Shaw's Sense of History* (Oxford: Clarendon, 1988), p. 50.

25. Shaw, *CL 1874–1897*, pp. 644, 634.

26. Ellen Terry, Letter to Mrs. Huddart, 15 Sept. 1895, Collection of Val Daley, Agua Dulce, California.

27. Gordon Craig, "Irving Seemingly Perplexed," *The Drama*, n.s., 43 (Winter 1956), p. 26.

28. Shaw, *CL 1874–1897*, pp. 634–35.

29. Shaw, *Man of Destiny*, in *Plays Pleasant*, p. 179.

30. St. John, ed., *A Corr.*, p. 35.

31. Shaw, *CL 1874–1897*, p. 650.

32. Shaw, preface to St. John, ed., *A Corr.*, p. xxii.

33. Shaw, *Our Theatres*, II, 126–28.

34. Craig, *Henry Irving*, pp. 151, 152, 153, 158.

35. Shaw, "On Gordon Craig's *Henry Irving*," in *Shaw on Theatre*, ed E. J. West (New York: Hill and Wang, 1958), p. 202.

36. Shaw, "How to Make Plays Readable," in *Shaw on Theatre*, p. 95.

37. Shaw, *Diaries*, II, 1023.

38. Meisel, *Realizations*, p. 221; the whole chapter, entitled "Napoleon; Or, History as Spectacle," is of interest.

39. Shaw, *Man of Destiny*, in *Plays Pleasant*, p. 164.

40. Laurence Irving, *Henry Irving*, p. 214.

41. Shaw, *Man of Destiny*, in *Plays Pleasant*, p. 164.

42. Craig, marginal annotations in Craig's personal copy of Laurence Irving, *Henry Irving*, Philbrick Collection, Honnold Library, Claremont, California.

43. Shaw, "How to Become a Man of Genius," in *Selected Non-Dramatic Writings*, p. 343.

44. Shaw, preface to *Plays Pleasant*, p. xii.

45. Shaw, *Man of Destiny*, in *Plays Pleasant*, p. 213.

46. H. A. Saintsbury, "Irving as Stage Manager," in Saintsbury and Palmer, eds., *We Saw Him Act*, p. 402.

47. Terry, *Memoirs*, p. 131.

48. Stoker, *Personal Reminiscences*, I, 261.

49. Victorien Sardou, *Madame Sans-Gêne*, adapt. J. Comyns Carr (privately printed edition), pp. 25, 53, 69, Philbrick Collection, Honnold Library, Claremont, California.

50. William Archer, rev. of *Madame Sans-Gêne* by Victorien Sardou, *The Theatrical "World" of 1897* (London: Walter Scott, 1898), p. 107.

51. See Henry Irving, Letter to George Bernard Shaw, 15 June 1896 (50538, f. 218), British Library, London.

52. Doyle, *Memories*, pp. 113–14.

53. Voucher list, [ca. 1902–3], box 3, folder 1, D. 181, Irving-Disher Collection, Rush Rhees Library, Rochester, New York; Doyle, *Memories*, p. 113.

54. Quoted in Pearson, *G. B. S.*, p. 138.

55. See Laurence Irving, letter to George Bernard Shaw, incomplete ms., [Dec. 1946] (50538, f. 215), British Library, London.

56. Quoted in Pearson, *G. B. S.*, pp. 137–38.

57. Shaw, *Our Theatres*, II, 198.

58. Shaw, *CL 1874–1897*, pp. 672, 701.

59. Ibid., p. 742.

60. St. John, ed., *A Corr.*, p. 127.

61. Shaw, *CL 1874–1897*, p. 742.

62. Ibid., p. 742.

63. Shaw, *Our Theatres*, III, 110.

64. Shaw, *CL 1874–1897*, p. 650.

65. Ellen Terry, *The Story of My Life* (1908; reprint New York: Schocken, 1982) p. 204. This passage does not appear in the 1932 edition of the memoirs.

66. Shaw, *Our Theatres*, III, 39.

67. Shaw, letter to Ellen Terry, 31 Jan. 1897, from transcript in the Philbrick Collection, Honnold Library, Claremont, California. This unpublished letter is said to remain with the Philbrick family.

68. Quoted in Laurence Irving, *Henry Irving*, p. 604.

69. Shaw, *CL 1874–1897*, p. 747.

70. St. John, ed., *A Corr.*, pp. 140, 139, 142.

71. "Theatrical Gossip," *Era*, 8 May 1897, p. 12.

72. Quoted in Shaw, *CL 1874–1897*, p. 753.

73. Henry Irving, letter to George Bernard Shaw, 8 May 1897 (43801, f. 91), British Library, London. This letter is probably misdated and should be 10 May 1897.

74. St. John, ed., *A Corr.*, pp. 147, 146.

75. Shaw, *CL 1874–1897*, p. 755.

76. Pearson, *G. B. S.*, p. 140.

77. Bernard Shaw, *Advice to a Young Critic*, ed. E. J. West (1955; reprint New York: Capricorn, 1963), pp. 76–78.

78. Shaw, *The Quintessence of Ibsenism*, in *Selected Non-Dramatic Writings*, p. 230.

79. Quoted in Laurence Irving, *Henry Irving*, pp. 534–35. Craig's comment in the margin opposite this same passage in Brereton's biography of Irving (the *only* place where Brereton refers directly to Shaw, and that without mentioning his name) is interesting: "Irving was beginning to be more & more provocative. Perhaps it's best to *begin* halfway & develop into the bigger thing" (marginal annotation in Craig's personal copy of Brereton, *Henry Irving*, II, 165, Philbrick Collection, Honnold Library, Claremont, California).

80. Shaw, *Quintessence*, in *Selected Non-Dramatic Writings*, pp. 295, 294. See Shaw's letter to William Archer, 23 April 1894, for further insight into Shaw's strategy, *CL 1874–1897*, pp. 425–28.

81. Shaw, *Quintessence,* in *Selected Non-Dramatic Writings,* pp. 303–4.

82. Philip Amory, "Mr. and Mrs. John Bull Pretend," *Comet,* May 1897, pp. 30, 36, 37, 39, 35, 43.

83. Shaw, *CL 1874–1897,* p. 768.

84. St. John, ed., *A Corr.,* p. 153.

85. Ibid., p. 214.

86. Shaw, *CL 1874–1897,* pp. 777–79.

87. Shaw, preface to *Plays Pleasant,* p. x.

88. Quoted in Shaw, *CL 1874–1897,* p. 791.

89. Shaw, *CL 1874–1897,* p. 779.

90. "Shaw," in Louis Kronenberger, ed., *George Bernard Shaw: A Critical Survey* (Cleveland: World, 1953), p. 179.

91. Bentley, *Bernard Shaw,* p. 111.

92. Saintsbury, in Saintsbury and Palmer, eds., *We Saw Him Act,* p. 402.

93. Quoted in Archibald Henderson, *George Bernard Shaw: Man of the Century* (New York: Appleton-Century-Crofts, 1956), p. 718.

94. Shaw, preface to *Our Theatres,* I, v.

95. William Archer, *The Old Drama and the New* (Boston: Small, Maynard, 1923), p. 342.

96. Bentley, *Shaw,* p. 111.

VIII. PERSONALITY

1. Beginning with its derivation from the Latin word for theatrical mask, the word has an interesting history. Raymond Williams includes it as one of his keywords but makes only indirect references to its usage in theatrical discourse: "The *private characters* of **personalities** who have created *characters* are also regularly looked into" (*Keywords: A Vocabulary of Culture and Society* [New York: Oxford University Press, 1976], p. 197). Warren I. Susman's "'Personality' and the Making of Twentieth-Century Culture" is also of interest, although he, too, overlooks usages in theatrical writings (as opposed to later cinematic writings) and more seriously neglects to situate his subject in the context of Le Bon's concepts of personal prestige and leadership of the crowd; see John Higham and Paul K. Conkin, eds., *New Directions in American Intellectual History* (Baltimore: Johns Hopkins University Press, 1979), pp. 212–226.

2. L. F. Austin, "Sir Henry Irving," *North American Review,* 181, no. 589 (Nov. 1905), p. 767.

3. Martin-Harvey, *Autobiography,* p. 332.

4. Ibid., p. 333.

5. J. A. Hammerton, ed., *The Actor's Art* (1897; reprint New York: Blom, 1969), pp. 11–12.

6. Leonard S. Outram, "The Actor's Personality," *Dramatic Review,* 1, no. 38 (24 Oct. 1885), p. 113.

7. Quoted in Daniel Farson, *The Man Who Wrote Dracula: A Biography of Bram Stoker* (London: Joseph, 1975), pp. 230–31.

8. See Shaw, *Diaries,* I, 392; Oscar Wilde, "The Soul of Man Under Socialism," in Wilde, *The Artist as Critic: Critical Writings of Oscar Wilde,* ed. Richard Ellmann (Chicago: University of Chicago Press, 1969), p. 278.

9. Wilde, "Soul of Man," pp. 279, 271.

10. Edward Gordon Craig, *Index to the Story of My Days* (1957; reprint Cambridge: Cambridge University Press, 1981), p. 148.

11. Quoted in Pearson, *G. B. S.,* p. 146.

12. Nina Auerbach, *Ellen Terry: Player in Her Time* (New York: Norton, 1987), p. 202.

13. Craig, *Henry Irving,* p. 95.

14. Oscar Wilde, "Puppets and Actors," in *Miscellanies,* vol. VI of *Complete Writings of Oscar Wilde* (New York: Nottingham Society, 1909), pp. 165–66.

15. Oscar Wilde, "*Hamlet* at the Lyceum," in *Reviews,* vol. IV of *Complete Writings of Oscar Wilde,* p. 17.

16. Shaw, "Oscar Wilde," in *Pen Portraits and Reviews,* pp. 285–86.

17. Max Beerbohm, *Around Theatres* (1930; reprint New York: Simon and Schuster, 1954), pp. 396, 398, 399.

18. Symons, "Great Acting in English," in *Plays, Acting, and Music,* p. 182.

19. Lane Crauford, *Acting, Its Theory and Practice* (1930; reprint New York: Blom, 1969), pp. 146, 147.

20. Jessie Millward (in collaboration with J. B. Booth), *Myself and Others* (London: Hutchinson, 1923), p. 61; "Henry Irving," *Edinburgh Review,* 209, no. 427 (Jan. 1909), p. 33; St. John, *Henry Irving,* p. 24. Edward J. West, "Henry Irving, 1870–1890," in *Studies in Speech and Drama: In Honor of Alexander M. Drummond* (Ithaca, N.Y.: Cornell University Press, 1944), pp. 167–95, offers a useful overview of ideas about Irving's personality.

21. Reviews of *Louis XI, New York Tribune* and *Boston Transcript,* quoted in *Mr. Henry Irving and Miss Ellen Terry in America: Opinions of the Press* (Chicago: Morris, 1884), pp. 4, 13.

22. Amy Leslie, *Some Players* (Chicago: Stone, 1900), pp. 123–24, 132, 136, 139.

23. Ibid., p. 123.

24. A. E. Wilson, *Edwardian Theatre,* p. 48.

25. Shaw, *CL 1874–1897,* p. 780.

26. Craig, *Henry Irving,* pp. 108–10.

27. Henri F. Ellenberger, *Discovery of the Unconscious* (New York: Basic Books, 1970), p. 115.

28. See Eric J. Dingwall, *Hypnotism in Great Britain,* vol. IV of *Abnormal Hypnotic Phenomena: A Survey of Nineteenth-Century Cases,* ed. Eric J. Dingwall (New York: Barnes and Noble, 1968), pp. 128–51; on the training of actors and methodological literature, see Michael Sanderson, *From Irving to Olivier: A Social History of the Acting Profession in England, 1880–1983* (London: Athlone, 1984), especially pp. 32–53; also see Michael Baker, *The Rise of the Victorian Actor* (London: Croom Helm, 1978).

29. Laurence Irving, *Henry Irving,* pp. 51, 37.

30. Mrs. Alec-Tweedie, *Behind the Footlights* (New York: Dodd, Mead, 1904), pp. 4–5.

31. Ibid., p. 38.

32. See Tracy C. Davis, *Actresses as Working Women: Their Social Identity in Victorian Culture* (London: Routledge, 1991).

33. Quoted in Alec-Tweedie, *Behind the Footlights*, p. 226.

34. Mrs. Aria, *My Sentimental Self* (London: Chapman and Hall, 1922), p. 104.

35. Shaw, *Our Theatres*, I, 113, 115. Shaw's reference is to Grant Allen, "The New Hedonism," *Fortnightly Review*, n.s., 55, no. 327 (1 Mar. 1894), pp. 377–92.

36. Peter Thomson, "'Weirdness that lifts and colours all': The Secret Self of Henry Irving," in Richard Foulkes, ed., *Shakespeare and the Victorian Stage* (Cambridge: Cambridge University Press, 1986), p. 105.

37. Irving, *The Drama*, pp. 32–33.

38. Alec-Tweedie, *Behind the Footlights*, pp. 224–25.

39. Aria, *My Sentimental Self*, pp. 103–4.

40. Craig, marginal annotation in Craig's personal copy of Laurence Irving, *Henry Irving*, p. 611, Philbrick Collection, Honnold Library, Claremont, California.

42. Aria, *My Sentimental Self*, p. 92.

42. Raymond Blathwayt, *Does the Theatre Make for Good? An Interview with Mr. Clement Scott* (London: Hall, [1898]), p. 4.

43. Quoted in Laurence Irving, *Henry Irving*, p. 616.

44. Blathwayt, *Does the Theatre*, p. 4.

45. Max Beerbohm, *More Theatres, 1898–1903* (New York: Taplinger, 1969), pp. 420–21.

46. Thomas Jay Hudson, *The Law of Psychic Phenomena* (Chicago: McClurg, 1908), p. 108.

47. Terry, *Memoirs*, p. 130.

48. Farson, *Man Who Wrote Dracula*, p. 164.

49. Maurice Richardson, quoted in Farson, *Man Who Wrote Dracula*, p. 211.

50. Stoker, *Personal Reminiscences*, II, 202.

51. Auerbach, *Ellen Terry*, p. 199.

52. Stoker, *Personal Reminiscences*, II, 203–4.

53. Bram Stoker, "The Censorship of Fiction," *The Nineteenth Century and After* 64 (Sept. 1908), pp. 481, 486, 485, 483, 485.

54. Shaw, *Our Theatres*, I, 115, 113.

55. Ibid., p. 241.

56. Ibid., p. 240.

57. Scott, *Drama*, II, 380.

58. Terry, *Memoirs*, p. 262.

59. See Bertolt Brecht, "Three Cheers for Shaw" [25 July 1926] in *Brecht on Theatre: The Development of an Aesthetic*, ed. and trans. John Willett (New York: Hill and Wang, 1964), pp. 10–13.

60. Quoted in Scott, *Drama*, II, 381.

61. George du Maurier, *Trilby* (London: Osgood, McIlvaine, 1895), pp. 310, 304.

62. Quoted in Richard Kelly, *George Du Maurier* (Boston: Twayne, 1983), p. 119.

63. Kelly, *George Du Maurier,* p. 22.

64. Shaw, *CL 1874–1897,* p. 746.

65. See Laurence Irving, *The Successors* (London: Rupert Hart-Davis, 1967) and *The Precarious Crust* (London: Chatto and Windus, 1971) for the rich stories of how Irving's sons came into their own as successors.

66. See Cary M. Mazer, "The Criminal as Actor: H. B. Irving as Criminologist and Shakespearean," in Foulkes, ed., *Shakespeare and the Victorian Stage,* pp. 106–119.

67. Doyle, *Memories and Adventures,* p. 114.

68. Shaw, *CL 1898–1910,* p. 188.

69. Ibid., pp. 199, 376.

70. St. John, ed., *A Corr.,* p. 287.

71. H. A. Saintsbury, "Irving as Stage Manager," in Saintsbury and Palmer, eds., *We Saw Him Act,* p. 412.

72. Laurence Irving, *Henry Irving,* p. 609.

73. Robert Hichens, "Sir Henry Irving," *Fortnightly Review,* n.s., 162, no. 972 (Dec. 1947), p. 457.

74. Quoted in Laurence Irving, *Henry Irving,* p. 609.

75. "Proceedings In Re 'The Medicine Man,' " *Punch* 114 (14 May 1898), p. 225.

76. Shaw, *Our Theatres,* III, 379–80.

77. Hichens, "Sir Henry Irving," p. 458.

78. Shaw, *Our Theatres,* III, 380.

IX. IRVING'S GHOST

1. Craig, *Henry Irving,* pp. 86, 180.

2. Craig, *Index,* p. 171.

3. See Auerbach, *Ellen Terry,* esp. chap. 4, on the "marriage" of Terry and Irving.

4. Craig, *Index,* p. 236.

5. Quoted in Edward Anthony Craig, *Gordon Craig: The Story of His Life* (New York: Knopf, 1968), p. 73.

6. Quoted in Auerbach, *Ellen Terry,* p. 161.

7. Quoted in Edward Anthony Craig, *Gordon Craig,* pp. 141–42; I have corrected what seems an obvious typographical error, putting quotation marks after "My Son" instead of after "my shoulders——."

8. Craig, *Index,* pp. 151, 152.

9. Shaw, "On Gordon Craig's *Henry Irving,*" in *Shaw on Theatre,* p. 203.

10. Gordon Craig, letter to *The Observer,* proof copy, [1931], Philbrick Collection, Honnold Library, Claremont, California. Shaw's reply is written on this proof copy, which was sent to him for comment.

11. Edward Gordon Craig, "A Plea for G. B. S.," in *Ellen Terry and Her Secret Self* (New York: Dutton, 1932), pp. 24–25.

12. Shaw, "Gordon Craig and the Shaw-Terry Letters," in *Shaw on Theatre,* pp. 208, 212.

13. Shaw, *CL 1874–1897,* p. 661.

14. Shaw, "On Gordon Craig's *Henry Irving,*" in *Shaw on Theatre,* p. 203; Craig, *Towards a New Theatre,* p. 66.

15. Craig, *Index,* p. 2.

16. Archibald Henderson, *Table-Talk of G. B. S.* (1925; reprint, New York: Haskell House, 1974), p. 35.

17. Craig, *Henry Irving,* pp. 1–2.

18. Ibid., pp. 2–3.

19. Craig, *Index,* pp. 4–5.

20. Quoted in David Cecil, *Max: A Biography* (Boston: Houghton Mifflin, 1965), pp. 470–71, except for the last sentence, which is here supplied from Max Beerbohm, letter to George Bernard Shaw, [attributed to ca. 1948], photostat of draft, Philbrick Collection, Honnold Library, Claremont, California.

21. Victor Hugo, *Victor Hugo's Intellectual Autobiography,* pp. 369, 370.

22. Gordon Craig, letter to Doris Hutton, 23 Oct. 1956, Philbrick Collection, Honnold Library, Claremont, California.

23. Craig, *On the Art of the Theatre,* p. 74.

24. Craig, *Ellen Terry,* pp. 90–91.

25. Craig, *Henry Irving,* pp. 168–69.

26. Ibid., pp. 170–71.

27. Benjamin, *Illuminations,* pp. 257–58.

28. Craig, *Henry Irving,* pp. 241–43.

29. Benjamin, *Illuminations,* p. 255.

30. Craig, *Henry Irving,* p. 247.

31. For Craig as historian see Irene Eynat-Confino, "Gordon Craig: The Artist as Theatre Historian," *Theatre History Studies* 11 (1991), pp. 167–74.

32. Craig, *Henry Irving,* p. 103.

X. "THEY COULD NOT SHOUT THAT CURTAIN UP"

1. Stoker, *Personal Reminiscences,* II, 329.

2. Quoted in Laurence Irving, *Henry Irving,* p. 666.

3. Quoted in Edward F. O'Day, "Henry Irving, as Seen by His Former Leading Lady, Maude Fealy," *New York Dramatic Mirror,* 76, no. 1963 (5 Aug. 1916), p. 1.

4. Fitzgerald, *Henry Irving,* p. 274.

5. Ervine, *Theatre in My Time,* p. 33.

6. Terry, *Memoirs,* p. 262.

7. Stoker, *Personal Reminiscences,* II, 353.

8. Edith Wynne Matthison, quoted in "A Real Tragedy," *Sunday Globe* [Boston], 11 July 1909, in Harvard Theatre Collection clipping file.

9. Campbell Rae-Brown, "Henry Irving: 1838–1905," commemorative print (London: Art Reproduction Co., 1905).

10. Shaw, *CL 1898–1910*, p. 570.

11. "Irving to Retire," *Dramatic World,* 1, no. 5 (15 Mar. 1895), p. 4.

12. Talcott Williams, "Sir Henry Irving," *Atlantic Monthly,* 96, no. 6 (Dec. 1905), p. 830.

13. "Henry Irving," *Times Literary Supplement,* 4, no. 197 (20 Oct. 1905), p. 349.

14. Austin Brereton, *In Memoriam: Father and Son: Henry Irving, Henry Brodribb Irving* (London: Miles, 1919), p. 8.

15. Ervine, *Theatre in My Time,* p. 101.

16. William Archer, *Real Conversations* (1903; reprint, n.p.: Folcroft Library Editions, 1978), p. 6.

17. Hugo, *Les Misérables,* II, bk. I, chap. 18 (p. 50).

18. Sigmund Freud, *Beyond the Pleasure Principle,* trans. and ed. James Strachey (New York: Norton, 1961), p. 32.

19. St. John, ed., *A Corr.,* pp. 287–88.

APPENDIX A

1. See Carr, *Life of Sir Arthur Conan Doyle,* pp. 285–95.

2. Henry Irving, letter to Bram Stoker, 12 March 1892, Bram Stoker Collection, Shakespeare Centre Library, Stratford-upon-Avon (reel 6, item 176 of microfilm edition).

3. Arthur Conan Doyle, letter to Bram Stoker, 15 March 1892, Bram Stoker Collection, Shakespeare Centre Library, Stratford-upon-Avon (reel 7, item 130 of microfilm edition).

BIBLIOGRAPHY

(Note: This bibliography is not intended as a comprehensive survey of relevant literature but rather as a listing of sources cited in the book, with the addition of a very few works of general importance.)

ARCHIVAL COLLECTIONS

The British Library. London.

Percy Fitzgerald Collection. Library of the Garrick Club. London.

Harvard Theatre Collection. Harvard University. Cambridge, Massachusetts.

Irving-Disher Collection. Department of Rare Books and Special Collections. Rush Rhees Library. University of Rochester. Rochester, New York.

Geraldine Womack and Norman D. Philbrick Library of Dramatic Literature and Theatre History. The Honnold Library. Claremont, California. (Hereafter referred to as Philbrick Collection.)

Clement Scott Collection. The Huntington Library. San Marino, California.

Bram Stoker Collection. Shakespeare Centre Library. Stratford-upon-Avon. (Also available on microfilm in *Series One: The Papers of Henry Irving and Ellen Terry from the Shakespeare Centre Library, Stratford-upon-Avon* in *Britain's Literary Heritage: Actors and Managers of the English and American Stage* (Sussex: Harvester Microform, 1987).

PUBLISHED SOURCES

"About 'A Story of Waterloo,'" Unidentified Boston newspaper. 14 Sept. 1897. Harvard Theatre Collection clipping file, Cambridge, Mass.

Alec-Tweedie, Mrs. *Behind the Footlights*. New York: Dodd, Mead, 1904.

Allen, Grant. "The New Hedonism." *Fortnightly Review*, n.s., 55, no. 327 (1 Mar. 1894), pp. 377–92.

Altick, Richard D. *The Shows of London*. Cambridge, Mass.: Harvard University Press, 1978.

Amory, Philip, "Mr. and Mrs. John Bull Pretend." *The Comet: A Magazine of Free Opinion*, 1, no. 1 (May 1897), pp. 30–43.

Archer, C. *William Archer: Life, Work, and Friendships*. London: Allen and Unwin, 1931.

Archer, William. *Henry Irving, Actor and Manager: A Critical Study*. [1884]; reprint, St. Clair Shores, Mich.: Scholarly Press, 1970.

———. *The Old Drama and the New: An Essay in Re-valuation*. Boston: Small, Maynard, 1923.

————. "A Plea for the Queue." *Dramatic Review*, 1, no. 12 (25 Apr. 1885), pp. 196–97.

————. *Real Conversations*. 1903; reprint, n.p.: Folcroft Library Editions, 1978.

————. "Some Recent Plays." *Fortnightly Review*, n.s., 55, no. 329 (1 May 1894), pp. 600–13.

————. *The Theatrical "World" of 1894*. London: Walter Scott, 1895.

————. *The Theatrical "World" of 1895*. London: Walter Scott, 1896.

————. *The Theatrical "World" of 1897*. London: Walter Scott, 1898.

Archer, William, and Robert Lowe. *The Fashionable Tragedian: A Criticism*. Edinburgh: Gray, 1878.

Aria, Mrs. *My Sentimental Self*. London: Chapman and Hall, 1922.

Arthur, George. *From Phelps to Gielgud: Reminiscences of the Stage through Sixty-five Years*. London: Chapman and Hall, 1936.

Auerbach, Nina. *Ellen Terry: Player in Her Time*. New York: Norton, 1987.

Austin, L. F. *Points of View*. Ed. Clarence Rook. London: Lane, 1906.

————. "Sir Henry Irving." *North American Review*, 181, no. 589 (Nov. 1905), pp. 767–76.

Ayres, Alfred. *Acting and Actors, Elocution and Elocutionists: A Book about Theater Folk and Theater Art*. New York: Appleton, 1894.

Baker, Michael. *The Rise of the Victorian Actor*. London: Croom Helm, 1978.

Beerbohm, Max. *Around Theatres*. 1930; reprint, New York: Simon and Schuster, 1954.

————. *More Theatres: 1898–1903*. New York: Taplinger, 1969.

Benjamin, Walter. *Charles Baudelaire: A Lyric Poet in the Era of High Capitalism*. Trans. Harry Zohn. London: New Left Books, 1973.

————. *Illuminations*. Ed. Hannah Arendt. Trans. Harry Zohn. New York: Schocken, 1969.

Bentley, Eric. *Bernard Shaw*. 1947; reprint, New York: Limelight Editions, 1985.

Berst, Charles A. "*The Man of Destiny*: Shaw, Napoleon, and the Theater of Life." *Shaw: The Neglected Plays*. Ed. Alfred Turco, Jr. Vol. 7 of *Shaw: The Annual of Bernard Shaw Studies*. University Park, Pa.: Pennsylvania State University Press, 1986.

Blathwayt, Raymond. *Does the Theatre Make for Good?: An Interview with Mr. Clement Scott (Reprinted from "Great Thoughts"), Replies from Leading Actors, Press Comments, &c*. London: Hall [1898].

Booth, J. B. *London Town*. London: T. Werner Laurie, 1929.

Booth, Michael R. *Victorian Spectacular Theatre, 1850–1910*. London: Routledge and Kegan Paul, 1981.

[Boucicault, Dion.] *The Old Guard*. New York: Samuel French, n.d.

Brecht, Bertolt. *Brecht on Theatre: The Development of an Aesthetic*. Ed. and trans. John Willett. New York: Hill and Wang, 1964.

Brereton, Austin. *In Memoriam: Father and Son: Henry Irving, Henry Brodribb Irving*. London: Miles, 1919.

————. *The Life of Henry Irving*. 2 vols. 1908; reprint, New York: Blom, 1969.

————. "Mr. Henry Irving in a New Play." *The Theatre*, 1 Oct. 1894, pp. 179–81.

Brombert, Victor. *"Les Misérables:* Salvation from Below." In *Modern Critical Views: Victor Hugo.* Ed. Harold Bloom. New York: Chelsea House, 1988.

Byron, George Gordon. *Lord Byron: The Complete Poetical Works.* Ed. Jerome J. McGann. Vol. II. Oxford: Oxford University Press, 1980.

Canetti, Elias. *Crowds and Power.* Trans. Carol Stewart. New York: Viking, 1962.

Carr, John Dickson. *The Life of Sir Arthur Conan Doyle.* New York: Harper, 1949.

Cecil, David. *Max: A Biography.* Boston: Houghton Mifflin, 1965.

Craig, Edward Anthony. "Gordon Craig and Hubert von Herkomer." *Theater Research,* 10, no. 1 (1969), 7–16.

———. *Gordon Craig: The Story of His Life.* New York: Knopf, 1968.

Craig, Edward Gordon. *Ellen Terry and Her Secret Self: Together with A Plea for G. B. S.* New York: Dutton, 1932.

———. "Extracts from a Diary." In booklet accompanying record album, *Edward Gordon Craig: Radio Talks.* London: Discurio, 1962.

———. *Henry Irving.* 1930; reprint, New York: Blom, 1969.

———. *Index to the Story of My Days: Some Memoirs of Edward Gordon Craig, 1872–1907.* 1957; reprint, Cambridge: Cambridge University Press, 1981.

———. "Irving Seemingly Perplexed." *The Drama,* n.s., 43 (Winter 1956), pp. 25–26.

———. Letter to *The Observer.* Undated proof copy [1931]. Philbrick Collection, Honnold Library, Claremont, California.

———. *On the Art of the Theatre.* 1911; reprint, New York: Theatre Arts, 1956.

———. *The Theatre Advancing.* 1947; reprint, New York: Blom, 1963.

———. *The Theatre—Advancing.* Boston: Little, Brown, 1928.

———. *Towards a New Theatre: Forty Designs for Stage Scenes with Critical Notes by the Inventor.* London: Dent, 1913.

Crauford, Lane. *Acting, Its Theory and Practice: With Illustrative Examples of Players Past and Present.* 1930; reprint, New York: Blom, 1969.

Darbyshire, Alfred. *The Art of the Victorian Stage: Notes and Recollections.* 1907; reprint, New York: Blom, 1969.

Davis, Tracy C. *Actresses as Working Women: Their Social Identity in Victorian Culture.* London: Routledge, 1991.

Dingwall, Eric J., ed. *Abnormal Hypnotic Phenomena: A Survey of Nineteenth-Century Cases.* Vol. IV. New York: Barnes and Noble, 1968.

Doyle, Arthur Conan. *Adventures of Gerard.* 1903; reprint, London: John Murray and Jonathan Cape, 1976.

———. *The Great Shadow.* New York: Harper, 1893.

———. *Memories and Adventures.* Boston: Little, Brown, 1924.

———. *Round the Red Lamp: Being Facts and Fancies of Medical Life.* 1894; reprint, Freeport, N.Y.: Books for Libraries Press, 1969.

———. "A Straggler of '15." *Black and White,* 1 (21 Mar. 1891), pp. 214–17.

———. "A Straggler of '15," *Harper's Weekly,* 35 (21 Mar. 1891), pp. 205–7.

———. *Waterloo.* In *One-Act Plays of To-Day: Second Series.* Selected by J. W. Marriott. London: Harrap, 1925.

———. *Waterloo.* New York: Samuel French, 1907.

Du Maurier, George. *Trilby.* London: Osgood, McIlvaine, 1895.

Ellenberger, Henri F. *The Discovery of the Unconscious: The History and Evolution of Dynamic Psychiatry.* New York: Basic Books, 1970.

Erckmann-Chatrian [Émile Erckmann and Alexandre Chatrian]. *Waterloo: A Sequel to "The Conscript of 1813."* New York: Scribner's, 1903.

Ervine, St. John. *The Theatre in My Time.* London: Rich and Cowan, 1933.

Eynat-Confino, Irene. "Gordon Craig: The Artist as Theatre Historian." *Theatre History Studies,* 11 (1991), pp. 167–74.

Farson, Daniel. *The Man Who Wrote Dracula: A Biography of Bram Stoker.* London: Joseph, 1975.

Fitzgerald, Percy. *Sir Henry Irving: A Biography.* Philadelphia: Jacobs [1906].

Foulkes, Richard, ed. *Shakespeare and the Victorian Stage.* Cambridge: Cambridge University Press, 1986.

Freud, Sigmund. *Beyond the Pleasure Principle.* Trans. and ed. James Stachey. New York: Norton, 1961.

———. *Group Psychology and the Analysis of the Ego.* Trans. and ed. James Strachey. New York: Norton, 1959.

Gottschalk, Louis Moreau. *Notes of a Pianist.* Ed. Jeanne Behrend. 1881; reprint, New York: Knopf, 1964.

Guérard, Albert Leon. *Reflections on the Napoleonic Legend.* New York: Scribner's, 1924.

Hammerton, J. H., ed. *The Actor's Art: Theatrical Reminiscences, Methods of Study and Advice to Aspirants.* Prefatory note by Henry Irving. 1897; reprint, New York: Blom, 1969.

Harris, Frank. *Bernard Shaw: An Unauthorized Biography Based on First Hand Information.* Postscript by Bernard Shaw. New York: Simon and Schuster, 1931.

———. *My Life and Loves.* Ed. John F. Gallagher. New York: Grove Press, 1963.

Hatton, Joseph. "Sir Henry Irving: His Romantic Career On and Off the Stage." *Grand Magazine,* 2, no. 11 (Dec. 1905), pp. 992ff.

Henderson, Archibald. *George Bernard Shaw: His Life and Works.* Cincinnati: Stewart and Kidd, 1911.

———. *George Bernard Shaw: Man of the Century.* New York: Appleton-Century-Crofts, 1956.

———. *Table-Talk of G. B. S.: Conversations on Things in General Between Bernard Shaw and His Biographer.* 1925; reprint, New York: Haskell House, 1974.

"Henry Irving." Rev. of Austin Brereton, Bram Stoker, Ellen Terry, and Walter Herries Pollock, [books about Henry Irving], *Edinburgh Review,* 209, no. 427 (Jan. 1909), pp. 29–48.

"Henry Irving." *Times Literary Supplement,* 4, no. 197 (20 Oct. 1905), p. 349.

Herold, J. Christopher. *The Age of Napoleon.* New York: American Heritage, 1963.

Heslewood, Tom. "Relics and Memories of Irving." *Birmingham Post,* 11 Feb. 1938, p. 1.

Hiatt, Charles. *Henry Irving: A Record and Review.* London: George Bell, 1899.

Hichens, Robert. "Sir Henry Irving." *Fortnightly Review*, n.s., 162, no. 972 (Dec. 1947), pp. 455–60.

Higham, Charles. *Adventures of Conan Doyle: The Life of the Creator of Sherlock Holmes*. New York: Norton, 1976.

Holroyd, Michael. *Bernard Shaw: The Search for Love, 1856–1898*. New York: Random House, 1988.

———. *Bernard Shaw: The Pursuit of Power, 1898–1918*. New York: Random House, 1989.

Houghton, Walter E. *The Victorian Frame of Mind, 1830–1870*. New Haven: Yale University Press, 1957.

Howarth, David. *Waterloo: Day of Battle*. New York: Atheneum, 1968.

Hudson, Thomas Jay. *The Law of Psychic Phenomena: A Working Hypothesis for the Systematic Study of Hypnotism, Spiritism, Mental Therapeutics, Etc.* Chicago: McClurg, 1908.

Hughes, Alan. *Henry Irving, Shakespearean*. Cambridge: Cambridge University Press, 1981.

Hugo, Victor. *Victor Hugo's Intellectual Autobiography (Postscriptum de Ma Vie) Being the Last of the Unpublished Works and Embodying the Author's Ideas on Literature, Philosophy, and Religion*. Trans. Lorenzo O'Rourke. New York: Funk and Wagnalls, 1907.

———. *Les Misérables*. 5 vols. Trans. Lascelles Wraxall. New York: Heritage, 1938.

"In the Provinces." *The Theatre*, 1 Nov. 1894, pp. 256–62.

Innes, Christopher. *Edward Gordon Craig*. Cambridge: Cambridge University Press, 1983.

Irving, Henry. "Acting: An Art." *Fortnightly Review*, n.s., 57, no. 339 (1 Mar. 1895), pp. 369–379.

———. *The Drama: Addresses*. 1893; reprint, New York: Blom, 1969.

———. Preface. *The Paradox of Acting* by Denis Diderot. Trans. Walter Herries Pollock [1883]. Published in one volume with *Masks or Faces* by William Archer [1888]. New York: Hill and Wang, 1957.

Irving, Laurence. *Henry Irving: The Actor and His World*. New York: Macmillan, 1952.

———. *The Precarious Crust*. London: Chatto and Windus, 1971.

———. *The Successors*. London: Rupert Hart-Davis, 1967.

"Irving to Retire." *Dramatic World*, I, no. 5 (15 Mar. 1895), p. 4.

Jones, Henry Arthur. *The Shadow of Henry Irving*. 1931; reprint, New York: Blom, 1969.

Keegan, John. *The Face of Battle*. New York: Penguin, 1983.

Kelly, Richard. *George Du Maurier*. Boston: Twayne, 1983.

King, W. D. "An 'Exquisite' Memory: Bernard Shaw and Henry Irving at *Waterloo*." In *Before His Eyes: Essays in Honor of Stanley Kauffmann*. Ed. Bert Cardullo. Washington, D.C.: University Press of America, 1986.

———. "History and Theatre: Reweaving the Afterpiece." In *History and. . . .* Ed. Michael Roth and Ralph Cohen. Charlottesville, Va.: University of Virginia Press, 1993.

―――. "The Portrayal of Darkness and Sixth Sense on the Nineteenth-Century English Stage." *Theatre Survey,* 34, no. 1 (May 1993).

―――. "When Theatre Becomes History: Final Curtains on the Victorian Stage." *Victorian Studies,* forthcoming, 1993.

Kingsmill, Hugh. *Frank Harris: A Biography.* New York: Farrar and Rinehart, 1932.

Kronenberger, Louis, ed. *George Bernard Shaw: A Critical Survey.* Cleveland: World, 1953.

Le Bon, Gustave. *The Crowd: A Study of the Popular Mind.* London: Unwin, 1903.

Lellenberg, Jon L., ed. *The Quest for Sir Arthur Conan Doyle: Thirteen Biographers in Search of a Life.* Carbondale, Ill.: Southern Illinois University Press, 1987.

Leslie, Amy. *Some Players: Personal Sketches.* Chicago: Stone, 1900.

Lewes, George Henry. *On Actors and the Art of Acting.* Leipzig: Bernhard Tauchnitz, 1875.

Low, Edward Bruce. *With Napoleon at Waterloo and Other Unpublished Documents of the Waterloo and Peninsular Campaigns: Also Papers on Waterloo.* Ed. Mackenzie MacBride. Philadelphia: Lippincott, 1911.

McArthur, Benjamin. *Actors and American Culture, 1880–1920.* Philadelphia: Temple University Press, 1984.

Martin, Everett Dean. *The Behavior of Crowds: A Psychological Study.* New York: Norton, 1920.

Martin-Harvey, Sir John. *The Autobiography of Sir John Martin-Harvey.* London: Sampson Low, Marston, n.d.

Matthews, Brander, ed. *Papers on Acting.* New York: Hill and Wang, 1958.

Maupassant, Guy de. *Sur l'Eau and Other Tales.* Vol. IV of *A Selection from the Writings of Guy de Maupassant.* New York: Review of Reviews, 1903.

Mayer, David, ed. *Henry Irving and "The Bells": Irving's Personal Script of the Play by Leopold Lewis.* Manchester: Manchester University Press: 1980.

Meisel, Martin. *Realizations: Narrative, Pictorial, and Theatrical Arts in Nineteenth-Century England.* Princeton, N.J.: Princeton University Press, 1983.

―――. *Shaw and the Nineteenth-Century Theater.* Princeton, N.J.: Princeton University Press, 1963.

Millward, Jessie (in collaboration with J. B. Booth). *Myself and Others.* London: Hutchinson, 1923.

Mr. Henry Irving and Miss Ellen Terry in America: Opinions of the Press. Chicago: Morris, 1884.

Moscovici, Serge. *The Age of the Crowd: A Historical Treatise on Mass Psychology.* Trans. J. C. Whitehouse. Cambridge: Cambridge University Press, 1985.

Nordau, Max. *Paradoxes.* Trans. J. R. McIlraith. London: Heinemann, 1896.

Nye, Robert A. *The Origins of Crowd Psychology: Gustave Le Bon and the Crisis of Mass Democracy in the Third Republic.* Vol. 2 of *SAGE Studies in 20th Century History.* London: SAGE Publications, 1975.

O'Day, Edward F. "Henry Irving, as Seen by His Former Leading Lady, Maude Fealy." *New York Dramatic Mirror,* 76, no. 1963 (5 Aug. 1916), p. 1.

Outram, Leonard S. "The Actor's Personality." *Dramatic Review*, 1, no. 38 (24 Oct. 1885), p. 113.

Pearsall, Robert Brainard. *Frank Harris*. New York: Twayne, 1970.

Pearson, Hesketh. *Conan Doyle*. 1943; reprint, London: White Lion, 1974.

———. *G. B. S.: A Full Length Portrait*. New York: Harper, 1942.

Pellissier, Eugène. Introduction. *Waterloo* by Erckmann-Chatrian. London: Macmillan, 1924.

Pollock, Walter Herries. *Impressions of Henry Irving. Gathered in Public and Private During a Friendship of Many Years*. Preface by H. B. Irving. 1908; reprint, New York: Blom, 1971.

Postlewait, Thomas, and Bruce A. McConachie, eds. *Interpreting the Theatrical Past: Essays in the Historiography of Performance*. Iowa City: University of Iowa Press, 1989.

"Proceedings In Re 'The Medicine Man.'" *Punch*, 114 (14 May 1898), p. 225.

Rae-Brown, Campbell. "Henry Irving: 1838–1905." Commemorative print. London: Art Reproduction Company, 1905.

"Readings and Recitals by Henry Irving and H. J. Montague." Theatrical program. Westbourne Hall, 23 Oct. 1869.

"A Real Tragedy." *Sunday Globe* [Boston], 11 July 1909. Harvard Theatre Collection clipping file, Cambridge, Mass.

Rev. of *A Story of Waterloo*. "Between Curtains." *Boston Standard*, 14 Oct. 1895. Harvard Theatre Collection clipping file, Cambridge, Mass.

———. *Boston Transcript*, 4 Oct. 1895. Harvard Theatre Collection clipping file, Cambridge, Mass.

———. *Bristol Mercury*, 22 Sept. 1894, p. 5.

———. *Bristol Times and Mirror*, 22 Sept. 1894, p. 8.

———. *Daily News* [London], 22 Sept. 1894, p. 7.

———. *Evening Times* [Glasgow], 12 Nov. 1894, p. 5.

———. *Glasgow Evening News*, 12 Nov. 1894, p. 3.

———. "Irving Takes Paregoric." *New York Times*, 2 June 1895, p. 5.

———. *North British Daily Mail* [Glasgow], 12 Nov. 1894, p. 5.

———. "Our Cantankerous Critic." *Quiz*, 15 Nov. 1894, pp. 18–19.

———. *Stage*, no. 850 (1 July 1897), p. 12.

———. "The Story of Waterloo at the Garrick Theatre." *Saturday Review*, 78, no. 2043 (22 Dec. 1894), pp. 679–80.

———. *Times* [London], 22 Sept. 1894, p. 6.

———. *Umpire* [Manchester], 9 Dec. 1894, p. 5.

———. Unidentified Boston newspaper, [1896]. Harvard Theatre Collection clipping file, Cambridge, Mass.

———. Unidentified newspaper, [1900–2]. Percy Fitzgerald Collection, Library of Garrick Club, London, vol. XIV, p. 63.

———. Unidentified newspaper, [May 1895]. Percy Fitzgerald Collection, Library of the Garrick Club, London, vol. XV, p. 54.

———. *Western Daily Press*, 22 Sept. 1894, p. 5.

Rev. of *Becket* by Alfred Tennyson. *Daily Graphic* [London], 1 May 1905, p. 4.

Rev. of *The Crowd: A Study of the Popular Mind* by Gustave Le Bon. *Athenaeum*, no. 3587 (25 July 1896), pp. 123–24.

Ribot, Th[éodule]. *The Psychology of the Emotions*. (London: Walter Scott, 1900).

Roach, Joseph R. *The Player's Passion: Studies in the Science of Acting*. Newark, N.J.: University of Delaware Press, 1985.

[Rook, Clarence]. "Mr. Shaw's Future. A Conversation." *The Academy,* 30 Apr. 1898, p. 476.

Roth, Samuel. *The Private Life of Frank Harris*. New York: William Faro, 1931.

Rowell, George. *Theatre in the Age of Irving*. Oxford: Blackwell, 1981.

Ruskin, John. *Modern Painters*. 3 vols. In *The Works of John Ruskin,* eds. E. T. Cook and Alexander Wedderburn. London: Allen, 1904.

Sachs, Edwin O., and Ernest A. E. Woodrow. *Modern Opera Houses and Theatres*. Vol. III. 1898; reprint, New York: Blom, 1968.

Saintsbury, H. A., and Cecil Palmer, eds. *We Saw Him Act: A Symposium on the Art of Sir Henry Irving*. 1939; reprint, New York: Blom, 1969.

Sanderson, Michael. *From Irving to Olivier: A Social History of the Acting Profession in England, 1880–1983*. London: Athlone, 1984.

Sardou, Victorien. *Madame Sans-Gêne*. Adapt. J. Comyns Carr. Privately printed edition. Philbrick Collection, Honnold Library, Claremont, California.

Scott, Clement. *The Drama of Yesterday & To-Day*. 2 vols. London: Macmillan, 1899.

[Scott, Clement]. "Mr. Irving in a New Play." Rev. of *A Story of Waterloo. Daily Telegraph* [London], 22 Sept. 1894, p. 5.

Scott, Mrs. Clement. *Old Days in Bohemian London: Recollections of Clement Scott*. New York: Stokes, n.d.

Shaw, George Bernard. *Advice to a Young Critic and Other Letters*. Ed. E. J. West. New York: Capricorn Books, 1963.

———. *Collected Letters, 1874–1897*. Ed. Dan H. Laurence. New York: Dodd, Mead, 1965.

———. *Collected Letters, 1898–1910*. Ed. Dan H. Laurence. New York: Dodd, Mead, 1972.

———. *The Diaries, 1885–1897: With Early Autobiographical Notebooks and Diaries, and an Abortive 1917 Diary*. Ed. Stanley Weintraub. 2 vols. University Park, Pa: Pennsylvania State University Press, 1986.

———. Draft reply to Gordon Craig letter to *The Observer* [1931]. Philbrick Collection, Honnold Library, Claremont, California.

———. *London Music in 1888–89 as Heard by Corno di Bassetto (Later Known as Bernard Shaw) with Some Further Autobiographical Particulars*. London: Constable, 1937.

———. *Our Theatres in the Nineties*. 3 vols. London: Constable, 1932.

———. *Pen Portraits and Reviews*. London: Constable, 1932.

———. *Plays: Pleasant and Unpleasant: The Second Volume, Containing the Four Pleasant Plays*. New York: Dodd, Mead, 1940.

———. *Selected Non-Dramatic Writings of Bernard Shaw*. Ed. Dan H. Laurence. Boston: Houghton Mifflin, 1965.

———. *Shaw on Theatre*. Ed. E. J. West. New York: Hill and Wang, 1958.

———. *Shaw's Dramatic Criticism (1895–98)*. Ed. John F. Matthews. New York: Hill and Wang, 1959.

————. *Sixteen Self Sketches.* London: Constable, 1949.

————. "To the Audience at the Kingsway Theatre: A Personal Appeal from the Author of John Bull's Other Island." Program insert. 1913.

Shaw, G. Bernard, with J. Fletcher Moulton, Justin McCarthy, H. W. Massingham, Sidney Webb. "What Mr. Gladstone Ought to Do." *Fortnightly Review,* 53, no. 314 (1 Feb. 1893), pp. 262–87.

Siborne, H. T., ed. *Waterloo Letters: A Selection from Original and Hitherto Unpublished Letters Bearing on the Operations of the 16th, 17th, and 18th June, 1815, By Officers Who Served in the Campaign.* London: Cassell, 1891.

Siborne, Capt. W. *History of the War in France and Belgium, in 1815: Containing Minute Details of the Battles of Quatre-Bras, Ligny, Wavre, and Waterloo.* 2 vols. London: Boone, 1844.

"Some Memories [of Henry Irving]: By London Playgoers." *Pall Mall Gazette,* 14 Oct. 1905, p. 7.

St. John, Christopher, ed. *Ellen Terry and Bernard Shaw: A Correspondence.* New York: Putnam's, 1932.

————. *Henry Irving.* London: Green Sheaf, 1905.

Stoker, Bram. "The Censorship of Fiction." *The Nineteenth Century and After: A Monthly Review,* 64 (Sept. 1908), pp. 479–87.

————. *Personal Reminiscences of Henry Irving.* 2 vols. London: Heinemann, 1906.

Susman, Warren I. " 'Personality' and the Making of Twentieth-Century Culture." In *New Directions in American Intellectual History.* Ed. John Higham and Paul K. Conkin. Baltimore: Johns Hopkins University Press, 1979.

Symons, Arthur. *Plays, Acting, and Music: A Book of Theory.* New York: Dutton, 1909.

Tennyson, Alfred. *The Poems of Tennyson.* Ed. Christopher Ricks. 2nd ed. Vol. II. Berkeley and Los Angeles: University of California Press, 1987.

Terry, Ellen. *Ellen Terry's Memoirs.* Preface, notes, and additional biographical chapters by Edith Craig and Christopher St. John. New York: Putnam's, 1932.

————. *The Story of My Life.* 1908; reprint, New York: Schocken, 1982.

"The Theatres of Varieties: Gossiping and Critical Notes." *Dramatic Review,* 17, no. 502 (17 Mar. 1894), p. 172–73.

"The Theatres of Varieties: Gossiping and Critical Notes." *Dramatic Review,* 17, no. 499 (24 Feb. 1894), pp. 124–25.

"Theatre Gossip." *The Sketch,* 30, no. 388 (4 July 1900), p. 498.

"Theatrical Gossip." *The Era,* 8 May 1897, p. 12.

"To George Bernard Shaw, Esq." *The Theatre,* 1 July 1897, pp. 8–10.

Towse, John Rankin. *Sixty Years of the Theater: An Old Critic's Memories.* New York: Funk and Wagnalls, 1916.

Trevelyan, George Macaulay. *History of England.* London: Longmans, Green, 1937.

Walkley, A. B. *More Prejudice.* London: Heinemann, 1923.

West, Edward J. "Henry Irving, 1870–90." *Studies in Speech and Drama: In Honor of Alexander M. Drummond.* Ithaca, N.Y.: Cornell University Press, 1944.

"Who Is the Future Actor?" *Dramatic World,* 1, no. 3 (Jan. 1895), p. 4.

Wilde, Oscar. *The Artist as Critic: Critical Writings of Oscar Wilde.* Ed. Richard Ellmann. Chicago: University of Chicago Press, 1969.

———. *Complete Writings of Oscar Wilde.* Vols. IV and VI. New York: Nottingham Society, 1909.

Williams, Raymond. *Keywords: A Vocabulary of Culture and Society.* New York: Oxford University Press, 1976.

Williams, Talcott. "Sir Henry Irving." *Atlantic Monthly,* 96, no. 6 (Dec. 1905), pp. 826–33.

Wilson, A. E. *Edwardian Theatre.* London: Barker, 1951.

———. *The Lyceum.* London: Dennis Yates, 1952.

Winter, William. *Vagrant Memories: Being Further Recollections of Other Days.* New York: Doran, 1915.

———. *The Wallet of Time: Containing Personal, Biographical, and Critical Reminiscence of the American Theatre.* 2 vols. New York: Moffat, Yard, 1913.

Wisenthal, J. L. *Shaw's Sense of History.* Oxford: Clarendon, 1988.

Zola, Émile. *The Experimental Novel and Other Essays.* Trans. Belle M. Sherman. New York: Haskell House, 1964.

INDEX

Achurch, Janet, 143, 146, 147, 155, 276n.18
Acting: end of the era of, 34–36, 119, 138–39, 142; ephemerality of, 11, 36–38, 235–36, 238–39; and hypnosis, 191, 194, 200, 209; and naturalism, 92; and personality, 183–86; and sex, 196, 197–200; Shaw on, 156–58
"Actor and the Über-Marionette, The" (Craig). See Craig, Edward Gordon: "The Actor and the Über-Marionette"
Alec-Tweedie, Mrs., 196–97, 198
Allen, Grant, 197, 281n.35
Allen, J. H., 226–27, 232
Alma-Tadema, Sir Lawrence, 163
Amory, Philip, 176–78
Archer, William, xviii, 43, 147, 276n.18; on antagonistic criticism, 22–26; on Irving, 14, 35, 48–50, 61, 236; on the Lyceum pit, 42; on Madame Sans-Gêne, 163–64; on Shaw, 25, 179, 182, 267n.41; on Waterloo, 24–25; picture of, 47
Aria, Eliza, 197, 199
Arliss, George, 40
Arms and the Man (Shaw). See Shaw, George Bernard: Arms and the Man
Arthur, Sir George, 10, 11
Athenaeum, 49, 273n.45
Atlantic Monthly, 235
Auerbach, Nina, 188, 201
Austin, Louis Frederick, 81, 172, 183
Ayres, Alfred: quoted, 14

Baird, Dorothea, 205–7
Ball, Meredith, 128
Balsamo, Joseph, 194
Barrett, Wilson, 176–78
Barrie, J. M., 49
Bartlett, F.: quoted, 63
Bateman, Hezekiah Linthicum, 106

"Battle of Blenheim, The" (Southey), 128
Beaconsfield, Benjamin Disraeli, Earl of. See Disraeli, Benjamin
Becket (Tennyson). See Irving, Henry: in Becket
Beerbohm, Max, 22, 129, 190–91, 200, 221–22, 239
Behind the Footlights (Alec-Tweedie), 196
Bell, Dr. Joseph, 90–91
Bells, The (Lewis). See Irving, Henry: in The Bells
Belmore, Lionel, 211
Benjamin, Walter, xx, 107–12, 227, 228
Bentley, Eric, 181–82
Berst, Charles A., 152, 276n.18
Betterton, Thomas, 235
Blake, William, 222
Boer War, 130–31, 135
Booth, Edwin, 34, 70
Boucicault, Dion, 87; The Old Guard, 104–6
Brecht, Bertolt, 204
Brereton, Austin, xii, 20, 41, 278n.79
Brewster, Corporal Gregory. See Story of Waterloo, A: Corporal Brewster as character within
Bright, Golding, 157, 172–73
Brombert, Victor, 124–26
Brown, Ford Madox, 77–78, 80, 82, 94
Bryan, Alfred, 129, 135, 167, 275n.17
Buffon, Comte Georges Louis Leclerc de, 235
Burford's Panorama, 119
Burne-Jones, Sir Edward, 80, 163
Bygones (Pinero), xi
Byron, George Gordon, Lord, xviii, 140, 263; Childe Harold's Pilgrimage, 53, 54, 115–16; Don Juan, 54

Cagliostro, Count Alessandro di (Giuseppe Balsamo), 194

in *Madame Sans-Gêne*; *Madame Sans-Gêne* (Sardou)

Saturday Review, The, xi, 12, 26, 28, 77, 129, 156, 179, 190, 208; Frank Harris as editor of, 21–22

Saxe-Meiningen, Georg, Duke of, 71–72

Scott, Clement, xviii, 34, 136, 168, 208, 214, 269n.25; Philip Amory on, 176–77; editorship of *The Theatre*, 46–48; on Ibsen, 23, 173–74; on Irving, 199; on Irving's *Louis XI*, 83–84; scandal of, 199–200, 202; Shaw's opinion of, 50, 173–74; on *Trilby*, 203–5; on *Waterloo*, 89–90; picture of, 47

Scribe, Eugène, 27, 144, 146, 163, 268n.56

Sensibility: actor's, xix, 15, 141, 184–86, 198; critical, xix, 13, 15–18

Sentiment and sentimentality, 141, 145, 199, 237; and anti-sentimentalism, 10, 49–51, 161, 174; in crowd psychology, 2, 12–13, 39, 54, 61, 62–63, 66, 69, 73, 186; and Doyle, 22; and Irving, 35, 83, 160, 220; and *Waterloo*, xvii, 59, 75, 85, 93

Seymour, Captain Horace, 99

Shakespeare, William, xi, xvii, 22, 149, 155, 156, 166, 173, 174; as validator of artistic merit, 37, 44

Shaw, George Bernard, xvii–xviii, xix, 278n.79, 278n.80; and the antiromantic, 13, 21, 25, 27, 77–78, 80–81, 85, 123, 126, 147, 159–61; on applause, 52–53; on William Archer, 25–26, 50; and censorship, 202; on Craig, xvii, 136, 139, 215–18, 220, 221–22; Craig on, 215–18, 221, 228–29; death of, 217; on dramatic criticism, xi, 13, 16–18, 20–30, 175–76, 267n.41; on Irving, xi, xiii, 14, 69, 77–78, 80–81, 84–85, 90, 94, 133, 139–41, 155–57, 161, 164–65, 174, 178, 183, 192–93, 200, 207, 222, 233–34; on *Madame Sans-Gêne*, 143–44, 146, 165–69; as Napoleonic figure, 31–32, 153, 160, 169, 171, 217–18; and the New Drama, xvi–xvii, 35, 119, 145, 148–49; as playwright, 28, 154–56, 204, 236; and politics, 21, 65, 69, 187; on realism, 77–78, 80–81, 85; resistance to Lyceum publicity mecha-

nism, 45, 48–51; on Clement Scott, 50, 173–74; and stage directions, 156–58; on Ellen Terry, 94; on *Trilby*, 203; on Oscar Wilde, 187–89; picture of, 145

— *The Man of Destiny*, xvii, 201, 202; analysis of, 158–62, 186; Craig on, 157; Irving and, 147–50, 152–55, 162, 164–65, 170–73, 176; performances in Croydon, 179–80; sources of, 147, 150, 152, 158, 276n.18; summary of plot, 151–52; Terry and, 148–55, 157, 180; writing of, 143–44, 146–47

— "Mr Irving Takes Paregoric" (review of *Waterloo*), xi–xv, 11–13, 18–20, 23–24, 27–30, 53, 54, 95, 97, 120, 143, 203, 206, 227; and Shaw's other comments on *Waterloo*, 203; text of, 260–63; *Waterloo* as "good acting play," 61, 154, 156, 166, 180; quoted, 93, 106, 112, 140, 149, 153, 178, 197, 203

— Other writings: *Arms and the Man*, 21, 25, 73, 145, 146–47, 150; *Caesar and Cleopatra*, 152; *Candida*, 146, 153, 165; *Captain Brassbound's Conversion*, 206–7; *The Devil's Disciple*, 165; "A Dramatic Realist to His Critics," 21; "How to Become a Man of Genius," 161; *John Bull's Other Island*, 53; letters to Ellen Terry, 18, 54, 78, 81, 148–50, 152–55, 165–72, 178, 180–81, 216, 218; preface to "Pleasant Plays," 20–21, 149, 161, 179, 181; *Quintessence of Ibsenism*, 78, 173–75; review of *The Medicine Man*, 208–9; "What Mr. Gladstone Ought to Do," 134, 136; *You Never Can Tell*, 165; quotes from other writings, 26–27, 133

Siborne, Lt. William, 113, 117–21

Sims, George R., 179

Sketch, The, 131

Sloane, William A., 152

"Soul of Man Under Socialism, The" (Wilde), 186–87

Southey, Robert, 128

Spirit, inspiration, and spiritualism, xiii–xiv, xvii, 10–11, 13–17, 24, 39, 55–56, 66, 91, 124, 133, 138, 154, 185, 225, 227–29; and crowds, 21, 43, 45, 73–74, 76, 237

Stanislavsky, Constantin, 31, 51

Compositor: Graphic Composition, Inc.
Text: 10/13 Times Roman
Display: Times Roman
Printer: Thomson Shore
Binder: Thomson Shore